THI

CATRIONA KING

This is a work of fiction. Names, characters, places and incidents are used fictitiously and any resemblance to persons living or dead, business establishments, events, locations or areas, is entirely coincidental.

No part of this book may be used or reproduced in any manner without written permission of the author, except for brief quotations and segments used for promotion or in reviews.

Copyright © 2019 by Catriona King

ISBN: 978 1075370557

Photography: Images by polkadot_photo (Businessman), Dean Fikar (Glacier), JillWellington (Girl)

Artwork: Jonathan Temples:
creative@jonathantemples.co.uk

Editors: Andrew Angel and Maureen Vincent-Northam

Formatting: Rebecca Emin

All rights reserved.

Hamilton-Crean Publishing Ltd. 2019

For My Mother

About the Author

Catriona King is a medical doctor and trained as a police Forensic Medical Examiner in London, where she worked for some years. She returned to live in Belfast in 2006.

She has written since childhood and has been published in many formats: non-fiction, journalistic and fiction.

'The Depths' is book twenty-one in The Craig Crime Series. Each book can also be read as a standalone.

The Craig Crime Series So Far

A Limited Justice
The Grass Tattoo
The Visitor
The Waiting Room
The Broken Shore
The Slowest Cut
The Coercion Key
The Careless Word
The History Suite
The Sixth Estate
The Sect
The Keeper
The Talion Code
The Tribes
The Pact
The Cabal
The Killing Year
The Running of The Deer
The Property
Crossing The Line
The Depths

'The Depths' is the twenty-first book in the series. The twenty-second will be released later in 2019.

The audiobook of the first Craig Crime novel, A Limited Justice, is now available on Amazon ACX.

Aurora, the author's first Irish fantasy/mythology novella was released in August 2017.

She has also released a science fiction novel set in New York City, entitled The Carbon Trail.

****

Acknowledgements

My thanks to Northern Ireland and its people for providing the inspiration for my books.

My thanks also to: Andrew Angel and Maureen Vincent-Northam as my editors, Jonathan Temples for his cover design and Rebecca Emin for formatting this work.

I would also like to thank all the police officers I have ever worked with for their professionalism, wit and compassion.

Catriona King
June 2019

Discover more about the author's work at:
www.catrionakingbooks.com

To engage with the author about her books, email:
Catriona_books@yahoo.co.uk

The author can also be found on Facebook and Twitter: @CatrionaKing1

Chapter One

The West Mountain Quarry. Thirty miles Outside Omagh, County Tyrone. Northern Ireland.

Tuesday 5th February 2019. 2 p.m.

"BREAK THE ICE, STUPID!"

Fourteen-year-old Ricky Murphy dragged his attention away from his tangled fishing rod towards the origin of the shout, to see his two friends since nursery standing on the margin of the quarry's excavated cliff two hundred feet above him. One of them on the free end of a narrow granite prominence edging precariously out over the frozen pool where they'd been messing about for an hour, their favourite spot for a day's truanting because of the lack of nosey passers-by likely to snitch to their parents; and the other one, the smallest of the group, almost a year younger but already with the strut of a teenager, more sensibly bestriding the springboard's secure attachment to the cliff's face, both hands planted solidly on his hips the better to project his yell.

The fisherman's turn brought with it swift anxiety, the fear of his taller, heavier friend launching himself without warning from nature's diving board, goaded on by the smaller, shouting second. Placing his thick arms together with hands pointed as he crashed through the ice into the freezing water below, perhaps never to re-emerge. Confusion joined Murphy's anxiety as he puzzled why the scene was playing out at all, knowing how out of character such behaviour was for both his mates, but he understood a few seconds later when the shouted instruction was repeated and he realised that the words had only *ever* been meant for him.

"BREAK THE ICE, RICKY! IT LOOKS THIN WHERE YOU ARE."

Paul Rontgen picked his way down to where the fisherman was hunkering on the rocky shore below, his voice quietening as he approached.

"That way we can see if it's worth dropping the lines."

A moment later they were a chuckling group of three as Ricky regaled them with his story.

"I thought you were telling *Shamie* to jump!"

The slim-framed Rontgen glanced up at the shadow-inducing bulk of Shamus Wright, the erstwhile high diver, and snorted, "Not even *his* big head could crack ice that hard." He gestured to the others, clearly the boss of the group despite his size and youth. "One of you use a rock to break it... there. You can see the weeds through it so it can't be that thick."

It wasn't, and minutes later six trainer-clad feet were dangling over a small outcrop, fishing lines strung from the borrowed rods in their hands and flasks of hot chocolate filched from home by their sides as they sat contentedly ice-fishing, or as close an approximation as they were ever going to achieve in Ireland anyway.

Nature clearly being aware of their hierarchy it didn't take long for Rontgen to get a nibble, and after a cursory attempt to reel it in by himself he enlisted the help of the other two. Even so, it was still a challenge; three adolescents braced against a block of half-hewn stone abandoned at the close of the quarry four years before, biceps and quads tensed to hardness as their not-quite-grown-man hands gripped and slipped up and down the rod.

"It's bloody enormous this fish!"

"Looks like we've got our own Loch Ness monster, lads!"

Ricky squeezed out a focusing, *"Shut up and pull"* which was rewarded by the surrounding, already splintering ice fracturing further, and the surface of the freezing black water below breaking abruptly to reveal the ghost of a pale, almost oval shape. A further united tug and more of their catch appeared above the murky surface; a bloated, blue-white outline that distorted though it was resembled something familiar; a human face.

It was followed immediately by something larger and heavier and unmistakably clothed, the extremity of the first tranche of material revealing a degraded stump that had once been a hand. The next pull, using strength generated by bravado, fascination, and fear now, was strong enough to display a man's torso and legs, with whatever feet there were still remaining left hidden in the pool.

One by one the teenagers' clenched muscles shuddered, weakened and failed, at first just halting their efforts and then making each hand release the rod in turn as its owner waited for the others to state the obvious; that their afternoon's illicit fishing had just come to the worst unwelcome end.

****

The Atlantic Way Merchant Bank. Dublin Docklands.

Róisín Casey closed down the cryptocurrency site that she'd been accessing on her office computer, completely against company regulations but so well firewalled that no-one at the bank could possibly suspect, and picked up her large, expensively unwieldy handbag, setting it on her desk with the same reverence that a museum curator might attach to placing an exhibit on a plinth. But then she honestly believed that the item deserved such treatment. After all, it *was* a Chanel, and its kilogram of calfskin and metal had cost her the equivalent of one of her junior staff's monthly wage.

As the slim brunette drew an elegant finger over the bag's smooth beige leather she mused about how little *she* had earned when she'd first started out at the bank; nothing close to even the cost of her purse never mind her bag. Now she was its first female Vice President, she lived in an apartment on the capital's prosperous south riverside, and she had so much money that she hardly knew what to do with it.

Which didn't stop her wanting more of course. To her, wealthy people who said that they had enough money were beyond the pale. Scarcely credible and traitors to her adopted class. *She* was a *real* capitalist; always on the lookout for the next big thing.

Money was more to her than mere numbers on a page, it was her religion, and like all zealots *anything* was justifiable in the name of her God. Little did she know that belief would be tested very soon.

****

The West Mountain Quarry. 5 p.m.

"What the hell are we doing here, John? It's freezing, and I've a lot to get on with back at the office."

Pathologist John Winter didn't even glance up at his interrogator, well used to police officers grumbling when he summoned them to cold, inconvenient places, as if everyone should meet their maker in a nice centrally-heated bedroom, or at the very worst a slightly colder integral garage.

The idea became even more absurd if you factored in that *any* death could be a murder. Killers weren't known for their tendency to plan far enough ahead to choose a nice venue unless they were hit men, *or* for any consideration for the people who might come after and preferred to be comfortable as they did their jobs.

The medic's lack of response and the silent disdain that accompanied it left D.C.S. Marc Craig with two choices: ask his question again, or ask a different, more useful one.

As a prequel to the second he hunkered down on the rocky pedestal on which he'd been standing, grateful at least for its man-made smooth surface, being careful not to contaminate the senior pathologist's field.

"OK, let me rephrase that. I know we're down here because you told the local coppers to request some Murder Squad input and *we* were on the Rota, but can you at least tell me *why* you think this was a murder rather than an accidental death? And even if it is, why it necessitated calling us down here to bloody Ballygobackwards, when we could *easily* have viewed the body in the morgue?"

This time John Winter *did* lookup. "You mean apart from the fact this man was found dead in a quarry that hasn't been worked in four years?"

As Craig didn't believe the question deserved *quite* the amount of sarcasm and pride with which it had been asked, he came back just as snappily.

"I'll need more than that! Like something that tells me he didn't just fall in drunk and drown."

The pathologist conceded the point with a shrug, rising to his feet and stripping off his latex gloves as he did.

"Fair enough."

Never a man to cling to pride as a defence he indicated

their charge. "What you *can't* see, because he's covered now, is that he has bruising on both shoulders."

Craig stood up again and gazed high above them at the quarry's excavated cliff edge. "Couldn't those just have happened on his way down?"

John shook his head. "You're *assuming* that he fell from up there. And anyway, no, not the bruises that *I've* just seen."

He lifted his bag and began his ascent up a steep stone track hewn years before by quarry workers beckoning the detective to follow, and they eventually reached its pinnacle where Craig's deputy, D.C.I. Liam Cullen, was busily running on the spot for warmth and wishing that he'd bought a winter coat like his wife had nagged him to months before. As they reached him John Winter restarted his report.

"OK, so it looks like our man's been in the water for months, but insects will give me a more accurate dating. We're very lucky there's even that much left of him. If it had been a real lake the fish would have devoured his flesh after-"

Craig interrupted him. "So because the pool was created by rainwater filling the quarry pit there are fewer fish?"

"None at all would be my guess, not unless someone put them there. The kids that found him..." He paused to point to a liveried patrol car parked a short distance away, where the three erstwhile happily fishing teenagers were sitting huddled and white-faced in the back, "...would have been waiting forever to catch anything. That's what they told the local cops when they arrived, that they came here to fish, although my guess is they just fancied a day off school."

"I'll ask them later." Craig brought him back to the point. "OK, so if there are no fish what took his fingers off?"

"Maceration, but perhaps insects as well. We don't know what sorts are in there yet. There seems to be a lot of vegetation in the water, some of which was probably on the rocks already and grew, but some could have been blown in on the wind and brought insects along with it. And there might be small animals around here, rodents. They'll *always* have a nibble. But the flesh on his hands would have dropped off eventually anyway because of the water. Maceration, like I said." He held up a hand. "A few days' pruning in the bath would loosen mine, and after that it's just a matter of time before it all sloughs off."

Craig shuddered. "Never *ever* say slough to me again, John. It's a revolting word."

Liam was also shuddering, but not at the thought of a fingerless John. He'd stopping jogging now and was freezing. He was also *really* irritable because he couldn't understand why they were having their conversation standing in a biting easterly wind instead of inside a nice warm car!

To underline the point he led by example, walking across to his Ford, yanking open its doors and jerking a thick thumb inside. A minute later they were all a lot more comfortable and Craig had returned to the case, trying to keep his cynicism out of his voice.

"OK, so, he's been down there for months, and you're basing your view that he was murdered on the fact that you saw bruising on his shoulders?"

He already knew the medic had to have seen more than that, but he needed to know exactly what.

John employed his slowest and most tolerant, 'I'm obviously talking to an idiot today' tone.

"Well, first... the bruising was on the *front* of both shoulders, which is odd as there was nothing on his shins or anterior thighs that I could see. But let's go with your theory and say he *did* fall from up here into the water. Try to picture that. He'd have had to pirouette in mid-air in order to have bounced off the cliff wall face-on. Even an Olympic diver couldn't manage that!"

He contorted his body in the car's back seat trying to make it work, then gave up and shook his head.

"But OK, let's say *some* bruising on the front of someone's shoulders *could* possibly be explained by a fall." His sceptical expression said that he was just humouring the detectives now. "This *wasn't* just some random bruising that could have been explained by him banging against something, these bruises are on the front of *both* shoulders over his clavicles with no abrasions in or around them. Most importantly they look like they're in the shape of hands. Granted, I could only see a couple of finger outlines, but this is an awkward place to examine someone so you'll have to wait until after the post-mortem for the rest."

Liam was feeling warmer and less irritable so he decided that it was time to join the debate. "So? What? Someone gripped him and threw him off the top?"

It was Craig who answered, shaking his head. "It's far too uncertain a method if you're trying to murder someone. What if he'd survived the fall? Plenty have, even from this height. And if the water had been deep enough he could just have hidden beneath the surface until his attacker had left and climbed out."

Something occurred to him. "He couldn't have died of a head injury, John, could he? Banging it on the way down?"

"Or on the bottom of the quarry if the hole was dry when he'd fallen in, Doc?"

The pathologist waited until both detectives had nodded eagerly and then said, "No" with a smug smile. "There was no head injury that I could see." He relented, deciding to be slightly kinder to them. "But it is just *possible* that there might be a concealed one, and the local rainfall patterns should tell us how dry the hole was likely to have been when he went in. On the other hand, if he died from drowning I should be able to tell you what time of year it happened from the vegetation and insects in his lungs."

Liam nodded, gesturing back towards the pit. "There's a lot of limestone in that rock, so my guess is it sucks in the water like billy-oh."

"Meaning?"

"In summer that watering hole's probably as dry as a bone."

One thing was sure; this victim's time of death was going to be listed in months not days.

John picked up his report. "OK... I'm loath to stick my neck out on the cause of death this early, and I'm caveating *everything* I say now with 'wait for the PM', but if I was *pushed* I'd say that by the look of him he drowned. *Was* drowned by someone."

"Hence murder and the reason you called us down." Craig nodded. "OK. It'll do as a working theory anyway."

He turned to his deputy. "There couldn't have been any guarantee of death just by pushing him in from the top, so those bruises *must* have come from someone holding him under water until he was dead. He was small but muscled, so we're talking about someone strong. Definitely a man."

John shook his head in warning. "That all depends on whether I'm right."

Liam gazed at him like a groupie. "I believe in you, Doc. You're my hero."

That earned him a derisive snort as the pathologist climbed out of the car. "I'll do the PM early, so if you drop down late morning I should know for sure. Oh, by the way, look out for gold when you're nosing around."

"What?"

"This place might look like a quarry now, but there was a gold mine sunk here for a few years. One of the local cops told me. So, you *might* find a lump or two of the stuff lying around if you're lucky. Who knows?"

The door closed behind him to snorts of scepticism, and the detectives were left staring out through the windscreen in silence until Liam spoke again.

"OK, so, the nearest village is called Rownton, about five miles from here. I've asked the sergeant there to get reinforcements from Omagh and start questioning the locals on what they know."

"Good."

"That leaves *us* with three choices, boss. We can sit here and speculate why someone wanted our floater dead, we can get out and ask those kids what they saw, or we can do both of those *after* we talk about Annette."

It was a neat synopsis and Craig couldn't have put it any better. Annette Eakin, the Murder Squad's long serving detective inspector, had been involved in a fatal shooting just before Christmas. Her ex-husband Pete McElroy, who'd been imprisoned for assaulting her and then had his stay at Her Majesty's pleasure extended and moved to a high-security nick for shivving another inmate, had been released on a short pre-release leave just before Christmas and had immediately broken into the home that Annette shared with her new partner Mike Augustus and their two-year-old child.

Unfortunately, the shock of seeing Pete standing over

their bed in the middle of the night had made Annette reach for her Glock, a personal protection weapon that she *should* have locked away as soon as she'd come home that evening after the squad's Christmas party but hadn't because it was late, and a weapon that she'd then shot him dead with after having consumed alcohol at said party, something that had unfortunately shown up in her blood results.

The upshot was that an investigation had been launched by the Police Ombudsman, and Annette had been suspended pending investigation. She was at home now on the euphemistically nicknamed 'gardening leave' until everything was, *hopefully,* sorted out.

The less hopeful part was covered by Liam's next words.

"What if she goes down, boss?"

Craig's head whipped round as fast as his answer snapped out. *"For what?"*

"For not locking her gun away as per the licensing terms, for being in charge of a weapon while under the influence of alcohol, for discharging that weapon, for-"

Craig cut across him angrily. *"For shooting an intruder?* A burglar, a man with a history of violence not just against her but against other people, against other *men* in prison? A man who'd almost killed another inmate with a shiv? And for coming home late and exhausted after the end of a major case?"

He sucked in a mouthful of air and continued. "OK, yes, so she had alcohol on board, but she was only one percent over the drink-drive limit, so still within the margin of error, and I'm surprised that she was even that! You *know* how little Annette drinks. Anyway, she wasn't driving *that* night and she *wasn't* drunk. They'd have to prove she was and it would never stick. And you and I both know how careful she is with firearms. She's only ever shot someone once before, and that was because he was about to kill you! And me-"

Liam stepped up to his role as Devil's Advocate.

"Pete's dead though!"

"She can't be penalised for being a crack shot!"

The D.C.I. allowed himself a small smile that made his boss scowl.

"What are you smirking about?"

"I'm not smirking, I'm smiling, and it's because I was just messing with you to see what you'd say. After *that* defence I just hope that you're in my corner when my time comes."

Craig managed a chuckle. "Planning on shooting someone are you?"

"That woman in the staff canteen if she burns my sausages one more time. No, but seriously, boss, we'll both be called to testify if there's a hearing, seeing as we were with Annette just hours before."

Craig opened the car door to climb out. "Then we tell the truth."

And the truth will set Annette free. *Hopefully*.

****

The Rocking Chair Pub. Rownton Village. 5 p.m.

The Rocking Chair Pub was a vision of kitsch and cosiness; the sort of hostelry you see in brochures for Irish Tourism, with polished mahogany beams, well-shone brasses and sparkling glasses, all lit by the flickering red-orange flames of an open fire.

In the brochure all of this would be set against the background of a tune singing out from a fiddler's strings and a dark-haired colleen in the corner beating out a leaping rhythm with her feet, but even without those additions the pub was a cliché, yet its customers loved it no less for that. It was their retreat when their hard day's work ended at the farms, shops and small factories nearby, and a place to meet neighbours, romantic partners and perhaps even the odd vicar or priest.

Such places are the hearts of villages not deemed fashionable enough to have chi-chi restaurants that attract the country's gourmets and those so small that their pulse, the village post-office, has long ago been stopped. But anthropomorphically a pub isn't just the heart or pulse but the ears and eyes of a village; the place where every local's secrets become common discourse, and every stranger runs a gauntlet of curious looks or stories trotted out for a new audience because the old ones are either disinterested or dead.

But that afternoon there were no strangers amongst The Rocking Chair's occupants, its public bar quiet and sparsely filled. An elderly couple, the village's oldest inhabitants, had taken up prime position by the fire and were sipping quietly at the two half-pints that their pensions allowed them, while a pair of weather worn, middle-aged men drinking Guinness stood propping up its long wooden bar.

So quiet was it that when the oil-starved street door screamed open, every occupant turned to see who was entering, their gazes lasting only long enough to welcome the newcomer as someone familiar before they turned to their drinks again, all except for Finbar Brolly, the pub landlord, who broke the silence to ask the question that he asked scores of times each day.

"What'll you be having," the name of the prospective drinker inserted almost as an afterthought, "Derek?"

The anxious looking man walked straight to the unoccupied end of the bar, answering, "Lager" as he did, and as the honey-coloured liquid appeared in front of him he beckoned his host closer and lowered his voice. "Have the police been in yet, Finbar?"

Brolly took a step back and lifted an empty glass to polish as he answered the question with another.

"How'd *you* hear about them, Derek? Tucked away in that office of yours."

The aging builder responded irritably. "Word travels around here, you know that! People saw the cars. Now, have they been in or not?"

His tone made Brolly raise a greying eyebrow, and on another day and with a different customer the landlord might have turned and walked away. But Derek Morrow was no ordinary local, he was the boss of the only construction firm for one hundred miles, and if Derek gave the word all his workmen would stop spending their pay packets in the pub.

So Finbar Brolly bit his tongue and shook his head obligingly, although spite made him add a predictive, "Not yet", and experience a frisson of pleasure when he saw a flash of sweat appear on the builder's top lip.

"When did they arrive?"

Morrow's tone was even more intense than before.

"No idea why they're here, but they turned up around an hour ago. All the commotion they made too, with their nee-naw nee-naws and flashing lights." The landlord shook his balding head. "I don't know why people can't just do things quietly, instead of running around disturbing the peace like that."

The construction boss wasn't about to be drawn into a debate on noise pollution and focused instead on what mattered to him, his next question an insistent hiss.

"Does anyone know why they were called?"

It earned him another elevated eyebrow from his host, who was now rubbing so hard at the glass that he was holding to prevent himself punching the builder that it was a wonder that his tea-towel didn't pass right through.

After he'd deemed enough time had passed to convey his feelings Brolly stopped rubbing and gave his customer a look of implied knowing, that reflected nothing so well as his confusion about why Morrow was asking such a thing plus a growing desire to find out.

In view of the businessman's obviously taut state of mind Brolly decided to meander as he did so to wind him up.

"I hear there are Belfast cops here too."

It brought a satisfying tightening of Morrow's sagging jaw so he pressed the advantage.

"Sergeant O'Hare was in ten minutes ago saying they want to interview everyone local, but he doesn't know why. *Everyone,* mind you."

As the tightening became a clench the pub landlord stared hard at his customer. "Do *you* know why, Derek?"

The builder jumped back as if the bar had just been electrified and his response this time was loud.

"I DON'T KNOW ANYTHING! THAT'S WHY I'M ASKING!"

It earned him glances from the bar's other occupants and a quiet tut from the old woman, who had never in her life liked loud people, or her peace and quiet being disturbed.

Brolly gave a twisted smile, the bill for Morrow's earlier bad temper now well and truly paid.

"If you shout like that people will think you know

exactly why the cops are here, Derek. People will think *you've* been up to no good."

The taunt earned him a fiver slapped down on the bar and a view of Morrow's back as he exited, and it left The Rocking Chair's regulars a lot more curious about life than they'd been ten minutes earlier, and with plenty to tell the folks at home that night.

****

The West Mountain Quarry. 6 p.m.

By six o'clock the detectives had heard three versions of that afternoon's happenings from the teenagers, in various shades of breaking voice but all of them adding up to the same thing; the quarry was their favoured venue for an afternoon spent bunking off school. Whether they used it for exploring, swimming, skating or fishing depended on the solidity of the water's surface and the weather, but all three agreed that today's was the biggest adventure they had *ever* had.

When asked if they'd ever actually *caught* a fish, Craig had stifled a smile as the one called Ricky had held his hands two feet apart and described the one that had got away. But further probing had confirmed John's hypothesis; the only aquatic creatures the boys had ever seen were fronds of vegetation beneath the water's surface and the only catch they'd ever made was the unwelcome human whale that they had landed that day. A whale that none of the three had ever seen when he was alive. There was only one version on that.

Craig beckoned his deputy to one side and dropped his voice. "What do you think? Can we trust them not to tell everyone what they found?"

Liam snorted in derision. "Not a hope in hell! They'll be down to the nearest street corner or youth club, or wherever the kids hang out around here, bigging up their psychological trauma at finding a corpse for all it's worth."

"Except *that* would tell their parents that they'd been mitching school and they *definitely* don't want that. They're still refusing to give their surnames and they screamed blue murder earlier when the uniforms said they'd have to call their folks. The one that I was just questioning is *still* saying he's twenty-five, just small for his age."

Liam wasn't persuaded.

"Nah. By tomorrow morning they won't care about any of that, they'll just be busting to tell their mates. Anyway, my bet is that their folks won't be that surprised. This won't be the first time bunking school for any of them."

Craig sighed, knowing that he was right. Kids were always kids.

The D.C.I. hadn't finished.

"And another thing, boss. My bet is they'll call the papers and try to flog their stories as well. That's what kids do these days."

Newspapers or no newspapers, Craig knew the discovery might be all over *social* media in a few hours, if it wasn't already. Only the rural nature of their location might have slowed things down.

As soon as the thought occurred to him he strode back to the car where the three boys were now play-fighting in the back seat and motioned them to get out. They emerged warily, Craig's expression telling them unambiguously not to mess about.

"Phones."

He held out a hand, and as the ubiquitous smartphones appeared, variously adorned with football, rugby and zombie stickers, he passed them to his deputy to inspect while he went on.

"Did any of you boys photograph the body after you found it?"

Averted eyes and shuffling feet said that the answer was yes.

"Right. Which of you?"

A tightening of each smooth face in turn said that all three had, prompting Craig to give a disgusted tut.

"For God's sake, were none of you brought up to respect the dead?"

Perhaps a stupid question of a generation whose computer games mostly revolved around killing and maiming to achieve a goal.

A roar from his deputy put paid to Craig's follow-up question.

"WHOSE PHONE IS THIS?"

The detective turned to see Liam brandishing the zombie phone in the air and walked across to take a look. He saw a photograph of their victim's face, bloated and macerated but still potentially recognisable by someone who'd loved him, with a banner beneath it saying, 'Found a real zombie at the quarry today. Ace!'

Craig swung back to see the smallest of the three amigos staring at the ground so hard he looked like he was trying to bore through to Australia, so he leant down to glare right into the teenager's face.

"This is your phone?"

A weak nod from Paul Rontgen said yes.

Craig stepped back, fighting an urge to shake the adolescent like some public school master in a black and white movie.

"Look at me when I'm talking to you."

The boy's closely shorn head rose sharply and to Craig's fury he caught a glimpse of defiance in his eyes. The teenager made the mistake of giving it voice.

"It's a free country! I can post anything I want!"

Liam closed his eyes and waited for the explosion. It didn't take long.

"AND I CAN HAVE YOU ARRESTED FOR INTERFERING WITH A POLICE INVESTIGATION!"

Craig swung round to face the other two, whose faces had turned a sickly grey.

"Will we find similar posts on *your* phones?"

He was almost blown over by the breeze from the teenagers' shaking heads.

But the haste of their garbled, "No way. Just photos", and already having been bitten once meant that he didn't trust them, so he looked to his deputy for confirmation and eventually received a weary nod.

"There are photos of our man on all three, but that's the only thing I found that looked like an actual post. We'll need them to sign in to all their media and emails so we can check if they've written about their find too."

Five minutes later they knew that Shamus Wright had done nothing but take and save the photograph and Ricky Murphy had emailed his pen pal in New Zealand about the find, but thankfully with no image attached so the squad's senior analyst, Davy Walsh, could easily do damage limitation on that.

That just left Paul Rontgen's zombie post.

Craig turned back to the short teenager. "Show me where you posted this." At the boy's hesitation he added, *"Now"* in such a stern tone that Liam mused he might have been practicing for his impending fatherhood in front of the mirror.

It brought a grunt from Rontgen and a lackadaisical stabbing at his mobile but soon they were in his email account.

"What about any others accounts, like FaceChat? Did you post it on any of those?"

It was Murphy who answered. "We didn't get time, honest. Your lot turned up too fast."

Evidently only the local cops' rapid response to the boys' nine-nine-nine call had prevented a full-on social media fest, meaning that lack of time and not morality had saved the day.

The fact depressed both detectives more than they could say.

Craig turned back to Paul Rontgen.

"The banner underneath suggests this is an internet post, so where has it been posted?"

"Nowhere. I emailed it."

"To?"

The response was mumbled. "My mum."

It could have been worse he supposed, but given the behaviour of her offspring the woman's own common sense had to be seriously in doubt.

"Liam, get her name, work and home addresses and send a uniform to each to get it deleted before she passes it on."

The boy's mouth opened immediately to protest, but a warning glance clamped it shut again.

"I'll see what Davy can do from his end."

Two minutes later Davy Walsh the squad's senior analyst, who'd just been packing up for the night and planning what he was going to steam for dinner, going through as he had been since his trip to Iceland at Christmas a healthy eating phase involving a lot of rice and fish, knew that whatever meal he'd been planning on having that night was going to be delayed for at least an hour.

He rebooted his PC and noted down the relevant information, waiting until Craig had finished to say, "OK, I can delete S...Shamus W...Wright's and call back Ricky Murphy's email now, that provider gives the facility."

Noticing that his usually mild stammer on 's' and 'w' was more pronounced than usual, something that sometimes happened when his blood sugar dropped, he reached into his drawer for a piece of chocolate from his secret stash before going on.

"It was after two a.m. in New Zealand when he sent it so it's unlikely it's been opened, but I'll call at a decent hour just to check." He stared at his screen and shook his head. "I'm just looking, chief, but it looks like Paul Rontgen's mail provider doesn't have a recall facility, s...so you'll have to get his mum to delete it from hers as well. If she w...won't do it, are you OK with me asking the providers to freeze the whole family's accounts?"

"Will it stop them downloading or forwarding the photo to anyone?"

"Yep. And I can't promise, but I'll try to delete the image remotely from her email as well. I'll tell you how to w...wipe it off the phone now."

Ignoring Rontgen's outstretched hands and noisy objections Craig did just that and then left his analyst to it, using the twenty minutes until he called back to put the fear of God into the three youths. An eventual nod from his deputy told him that Mrs Rontgen had cooperated, although not without objections judging by his expression. When Liam held out his phone indicating that the loving parent would like a word with her son Craig could hear her shouting from several feet away.

The D.C.I. chuckled. "The other two might get some sympathy for finding a corpse when they get home, but that one's looking at a thick ear for getting his ma paid a visit by the cops."

Craig gave a small smile, and then confused his deputy by immediately shaking his head.

"The problem is it *still* doesn't solve our problem, Liam. Short of gagging the boys this will be all round the area tonight, and that means if the killer lives locally they'll be forewarned and have plenty of time to concoct an alibi."

Liam shrugged. "There's nothing we can do about that but warn the lads to keep schtum and get our own statement out. I'll sort them while you make a plan."

It only took Craig five minutes to formulate one, but he knew it wasn't going to be popular with his deputy. He wasn't exactly thrilled about it either, because it entailed staying in Tyrone late and he and Katy were supposed to be viewing a house to buy that night. But needs must, so he made a note to ask her mother to go along instead and started to draft a holding press statement.

When Liam returned he was rubbing his hands and looking satisfied.

"Scared them into silence have you?"

"And then some. Even that wee skitter Rontgen looks subdued."

"Good. I've spoken to the press office so they'll put out an interim statement, but that doesn't alter the fact that those three will contaminate the interview pool as soon as they leave here. We'll need-"

The D.C.I.'s face lit up. "To lock them up?"

His optimism made Craig laugh. "I wish. But no. We-"

Liam cut him off again, this time with a groan. "We're not going home yet, are we? And it's steak night too. "

Craig shook his head apologetically. "Sorry to interfere with your dietary needs, but I think we need to take their statements in front of a solicitor to discourage them from telling the world what they found."

"We'll be here all bloody night!"

"If necessary, yes, and if we are I promise I'll buy you dinner. But it all depends how fast we work, so instead of standing there moaning go and gather the uniforms together so I can brief them, while I inform our young discoverers that we'll be inviting *all* their parents down to the local station so we can get their statements again on tape."

Chapter Two

The Atlantic Way Merchant Bank. Dublin Docklands. 6 p.m.

Róisín Casey was just reapplying her lipstick ready to leave for dinner with her lover when the ID of a man who ran one of her minor enterprises flashed on her mobile phone.

She answered the call in a surprised tone.

"Arthur! How nice to hear from you, it's been ages. But I wasn't expecting your call and I'm in a bit of a hurry, so could we reschedule for another time?"

"We really need to talk now, Róisín."

A sudden shard of anxiety brought with it a question, asked as calmly as she could muster.

"Something's wrong?"

His answer confirmed her fears.

"In a way."

This time her anxiety was obvious.

"The mortgage company isn't going well?"

Small though it was she'd made a hefty investment in their joint Northern Irish mortgage business, persuaded by reports of increased house building in Belfast, and the thought of losing money was worse to her than the possible loss of a limb.

She felt an overwhelming urge to cry as she waited for his answer.

"The company's doing so-so, but that's not why I called you."

The tension in the elderly businessman's voice took her aback, but not as much as his next words.

"The police are in Rownton."

The banker inhaled sharply, picturing the isolated Tyrone village, and the limited reasons that *anyone* bar a shepherd or a dairy farmer might have for visiting there. Hope rose again at the thought that he might just have meant the local Bobbies, but when, "No. They're definitely *Belfast* coppers" was the response to the question she squeezed out a, *"Do you know why?"* that was heavy with blame.

Arthur Norris heard it but fought his immediate urge to cower to reply, "No, not yet."

The banker's silent chastisement lingered so he rushed to add some information that, had he only but known it, was about to make things worse.

"Marked and unmarked cars were seen driving through the village earlier, heading south-west, which is why I'm so worried. Then the village sergeant started questioning the locals. My mole says no-one's come out looking worried yet, but..." He braced himself for her reaction to his next words. "...no-one's saying what questions they were asked."

Róisín was still on 'south-west' but this time she hid her concerns behind a casual tone.

"The south-west... isn't that old mine we dug around there?"

"Yes! That's *exactly* my point. There's nothing else that side of Rownton, so what if the police visiting has something to do with *that*? I always said environmental pollution there might come back to bite us."

The businesswoman glossed over his anxiety with a laugh. If he only but knew it, environmental issues were the *least* of her worries.

"They won't, Arthur, you're just being paranoid. Hold on for a second while I pull up a map. I need to get my bearings. I only visited the damn place once."

Although by association far more often than that.

Her land agent come gofer talked on as he waited. "That gold mine you sank was *always* a dud investment, Róisín. I told you that at the time. Three years getting permission to excavate, another three digging and all you got back was a ton of gold over its whole life. You should have just run it as the quarry it was originally."

She chided him for his negativity, pleased by his obvious ignorance of the quarry's real significance to her.

"Now, that wasn't *quite* all, Arthur. That's how we met, remember, when I engaged you as my agent to scout the land. If we hadn't then we would never have gone on to bigger and better things."

"Well, the mortgage company's bigger maybe, but I'm not sure how much better it is."

This time her admonishment was swift. "Are you getting cold feet about working for me? I need to know *right now* if you are."

He backtracked hastily, sensing that his pension was about to disappear. "No, no, I'm fine. It's just that I get nervous when I hear the police being mentioned, that's all."

"So does everyone. It's conditioning." Something occurred to her. "Your mole down there... surely *he'll* be called in for interview too? Then he'll be able to tell us exactly what the cops want."

"That's what I'm banking on. It'll probably turn out to be a whole lot of nothing, but I still don't like it. If the quarry *is* why the cops are in Rownton and there's a pollution problem, they'll find your consortium liable as the owners and me as the agent, and that could cost us all *hefty* fines."

The banker made soothing noises but her thoughts were on his words; *'Pollution problem.'* Yes, well, she supposed you *could* describe a dead body like that.

****

Rownton Police Station. Midnight.

It had been after ten p.m. when the Belfast detectives had shut up their interviewing shop for the night after sorting out their teenage witnesses, and then the local sergeant had decided to pay them back for making him interview people that he played bowls and drank with, by handing them two hours extra work listening to complaints from the locals about the lack of neighbourhood Bobbies, the state of the roads, and the festival that was held in a field fifteen miles away every summer that, "Was almost enough to turn people deaf."

Craig noticed that *no-one* was complaining about people speeding down country roads in their tractors, the rural cash-in-hand economy, or the late opening hours at the village pub, which he was *sure* happened there as it did in practically every village in the land; but then all of *those* things probably suited the local people, especially the last.

The evening had almost been a bust, with the interviews held drawing a blank on their dead man's identity using his general description, his face far too distorted to try for a photo ID, but as nobody in the ten-square-mile hinterland that the village served was known to be missing they could probably rule their victim out as being a local man.

What they *had* confirmed, just in time to warn everyone not to speak to the press as the national newspaper journalists' and TV stations' cars and vans had pulled up, was that John had been right and the quarry hadn't been worked in over four years, and when it had been, most recently from twenty-twelve to twenty-fifteen, it hadn't just produced granite or limestone like most in the country but had functioned as one of Northern Ireland's first open-cast gold mining enterprises, which even though it had provided some local employment had been *very* unpopular.

Possibly something to do with Irish gold rightly belonging to the Leprechauns and the removal of it therefore being bound to bring a heap of magical mischief down on their heads, or so Liam had announced in a manner that had allowed for no dispute. The pub landlord, Finbar Brolly, had been equally forthcoming on the supernatural subject, probably because he and Liam, both being large and robust country men, had hit it off immediately, bonding over their love of Celtic myths as well as GAA football.

What Craig had learned that was *factual* was that there'd been a running battle with government planners and years of protests against the mine ever being sunk in an area of such natural beauty, and that more than one of those protests had turned to blows.

When Brolly had finally left the interview room he turned the tape off with a smile.

"You realise what that means don't you?"

Liam yawned loudly as he answered; his, "No, what?" emerging muffled, as if he was speaking through cotton wool.

"It means there'll be police reports on the quarry protests and maybe even tapes. The television companies wouldn't have missed being here to report that. Our dead man might even be on one of them."

"Thrilling, I'm sure."

As Craig reached into his pocket for his mobile his deputy deliberately allowed him to dial and listen impatiently as the call rang out before pointing at the clock.

"It's midnight, boss! You didn't *seriously* expect anyone to still be in the office, did you?"

The D.C.I. realised halfway through the question that he really had. To him investigating a murder was a twenty-four-seven job.

Craig's only response was, "OK, so tonight..."

When the sentence tailed off there, Liam made a guess at its ending.

"Tonight, Matthew, I'm going to be Cher?"

It made his boss chuckle. "Very witty, although Dean Martin's more my style."

"You wish."

Craig didn't dignify the jibe with a comeback. "Right, so, *tonight* we need to make the decision whether to go home or stay here."

"That depends on whether we need to be here in the morning, doesn't it, Dino. So do we?"

Craig considered his options for a moment then he shook his head and rose to his feet.

"No, we don't. The first interviews on the villagers have almost been completed, and they've been warned about the press. But we can't gag them, so that'll work out whatever way it's going to. There are still farm people in the hinterland to speak to, especially out near the quarry, but I think I'll get Andy and Aidan to take those."

Liam smiled at his use of 'farm people' as opposed to just 'people', having been a 'farm person' himself in his youth. It was as if they were a different species and it was such an obviously city term. Mind you, *he'd* referred to city folk far less politely than that when he was a boy.

He clambered to his feet. "OK, so home now and tomorrow we head to the lab for the PM results. Meanwhile the geeks can dig out your protest footage and let's hope all that puts a name on our man."

He kept talking as they walked to the car. "It's a bit odd that after getting through all that protesting the owners abandoned the mine after only three years isn't it."

Craig shrugged. "I suppose. Maybe the gold ran out. Even the gold rush in the Klondike ended eventually."

"The Leprechauns will have had a hand in it, although I

suppose it still needs checked out. If they left the mine because of harassment from the locals we might get something tasty on our Vic."

"Good thinking, Batman."

Craig lifted a comic bearing that very title off from the car's rear shelf, then placed it over his face and reclined his seat.

"Right, I'm going to sleep. We'll talk about it tomorrow morning." He made a sweeping 'wagons-ho' gesture. "Home, James."

****

Rownton Village. Morrow's Construction Works. Wednesday, 1 a.m.

Derek Morrow had a calculation to make and he knew that it wasn't going to work out neatly; not like the precise maximum weight that a crane could carry or the tallest point from which a boulder could be dropped before it broke. He *liked* calculations like those and experienced an almost visceral pleasure from getting them right, thrilled when a wrecking ball hit a wall on the perfect spot to bring it down with one blow, or when a concrete beam slotted into position in a way that demonstrated just how a new house would take shape.

But *those* things involved processes that he could control; empirical measurements and machinery, any element of human error all but removed by employing only people that he'd worked with for years. But this other thing... this thing that he'd *stupidly* decided to get involved in; *it* had been messy and risky and unclean from the start.

God only knew why he'd done it, risked *everything* for the promise of money, and pushed every principle that he'd held aside for gain. But even as the construction boss was asking himself the question he knew the answer; he'd done it because the cushy job that Arthur Norris had arranged for him at the quarry had presented him with an unexpected opportunity that he hadn't had the moral fibre to refuse.

Morrow stared in the site portaloo's mirror and saw a sixty-year-old face that looked seventy staring back, its contours long buried beneath fat and weathered sagging, and further blurred now by the whiskey he had on board. He'd been drinking his work stash solidly since he'd left the pub that afternoon and now his drunkenness was forcing him to be honest. No, he hadn't *just* done it because Arthur had given him a job; *his* offer had been innocent and his knowledge of their sordid business nil. Arthur's work was limited to advising on property: bricks and mortar, quarries and houses; but the thing that *he'd* chosen to get involved in was evil and he'd done it purely for gain.

Despite all the years that he'd slogged and worried his construction business had barely kept his family afloat, and the money that he'd been offered to keep his mouth shut had simply been too much to pass up. It had made their past few months enjoyable and it would make his wife and children secure when he was gone.

And even though he knew that he *should* have been a better man than to make an easy life his priority, he obviously wasn't; what he'd done had *proved* that he was greedy and amoral, and if there *was* a God he fully expected to pay the price for those failings after his death.

As the reality of his situation hit him Morrow felt nauseous and turned quickly to the sink, closing his eyes tight and splashing his face with cold water until the wave had finally passed. It didn't help much; the images that had dogged him for weeks had reappeared the moment his eyes had shut, and they were joined now by a certainty that whatever the police were up to in the village it would have something to do with him.

As the builder's eyes sprang open again he made a decision; he'd done his duty and warned Arthur but now he had to take care of the people that he loved. He grabbed for the door handle and exited the tiny lavatory, storming across the muddy site to his portakabin office and locking its door. If the police were planning on questioning everyone then they would reach him tomorrow and he knew that he would buckle and betray people; he also knew that he *couldn't* do that, for his family's sake.

And being the precise man that he was Derek Morrow had anticipated such an event and had everything ready, so he took a seat behind his desk, opened a drawer on one side and removed two envelopes. A bulky one filled months before with bank account details, his Will and funeral arrangements, and a second, slimmer one that he replaced each week containing an updated letter to his wife and kids.

The construction boss set the missives neatly on the desk in front of him, pushing them far enough away that they wouldn't be contaminated by what he planned to do next. He'd phoned home hours before to explain that he'd be working all night, not unusual if he was trying to finish a job, so he was certain that he wouldn't be disturbed.

Before he could change his mind the builder opened a second, locked, drawer, removed a revolver and quickly loaded it, and then the man who hated mess but had got himself into a huge one placed the barrel in his mouth and blew out his brains.

Chapter Three

The Labs. Wednesday, 9.30 a.m.

John Winter was humming to himself as he entered his main dissection room, pleased to be back in his comfort zone. He didn't mind attending crime scenes; in fact he normally quite enjoyed it, giving him as it did a different perspective on the world generally and an additional one on the crime's victim which helped him put their last living moments in context.

But yesterday's visit to a frozen quarry way out in the country had been both physically uncomfortable *and* had cost him brownie points at home, causing him to miss his weekly couples counselling appointment with his wife Natalie. They'd been attending the sessions with Doctor Amanda Beresford for months now and he had to admit that they *were* doing their challenging marriage some good, moving their relationship from outright conflict bordering on possible separation to an entente, that in the bedroom at least, had become *decidedly* cordiale, although part of him did wonder whether *that* hadn't more to do with his newly long hair, waving almost to his collar, and the Balbo beard that Natalie had encouraged him to grow.

He thought the combination made him look like a musketeer, but he wasn't knocking the look because the effect on their love life had been astounding; although if hair growth *had* been all that was needed then he wished he'd known that the year before because it would have saved them over two grand in psychologist's fees.

But it was probably a good idea that they *were* still attending the sessions, because another and potentially even larger family problem looked as if it was about to rear its head; that of their not yet two-year-old daughter Kit, an absolute angel in his eyes. She was cheerful, playful and affectionate, but for her high-achieving mother that didn't seem to be enough. Natalie was a surgeon and she expected her daughter to equal her achievements in a man's world if not surpass them, so a nuclear physicist, a professor, perhaps even an astronaut were all on her favoured career list. But they *weren't* on his. All *he* wanted was for Kit to be the same happy, loving, affectionate person at ten, twenty, fifty and eighty-years-old as she was now, and if Natalie's absurd ambitions threatened that in *any* way then they were going to have problem number two.

John had to admit to being surprised by the ferocity of his protectiveness towards their daughter, always imagining that as a man it would have reared mainly or perhaps even only in the event of a perceived physical threat. But the idea that Natalie might ever pressure, harangue, stress or in any way make unhappy their adorable infant was making him want to roar already, and before that happened he wanted Doctor Beresford to deconstruct the problem calmly and logically and then to put his wife firmly back in her box!

But that would have to wait for next week's appointment because as he entered the cool dissection room John Winter the professional pushed all personal thoughts to one side. By the time he'd drawn back the sheet covering his patient his mind was only on the man lying in front of him, and the next ninety minutes were a dance of X-raying, dissection, photography and recording, so that by the time it drew to a conclusion he had the man's definite cause of death diagnosed and taken the samples that would tell the police all they needed to know about their victim's final day.

To help even more he decided to carry the evidence the three floors up to the forensic department himself, where he found his partner in criminology, Doctor Des Marsham, polishing a shiny nameplate on his door.

"Is that new, Des?"

The forensic scientist turned in surprise at the words, so absorbed that he'd completely missed the pathologist's clog-heavy footsteps approach.

"Oh, hello, John. I didn't hear you coming. Yes, it's my first nameplate with 'Head of Government Forensics' on it. You'll be getting a new one as well. *Government, eh?* Sounds important, doesn't it?"

As they'd *always* been the government leads John didn't quite get the thrill, so as he slipped through the half-open door into the scientist's office he responded in a droll tone.

"Be still my beating heart."

Before Des could retort the pathologist held up their victim's X-rays and a plastic bag full of samples by way of explanation for his visit, forcing the forensic scientist to cast one last loving look at his nameplate and then join him inside the room.

"I was just going to ask you why you were here. Who are those from?"

The medic set everything down on the desk. "The man found in the quarry in Rownton yesterday. Your on-call CSIs came down to help."

Des' brown eyes widened as he remembered something. "If it's him then I have something for *you* to look at too."

Just as he reached into his desk drawer to retrieve the item in question the door flew open again, and the room suddenly seemed crowded as the combined bulk that was Liam and Craig forged in.

"Hold that thought for a minute, Des." Craig scanned the office. "Where's your coffee?"

"I don't drink it, remember. But I can offer you a nice cup of tea."

As his deputy said, "That'll do", Craig shook his head and beckoned everyone to follow him, and in less than a minute they were downstairs in John's office, re-running the drinks conversation with more success.

Once Craig had a mug of coffee in his hand and had found himself a chair, he gave an apologetic smile.

"Sorry, Des, but I can't think without caffeine."

An arch, "How *did* you manage at school?" prompted John to reply.

"Ah, now that was in the years *pre* addiction. It was controllable until we went to Queen's but ever since then he's been hooked."

Bored with the debate about his coffee habit, not his worst it had to be said, Craig moved the conversation on.

"So what were you two about to discuss upstairs?"

Des motioned for permission to sit at the pathologist's computer and withdrew some small X-ray films from his pocket.

"I'll show you once John scans in these dental X-rays."

A minute later they were logged into the police missing persons' database and the central repository of dental X-rays and their victim's information was running against both. Meanwhile Des brought an image file up on the screen.

"While we're waiting for those to run, this is the scan of a photograph my CSIs found in your victim's pocket. Thankfully it was tucked into the small coin pocket inside his jacket, so it was soggy but not completely wrecked."

Liam nodded sagely. "Wrecked. A solid technical term that. Trashed is another one."

"And both apply to us when we've been out on the lash."

As the forensic scientist tweaked the image's contrasts Craig asked the question that he knew he *should* have asked the CSIs the day before.

"Did your team find any ID on him, Des? A driving licence or credit cards maybe?"

The reply was coolly logical. "If they had done I wouldn't be wasting my time running his dental X-rays, now would I?"

The retort made the detective smirk. "Fair point. I *was* teaching my granny how to suck eggs." He gestured at the computer screen. "So there was nothing but this photo?"

The scientist shook his head as he continued typing. "Nothing. His wallet was gone."

John cut in. "And his watch. There was a tan line where it should have been. They left his wedding ring behind."

Liam nudged his boss. "His cards and watch might have been worth something."

Craig nodded slowly. "There *could* have been an element of robbery here, or they might just have been taken as an afterthought."

"*Or,* the killer might have chucked them in the water. We'll need divers to check."

Craig nodded. "Organise that, will you, Liam. Brief them as-"

He was cut off by Des announcing, "Here we go" and turning the computer around to face them. On it was a blurred image of a small girl, wearing a summer dress, sandals, and a flowery sunhat pushed back from her face.

There was a stunned silence in the room, which didn't mean that there was no activity. Thoughts and feelings don't make a sound.

Then, because everyone's perspective in life is shaped

by their experiences both detectives shuddered violently and Des Marsham looked sad. In light of the policemen's reactions he tempered his expression almost immediately with defensiveness.

"I know what you're thinking, but she could have been his daughter! *That* might be why he kept the photo with him."

Craig threw him a bone. "You're right, Des, she *could* be his daughter. Let's think positively."

John was looking confused. "Sorry, but why do we need to think positively? Does that mean you were thinking something *negative* about the picture? I mean what could there possibly be..."

His words tailed off as he realised what had been on the policemen's minds. "Oh God, you think he was a paedophile!" He felt sick. "I might just have PM-ed a paedophile!"

They all knew that his horror was irrational because after death we're all just a bag of bones, but at the same time *everyone* understood.

Liam cut in. "Not a paedo for sure, Doc, it *could* just be our warped minds. I mean any of *us* could be carrying a photo of our kids when we die and it wouldn't make *us* one." The D.C.I. winced slightly before going on. "But it's just... because the photo was being hidden... well, it *is* something we need to chuck into the pot. Considering that he was murdered and all."

Craig agreed his deputy's softening caveat with a nod. He knew he was growing more cynical with age and he also knew that he needed to rein it in, so he might as well start now.

"Liam's right, so let's agree for now that the girl *could* be our victim's daughter. How old does she look to everyone?"

Des offered his opinion first. "Four maybe."

Liam shook his head. "Nah, not much older than two there. She's still a wee bit bow-legged and that starts to straighten out about two."

Craig turned from the dad-experts to the anatomist in their midst. "John?"

"Liam's half-right. Genu varum, bow-legs, are a normal variant until around two when they should start to straighten. But hers *are* almost straight, Liam, so I'd say she's nearer three-years-old."

"How old do you think our dead man was?"

"Forty maybe." He added hopefully. "So still in the usual age-range to be her dad."

"Especially as..." Craig leaned in closer to the computer's screen as he continued. "I know the photo was underwater for a while but do those colours look strange to anyone? Dull, like old-fashioned pictures."

He was thinking of photos he'd had taken as a kid in the late seventies and eighties which, even allowing for the fact that the whole world seemed to have been painted brown and orange at the time, had always seemed to bear an ochre tinge.

John made a face. "I don't think it was taken a long time ago if that's what you mean. I think the colours might look strange to us because it was taken with an actual camera, and we're used to brighter digital images now. Also, maybe it was already an old photo of the girl so it was faded? A favourite of her when she was young that he just didn't want to put away. She could be a teenager now for all we know."

Craig conceded the points and turned back to the forensic scientist. "Can you see what you can find out from the original? And you said it was in his coin pocket?"

"Yes and yes."

Liam interjected. "Coin pockets are small, so were the edges curled up?"

"Actually, it was folded in two. I photo-shopped out the crease in its centre."

"Folded so it would fit in his coin pocket..." Craig took a sip of coffee as he considered what they had.

"OK, so... by virtue of the fact our victim was carrying the photo at all, it was obviously important to him. So why risk ruining it by folding it in two? From memory, his jacket looked like most other jackets..." He glanced at his deputy for confirmation and got a nod, "...so there *were* several larger pockets in which he *could* have carried it, inside his wallet would have been the usual place, yet he stuffs it into a tiny coin one, damaging it. Not the usual place for a photo, is it? Not unless..." He gave a small smile as he continued, "... not unless you're afraid that you might *lose* the contents of your other pockets."

Liam smiled. "Because they're the first place that someone mugging you would search for cash."

"Yes. *Or* look to remove anything that might identify you once they'd killed you."

John shook his head. "By that reckoning why not burn off his fingertips and yank out all his teeth?"

Liam's eyes widened. "Frick me, Doc! Remind me not to piss *you* off."

The interaction made Craig laugh. "Have you been at the gangster box-sets again, John?"

The pathologist gave an embarrassed smile. "All right, you've caught me. But tell me how I'm wrong? If his attacker *really* hadn't wanted our John-Doe identified then surely they would have done the job properly?"

Craig shrugged. "There could be lots of reasons why they didn't. Maybe they were in a hurry, or squeamish, or they were amateurs so they didn't think of it. Or perhaps they just don't watch as much TV as you."

"Funny man."

Liam had another suggestion. "More likely they thought our Vic would never be found at the bottom of a quarry pool. Although... why didn't they, boss? They couldn't have expected him *not* to float unless he'd been weighted down. He wasn't, was he, Docs?"

The scientists shook their heads simultaneously and a jumble of, "No weights found" and "No marks to indicate it" emerged.

The debate made Craig sit up straight.

"That's actually a good point, Liam." He turned back to the pathologist. "John, allowing for the fact that we *might* find metal weights if we trawl the water, or the killer might just have put some handy rocks in our Vic's pockets that fell out over time, why do *you* think he hadn't floated to the top?"

"The most likely reason is that he got caught on sub-surface vegetation. It looked like there was a lot in there."

"Maybe..." Craig turned back to his deputy. "But the killer couldn't have *relied* on that, so in the event of our man floating to the surface why didn't they *expect* him to be seen?" He answered his own question. "They thought no-one went near the quarry because it was closed. They didn't reckon on the local kids."

"That's careless, boss."

"It's a pretty isolated area."

Liam took out his notepad and scribbled a memo to himself. "I noticed some huts near the old entrance gates so I'll get those checked out. There could be a guard for the site. But even if there is, they might not be that fussy about doing their rounds and never have checked the pool."

Craig frowned as something occurred to him. "Or maybe the guard was in on the killing so he didn't *need* to check. He already knew that our Vic was there."

The detectives were still debating the point when John returned to the photograph.

"So you think our John Doe was definitely hiding the girl's photo, Marc?"

"What? Oh, yes, hidden would be my choice, unless anyone can think of another reason it might have been folded up in that pocket?"

There was a shaking of heads as the pathologist went on.

"OK, so *why* hide it then? Apart from thinking he might get mugged."

Liam volunteered an answer. "Maybe he loved her and wanted to keep it close to his heart?"

Craig shook his head. "Nice idea, but then why destroy it by folding it? John's right, if he *was* hiding it we need to find the reason why. Mugging's one idea and your suggestion that he loved the girl is another. Anything else?"

As Des moved away from the computer and waved John back to his desk, his expression turned morose.

"Because he knew he shouldn't have had it at all and didn't want it discovered."

"Go on."

"Because she *wasn't* his daughter and you two were right about him being a paedo, in which case I'm glad he's dead."

Liam gave a cheer. "Yeh! A man after my own heart."

Craig rolled his eyes. "We're supposed to be the ones *upholding* the law. Remember? Although I can't say that I disagree."

He took a sip of coffee and regrouped. "OK, so maybe

she was his daughter and he hid it because he wanted to keep it close to his heart or was afraid it would be stolen, or maybe he was a paedophile and he was hiding it because he didn't want to get caught. In *any* case, I want to return to whoever killed him and dumped his body for a moment. There's another reason why he mightn't have been weighed down-"

Liam jumped in. "They didn't *care* if he was found."

"Yes. So *why* didn't they care?"

The D.C.I.'s eyes widened in realisation. "Because whoever killed him doesn't think the body will ever lead back to them." His forehead furrowed. "Aw hell, that means our Vic'll have no connection with his killer."

Craig shook his head. "Not so fast. He may *not* think the body will lead back to him because there's no connection, or not an obvious one anyway, or he *may* just be an arrogant bastard who thinks that all cops are thick. It's clear it's going to take hard work to work out who this killer is, but then if our jobs were easy we would all get bored."

Not everyone looked so sure about that, but Craig ignored any lack of enthusiasm and went on.

"OK, so our man hid the photo where it wouldn't be found, either to protect it, from sentiment, or because he shouldn't have had it. Let's take the first and last. Hiding it for those two reasons means that he either feared or *expected* someone to go looking for it. Who? Who would have looked in his pockets?"

He scanned the small group impatiently. "Suggestions? Oh, come on, wake up you lot!"

Des' interest was piqued. It was like one of the murder detective dinner parties that he went to with his wife; the ones that he never solved and she, frustratingly, *always* did.

"You mean who would have looked in his pockets *apart* from his killer?"

Craig shrugged. "Apart from, or as well as. We can't know when our victim hid that photo in his coin pocket."

John's mind went immediately to Natalie. "His wife." At Liam's smirk he added hastily, "If she was checking his jacket before she took it to the dry cleaners, that is."

The smirk widened.

"Natalie do that often, does she?"

The thought of the feminist surgeon doing anything so domestic made everyone but her husband laugh. Instead, the pathologist tapped his nose mysteriously in a show of machismo that none of them, not even his best friend, believed.

"You don't know *half* of the things that Natalie does for me."

He gave a knowing laugh that made Craig, seeing his deputy preparing to demolish the medic with a pointed retort, direct everyone hastily back to the case.

"Focus, please. OK, more suggestions? So far, we have wives looking in pockets for domestic reasons, or perhaps even because they're suspicious of their husbands. OK, our John Doe might *not* have wanted his wife to find the girl's photo if he was up to no good, but it's unlikely that a woman could have exerted enough force to hold him down and drown him. John?"

"Not unless she was a body builder. It took considerable force to leave those bruises *and* they were man-sized."

"So you're *confirming* now that our killer was a man?"

"Yep."

"OK, good. That rules out half the human race anyway. More suggestions, please. If John Doe *wasn't* hiding the photo from his wife, then who else did he think might have been looking for it, and why?"

Des interjected thoughtfully. "*Who,* might have been one of the girl's male relatives. *Why,* could have been them searching for proof of what our John Doe had done to her."

Liam shook his head firmly, which finally removed his lingering smirk about Natalie. "Except he obviously *didn't* find the photo, hence no proof our Vic was a paedo. So why kill him?"

"But by then the father or brother might have been so wound up that his suspicions might have made them kill anyway."

Craig furrowed his brow for a moment and then turned to his deputy again. "Tell everyone why that doesn't work, Liam."

"Because an angry male family member would have given our John Doe a hiding before he drowned him-"

Craig raised a hand to halt him so he could check the

point.

"*Any* signs of a fight on the PM, John?"

"None. There could have been some on his hands I suppose, but they've gone. There were a few abrasions and cracks but they fit more with bashing against stones in the water and they happened *after* death. And before you ask, no, there were no prints anywhere on the body. Des can tell you if there were fibres."

Craig glanced at the forensic lead and he shook his head.

"Just vegetation and a few dead insects. Sorry."

Craig nodded his deputy to continue.

"So with a male relative of the girl there's no way our Vic would have got off *without* having his head beaten in. In fact, violent assault would have been a more likely way of killing him than drowning; it fits better with a crime of emotion. Just holding him down in the water till he drowned would be too clean a death for someone suspected of killing your child."

Craig grinned with pride. When Liam concentrated he was a damn good cop.

"Exactly. Liam's right; the death was far too clean. Our victim was killed calmly and in cold blood by someone *unrelated* to the girl in that photo. Which tells us that either the girl's photo had nothing to do with the reason he died, or it had but the killer wasn't a *relative* of the girl. And if they *were* looking for the photo, which we can't *know*, we *can* say that although its discovery might have been something that our John Doe feared, they definitely failed to find it. OK, Liam-"

John gave a low whistle, something that was sufficiently rare to stop Craig in his tracks.

"That confirms it..."

"What?"

"The reason for the bruises' positioning." He stood up. "I'll show you. Stand up, Marc."

The detective obliged, looking bemused.

"OK, now face me, and bear with me while I demonstrate something."

Craig moved into position. "Crack on."

He was surprised when a moment later the pathologist gripped his shoulders with such strength he would never have credited it as coming from his slim frame.

"Blimey, John, when did *you* start working out?"

The medic gave a smug smile. "Six months ago, but I didn't mention it because I knew you lot would just take the piss."

He tightened his grip and tried to push Craig vertically down towards the floor. That was where he reached the limit of his strength; the detective merely smiled at him and didn't shift.

"Sorry, but I started gym work thirty years before you, remember. But go ahead and make your point."

John conceded defeat and removed his hands.

"OK, so, if I attack you, grip your shoulders and try to push you down under the water to drown you, first, I'd have to be taller than you, and second I'd have to be considerably stronger. Also, you *would* struggle and try to fight back."

"OK...so, what height was our John Doe?"

"Five-eight and slim, although he's pretty wiry, so fit I'd say. That means his attacker was taller, quite a lot taller I'd say, and a great deal stronger too."

"And if the killer had attacked face-on and we'd found him soon after the attack *he'd* likely have had some injuries, probably on his face or torso, yes?"

Liam chipped in. "Or legs if our man had kicked him before he'd managed to shove him underwater. But none of that helps us, Doc, 'cos those injuries would've healed ages ago."

"True. But this *wasn't* a frontal attack. Look at the bruises I would have left on Marc's shoulders coming at him from the front. My finger bruising would all have been on his back, except for my thumb gripping the front just above his clavicle." He motioned to Craig. "OK, now turn around." After repeating the experiment for a moment both men retook their seats and the pathologist continued speaking.

"The finger bruises I found on our John Doe were all on the front of his shoulders, so they could *only* have been made if his assailant had pushed him under the water *from behind*."

The words made Craig frown. "I could see that being easy if he'd already been in the water and *then* someone had come at him from above and behind, but no-one goes swimming wearing a suit! And the odds of someone being suicidal and already having walked into the water to drown themselves, then being coincidentally killed by an obliging passerby are... well, absurd."

John shook his head, "What if our victim was on the shore by the water looking around for something? His attacker could have run at him from behind, caught him by surprise, and then pushed him quickly into the water and straight down."

Liam nodded. "Coming from behind's another thing that goes against a passion based assault. Those come face-on. This wasn't personal, boss."

"Mmm... except..." Craig considered for a moment. "I can picture your scenario working physically, John, and it may *not* have been strictly personal, Liam, I agree, but there *is* another dimension here, I'm sure of it. Assaults from behind are usually unemotional, yes, but *rarely* hands on. Why *bother* to run at someone and push them down into the water when you could hit them with something or shoot them in the back? Once you initiate physical contact with your victim you're adding another layer to a killing."

"Maybe he didn't want to shoot him in case we did ballistics on the bullet?"

Des shook his head. "He could have dug it out before he left."

Suddenly Craig palmed his forehead. "*Of course!* I'm stupid. There was no extraneous violence here and no sign of a fight, and coming at our Vic from the back suggests an unemotional, efficient dispatch, OK. But more than that..."

He locked eyes with his deputy and they both nodded. "The killer didn't want to face him because they *knew* each other somehow. But not well, not enough to have strong passions involved. The killer knew his victim peripherally somehow, but the motive for *killing* him wasn't emotional, it was something else. Practical. Our victim wasn't just murdered he was *dispatched*."

Liam nodded. "I'm not even sure that he wanted to kill him."

Craig nodded furiously, his mind a skein of thoughts that he was trying to unravel. "Yes, yes, you're right. But he thought he *had* to kill him for some reason, and he couldn't look in his eyes as he did."

Des had been listening with widening eyes. "A lot taller, much stronger, no struggle, dispassionate, and not a relative of the girl. And now you're saying they knew each other peripherally, and he probably hadn't really wanted to kill him but needs must! That's quite a theory without even having your victim's name. Now you just have to prove it."

Liam sonorous chuckle filled the room. "Aye, well, there's always that."

John was shaking his head. "No. I don't believe it. If someone tells me to turn my back and they're planning to kill me I'm not going meekly, I'm going to fight!"

"And maybe he did, John, and the months in the water have destroyed the signs, or maybe he was caught unawares and our killer ran at him and shoved him in and under. But I stand by what we've said and only time will show whether we're right or not."

Craig smiled and returned to a thought he'd had earlier. "Liam, make a note that I need Davy to check out the original of the girl's photo in more detail, will you. Right, let's move on. Why was our dead man even in the area in the first place? Looking at his suit I'd have said he was an office worker. It certainly wasn't country gear."

John nodded excitedly. "It was an Armani. They're fifteen hundred bucks a pop."

Craig smiled at the *'bucks'*. Cowboys and gangsters; exactly the same as when they'd been at school.

"OK, so, *that's* an anomaly. A wealthy office type found dead in an abandoned country quarry. Anything on his time of death, John?"

"He's been dead between three and four months, and cause of death was straightforward drowning. His lungs were full of water and algae, definitely inhaled as he died and was gasping for breath because the algae was so far down in his airways. And like I said, the size and location of the shoulder bruising fits with a man's hands holding him under from behind. There were no other injuries other than the odd skin tear that fits with banging against the rocks, and a couple of broken ribs. Contact fractures."

"Contact from a fist?"

"No. They weren't displaced inwards, just hairline

cracks. I'd say he hit the rocks as he went under or bobbed against them later. He was dead when they happened."

Craig rubbed his chin thoughtfully. "OK, good. We've got an initial picture of what happened. We'll need his stomach contents and blood analysis to see if there's anything interesting there, Des. Maybe we'll find something useful on his last meal. Do a mineral analysis on his bones too, please. Let's see where he was from if it wasn't Rownton." He motioned at the screen. "Now, can you sharpen up the girl's photo any?"

"I can't but Davy could. I'll send it across."

"What about our Vic's prints and facial features, John?"

"His fingertips were taken by insects or maceration, and so was some of his face, but I can try to reconstruct that from his skull X-ray if you give me a day."

"Half-a-day."

The bartering was interrupted by a loud jingling of bells that startled Des and made Liam laugh.

"Is that your computer alert, Doc?"

The pathologist gave a sheepish nod. "I had Kit down here on Sunday so I changed it to one she liked and forgot to put it back."

The D.C.I. snickered. "I wouldn't bother. It suits you."

Craig got back to the point. "What was the noise *for*, Tinkerbell?"

John glanced at his screen.

"It's the dental X-rays. They've thrown up a result!"

Des was impressed. "That was quick! It never does that upstairs."

Before the difference in broadband speeds between the pathology building's floors sparked an argument about medical privilege, Craig asked the important question.

"And our victim's name is?"

John scanned the screen hurriedly, the tone of Craig's question saying that he didn't want to wait.

"Stuart Kincaid. Date of birth the first of August nineteen-seventy-five. Forty-three-years-old. I was right about his age." He tapped a few keys and shook his head. "OK, I've only run a first level check but he doesn't seem to have a criminal record."

Craig nodded. "Davy will dig deeper. Google him and see what else you can find, John."

A few taps later and an image of their victim in better days appeared. The biography beneath it declared him to be the managing director of a company called Kincaid Holdings in Portaferry, a small fishing and sailing town on the tip of the Ards Peninsula.

John read aloud. "It's a shipping and export company. Do you want me to check it out at Companies House?"

Craig shook his head. "Our lot can do that."

"Fine. Well, at least ID-ing him saves me having to reconstruct this skull."

Des nodded. "And me a mineral analysis."

Liam sat forward eagerly. "Is there anything on there about his family? Did he have a daughter?"

The medic scrolled down swiftly. "Nothing on his company bio... but let me search again."

A longer wait this time yielded Stuart Kincaid's personal information.

"OK, this is from twenty-seventeen's Ulster Bazaar, a piece on the Down Royal races. It looks like Kincaid's company hosted a hospitality event at it."

He moved down the page, reading aloud, "Wife Luisa... a veterinary surgeon. And...they have two children." He took a deep breath before adding, "Sons. Fourteen and sixteen."

No-one spoke, all of them watching Craig's rapidly changing thoughts hurtle across his face.

Stuart Kincaid had only had sons, and unless they were extremely precocious neither was old enough to have fathered the little girl in the photograph. So was she a child that Kincaid had fathered by someone else? And if she wasn't Kincaid's daughter or granddaughter then what was she? A cousin or a niece perhaps?

The detective breathed in and out slowly, trying not to let his thoughts return to the dark place where they'd originally jumped. But it was unavoidable. Stuart Kincaid had had a photograph of a small girl *hidden* in his pocket so the possibility had to be faced; their dead man *might* have been a paedophile.

He shuddered, remembering the day when someone had tried to take his younger sister Lucia from their garden in Holywood; a convicted paedophile they'd discovered later, but at the time just a pervert that his nineteen-year-old self had caught and beaten half to death. It had almost landed him in jail and with a very different life to the one that he had now, and he remembered every day just how lucky he was. It made him think of Annette again as well; she was the only member of his team that knew the truth about that period in his life.

The episode had left him with a particular loathing of anyone who harmed children, almost above any other sort of criminal, and in a thought that he kept firmly to himself Craig decided that if Kincaid *did* turn out to be a child molester, he would buy his killer a drink before he locked them up.

But the possibility that their victim was a paedophile was still only one of many that they had to explore, so to make sense of things the detective motioned his friend to let him at the computer and logged into the UK and Ireland wide missing persons' databases as well as Interpol's and Europol's.

After minutes of search screens flashing past in silence, the thought of what might appear stopping all conversation, Craig paused on a screenshot and typed in some additional parameters, launching a much slower search. Finally, he sat back and gave a nod as an image identical to the photograph that they'd found in Stuart Kincaid's pocket appeared.

He turned the screen around to face the others, speaking in a subdued voice. "Bella Mary Westbury, born May twenty-twelve-"

Liam cut in, determined to find something positive to say about the little girl before the axe dropped.

"Almost seven now. Lovely age."

Craig carried on reading as if he hadn't heard. "Missing since the twenty-ninth of August twenty-fifteen when she was aged three and three months. She disappeared from the back garden of a house in Nice in the South of France and hasn't been seen since. Her father and all male relatives and neighbours were ruled out early on, so the case was labelled a stranger abduction..." His voice quietened further and faltered... "She's... presumed dead."

"Fucker!"

There was no disagreement with Liam's description of the girl's abductor, in fact Craig added to it himself.

"Anything that involves children deserves the death penalty."

John's eyebrows shot up. "A minute ago you were telling us off for that!"

"That was vigilantism. This wouldn't be. The courts would try them fair and square first."

"But you've always been anti death penalty."

"Where kids are concerned I could be persuaded to make an exception."

He darkened the screen, seeking solace in logic.

"OK, let's think about this as unemotionally as we can. Bella Westbury was abducted in France almost three and a half years ago-"

Des had been quiet since the computer searches had started, but now he interrupted in a quizzical voice.

"Hang on, Marc." He glanced around the group. "Westbury? Does no-one but me think it's strange that she has an Irish surname?"

Both detectives' foreheads creased but Liam spoke first.

"Why wouldn't she? We're in Ireland."

"But *she* wasn't. Only her photograph is *now*."

Craig's eyebrows lifted in realisation. "*Of course...* Why would she have an Irish surname when she was abducted in France?" He smiled at the scientist. "Well spotted, Des. I'd completely missed that. If she *was* Irish then that gives us a possible link to Kincaid."

The forensic expert made a face. "Is."

"What?"

"Can we please say she *is* Irish instead of was? At least until we're sure that she's dead."

Craig smiled. "Fair point. We'll only speak of her in the present tense unless we prove otherwise."

John interjected. "OK, but what was she doing in France then?"

Des took that one as well. "She could have been there on holiday. Or maybe she had a French mum and an Irish dad and was there visiting relatives."

Craig joined in. "Or she *might* actually have been living there at the time. I know it's hard to believe that anyone would ever want to leave God's own country, but some people *do* leave Ireland to emigrate."

He smiled at Liam as he said it, knowing that while the

D.C.I. would spend the odd couple of days outside Ireland if he had to for work, Germany being one trip they'd taken together, getting him to leave the country for any longer than that would take a miracle; his long suffering wife Danni had to fight him for even a week's holiday abroad! His deputy was unambiguously Irish and had both feet firmly planted in his country's soil.

Craig stretched his arms above his head and yawned before he examined the possible scenarios; the night before had been another with little sleep because Katy had found getting comfortable nigh on impossible. The latter stages of pregnancy were no joke for the mother; in fact, he imagined that pretty much none of it was.

He sat forward briskly in an attempt to wake himself up.

"OK, so we have Bella Westbury, Irish, possibly abducted-"

Liam cut in. "Hang on, boss. The file said *presumed* dead. So no body found? In three years?" As he said it he tried not to picture the image the words conjured.

Craig shook his head. "That's a good point, but-"

"Davy'll need to check. Boys-oh, *he's* going to be busy."

"Ash can do some of it..."

Ash Rahman was the squad's junior analyst, although no-one would never have known it from the way he carried on with his boss, with a cheeky familiarity that came from him and Davy doing their masters degrees in computing together, and Davy was far too modest to point out their current difference in rank unless forced.

"... Davy's got some big presentation to do this week as part of his PhD, and he needs time to prepare. Anyway, so this little girl disappeared in France three and a half years ago without a trace... Liam, I want you to work with the analysts and find out the extent of the French investigation. Get a copy of their file sent over and let me know of any trail you think we should pursue. Anything that we can dig deeper on..."

The D.C.I. gave a brisk nod.

"...We need to find out *why* Stuart Kincaid might have had her photograph, legitimately or otherwise." He looked at the scientists, "Any ideas? Just throw them out."

Des went first. "OK, so, the girl was very young in this

photo, three or even a bit less?"

He was answered by a nod from John.

"And she was taken at three and three months, so the snap was obviously taken not long before she disappeared, wasn't it?"

John frowned. "What's your point?"

"Well, if she isn't dead and Stuart Kincaid *was* the paedophile who took her, shouldn't he have been carrying a more recent image of her than that?" The scientist swallowed hard, "And... maybe not such an innocent one."

Liam grimaced. "So she *could* be dead and they just haven't found the body."

Craig was less negative. "I think he's suggesting Kincaid might not have seen her since *before* she was abducted."

Des chewed his bottom lip, and part of his beard with it, which made John want to gag and decide never to grow his own as long.

"It's just a thought. It's just... well that photo seems more like a memento to me." The forensic lead's round face became glum. "But then why did Kincaid have it at all? I mean most people don't carry around photos of kids unless they're related to them, do they? And Kincaid only had sons-"

"Remember that we still need to rule out that Bella *wasn't* his child as well, Des."

John interrupted eagerly. "So if she *was* Kincaid's long-lost daughter and he was searching for her, *that* could be why he was carrying it."

Liam rolled his eyes cynically. "How old are you that you still believe in fairytales?"

Craig ignored him, interested. "Go on, John."

"Maybe *hunting* for the girl got Stuart Kincaid killed."

Liam made a face. "But *why* hunt for her? Leaving aside your fantasy that he might be her dad, Kincaid was in shipping! He wasn't a cop or even a private eye who was *equipped* to investigate. And anyway, there's other stuff that says no."

"Outline it."

"OK, well, for one thing, how would Kincaid have found the abductor when the police case had obviously gone cold? Seventy-four percent of abducted children are found dead within three hours, eighty-nine percent within twenty-four, and the trail usually dies with them. And this is *years* later without even a body to give up evidence, so where would Kincaid even have found enough info to pursue?" He gestured at John, on a roll now. "And then there's Kincaid's lack of injuries. If a relative's hunting for-"

Craig cut him off. "If Kincaid wasn't a relative, your earlier comments about that don't apply."

Liam gave an irritated tut. "OK then, then why hunt *at all* if he wasn't a relative? And why hunt in Ireland when the abduction was in France?"

He looked at Craig so triumphantly that it earned him a smile.

"OK, maybe you're right and maybe you're not. For now let's just agree there was something odd about Kincaid's death. I'm not sure yet what that was, but there may well be a link between this girl's disappearance and his murder."

He scanned the group for other ideas and when none came he rose to his feet.

"Thanks, everyone, that was useful, but we won't get any further without some facts, so we'd better go and find them." As he turned towards the door he glanced at his deputy. "Next steps?"

"We need more on the girl, *and* what's been going on in the Kincaid family since twenty-fifteen, particularly with the dad."

Craig nodded and then left the office deep in thought, leaving Liam to say their goodbyes.

Chapter Four

The C.C.U. The Murder Squad. Wednesday, 1 p.m.

Craig had originally called a briefing for twelve o'clock, but Liam's growling stomach and moaning mouth had stymied *that* plan, so it was fish and chips and an hour later when they finally pitched up at the squad-room, to be greeted by another person moaning; Alice, Craig's temporary PA.

She hurtled across the floor to greet the detectives as they entered, demonstrating her ballroom dancing honed fleetness of foot.

"There's a lawyer in your room from the Police Ombudsman's office, sir! And you need to return these calls."

The words were accompanied by a sheaf of yellow stickies being thrust into Liam's hand, Craig already having bolted for his room before she'd reached the end of 'Ombudsman.'

The detective threw open its door panicked, knowing that within the next minute he would learn what fate awaited his inspector and already girding himself for a fight. In the five seconds between entering and meeting his visitor's gaze he sent up a silent hope, which hit the floor with a smash the moment he read what was in her eyes.

By the time the solicitor opened her mouth to speak Craig was already slumped in his chair sighing, but as her name, "Sorcha Weller", hit the air he straightened up and readied himself to battle on.

"Thank you for coming, Ms Weller. I take it you don't have good news for me."

The thirtyish woman didn't bother to ask how he knew, merely shook her neatly bobbed head.

"I'm sorry, but no. The Ombudsman wanted you to know of the outcome of his investigation quickly so that you could support D.I. Eakin."

Craig waved her to a seat, replying caustically, "Very considerate of him, I'm sure. Do pass on my thanks." His tone changed from sarcastic to brisk. "OK, so what are his feelings on the matter?"

It was Weller's cue to remove a sheet of paper from the sleek handbag on her lap.

"You'll understand that the Ombudsman has merely laid out the findings of his investigation, but based on those the Public Prosecution Service's view of the most likely charge is... well, you'd better see for yourself."

She slid the page across the desk and Craig scanned it swiftly, his eyebrows rising incrementally as the eyes beneath them moved down the page.

"Manslaughter? They've got to be bloody kidding!"

The solicitor was taken aback. Kidding wasn't a word that she often associated with the work that she did, and she was also used to a *much* more deferential response from the police. But shocked though she was her exhibition of the feeling was restricted to a slight reddening of her cheeks as she responded primly.

"The office of Ombudsman and the PPS *never* joke, Chief Superintendent, and I urge you to take this matter seriously."

Craig only half-heard the words, barely aware of and definitely un-chastised by her finger-wagging tone. When he eventually set down the page he stared straight into the solicitor's eyes, in a way that had made serial killers quake.

"I understand that this is your job, Ms Weller, and thank you for alerting us early, but Detective Inspector Eakin is an exceptional officer, her husband was a violent offender who appeared in her bedroom on his first night's leave from prison, and she reacted on instinct and training when she fired."

He leaned forward just enough to underline what he said next without being intimidating.

"So, first: contrary to common opinion the Ombudsman *isn't* infallible, he merely investigates and writes reports; and although this *may* be the PPS' first thought on charges they'll have several hurdles to overcome before *any* are brought. We'll be supporting D.I. Eakin on a plea of self defence and she'll have the best barrister in the country defending her," his voice hardened slightly, "even if I have to pay for them myself."

He stood up abruptly and extended a hand, taking the lawyer aback.

"I don't shoot messengers, so thank you for coming all this way, Ms Weller. By all means report my words *and* their tone to your boss, but I would be grateful if I could tell D.I. Eakin of these findings myself."

He was surprised when Weller shook her head.

"I'm sorry, but a copy of this letter was hand-delivered to her this morning."

Shit! He needed to see Annette PDQ before she had a meltdown. She was a sensible woman not given to panic, but even sensible people can only deal with so much.

The solicitor managed a small smile of sympathy as she shook his hand. "But I'll tell the Ombudsman what you said about her innocence and I really hope that it all works out."

The squeeze she gave before she dropped the grip said that she'd meant the words despite his brusqueness towards her, perhaps recognising that his anger came from concern.

As Craig opened the door for the lawyer to exit, she was almost knocked over by his deputy barrelling in.

"Liam! Watch out!"

The D.C.I. caught the now red-faced Weller just as she threatened to fall backwards over her chair. He straightened her up and waved her out past him, then turned urgently to his boss.

"We need to get back to Rownton."

Craig shook his head. "I need to brief everyone and then we have to go and see Annette."

As the D.C.I.'s sandy eyebrows shot up questioningly, Craig shook his head. "I'll tell you about it on the way. Anyway, what's the hurry to get back to Omagh?"

He could have sworn that his deputy was stifling a smile as he answered.

"Because a local builder's gone and shot himself in the head!"

****

The C.C.U. 2.30 p.m.

By half-past-two everyone on the squad knew that the dead man in the quarry was named Stuart Kincaid, his cause of death was forced drowning by a strong assailant months before he'd been found by the teenagers, and that the rest of the PM evidence would have to wait.

Craig deferred telling them about the girl's photograph

until he'd dispatched Aidan Hughes, one of the squad's three Chief Inspectors and undoubtedly its fittest, to Rownton, to interview the farmers in its hinterland and check what more the local uniforms had found. Ryan Hendron, the squad's detective sergeant was going with him to lead some of the interviews. The D.S. had joined the squad from Strangford the year before and had spent a lot of his time so far in court on a joint Belfast/ Strangford murder case, but now with Annette's, potentially lengthy, absence it was time for him to step up.

Craig gave the two men an add-on instruction to save himself a trip, that they were to, "See what the hell that builder's suicide was about" while they were there.

His next order came after he'd given Liam time to outline the discovery of the girl's photograph and the details of her abduction, plus their thoughts so far on what it meant.

"Andy, I'd like you to go and see Stuart Kincaid's family and get them to ID his body. While you're with them dig gently, *very* gently please, on any possible links that there might be with the girl. Show them her photo, but keep it casual, I don't want any dropped hints about anything sordid. They'll be distressed enough about the man being dead."

Andy Angel, the most laid back and artistic of the squad's D.C.I.s, frowned.

"You don't mean the photo that you found with Kincaid, do you?"

"No. It's a mess for one thing, and for another there's a chance that it was used in the appeal when she went missing in twenty-fifteen and so, even if it's a stretch, they might catch on. One of these two can find you a better picture than that. From social media or somewhere."

He indicated the team's two analysts, who were both lounging halfway down in their seats and variously, in Ash's case fiddling with his gold earring, and rubbing at his bare neck with apparent nostalgia in the case of Davy, his boss, who after several years as a long-haired, bearded EMO come hipster had, with his fiancée Maggie's encouragement, had everything shorn off the evening before.

The longing with which he was stroking his nape said

that he was reconsidering the wisdom of the choice already, although the fact that every woman in the building had been dropping in all morning to speak to him on pathetic excuses would have been enough in most men's minds to say that the change had been for the good. But for the shy, and unfortunately, as far as he was concerned male-model handsome analyst, it was *way* too much attention for comfort and his hair couldn't grow again fast enough.

On Craig's follow-up, "And take Mary along with you", Andy's frown turned to a smile, and it was the squad's detective constable, Mary Li's turn to look less than amused.

Andy's happiness came from the fact that he liked company, and her unhappiness was because she hated the cold and February in Ireland was *definitely* that. The desire to avoid the big chill prompted her scowl to convert to an obsequious smile so fast that a lesser boss would have struggled to keep up, but Craig knew *exactly* what it heralded and pre-empted her coming plea before it had emerged from her mouth.

"And no, Davy *won't* need you to remain in the warm office for your computer expertise this time, Mary, but thank you anyway."

The constable had a computing degree and sometimes helped the team's analysts when they were stretched.

"Anyway, it'll be good experience for you to meet Kincaid's family."

He cast a pointed look at her bare arms and legs. Having to cover herself up outdoors was yet another reason why winter wasn't Mary's favourite time of year.

"I suggest you wrap up warm. It's cold out there."

Not even a father yet and already he was starting to sound like his dad.

Craig cut the plea bargaining short by turning back to his analysts.

"Davy, we'll need the photo that Des found sharpened up and the original print looked at for clues. It's not old but there's something strange about the colour quality. We'll also need the girl's French police file, and any CCTV from the village and environs in Nice. I'm particularly interested in the gendarmes' *non*-discovery of her body.

Also, dig into Stuart Kincaid's business and life. I want to know what, if anything, he had to do with that girl." He paused for breath and went on. "Did you manage to sort the Rownton teenagers' phones and emails out?"

The analyst nodded briskly. "Yep."

"OK, good. Do you need me to repeat any of that?" He looked pointedly as the analyst's hand, which was still rubbing the back of his neck. "You didn't write anything down."

"Nope." The computer expert tapped his temple. "Memory. It's a wonderful thing to be young."

His cheekiness became a laugh that Liam cut short by adding more items to his workload.

"And the quarry, find out about that too. Rock types, when it was dug out and all that stuff. Oh, aye, and who owned it and owns it now as well. That could be important. And there are those huts near the entrance, so what's that all about-"

Craig cut back in. "Good, yes. And also, Davy, the violent suicide in Rownton last night that Aidan and Ryan are going to pick up on; see if there's anything useful on the victim." He turned to his deputy. "What was the name, Liam?"

"Derek Morrow. He ate his gun."

Craig waited for a cry of dismay or a tut of disgust at the graphic description, and was saddened when none came. Not only because it showed that the rest of his team were just as jaded as he was, but because it reminded him that Annette, the person who would have been *guaranteed* to give such a reaction, wasn't there.

"Isn't *anyone* revolted by that image?"

A series of shrugs and grunts said not.

"Then you're all either watching too many box-sets or you're burning out. I'm ordering anyone who has holiday owing to take it before the end of the financial year in April."

He glanced across to his PA, "Alice can make up a Rota," and then back at his analysts, returning to the case. "Davy, can you get through all that work?"

The model shook his head, which he was starting to realise felt cold as well as naked. Maybe he should buy a hat and wear it until his hair grew back.

"Not me, chief. Ash will be doing most of the work. I've a presentation to organise."

Craig nodded, "Sorry, yes, I did remember that earlier. Where are you giving it again?"

"Geneva. On the fifteenth. It's the annual W...World IT in Criminology Conference. WICC for short. They've asked me to talk about my research."

It brought a smile to both Craig's and his deputy's faces, but for different reasons.

"Excellent, Davy. Well done."

Liam was positively grinning now so the analyst felt compelled to ask. "Are you just happy for me, Liam, or what?"

"No. I mean, yeh, well done and all that shit, but I was just picturing what your audience would look like. It'll be wall to wall specs, ponytails, beards and headphones. Nerds International."

"We're not nerds, we're *geeks*, because we're interested in technology. Nerds are just obsessed with any old stuff, like Des is obsessed with finding lumps of metal in the ground."

The forensic scientist went metal detecting in his spare time.

The analyst added breezily. "And I'll have you know that we're a very sexy bunch."

As Liam's jaw dropped at his unaccustomed boldness, Craig took advantage of the pause to change the subject before his PA told them off for their language again. Alice had, perhaps not unreasonably, an objection to people contravening work regulations by swearing, being lewd or eating at their desks. He wasn't about to censor his team, who worked far too many hours for far too little pay, but as a concession they'd built a new staff-room at the back of the office before Christmas, and although so far attempts at getting people to limit their use of expletives to the small enclosure had failed abysmally they *had* stopped eating at their desks so he supposed that was progress of a sort.

"OK, Davy, I don't mind who does the work as long as it's done."

He jumped off the desk he was seated on and turned towards the floor's exit.

"Right, you all know what you're doing, so get to it.

Liam and I have somewhere to be. Call me as and when."

On his way out he stopped at his secretary's desk. "Alice, if Doctor Marsham rings through with any forensics please pass him to Davy." He called back to the analyst. "Davy, phone me with any updates, please. We'll brief again either at six or first thing tomorrow. I'll let Alice know which."

Even as he said it he knew that Aidan and Ryan wouldn't be back from Rownton that evening, so he changed his mind.

"Make that tomorrow."

Then the two murder detectives disappeared into the lift, on their way to see a third who'd just received some very bad news.

****

Dublin. 3p.m.

Róisín Casey wasn't showing half as much reverence to her Chanel courts as she had to their matching handbag earlier, kicking her office wall hard in frustration again and again. It wasn't because she had so many pairs of shoes that she didn't care; well, she did have, but each pair was like a work of art so to damage them in any way was a crime in her eyes, unless... something *so* bad had happened that her rage was uncontrollable, which was the state in which she found herself now, prompted by some information she'd received hours before about a builder called Derek Morrow that had the potential to bring her carefully constructed world tumbling down.

Carefully constructed and meticulously crafted in every way. From the money she spent on her elegant appearance: hair, face, teeth and style, the total each year something that she couldn't bear to think about; to the even greater amount of time and effort she'd invested in the past on deportment, elocution lessons and reinventing herself, converting the girl from the slums of Limerick into the grand Dublin lady that she was today.

She'd been what they used to call on the London Stock Exchange 'a barrow boy'; a working class, street-wise kid who'd made it big. In her case she'd taken the skills she'd learnt from generations of her family who'd made a living selling their wares in Ireland's street markets, all of them Travellers until her parents, and applied them to trading on the world's markets, and it had brought her some of the financial stability that she had today. *Some*.

Now, between her looks, her job and her apartment in the right part of town, Dublin's elite thought of her as one of their own, and that was the way that she intended it to stay. And no stupid bloody builder who'd lost his nerve and decided to blow his head off was going to bring her down.

Her frustration vented and the toes of her beige stilettos irreparably damaged, Róisín kicked them off and slumped down behind her desk, swivelling her high-backed chair around to face Dublin's arterial river, the Liffey, as she replayed her earlier telephone conversation in her head.

Arthur, frightened and anxious, and desperate to pass on what he'd heard to someone who knew Derek Morrow, even though he had *no idea* of the information's potential significance to her. He'd simply chosen her because Morrow had worked on their quarry.

She knew that her initial reaction had shocked Arthur; swearing and shouting and then giving him a list of orders to follow and call her back. When he *had* done she'd wrecked her shoes, but now that she was a little calmer Róisín Casey was wondering just how worried she *really* needed to be. Derek Morrow had reportedly left behind a goodbye letter for his wife, a list of his important documents and that was all, and the reason she knew that much was because she'd insisted that Arthur pay the local undertaker a bung to tell him.

But now she decided that she needed two more things to make *certain* that Morrow's death didn't incriminate her: *sight* of the documents that the builder had left, and a way to pin the reason for his suicide on something completely unrelated to the truth. Something feasible but something that could never *possibly* lead back to her.

It was Róisín's eureka moment and prompted her to call back the elderly man that she'd sworn at earlier. Arthur Norris recognised who was calling him immediately and swallowed hard before he answered in a subdued voice.

"Yes, Róisín."

His timorousness made the banker purr inwardly with satisfaction. She liked her subordinates frightened; it made them far more likely to do as they were told.

But charm had its role to play in coercion as well, so Róisín decided to employ some and adopted her silkiest tone.

"Arthur... I think perhaps I was a little naughty when you called me earlier about Derek."

Naughty? Never mind the word's wide-ranging and sometimes enjoyable connotations, even using it made her smile. It was a middle-class word, a semi-cultured word, a word that would never have passed her impoverished mother's lips and probably still hadn't; she wouldn't know because she never saw her family now, their every word and gesture so working-class that they would have proved an impediment on her ascent to the top.

Norris' response was huffy.

"Yes, you were. I was only passing on information."

"And I realise that now, Arthur. I'm *so* sorry I overreacted."

She doubted that her emollience would have been enough to sooth him if she hadn't also slept with the old man; she made it a point to sleep with every man in her employ soon after she hired them, finding that the promise of it happening again, which it rarely did, was usually enough to keep them sweet for life. For her female employees she bought a matching bag and shoes.

Norris was still unimpressed.

"Huh."

Time to bring in the big guns.

"Won't you forgive me?" emerged in a saccharin, wheedling tone that even though it made her teeth ache she knew turned him on. It did the trick.

"Well, OK then. *I suppose.*"

Her tone immediately became brisk. Teasing men with the goodies didn't mean that you had to deliver them.

"Good. Now, tell me again what happened with Derek."

Norris waved bye-bye to any faint hope of sex and answered with a resigned sigh.

"One of his men knocked at the site portakabin, that was Derek's office, this morning, and opened the door to find his head spread all over the wall." *Delightful.* "As I said earlier, he left two envelopes addressed to his wife, and my undertaker got a look at them before the body was removed to the morgue. He said that one letter was Derek saying sorry to his wife for killing himself but he just couldn't cope with his work stress anymore, and the other was his bank details, Will and funeral papers."

Róisín waited for what she thought was an appropriate time to pretend respect for the dead and then gave an order.

"I want copies of everything."

Norris frowned, partly at himself. He should have anticipated the request; after all he knew how controlling she was. But all the same... it seemed a bit rich to photocopy a man's last words to his wife.

"The undertaker won't like it."

"Then give him a bonus. And we'll need to invent a better reason than work stress for why Morrow did himself in. It's far too thin."

He didn't think so, but then his was *never* the last word. "Why? And like what?"

"Why, is *my* business. As for what..."

She thought for a moment, remembering Morrow's request that she dress up in a bunny girl outfit the second and absolutely final time that they'd gone to bed.

"Right. I want you to find a girl, young and tarty. A stripper's probably best, but whatever. Just as long as she's prepared to tell the local papers that she and Morrow were having an affair and she'd ended it the day before he took the shot. They'll think he killed himself for love and that should be enough to stop people digging further. She can say that they were planning to run away together or some other tripe and she broke his heart."

Norris' mouth had been opened to object since "girl" and now he did.

"We can't do that! What about his wife? They'd been married for twenty years! It'll break her heart if she thinks Derek was unfaithful." He crossed his arms mentally and his next words reflected the defiant stance. "I won't do it."

Róisín's previously efficient tone became a hiss. *"Yes, you will, Arthur. And do you know why?"*

He gulped out a response, *really* not wanting to hear

what she said next. "Why?"

"Because if you *don't* do this to Derek's wife then I'll make damn sure that it happens to *yours*."

It was her backup approach with her married male employees and it *always* kept them in line.

****

Annette Eakin's Home. East Belfast.

Craig didn't know which concerned him more, the fact that his normally neatly presented inspector had answered the door to them wearing an un-ironed dress over a pair of worn leggings and with hair that obviously hadn't seen a comb for days, or the fact that she'd walked into her pretty living room ahead of them so slowly that both he and his deputy had pretty much been stepping on the spot. Both things were worrying indications of her low state of mind, something that despite the depressing letter that she'd received that morning he intended to change.

When she slumped into an armchair and pulled a fake-fur throw around her without even offering them tea Craig knew that it was time to take charge, something that out of good manners he *usually* tried to avoid doing in someone else's home.

Liam had no such qualms and headed straight for the kitchen. "Tea or coffee, you two?"

Seeing that his D.I. wasn't going to reply, Craig did so for them both.

"One of each, Liam, and make them strong and sweet."

As his deputy got to it Craig glanced around and found a footstool, planted it in front of his inspector's chair and sat down, then without asking for permission he reached out and enfolded her only visible hand in his.

"OK, Annette. I know you've received a notice of the likely charges and you probably feel like the sky's about to fall in, but it isn't." When there was no response he carried on. "The PPS have to assess two things before they proceed: is it in the public interest to prosecute you and is there enough evidence to convict?"

Just then Liam reappeared and pushed a coffee into his free hand, setting Annette's tea down by her side. She still wasn't looking at either of them, but Craig forged ahead.

"There's no public interest in prosecuting you, Annette, and I'm not even sure what *value* anyone would find in it, given Pete's behaviour towards you in the past."

At the mention of her dead ex she winced and jerked her hand away, but Craig continued undeterred.

"Not even the gobby politicians who usually want the police hauled over the coals for breathing the wrong way are calling for it. *Everyone* accepts that Pete was put in prison for being violent to you, *and* that while he was in there he shivved another inmate."

The D.I. opened her mouth to speak and her voice when she did was weak. "But he hadn't been violent for a year."

Craig shook his head at the implication.

"He hadn't been violent in *Mahon*, a high-security male prison, but he'd shivved a man in his first low-security placement, remember. That's why he was sent to Mahon in the first place."

Her Majesty's Prison Mahon in Armagh housed some of the most dangerous men that Northern Ireland had ever produced, which was saying something in a place where people had shot and bombed each other for thirty years.

"And remember that there were no women to assault in prison, Annette, and in particular *you* weren't there, the person that he was really angry with. The person that he *blamed* for getting him locked up."

Liam nodded in agreement. "Ach, sure the dogs in the street know that when Pete broke in here in the middle of the night it wasn't to bring you Christmas presents!"

She shook her head morosely. "He wasn't carrying a weapon either."

The D.C.I. tutted noisily. "You didn't know that, for God's sake, and there were plenty of things in that bedroom he could have used! He could have knocked Mike out with a lamp in a second and cut your throat with the broken bulb."

She winced at the imagery.

"Or even started on Carrie asleep next door. Everyone knows that, woman, so why don't you?"

Annette sprang forward in her chair, showing the first sign of energy since they'd arrived.

"Then why are they talking about manslaughter? Pete

broke into my house and I acted on reflex! He was looming over Mike so I shouted a warning, and then I shot at his arm to *stop* him, not kill him! But he turned just as I fired and..." Her next words were a wail... "*Oh, God, I killed him...I killed the father of my children.*"

Craig reached for her hand again to soothe her, but she shook her head. "Amy and Jordan are devastated. They say they're on my side, but maybe I *deserve* to go to jail-"

Liam cut her off with a shout. "YOU DON'T BLOODY DESERVE JAIL! STOP TALKING RUBBISH." He carried on more quietly but still sternly. "Pete McElroy was a scrote, a cowardly wife beater and a burglar, and you can't *know* what he would have done to Mike and you if you hadn't woken up. I'm sorry for your kids and I'm sorry for you, girl, but you doing time won't bring the bastard back."

Craig smiled inwardly as tortured Annette suddenly transformed into the reproving Annette of old.

"Don't you shout in my house!"

"Well, stop talking tripe then!"

Craig thought he caught a flicker of amusement on her face, but it faded as fast as it had appeared so he drove the conversation on.

"The PPS need evidence to prosecute. So, OK, I know this is repetition, but how did Pete get in?"

"The French doors in the sitting room were lying open, but the glass was intact and the lock wasn't damaged so he must have slipped it." She gave a shrug. "This used to be his house too, remember, so perhaps he knew that it was weak."

The information made Craig frown. "*Was* it weak?"

"I hadn't thought so, but I'd never looked at it much. Pete did all the house maintenance when we were together."

He parked the information for future reference and went on.

"Did the police get any prints from the door?"

"Yes. A full set. He didn't bother to wear gloves. Probably thought his prints would be in the house anyway from years back so that would cover him."

The explanation, while logical, didn't please Craig, but when he chased for the reason why it slipped away.

"OK. They have you on discharging your weapon, which

yes, you *should* have had in a lockbox, but let those of us who haven't done it cast the first stone. There won't be many when they've arrived home in the early hours at the end of a big case. Was the room pitch-black when you fired?"

Annette shook her head immediately. "No, there's a lamp down the street a bit. It casts a little light into our bedroom."

"So you saw that it was Pete, and what else?"

She shook her head again, more firmly. "No. I didn't *know* it was Pete then, I just saw a big man hunched over Mike."

Craig's eyebrows lifted and he felt a spark of hope. "You *definitely* didn't know it was Pete? You didn't mention that to me when it happened!"

"I could barely remember my name back then, sir."

"And you told the cops who first interviewed you that?"

She answered him in an exhausted tone.

"Yes, and I said it at my re-interview as well. I told them everything, but they mustn't have believed me."

"Then tell us now."

Her expression said what was the point but both men urged her on, so she told her story again in a resigned voice.

"Mike woke and must have moved, which woke me, so I turned and I saw the outline of a tall man looming over him. His left arm was slightly raised but I couldn't see his hand clearly, so I didn't know if he had anything in it. He could *easily* have been holding a knife or a gun. I called out for him to show me his hands but he didn't, so then I thought about jumping across the bed at him but he was too big, and that still would've given him time to shoot or stab Mike if he'd *had* a weapon, so I grabbed my gun and shouted. 'Stop. Armed police-"

"And then you shot at his arm."

"Yes, his left side was towards me so it was his left upper arm that I shot at. But just as I shot to *stop* him he turned towards me." She dropped her eyes to the floor and shook her head. "The bullet went through into his chest and tore his aorta."

Craig gazed at her intently. "Look at me, Annette."

She did so reluctantly.

"This is *really* important. Exactly *when* did you realise that it was Pete?"

"When he was on the floor. As Mike jumped out of bed to look after his wound I switched on my bedside lamp and ran around to help. That's when I saw who it was."

Her face crumpled and reddened, and Craig knew that tears and retreating into herself again would come next. He focused on the facts to keep her with them.

"Every part of this smacks of you acting in self defence. They're leaning on the fact you were slightly over the drink-drive limit and handling a gun, which as you weren't drunk, driving or on duty any good barrister should be able to get thrown out. Also that your gun wasn't locked away as per regs, which yes, you *might* get disciplined for. But to generate a manslaughter charge it sounds like they're also implying that you had an *enhanced motive* to shoot because it was Pete, but *you* didn't know it was him until he was on the ground!"

Annette's response came in a wretched voice. "But I've already *told* them all this, so why are they doing this to me?"

Liam gave a disgusted grunt. "Because the bastards are just looking to nail a copper. They're probably doing a happy dance at the thought!"

Craig gave him a wary look and shook his head. "Because the Ombudsman and PPS *have* to be seen to be even-handed and treat the police the same as everyone else, which is right until it tips over into trying too hard to be seen to be equitable or making an example of someone just for the sake of it. You didn't know it was Pete, he wouldn't show you his hands when you called out so he could easily have had a weapon, and you assessed that he was too strong for you to overpower, which we all know is right. He was a fit PE teacher, probably even fitter after years working out in a prison gym."

He sat up straight with a defiant look on his face. "Basically they're overcompensating. A strong, fit, man with a history of assaulting you broke into your home in the middle of the night, a home where your child was asleep. And not just into your home but into your bedroom, where you were at your most vulnerable."

Just then Liam thought of something and went to

interject, but Craig cut him off with a shake of his head and rose to his feet.

"Leave this with us, Annette."

A panicked expression appeared on her face. "You can't interfere, sir! They'll penalise *me* if you do."

"We'll be very careful, I promise. We're just going to dig around a bit in the background. The PPS and Ombudsman won't find out about it until or unless we turn something up."

Before she could ask what that something could possibly be the two men were out the front door and walking towards the car, with Liam shooting Craig knowing looks.

"You knew what I was going to say, didn't you?"

"Maybe. What *were* you going to say?"

"That Pete didn't care if his prints were found because he wasn't planning on going back to jail. He was going to do a runner."

He was partly right; Pete McElroy *hadn't* been planning on a return to Mahon, but perhaps not for the reasons that Liam thought. But Craig wasn't ready to say what those reasons might be just yet so he stuck to generalities.

"If he wasn't then we need to prove that before we give Annette false hope. By the way, I agree with your opinion on the motivation for the charges, but I didn't want to encourage her to say something to the PPS she might regret."

Liam smiled and climbed into the driver's seat, leaving his boss in the street for a minute to think.

They needed to find evidence to support their hunches and be quick about it, or the *process* would destroy Annette and the team would get a shell of its inspector back, if she ever returned at all.

****

The M1 Motorway

Aidan and Ryan were on the slow road to Rownton, not intentionally slow you understand, because they were on a motorway, but impeded by a lorry discharging its load of baby wipes all over the westbound carriageway, prompting rubberneckers to slow down as they passed and several amateur movie-makers to exit their vehicles and video the spectacle with the resultant queue of cars stretching back to the last junction but one. Bright yellow packets adorned with a cute infant skittered wildly across the lanes and into the adjacent hedgerows, sent flying there by people innocently driving into the fiasco and becoming pool players potting in a giant rule-free game.

After twenty static minutes, and bored waiting for the expected patrol car to siren and flash its way up the hard shoulder and sort things, Ryan nodded at the windscreen in a way that suggested they should get out and do the job themselves. The response was a grudging sigh from his senior officer, whose following glance at his dashboard clock said that although he was reluctant to exit the car, it being February, which in Ireland was a month that his late mother had often said 'would skin a fairy', such mythical beings obviously being sensitive to extreme cold, and he was only wearing a suit, time *was* moving on so he knew that the D.S. was probably right.

A second sigh, accompanied by a frown at the darkening afternoon sky, eloquently conveyed Aidan's thoughts that with the delay and the list of interviews they had ahead of them they would probably now have to stay in the sticks overnight.

Without a word he hit his car's blue lights and sirens and pulled across the middle and outer lanes of the carriageway then they exited his BMW cabriolet, a ten-year-old but spotless vehicle that he prided himself would be a classic someday. They held up their warrant cards as they did so and while Aidan walked ahead to speak to the driver of the lorry, a swarthy, heavily-set man who the D.C.I. imagined lied to his friends about the nature of his load, probably hinting that he only ever carried something macho like booze or heavy machinery and even then just the hardiest versions bound for Siberia, Ryan opened the car's boot and withdrew a hazard sign and several cones, dodging the skittering wipe packets skilfully to place them in the outer lanes, where he bravely positioned himself to perform the traffic handling drill that he'd learned twenty years before as a probationer.

He waved his arms and pointed his hands with the grace of a ballerina directing the now crawling traffic into the slow lane, and then motioned brusquely to the budding Spielbergs to get back in their cars. Fifteen minutes later the detectives were rewarded by only a ten-mile tailback and some blue-lighted allies who arrived, took over and waved them on their way, bathed in the glow of a good deed done and only fifty minutes behind where they might have been.

It prompted Aidan to speak for the first time in an hour. "We might be in luck and make up the time. I really don't fancy staying overnight in a one horse town."

Ryan took it as a sign that conversation was being encouraged. "How many farmers are there in Rownton's hinterland?"

"Four main ones so we'll do those first." He gestured towards the sergeant's top pocket. "Call the village station and see how the locals are doing with the rest."

After five minutes of listening on speaker they knew that every person in the village had been interviewed since the day before, and the only ones warranting their attention were the landlord of the pub and Derek Morrow's deputy foreman, Jimmy Rushton.

Aidan shouted into the phone in response. "Line them up for three hours' time, will you."

A rural voice that they hadn't heard before shouted back. "Here?"

Ryan said it first. "Who are you?"

The man replied in an offended tone, "I'm Sergeant O'Hare. And who are *you*?"

Aidan shook his head as a sign not to rise to the bait and intervened.

"It's D.C.I. Hughes here, Sergeant, and D.S. Hendron. We've been tasked to take over the interviews. We'll have the two men mentioned at your station then, please. Thanks for that." He signalled Ryan to end the call before the, now no-doubt doubly offended, village bobby could retort.

"He won't have liked that."

"Tough."

To underline his assertiveness Aidan put his foot down and thirty minutes later the sat-nav narrator informed them that they were approaching their destination in such a seductive tone that it sounded like she was suggesting a ménage a trois.

Ryan raised an eyebrow. "Did she come like that?"

Aidan cracked a smile, a rare enough occurrence that week because his nicotine addiction was giving him gip and he absolutely refused to vape, believing that the contraptions looked like old-fashioned cigarette holders and with his gangly appearance he would look like an escapee from a Noel Coward play.

"No. One of my mates at the gym programmed it in for me. The usual voice was giving me a headache. She sounded just like our English teacher at school."

A debate on the merits of sexy voices would have to wait, because the seductress had directed them down a narrow lane that deteriorated into such a mud-filled shuck the BMW's windscreen was splattered with the material, and the absence of any visible footpath said that they'd be knocking on their first interviewee's front door covered in a solid coating of the same.

****

Belfast City Centre.

Craig was openly vacillating between asking Liam to drive to Mahon Prison to see what they could uncover about Pete, to the Ombudsman's office so he could march in and give the old duffer a piece of his mind, or to the PPS' offices to see what, if any, pressure he could exert. In the end it was his deputy who made the decision to drive to the fourth and currently *only* sensible option, because handily enough they'd taken *his* car to Annette's.

"Which one are we going to first, Liam? Ombudsman or PPS?"

It was a genuine query by Craig as the route to both led them down Belfast's Victoria Street and they'd just hit that very road. His deputy didn't even make a pretence of answering, reckoning that in around thirty seconds his boss would have worked things out for himself.

Craig thought that he had when the PPS offices flew past them, but a different answer was hammered home thirty seconds later as the Ombudsman's office went the same way.

"Why are we heading back to the squad-room?"

Liam stared straight ahead and gave a long-suffering sigh before he responded. "I'm saving you from yourself."

Craig sat up sharply in the passenger seat, an irritated look on his face. "When I need you to save me from myself I'll tell you!"

The comment elicited a loud tut.

"Ach now, you see that's not even logical, is it? If you'd *known* you needed saving then you would've told me to go straight back to the ranch yourself, wouldn't you."

The D.C.I. nodded firmly to himself; convinced that he was right.

"Anyway, never mind about saving *you*, I'm saving Annette. Look, I'm with you on this. We definitely need to look into things, because there was a lot more to Pete turning up that night than meets the eye, but the last thing that lassie needs is you going in there shouting your big mouth off and putting your foot in things, prejudicing her case!"

Given that Craig wasn't known either for having a big mouth *or* putting his foot in anything, Liam had the decency to end the sentence with a laugh. Although his boss didn't *quite* join in, he did, after a moment's thought, give a desultory nod that said the D.C.I. was probably right.

"I'm *still* going to see them, Liam, but OK, we need to check things out first. And in this mood I could have made things worse, couldn't I?"

"Would, not could. You know lawyers; they're even more up their own asses than we are. Try telling them what to do and they'll throw the book at her, and it won't be one she'd like, like Fifty Shades of Grey."

That *did* make Craig laugh and by the time the two men reached the squad-room they still were, so it was with reluctance that Davy greeted them with, "I've more on the girl's abduction for you. Do you w...want to take it in your room?"

A minute later they were in Craig's office with three hot drinks and some biscuits in front of them courtesy of Alice, who was feeling better disposed towards the world because her daughter had just given birth to her first child, a photograph of whom was whipped out to be admired immediately, something that made Craig wonder how *he'd* be behaving in a few weeks time.

When the PA paused for breath he passed her a note asking her to set up a call with the governor of Mahon Prison around six, earning him a suspicious look from his deputy.

"What was that?"

Craig ignored him and waved the analyst on.

"What do you have for us, Davy?"

The computer expert woke up his smart-pad and turned it so that both detectives could see what he then recited from memory.

"Bella Mary Westbury, daughter of Edgar and Nicola Westbury, née Kincaid-"

Liam cut him off. "Kincaid? So-"

Davy returned the favour. "Yep. The girl's mother was Stuart Kincaid's s...sister."

Craig frowned. *"Was?"*

The analyst nodded glumly. "Nicola Kincaid killed herself in twenty-seventeen, chief. The file s...said she blamed herself for her daughter's abduction because she'd left her in the garden to get her some juice, and when she came back, no more than a minute later she was adamant about that, the girl w...was gone."

Liam shook his head slowly. *"Damn.* Poor woman. How do you ever get past that? And it's something that you'd do without thinking too. I know that I have with my two."

"That's how killers w...win, isn't it? They kill the whole family as well as their victim."

Craig shook his head briskly, pushing away the fury that he knew he'd feel if it was his child, and returning them to the point.

"We don't yet know that Bella Westbury *is* dead, but we do know that the chances of this being an opportunistic kidnapping have just dropped considerably. If the mother was correct, and I'm sure she was, that the girl had been left alone for less than a minute, then the likelihood is that someone had been watching her and just waiting for a chance to abduct."

He asked another question.

"Were there any other children, Davy?"

"Yes, a boy. He's thirteen now and lives with his dad in Monaghan. They moved back to Ireland after the mother died."

"What was the family doing in Nice?"

"The father, Edgar, was the manager of a luxury country hotel there. I checked it out online and it looks ace."

"Did the family live on site?"

"In a house in the grounds, owned by the hotel. Around a mile from the main building."

Craig gave a weary sigh.

"Damn... with all the hotel guests and staff there would have been hundreds of potential suspects for the abduction. Any CCTV covering the house?"

The analyst pulled a face. "I'm still trying to find out. There definitely w...was *inside* the main hotel and in its immediate grounds. The police checked every room and facility and interviewed all the staff and guests there at the time, but no-one jumped out."

Craig turned to his deputy. "I need you to go back over the witness statements and the French investigation file, Liam. You know what to look for."

Any guest or staff member, male or female, with sex convictions or even suspicions of strange behaviour with children, actually, make that *any* convictions at all. Plus anyone who'd left the country after the girl's disappearance in an uncomfortably hasty way.

"Ash can do any cross-checks that you need." He turned back to the younger man. "Did they search all their vehicles as well, Davy?"

The analyst hesitated for a moment before shaking his head. "I...I'm sure they must have, but I don't know for sure, chief, s...sorry. I'll go back and check. I should have done it immediately."

Craig smiled. "Your head's in Switzerland already."

Davy wasn't as easy on himself. "Well, it shouldn't be. I'll chase that for you now."

He made to stand up but Craig waved him down again. "Let's carry on for a minute. I'll need you to check if the searches were extended to nearby airports and ports too."

"I know France has an Amber Alert system like here, but I'll confirm exactly what they do."

"Good." The detective frowned suddenly. "The sooner they implement an EU-wide alert system the better.

Within the Schengen Zone her abductor could have moved the girl freely across twenty-six countries."

The geo-political diatribe was disturbed by a frown from his D.C.I.

"How soon after the mum's suicide did the Westburys leave France? I'd *never* move house if one of my kids disappeared, just in case they came back looking for me someday."

Davy nodded. "Six months. And that's exactly what I thought, s...so I dug deeper. It turned out their house was a perk of the manager's job, so when Edgar Westbury got so depressed that he couldn't work after his wife's suicide they kicked him out."

"Bloody hell! Not much compassion there, was there?"

Craig sighed. "There are no friends in business."

The analyst offered up a defence for the hotel. "They did say the family could stay on in the main hotel, but I suppose they didn't want to. Not the s...same."

After a lengthy pause while each of them pictured the nightmare that Edgar Westbury had found himself in, with a missing child and a dead wife, Craig changed topic to move things along.

"Tell me more about Stuart and Nicola Kincaid, Davy, and why Edgar Westbury wasn't our murder victim, if Stuart Kincaid *was* killed because he was hunting for the girl. *Westbury* was her father after all."

Liam looked at him curiously. "You don't think her photo was the reason for Kincaid's murder now?"

"I never thought it was the whole reason, Liam, but in any case that's not what I said. I'm just curious how Edgar Westbury reacted to his daughter's disappearance, and why it was her uncle who ended up hunting for her instead of her father, if that *was* what Kincaid was doing."

Davy shrugged. "I don't know much about the last bit yet, but the police reports mentioned that Stuart and Nicola Kincaid were very close and I know why." He tapped his screen again and two birth certificates appeared. "They were twins."

Liam grinned. "So our Vic was a loving twin brother and uncle, not a paedo."

"They're not mutually exclusive; but I take your point."

The analyst continued as if neither detective had

spoken.

"Nicola was born first and Stuart ten minutes later. They had no other s...siblings so Stuart must really have felt it when his sister killed herself." He shuddered. "I know I w...would if anything ever happened to Emmie."

Davy's five years older sister and only sibling Emmie worked as a lecturer in English at a London university.

Craig nodded. Although there was a ten year gap between Lucia and him, with it just being the two of them they were close despite that, more so now that they were adults. And even though she was getting married in a year's time to a man that he liked and was good to her, he still felt that it was his job to make sure she was all right.

Liam also had an opinion on the subject, as he had on almost everything in life. "Your folks should've had ten kids like mine did. No-one tried anything on with *us*. We were like the local mafia."

"With you as the Godfather I bet." Craig moved on before he could retort. "Perhaps Kincaid felt his sister's pain at Bella's disappearance as well. They say that some twins can."

Liam's expression said that he was persuadable. "It *could* explain why he carried the girl's photo."

"And why he was hunting for her if he was." Craig nodded at the smart-pad. "Good work, Davy. You and Ash dig as deep as you can on everything." He glanced at his watch. "How long will it take us to drive to Monaghan, Liam?"

The D.C.I. gave a snort. "What *am* I? Google maps?"

"You come from the country and country people know things like that."

Before Liam could argue about whether he was the rural equivalent of sat-nav, Davy had produced the answer.

"Sixty-five miles."

"OK, good, that'll only take us an hour or so. We'll go down tomorrow morning. Davy, get Edgar Westbury's contact details to me and ask Alice to set up the meeting for around ten. We'll need you to brief us again early so we have the latest facts before we go."

The analyst shook his newly shorn head, missing the familiar swish of his long hair as he did. He didn't care whether Maggie thought he looked like a young Jared Leto or not; he was growing it *and* his beard again ASAP.

"Not me, chief, I'm at Queen's first thing meeting my tutor. But I'll bring Ash up to speed. Eight o'clock OK?"

The early hour was his revenge for Ash's habit of dandering in late most mornings; having to be there for eight meant the lazy git would have to get up by seven at the latest. Maybe it would make him empathise with what *he* suffered every day, although he wasn't holding his breath.

"Eight's perfect."

As the analyst rose to leave, Liam couldn't resist a quip. "Who did it then?"

Davy knew instantly what he was talking about but refused to rise to the bait, instead staring innocently at him and pretending not to understand.

"Who did wh...what?"

The D.C.I. gestured at his head.

"Your hair, man, your hair. Who got at you with a lawnmower?"

Once again Davy responded in a way guaranteed to give Liam's joke a slow and painful death. He lifted a hand slowly to his neck and feigned shock.

"Oh my God! My hair's gone! Who stole it?"

He started to search frantically around the floor and beneath Craig's desk, making the detective laugh.

"He's just burnt you, Liam. There's no point taking the piss out of someone who doesn't care." Craig stared at the younger man's head for a moment and nodded. "I like it. It's more modern. That whole hipster look is getting old."

Liam wasn't half as amused as the other men were. He didn't like his punch lines ruined.

"Aye, well. It's...it's *too* short now! You...you look like... a convict, aye a convict, *that's* what you look like!"

The convict was already out the door with his best criminal cackle echoing back to them, so the D.C.I. turned on his boss.

"Anyway, what're you laughing at? You could do with a hair cut too. Those girly curls of yours are about to disappear down your back."

That jibe was thwarted as well when Craig smiled and rose to his feet.

"Thanks for reminding me. I think I'll go and get one

now. Tell Alice I'll be back at six, will you, and call me if there's anything urgent before then."

****

Eglantine Avenue. Near Queen's University Belfast.

It had taken Ash longer than Andy had hoped to find a photograph of Bella Westbury that was unlikely to have been used in the gendarmes' search and email it through, and when he *had* done the girl had been so young in it that she could simply have been any blonde toddler dressed in the fashion of a few years before. As a tool to identify her to anyone other than a family member the image was useless, but then as Ash had phoned through five minutes earlier to inform him that the Kincaids *were* actually that, perhaps it would be OK.

The second delay that the D.C.I. had encountered had held another, *very* tenuous, link with fashion, this time of the more modern variety. Mary had taken Craig's admonishments to keep warm to heart and had ordered a detour to her apartment near Queen's University to change outfit. While she was busy doing that on some storey of the redbrick Victorian terrace that she obviously called home, Andy waited outside in the car and entertained himself by playing the mix-tape his recently acquired girlfriend had made.

The relationship with Rebecca Wickes, a D.C. in the Vice Squad, was very new but already it felt serious, perhaps in part because it had been forged during an intense operation during which one of her informants had been killed. You can learn a lot about someone when you see them cry over a virtual stranger, and even more when they make the effort to attend the funeral and visit the family afterwards. Rebecca had a good heart that mattered to him more than her pretty face and sharp brain, so as the D.C.I. listened to the strains of Jack Savoretti playing in the background there was a definite bubble of excitement in his chest.

It was punctured quickly when the window was rapped to signal Mary's return, decked out in a pair of trousers so tight Andy wondered how she could sit down in them, and a pink, fake-fur jacket that made her look like she was planning to moonlight as a bunny girl. He responded to her request for entry with a shaking head and instead climbed out to join her on the street.

"I'm *not* taking you to see a bereaved family dressed like that! Go back and change."

The D.C. jutted out her chin defiantly. "There's nothing wrong with this! Show me the regulation that says I can't wear it! It covers me and I need to be warm."

"Then put on an overcoat! And make sure it isn't bright pink. We're about to tell someone they've lost a relative for goodness sake!"

He climbed back into the car to the sound of muttering and spent the next part of his wait pondering the wisdom of the force's plain clothes policy. To be fair, he couldn't recall *ever* having received guidance on exactly what *sort* of plain clothes he was allowed to wear, but most people's common sense seemed to stretch to it involving a suit or at least a decent jacket, and the general understanding was that it definitely didn't include pink fur!

But, people's craving for self-expression and narcissism being what it was nowadays, he decided to suggest to Craig that some team guidelines might be a good idea. He'd never understood the urge for individuality himself; personally he loved having the uniform of a suit to put on in the morning. It reduced his bleary decision making to the colour of his shirt, tie and socks, and at seven a.m. that was *always* a good thing.

The D.C.I.'s style musings were cut short by another rap on his window, and this time a navy coated and booted Mary was granted admission, making an irritating grumbling sound that made Andy crank up the volume on his music and which only ceased when they arrived at their destination, a leafy suburban park in Portaferry lined with detached villas and displaying a collection of SUVs and Hybrids that screamed 'middle-class family land'.

The D.C.I. knocked off his music mid-song and turned to the grumpy constable by his side.

"OK, this is the family of our murder victim, Stuart Kincaid, and while they *may* know that he's missing, although it hasn't been reported so we can't even be sure of that, they're *very* unlikely to know that he's dead, so leave the talking to me, please."

That suited Mary, who was preoccupied with snuggling as deep into her coat as was possible and hoping that the house they were about to enter was a lot better heated than his car.

A knock on the glossy front door of a mock-Tudor mansion and a quick flash of warrant cards saw them being shown into a comfortable sitting room by Stuart Kincaid's wife Luisa, an attractive, tanned brunette who looked older than Mary had expected from the approximate age they'd been given for her husband.

It was a prejudice Andy would correct another time when he enlightened her that twelve percent took place between older women and younger men, and many more than that if there was only a few years difference, and that he'd very much enjoyed being in one of them himself.

The D.C.I. waited until they were settled and then gazed kindly at the woman in front of him, asking a question that to anyone experienced in breaking bad news was a warning sign.

"Is anyone here with you, Mrs Kincaid?"

She smiled and shook her head. "My sons are both at school." She glanced at her watch. "Although the younger one should be home soon. My other son has sports practice today."

Just then they heard a key in the front door, and the sound of it banging open followed by a thud as something was dropped in the hall preceded a call of, "Mum?"

"In here, pet."

A lanky teenage boy flew in with his school tie and blazer half off and stopped in his tracks when he saw the detectives. His mother intervened quickly, as if fearing that he would let her down by saying something rude.

"These are police officers, Josh. Detectives."

The boy's abrupt, "What are they doing here?" said that she'd probably been correct in her fear.

"I haven't asked that yet, dear. The officers have only just arrived. Now," she rose and ushered him back out the door, "go upstairs and do your homework. I'll be absolutely fine."

His reluctant exit was accompanied by a quipped, "I bet

Kenny's done something" that said sibling rivalry was alive and well in the Kincaid home.

The words prompted Luisa Kincaid to ask quizzically, "Is he?"

"Kenny's your other son?"

"Yes. Is he in trouble?"

It prompted a shake of Andy's head and a sympathetic smile. "No, Mrs Kincaid, we're not here about your *sons*."

The slight emphasis that he'd tried to avoid placing on the final word made her eyes widen.

"*Which* squad did you say you came from again?"

There was no 'again' about it, because he'd deliberately omitted to say in the first place; but now he did, in as gentle a tone as he possessed.

"We're from Belfast's Murder Squad, Mrs Kincaid." After a short pause he added, "I'm very sorry", which he *really* was. The loss of a loved one was hard enough for families without the thought that someone had *deliberately* taken them away.

As the D.C.I. braced himself for a scream and tears, the constable beside him was scrutinising the new widow's face curiously, watching as each phase of realisation registered there: confusion, incredulity, and then, slowly, fear followed by shock. It wasn't that Mary was cold exactly; merely excessively analytical as perhaps befitted her degree background, breaking each human reaction but her own down into a binary sequence of ones and noughts. It was a useful ability in a detective if not in a human being.

Andy's anticipated scream and tears didn't materialise, Luisa Kincaid instead retaining the dull, staring, silence of the shocked phase, and yet somehow with enough clarity to murmur, "Stuart?"

The D.C.I. gave the smallest nod that he could manage, anything more vigorous unseemly, implying enthusiasm for the confirmation which was the last thing that he felt. He would've loved to have been able to prevent *all* the pain and suffering that he saw in the world but he knew that was impossible, so at the very least he tried to minimise it where he could.

He followed the nod with a soft, "We think so. I'm very sorry."

A lengthy pause without any further reaction from the widow was ended by a pained swallow as he moved to deliver the next blow. "We'd like you to come and perform the identification if possible."

Once more he braced himself for cries, but her walled-off, stunned restraint held and she rose robotically to her feet.

"I'll get my coat."

And tell her young son that she wouldn't be long.

Eighty minutes later the D.C.I. was standing beside the widow in the mortuary as John Winter uncovered the least damaged side of her husband's face, Luisa Kincaid's silence still so persistent that both men's experience told them that she might never unfreeze.

****

The C.C.U. 5.20 p.m.

"Right. I'm back. What's been happening?"

A newly shorn Craig appeared in front of his deputy's over-loaded desk, almost tripping over a heap of files as he did, and wondering why he'd never noticed how warm his hair had kept his neck until he felt nostalgic for it now. If his rank hadn't come with expectations of upholding the highest police standards of presentation the chill would almost have been enough to tempt him into a long-haired musketeer look like John's; he was so dark he had to shave twice daily so he could probably grow it in a few weeks but it would inevitably bring with it slagging about curls and ribbons from the squad. Or maybe a moustache just for a change, although *then* he'd have to deal with Katy making jokes about how he looked like a seventies porn star.

As Craig was speculating about possible uses for his natural hirsuteness Liam was scrutinising his newly short hair approvingly; *he'd* never been able to grow his sandy scrub any longer than an inch without it looking like a Brillo Pad, so he didn't see why any other bloke in the force should sport flowing locks.

Eventually he broke off his scrutiny to answer his boss' question.

"Andy phoned through. He's at the morgue with the widow and she's confirmed that our Vic is Stuart Kincaid.

She's in shock so he's going to question her in one of the offices there and tape it on his phone before he drives her home."

"Fine. Anything else?"

"Aidan and Ryan are staying down in Omagh tonight. They've four farmers and two locals to interview and most of the farmers are out on the land till sunset." The D.C.I. snorted pityingly. "Hughesy sounded surprised about it too. City boys. Huh! *I* could've told him they'd be out in the fields till it was dark."

"Why didn't you then?"

Without waiting for a reply Craig turned to scan the open-plan office, in particular an area in the far left corner behind the last of the desks. After a minute he nodded to himself and entered his office where his deputy hot-footed it after him, suddenly curious.

"What were you looking at near the back just then?"

"Nothing. Hang on a minute." Craig stuck his head back out his office door. "Alice, is that call with Mahon's governor set up for six?"

On her nod he stepped back in and took a seat behind his desk, nodding his now suspicious deputy to a chair.

"Why're you talking to the Governor, boss? You're going to land Annette in the shit!"

"I'll tell you later. And I *won't* add to her trouble because I've had an idea. Now, what have you found on those witness statements from France?"

"I'm only halfway through them."

"Give me whatever you've got."

In response Liam left the room for a second and reappeared with two sheets of paper in his hand. He retook his seat and set them side by side on the desk.

"OK, so both pages are a mixture of staff and guests, and this lot..." he tapped the left hand sheet "...are all in the clear for convictions. Ash has run them through every database he can find-"

"That was quick."

"Aye, well, to be fair the wee geek *was* ahead of us. The Doc phoned through the girl's name as we left the lab so he started then."

Craig made a mental note to give the analyst a glowing annual assessment and nodded his deputy on.

"Anyhow... *they're* all clear. But this lot." He lifted the right hand page into the air. "Aren't."

When Craig saw a list filling half the page his eyes widened. "You're telling me they've *all* got sex convictions?"

"Well, not *all* the convictions are for child sex and some just have suspicions and reports." The D.C.I. took out a pen, "But anyway, forget the rest of them, my gut says that *this* is the most interesting one." He circled a name and turned the page for Craig to read.

"Pierre Galvet. OK, so why him?"

"He's the only *serious* possibility. The others are mainly rumour and gossip, and what convictions they do have are mostly petty theft, public nuisance and the rest. My gut says most of them just pissed off the locals in some way so they squealed on them to the cops."

He underlined a different name. "I mean, look at this guy. Belgian, stayed at the hotel every year in their cheapest room, and was always shouting at the staff and complaining. I think he just got up the management's nose so much that they put his name on a list for the cops to harass."

Craig rolled his eyes; a contemporary version of the witch trials.

"So tell me more about Galvet."

Liam rested back in his chair and spoke from memory, which was still teenager sharp despite his fifty-three years. He could remember the name of every person that he'd ever arrested, *and* of the thankfully far smaller number that he'd been forced to shoot.

"Forty-four, born in Paris. Ran away from home at fourteen and ended up on the streets, where he mostly survived by thieving and scamming people. When he was nineteen he was done for the first time for sex offences, flashing, and the gendarmes banged him up for a short stay. He left Paris as soon as he got out of Le Nick."

Craig chuckled at the Franglais. There was more of it as the D.C.I. went on.

"The mademoiselles in Par-ee must've seen enough of Galvet's dingaling to do them."

Craig asked a question through his laughter. "OK. So where did he go next, and what were his other offences?"

When his deputy made a face Craig knew instantly that Galvet's crimes had become serious and his laughter died in his throat.

"There were multiple reports from small towns from Paris down to some place called rocket server..."

Craig considered enlightening him that it was La Roquette-sur-Var but decided to leave it alone.

"... of lewd behaviour, public urination and more flashing, but no charges. Then he got done for the second and third times, once for groping a twelve-year-old girl in a park where there was a witness to it, and then in twenty-ten he was suspected of trying to abduct a girl from outside a shop."

Craig's eyebrows rose. "Was he locked up for it?"

"Not for long, unfortunately. They couldn't prove attempted abduction so they just did him for groping again. The mother came out of the shop just in time to catch him with his hand on the girl and called the cops, but Galvet argued that he'd just been chatting to the kid because he was worried that she was standing on her own. Both times he got short sentences and was sent on his way."

"How old was the second girl?"

"Eleven."

"He's a hebephile then."

Hebephilia is a strong sexual interest by adults in early adolescent children, typically aged from eleven to fourteen.

"Yep, well the cops in Nice obviously didn't bother checking his records in other regions after Bella Westbury was abducted."

"Probably because when they were searching for known paedophiles they checked for those whose preference was for Bella's age range, not for older children like Galvet."

Liam nodded glumly. It was a mistake he'd seen cops make before, assuming that sex offenders chose their type and stuck to that. Some did but plenty didn't and it turned out to be a fatal mistake.

"OK, so the next that was heard of the scrote was more petty offences in Cross de Cagney..."

Cros de Cagnes.

"...that's down the coast from the hotel where the Westbury girl lived. The offences always happened between August and October and each time Galvet was interviewed he said he was in the area to pick grapes."

"What did he do to gain police attention this time?"

"Theft. Skimming credit cards and nicking cars mostly. There are no more sex convictions recorded."

"So either he got more cautious about his approaches or he learned to cover his ass."

"Do you want me to check if any other girls went missing locally?"

"Ask Davy to run a search when he has time, but let's focus on Bella for the moment."

"Will do."

The D.C.I. stretched his long arms above his head and yawned loudly before continuing, giving Craig a view of his rather large tonsils that he could well have done without.

"Anyway, *I* think that his history of attempted abduction and his proximity in the summer to the Westbury's house makes Galvet a suspect for Bella, boss, although his interview with the cops after her abduction gives him an alibi. He said he was in the field picking fruit all day."

Craig nodded. "I agree. We definitely need to dig deeper on him. OK, great work, Liam. Finish checking the rest of your list and then we'll make a plan."

The D.C.I.'s eyes lit up. "France?"

The suggestion made Craig's heart leap too. A trip to France would be wonderful; he hadn't visited the country in years. His family had spent every summer when he was growing up between Rome where his mother came from and Tuscany where they had cousins, and they'd often nipped over the border to Nice. It had done far more for his French than all the lessons he'd had at school and he would love the chance to speak it again.

But... sadly his mistress was the police finance department and she wasn't a generous one, so without serious justification they would never sanction the trip. Although of course that didn't mean he couldn't pay for it himself.

Craig's rationalisation had only taken seconds so his deputy was still looking at him hopefully for a yes.

"I'm not ruling a trip out, Liam, but it depends on what we discover here over the next few days." He lifted his desk phone. "OK, bugger off now. I need to make some calls before Alice puts Mahon through."

The D.C.I. didn't need to be told twice, especially as he guessed that at least one of the calls would be to Katy and might involve unnecessary, in his opinion, expressions of romance.

In fact none of Craig's calls were to his new wife, despite the advanced state of her pregnancy, because she'd told him very clearly to, "leave her alone", courtesy of his apparent tendency to, "fuss", something that he vehemently denied, although he supposed that phoning her every two hours in the previous month *had* been a bit much. It had seen Katy forbidding all communication between them between the hours of eight and eight, but thankfully he had the reassurance that she was in the care of her mother and he would have trusted Maureen Stevens with his life.

So his calls were in fact to the Ombudsman's and PPS' offices making appointments to see them the following week, by which time he'd hopefully have found out a lot more about Pete McElroy's burglary and also be less inclined to take a swing at their staff.

He followed up with a third call to the police works department, querying the price of an alteration to the squad-room's infrastructure which he'd just realised fifteen minutes before was long overdue. When he'd recovered from the quote that he was given for doing the work, *and* doing it that weekend, he gave them the go ahead. Even if the new structure didn't end up being utilised for its intended purpose all the time, they'd lost their quiet space to write reports and view CCTV tapes when the staff-room had been built so it would never go unused.

At the very least it would give his team a surprise on Monday and cheer them up, which they badly needed. While the main impact of Pete McElroy's death had definitely been on his immediate family Annette was a member of another family as well, his team, and although they dealt with death and tragedy every day in their work it was very different when somebody that they cared about was involved.

Whether she liked it or not, and he knew that

sometimes she viewed it as a pain in the ass, Annette wasn't only a gifted detective she was the squad's surrogate mum, just as his permanent secretary, Nicky Morris, currently only working occasionally because she was caring for her teenage son who had a drug problem, was their ever present nagging aunt. With both of them away now for an indeterminate length of time it was knocking the team's balance off, and he needed to find some way to rectify that while still keeping his eye on the prize; finding Stuart Kincaid's killer.

Craig's thoughts were disturbed by his desk phone ringing, normally only something that happened after he'd heard Alice receive a call to transfer. Rather than waste time wondering who might be bypassing the PA he answered the call quickly in case it was about Katy, and was surprised to hear a voice that he wasn't able to put a name to but sounded familiar enough that he thought he probably should.

"D.C.S. Craig?"

"Yes. Who's calling?"

"It's D.C.S. Pine. Counterterrorism."

Craig's thoughts ping-ponged from, 'What the hell does counterterrorism want with me?' to 'now *why* is that name familiar?' and back again, before he realised who she was.

Catherine Pine was one of three Chief Superintendents, with himself and Andy White, the Drugs lead in Derry, that Sean Flanagan had in his questionable wisdom decided to make into an informal team. Their task was to provide ad hoc consultation and expertise for the Serious and Organised Crime unit, its day-to-day operational running being the job of SOC's dedicated team and the Assistant Chief Constable who was their lead. Flanagan also utilised their joint expertise as and when any of their own cases revealed links to something bigger, as in the squad's murder case before Christmas which had yielded leads to counterfeit drug importing and dealing networks in prisons, and paramilitary gangs.

But Craig was struggling to think of anything that linked his work currently to counterterrorism and his heart sank at the only other possible reason he could think of that Cate Pine was giving him a call. He tried not to let it show in his response.

"Hello again, Cate, how are you?"

There was a momentary pause at the other end of the line during which he realised that she couldn't remember where they'd met before. He refreshed her memory.

"We were both at the joint forces conference in Dublin last year. The one with the Gardaí."

A drawn out, "Yesss..." said that the penny was taking an unflatteringly long time to drop. When it did it was with a clang. "You were the one who wouldn't switch your phone off and kept going outside to take calls."

It was said in a tone that implied phone answering was what secretaries were for, and he decided to move things on before she said something else to make him think she was a snob.

"What can I do for you, D.C.S. Pine?"

If she noticed the change in appellation she gave no sign of it.

"I thought we should meet up. I hear you've already worked with D.C.S. White in the new arrangement."

He'd been right about her reason for calling and it made his heart sink. He had enough to do at the moment without taking tea with a woman whose missing sense of humour was the talk of the force. So much so that one wit had even offered a reward for finding it and had had to be talked out of circulating a flyer to that effect. Being no craic was considered a crime in Ireland, and not a victimless one.

He deflected the meeting request with information.

"I had a case before Christmas that we needed his expertise on and it evolved into more, but I don't think anything we're working on at the moment overlaps with C.T." When he realised that he was sounding as reluctant to meet her as he felt, his good manners kicked in. "But I'm more than happy to meet up for a chat anyway."

"Information Technology."

"Sorry, what?"

He wondered whether he'd tuned out for part of the conversation and missed something; it *had* been known before when he was tired.

Her next words said that he hadn't.

"I'm leading Information Technology Crime now. I've left Counterterrorism. The only reason I mentioned it in my introduction was because I thought that was the only place you might know me from."

"Ah... well, I imagine tech is very interesting," he would rather have had his fingernails pulled out, "there's an IT component in most crimes nowadays." That part was true at least.

It was as if he hadn't spoken, as her voice, which Craig noticed was quite husky and attractive despite the words she was uttering, continued in exactly the same tone.

"When shall we meet? We won't need long, just enough for me to give you my perspective on how we might work together should the occasion arise, and you to give me yours."

The clipped nature of her last few words said that any meeting would be mostly about her, but Craig already had an idea how to defer the fateful day.

"I can't meet until the end of the week, and it may even be next week. We've just caught a case."

Her voice rose in the first sign of interest since she'd called him. "A murder?"

Diplomacy prevented him hitting back with, "No, shoplifting, because that's what a Murder Squad does," and he responded with a short, "mmm" instead.

As he made the sound Craig realised that there'd been something more than interest in her question; she was jealous of what she perceived was his exciting job. The sadness of it made him soften towards her slightly and he made up his mind to be more generous in their interactions, although as they hung up on, "Let's confirm later this week" he also decided to liven up their eventual meeting by bringing Liam along.

****

Rownton Village Hinterland. 7 p.m.

It was seven o'clock by the time Aidan and Ryan had completed their interviews with the local farmers and most of what they'd learnt could have been acquired by phone. The quarry had closed down four years before and the only people who ever went near it now were: a site guard who was paid to do occasional inspections, who even when he could be bothered to go there did little but drink tea in his hut near the entrance; people fly-tipping amongst the rocks on the cliff above the main pit; and evidently, although none of the farmers had been aware of it and the one who was Ricky Murphy's father had been less than amused, it had proved the perfect hanging out place for the local kids.

One thing that *had* made the personal visits worthwhile was being able to show Stuart Kincaid's photograph around, something that had caused their final interviewee, Gabriel McCusker, to narrow his eyes, momentarily rendering invisible the white squinting-in-the-sun lines that radiated from them and scored his mahogany skin like engravings in wood.

Aidan seized on his attention to Kincaid's photograph gratefully.

"You know this man?"

The farmer shook his head slowly. "Not *know*..."

Ryan jumped into his pause. "*Saw*. You saw him somewhere then?"

The response was a nod.

"Can you recall where that was?"

The closing of McCusker's eyes and screwing up of his face made the detectives hold their breath in anticipation. Their wait was finally rewarded by a hesitant nod.

"I think..."

As Ryan's mouth opened with a prompt, Aidan closed it again with a shake of his head that said, "Patience."

A moment's pause and then the local man's second nod was more definitive.

"Aye, aye, I did see him. Definitely. I saw him in the village. In the shop it was. He was talking to the post-mistress. Asking her something."

Aidan smiled encouragingly. "Do you have her name?"

"Aye, it's Biddy Evans, Bridget. She ran the shop and post-office for years. You can't miss it; it's the only shop in the place."

Rownton *was* the original one horse town.

Ryan signalled to speak again and this time his slightly controlling D.C.I. allowed it.

"Can you recall *when* you saw him? Was it last year for instance, or the year before?"

The farmer shook his head. "I'm not much for years and months, me. We mostly talk seasons here."

He rested back in his armchair in the warm room where they'd been sitting for the previous thirty minutes and continued, "Planting season, harvesting season, that's how we reckon time on the farm. But it was definitely in a harvest time I saw him, I know that because I was taking some veg to the church for Harvest Festival when I walked past Biddy's shop-"

Aidan cut back in. "Harvest happens in August and September doesn't it?"

"Mostly July to September, depending on the crop. The festival's in September."

Ryan had another idea. "Can you remember if he was showing the post-mistress something as he was talking to her? A piece of paper or...a photograph perhaps?"

McCusker's small brown eyes enlarged. "Now you come to mention it, he *did* have something in his hand. But I couldn't rightly say what it was. Biddy could tell you maybe."

"Maybe?"

"Aye, well, she's retired now." He tapped his temple with a weathered finger. "Not as sharp in her mind as she once was."

Aidan sighed heavily; if the post-mistress had a poor memory she mightn't even recall *seeing* Stuart Kincaid, never might remember what he'd asked her.

The farmer saw his downcast look and threw him a lifeline.

"But sure, Biddy was always cleverer than everyone else around here anyway, so she's probably just come down to our level now."

It was something perhaps, but there was only one way to find out. The D.C.I. rose to his feet and as he did so he saw Ryan withdraw the image of Bella Westbury that had been found in Kincaid's pocket, although considerably cleaned up by Des. It was worth a shot.

The sergeant turned to the farmer with the picture facing down towards the farmhouse's polished stone floor.

"We have another photograph that we'd like you to take a look at, if you would."

McCusker tugged at his long sideburns for a moment

and then nodded. "If I can help. Is it another man?"

"No." Ryan passed the picture across, watching the man's face closely as he did. "Do you recognise this little girl?"

Both detectives spotted the immediate upward flash of McCusker's eyebrows and then his narrowing gaze, so Aidan urged him on in an intense voice.

"You know her, don't you?"

The country man hesitated. "I...I'm... ach, it's not exactly a brilliant photo now, is it."

"Sorry, no." Ryan's tone became insistent as well. *"Who is she? Do you know?"*

In response McCusker pointed at the photograph's shadowed background, and to a woman standing about six feet behind the girl that no-one so far had paid any attention to.

"I'm not sure on the girl, but I'm nye on a hundred percent that's Nicola Westbury. So the girl must be her wee daughter, mustn't it? It'd make sense."

Aidan sat down again with a thud. Nicola Kincaid-Westbury had been in Rownton at some point! Was *that* why her brother Stuart had come there? And could it be a lead to how he'd died?

"How do you know Nicola Westbury?"

The farmer shook his head. "Well, I don't really; it's her husband I know. Edgar he's called. His family used to run the guest house on the edge of the village, and we went to the local school together. The parents are dead now; they passed in a car crash on the A28 in early fifteen." He shook his head solemnly. "Shocking road that. Course, I'm not surprised, the state of the potholes-"

Ryan heard a rant about government irresponsibility coming and cut in. "How can you be so sure which year the Westburys died?"

McCusker looked at him, surprised. "They announce all the local anniversaries for ten miles around at mass."

It was a stark reminder of how much closer rural communities were than those in the Big Smoke.

"They were nice folk too, the Westburys, so everyone round here was sad at their passing. I recognise Nicola because when they were alive Edgar used to bring her to Rownton to stay regular. Maybe they brought the wee lassie too but I never saw her. Mind you, I spend most my time in my fields. I don't go into town if I can help it."

His tone became conversational. "I heard Edgar's a bigwig in hotels now. They moved abroad somewhere, didn't they?"

Aidan steered the farmer back to the point. "So Edgar grew up around here and he used to visit with his wife Nicola until his parents died. What happened to the guest house then?"

McCusker shook his head morosely. "It got sold eventually and knocked down to build houses. Same fate everything has nowadays. No sense of history some folks."

Aidan steered again. "The rest of the Westbury family?"

"Aye, well, there was only one lad besides Edgar. His younger brother Blaine." He laughed maliciously. "A complete bloody waster he was. There were five years between them, but even so, him and Edgar were like chalk and cheese. Anyway, Blaine went off to fly his kite somewhere abroad years back so there was no-one interested in taking the guest house on."

"And you *definitely* saw Nicola with Edgar when he visited Rownton?"

"Oh, aye. Those two were real lovebirds. Like I said, I'm never in town much, but I remember meeting them once in the pub holding hands. Years ago it was."

Ryan was doing some calculations. Edgar Westbury's parents hadn't died until early in twenty-fifteen, months before Bella was taken. It was unlikely that Edgar and Nicola would have left their children with *her* parents every time they'd visited, the Westburys would have wanted to see their grandchildren after all, so... both Bella and her older brother *must* have been in Rownton at some point even if Gabriel McCusker hadn't seen them there.

He decided to try a more focused question.

"I appreciate that you're not sure of months or years, Mister McCusker, but could you tell us if you saw the man in this photograph," he held out the image of Stuart Kincaid again, "before or after the Westburys died?"

Both detectives held their breath while the farmer thought. This time it only took a second for him to nod.

"Aye, well, when you put it like that. He was definitely here after."

Stuart Kincaid had visited Rownton at some harvest time from twenty-fifteen onwards. Time to narrow it down further.

This time it was Ryan who stood up to leave.

"Thank you, Mister McCusker. You've been very helpful."

As he exited through the farmhouse door Aidan hurried to keep up.

"Where are you going?"

The D.S. waved his mobile in the air.

"To call Davy. If he can tell us the exact date the Westburys died in twenty-fifteen we might be able to form some sort of time-line. When they died, when Bella was abducted in France, when McCusker's harvest time sighting of Stuart Kincaid might have been; twenty-fifteen, sixteen, seventeen or eighteen."

Aidan was having some thoughts too and he pulled out his own phone.

Five minutes later they had reconfirmed with John Winter that Stuart Kincaid had been dead for no more than four months, which meant he *could* have been alive at harvest time the year before. They also knew that the elder Westburys' accident had happened in March of twenty-fifteen, so it was likely that Bella Westbury and the rest of the family would have been in the village that spring for the funeral, unless they'd left the children with Nicola Westbury's parents to spare them the grief.

That left them with another question for Gabriel McCusker so they knocked on his front door again, to have it answered by the farmer clad in his wellingtons and waterproof coat.

"I was just on my way to the cowshed."

"Sorry, just a couple more questions. The Westburys' road accident happened in March twenty-fifteen. Could you have seen the man in the photograph *that* harvest time?"

"No, it was more recent than that for sure."

That left sixteen, seventeen and eighteen.

"Did you see him in the village more than once?"

The local man shook his head. "No. Just the once with Biddy. But I was thinking, it must have been harvest time *twenty-sixteen* that he was here, because Biddy retired from the post-office that Christmas and it was taken over by her son."

"Excellent, thank you. Now, the Westburys' funeral. Did you attend it?"

McCusker nodded firmly. "Everyone around these parts did. To show their respects."

"Do you recall seeing Edgar and his wife there?"

"Oh, aye, and their two kids as well. Nice wee things. It was right sad what happened to that family-."

Ryan cut him off urgently. "Was Edgar's brother Blaine there too?"

The farmer's lips curled, telling them again what he thought of Blaine Westbury. "Aye, he was. *And* at the wake the day before, drunk off his head."

They had their timeline! Aidan wanted to cheer. The Westburys had died in the car crash March twenty-fifteen and Edgar and his whole family had attended the funeral at Rownton later that month. Then in August that year Bella had gone missing over thirteen hundred miles away in France, and at harvest time the year after that, in twenty-*sixteen*, Stuart Kincaid had been witnessed in Rownton talking to its post-mistress.

But that obviously hadn't been Kincaid's only visit to the village because he'd met his end there in the quarry only months before, so what had made the businessman return?

As the detectives returned to the car with their embryonic timeline they knew they would have three interviews to hold the next morning instead of two, now that Biddy Evans had been added to the list. While Ryan called Davy for some background on the post-mistress his D.C.I. phoned to update Craig.

****

The Labs. 7 p.m.

Identifying a dead body is never pleasant for anyone, but when someone has loved the deceased it can be a descent into hell; an amalgamation of chest tightening, stomach churning light-headedness and cold perspiration that makes the viewer want to vomit or run away.

But that is just the physical side of the ordeal, horrific

yes, but transient, and what remains can be far worse torment with its effects enduring for life; the loss of a companion, a child or a parent and every small and large aspect of them, from their laughter and support, their moods and foibles, through to the simple sound of their key in the front door and their call of, "I'm home" every night. All absent. Forever gone.

It would be tempting to say that nothing could possibly worsen that impact, but there is *always* the way in which the person died. Although not always true that a natural death with time for goodbyes is a comfort and mitigates the losses mentioned, the disappearance of a loved one ending in the news that they were brutally murdered is a horror that can steal even the most stoic's peace of mind.

That was how it was for Luisa Kincaid when Andy led her gently from the mortuary viewing room, so blank of expression and devoid of words that he knew he couldn't possibly interview her that day. Instead he'd ushered her into the warm, lamp-lit relatives' room that John Winter had indicated, guiding her to its couch and dispatching his junior to make tea while he sat opposite, saying nothing and allowing the wife who was now a widow to have whatever thoughts she chose.

The D.C.I. was no longer concerned about asking questions that could wait for another day, no longer willing to produce the photograph of the missing Bella at that moment and enquire about what Luisa Kincaid knew; instead his *only* concern was for the slim brunette in front of him, whose suffering was etching its name through her repeated scratching and gouging of her forearm and pouring out through her eyes, a river of pain and misery that made him shiver and offer up an entreaty that what had happened to this woman *never* became the lot of anyone *he* loved.

It was an approach that Craig would have agreed with had he been asked, but he wasn't. Couldn't be in fact, because at that moment he was engaged in a silent conversation of his own with George Royston, the Governor of Mahon Prison; an hour later than scheduled because some prisoner had decided to punch his mate.

Royston was a man that they'd encountered during a case at the prison in December, and one that Craig knew would cave and give him whatever information he needed if stressed enough. And he *needed* the name of Pete McElroy's cellmate; banking on him being the prisoner that McElroy had grown closest to inside, or at least the one that it was worth interviewing first.

So that's what the detective was trying to obtain through the strategic use of silence, and when Royston finally squeezed out, "Benjamin Frampton" in a grudging tone it became evident that the approach had worked.

"Pete McElroy's cellmate was called Ben Frampton?"

"Yes."

The detective could picture Royston's hand sweeping back through his hair repeatedly as he grudgingly yielded the information, just as it had done each time he'd been questioned during their case months before; although the stress in his voice suggested that this time it might be not so much a sweep as a rake.

"OK. Tell me more about Mister Frampton. How long is he in for, what was he convicted of, and the rest."

'The rest' being Frampton's general behaviour as a prisoner, and exactly how close he and Pete McElroy had become. The governor's grudging tone became defiant, but with a nervous undertone, as if he was insecure in his boldness and expecting to be shouted down.

"The Ombudsman's office contacted me and warned me to keep any information about Mister McElroy's time with us confidential."

'Time with us.' The man made it sound like he was running a boarding school, or at worst some sort of retreat.

It prompted Craig's first equivocation of the conversation; one that he was glad his deputy wasn't in the room to hear.

"The Ombudsman's office has been in touch with me as well and I'm au fait with everything."

If not exactly a lie it was a pretty big bluff to start on, but he'd made the calculation that either it wouldn't be caught, or if it was and he was proved right about the reason for McElroy entering Annette's house he would get a pat on the back. But even if he *wasn't* right, as long as he hadn't interfered with any possible prosecution it was likely he would only get his knuckles rapped.

His calculations were interrupted by the prison CEO

giving a relieved sigh at the other end of the line and then being so forthcoming it verged on incontinence.

"Well, if the Ombudsman's office says it's OK to tell you…"

Craig was tempted to point out that *wasn't* actually what he'd said but he held his tongue.

"Ben Frampton is a burglar. He's halfway through a ten year sentence with six offences being taken into account. No parole."

"Straight burglary with no weapon?"

"Yes."

Ten years and no parole for unaggravated burglary? Even with six offences, one of them must have involved a bloody bank!

Craig had guessed right.

"He was part of the big job on the NI Bank in Belfast's centre, and he did post-offices, shops, homes and even some cars as well. Anything with a lock really, and he was gifted at it; never left a mark. As far as his behaviour in here goes, it's been excellent. He's likable and does as he's asked with grace."

"And his relationship with Pete McElroy?"

"Good. Mister McElroy was put into the cell last January."

"Any particular reason for the pairing?"

Royston hesitated just a beat too long, making Craig's antennae twitch.

"None. Frampton's last cell-mate had been discharged and we needed the bed."

"Right…"

The detective left, "you're lying" hanging in the air as a subtext and continued on.

"You were about to tell me about their relationship being good."

"Yes, well, I'd go so far as to say it was cordial. Mister McElroy was a teacher before he offended as you know, and he spent a lot of time teaching Ben to read and write. To quite a good standard now actually. They shared for almost a year and became well nigh inseparable in McElroy's last few months here…"

Loyalty. Damn. It could make Ben Frampton a tough nut to crack.

As Royston's voice tailed away in either real or mock sympathy for his dead inmate, Craig was teeing up his most difficult query and already visualising himself hitting a brick wall.

"This may be difficult to answer, Governor, but I need to know if McElroy ever consulted the prison doctor?"

The defensiveness reappeared. *"Why do you need to know that?"*

"Answer the question, please."

It was said in his best interrogatory tone, which he'd noticed normally worked everywhere but at home.

But this time the stubbornness of the righteous joined Royston's defence.

"I'm not sure that I can, Chief Superintendent. Even by confirming such visits I would be breaching medical confidentiality."

"I could get permission from his family."

"Do that, and then *perhaps* I can help you."

He heard the governor's drawbridge being raised and locked. Apparently it wasn't *just* at home that particular approach could fail.

Shit. That meant involving Amy and Jordan, and he'd wanted to keep them out of things until he had proof to back up his hunch. Annette wouldn't want her kids upset, not even to save herself.

If there was no way around it that's what he would *have* to do to defend their mum, but before that Craig decided to play one last card.

"I need to interview Mister Frampton."

"For what reason?"

"That's confidential and to disclose it could prove prejudicial to an investigation."

That old chestnut.

But he'd deliberately said 'an' investigation not this specific one, so he only counted it as a half-lie and one that he was prepared to defend; exactly how he would work out later.

A note of stubbornness entered the governor's voice. "I'll need paperwork to release Frampton to you."

"You'll have it. I'll order him brought up to Belfast tomorrow afternoon. Make him ready for transport, please."

Ben Frampton didn't know it yet but he was about to help save a so-called 'pig's' bacon, and Aidan and Ryan didn't know yet that they would be making a detour on their way back to Belfast to pick him up.

****

Craig was just about to leave the office for the night when his mobile rang. He wasn't leaving to go home but to meet *yet another* estate agent, and be shown around *yet another* house that was for sale. Since their wedding six months before he and Katy had kept their own places, mostly because he'd been a bachelor for so long that an incremental transition to permanency, with all its overlapping living arrangements, was necessary to stop him, as Lucia had put it so pithily, "Freaking his dog'.

Logically the expression meant nothing, and yet it conjured up perfectly his likely state of mind on waking up one morning to find that he had no place to escape to for solitude, even though that place currently, his scruffy apartment at Stranmillis, was being visited less and less often every week.

Given that he wasn't carrying around a four kilogram embryo it made sense that he did most of the leg work of scouting for a house that met their minimum requirements: separate his and her caves as well as all the boring stuff like a kitchen, garden and so on; and then presented Katy with photos and his opinion to help her make a choice. But three weeks in and ten houses down he was bored rigid, not to mention left wondering how television presenters who did home makeover shows weren't tempted to run screaming for the hills.

One more sodding pine/Shaker/space-age/glossy kitchen with or without an 'island', or bedroom with 'a panoramic view' that could only be seen by hanging out a window with a pair of binoculars, and he thought he might actually shoot the agent. Left to his own devices he would just have had *them* produce a list and stuck a pin in it, but he acknowledged that Katy's view of buying their first home together carried a considerably more romantic tinge.

Either way the whole process was giving him a sore head, so when he heard his mobile springing to life he grabbed it like his sister would the last pair of boots in a Kurt Geiger sale and answered with a dramatic, "Thank you!" surprising Aidan who was on the other end of the line.

"What are you thanking me for, Guv?"

"Giving me a legitimate excuse to cancel a house viewing. You did call to give me some work, yes?"

The D.C.I. rolled his eyes at the sergeant beside him, eloquently expressing his view on the sanity of the higher ranks.

"Sorry, just information at the moment," he heard Craig's disappointment immediately and rushed to caveat with, "although of course you *might* decide to investigate it tonight."

Craig's sigh of pleasure coincided with someone knocking on his door that didn't wait for permission to enter, and even with his chair turned towards the window he knew exactly who it was.

"Sit down, Liam. I'm on the phone. OK, fire ahead, Aidan."

The D.C.I. outlined the discussion with Gabriel McCusker, and Stuart Kincaid's timeline in particular made Craig frown.

"Harvest time, that's August, isn't it?"

Before Aidan could answer Liam, who'd grown up on a farm near Banbridge, had obliged.

"July, August and September on most farms, although for some that grow barley it can stretch to November and veg can be planted to harvest in the spring. What sort of farm is it?"

Knowing the volume of his deputy's voice would have made his words audible in Rownton with or without a telephone, Craig said, "I take it you got that?"

It was Ryan who responded, he having asked that very question of McCusker when they'd arrived on his land.

"Wheat and dairy."

Liam nodded. "OK, then harvest's August and September mostly, although winter wheat *can* be harvested in May and June."

Craig's response was to swivel his chair around, set his mobile on the desk and put it on speakerphone.

"OK, as everyone seems to be joining in on this

conversation anyway, let's make it four-way. Aidan, you're saying Stuart Kincaid was in Rownton in the autumn of twenty-sixteen. Then he returned again, by John's reckoning, sometime in the final two to three months of last year, which is when he was drowned at the quarry."

"Yep. He came here in twenty-sixteen, about a year after his niece was taken, and then again a year after his sister committed suicide."

Craig frowned as the D.C.I. reached the end of his sentence, and noticing that his deputy had as well he waved him on.

"Tell everyone what bothers you about that, Liam, and then I'll tell you what I think."

The harvest expert cracked his knuckles loudly before he spoke, sparking a series of groans.

"OK... so Edgar Westbury grew up in Rownton and helped his folks run their guest house, then he grew up, went into the hotel business, did good, got married-" He stopped abruptly. "Here, when *did* he marry Nicola Kincaid?"

Craig tapped up a file. "Two-thousand-and-five."

"OK. So... most people get married in the girl's family church if they church it at all, so the wedding wouldn't have been in Rownton. It would have been..."

His boss filled in another gap. "In Ballycastle. That's where Nicola and Stuart Kincaid grew up."

"So...Nicola married Edgar Westbury in Ballycastle in oh-five and Stuart Kincaid would have been there for sure, but why would he have ever gone to *Rownton?* Does it say in the file that Edgar and Nicola ever lived there? If so, I could see Stuart going there to visit to see his twin, but-"

Craig scanned his screen quickly and cut him off, "No. They never lived in Rownton."

"Well, OK, then Stuart Kincaid would've needed a damn good reason to trek all the way to Rownton, seeing as it's halfway across the country from his home in Portaferry. Agreed?"

There was a murmur of agreement before he went on.

"So now the question becomes, what *was* that reason? *Why* would Stuart Kincaid have trekked to a place he had no link to, other than that his sister had married a guy from there? And *twice* in three years. At the time of his first visit in twenty-sixteen his sister was still living in France, and by the second visit last year she was dead."

The D.C.I. smiled decisively, as if a piece had just fallen into place.

"OK, so the first question we need answered is what were Stuart Kincaid's reasons for being in Rownton? Bearing in mind they could have been different for each visit."

Craig nodded him on.

"The second is... on Kincaid's initial visit to Rownton in twenty-sixteen, which was after his niece was taken from a country hundreds of miles away but while his sister was still alive, were Nicola or Edgar Westbury *with* him? And actually, I'd ask if Edgar was with him when Kincaid went there last year too."

Craig interrupted. "Aidan, are you taking all this down?"

He was now. "Yep."

"OK. Go on, Liam."

The deputy rested back in his chair and gazed up at the ceiling, knowing that it would help his thought processes more than staring at his boss' expectant face.

"OK, the third question is... if not why not? If Edgar or Nicola *weren't* with him and Kincaid went to Rownton alone both times, then why weren't they-?"

Craig shook his head. "Nicola Westbury probably didn't want to leave the house in France just in case her daughter returned home."

"OK, but why wasn't *Edgar* helping his brother-in-law to hunt in Rownton if he'd found some sort of lead?"

"*If* he had."

Ryan interjected. "Kincaid was seen talking to the postmistress in twenty-sixteen and showing her something, possibly a photo of the girl. We're meeting her tomorrow so we'll get more then."

Liam grunted his approval. "Good plan, but I'd ask in the pub and church as well. Between them the local shopkeeper, pub landlord and churchy types usually know everything that's happening in a small village and its surrounds, so you might find out more about Kincaid's visits from them."

He put his hands behind his neck for support and kept

gazing at the roof. "We can ask Edgar Westbury about it all when we see him tomorrow as well, boss. Now, next... if Kincaid *was* asking about his niece in Rownton in twenty-sixteen then it was probably because he was worried about his sister. He'll have loved the kid too, but bairns that age are seen as extensions of their mother and we know Nicola *must* have been in a bad way because she killed herself the following year. So...I think we can rule out anything sinister about Kincaid carrying the picture on either visit-"

He stopped dead and looked at Craig. "That's a thing, boss. If Kincaid was showing the girl's photo to the post-mistress in twenty-sixteen then by the time he died he'd have been carrying it around for years."

Craig nodded. "Or a copy. OK, you two, when you see the post-mistress tomorrow confirm that it *was* Bella's photo that Kincaid showed her and check if it was the same one he had in his pocket. You have a copy of that, don't you?"

"Yep" confirmed that they had.

Liam resumed his gaze at the ceiling.

"OK...but...the wee girl was stolen in France, so why did Kincaid think anyone at *Rownton* might have known anything about her whereabouts? Had he found something linking her abduction to the village, and if so, what?"

He dropped his gaze to Craig again and sat up straight, signalling that he was approaching his denouement.

"There must have been *something* to link her abduction with Rownton, boss, because when Kincaid went there again last year it got him killed."

As he said the words both men waved bye-bye to their trip to France. The answers to Bella Westbury's abduction lay in a chilly Northern Irish village and unfortunately *not* in sunny, picturesque Nice, city of al fresco dining and wine that slipped sensuously down the throat.

Then Craig thought of something that revived his hopes. "We might go yet, Liam. Remember Galvet."

It cheered the D.C.I. up again and encouraged him to finish his train of thought.

"We need to find out what Stuart Kincaid learnt that led him to Rownton."

Craig nodded. "Or what he *thought* he'd learnt anyway. For all we know Kincaid could have been barking up entirely the wrong tree by going there, but in the process inadvertently alerted someone dangerous in the village and got himself killed. We still can't be *certain* that his death is linked to the girl's disappearance."

A sceptical look from his deputy made him concede, "Although I grant you it looks likely. But I don't like that local builder's suicide. It's too much of a coincidence that happening just now." He leaned closer to the phone. "Aidan, have you had a chance to speak to anyone there about that yet?"

"No. Sorry, Guv. We spent the afternoon out at the farms. We've got the builder's deputy, the pub landlord, the post-mistress, and now thanks to Liam, the church on our list for tomorrow." He considered for a moment and added. "What time are you briefing? Because we won't make it back till the afternoon."

"Don't worry. Everybody has work to tidy up, so it won't be until six."

He glanced at his deputy to see if he had anything further to add and then asked the other two men the same. When the message was no all around Craig was just about to cut the call, and then he remembered something else. Loath as he was to hand Liam ammunition to fire at him he decided to mention it, shooting him a defiant look as he did.

"Before you go, Aidan, there's one more thing. I need you to take a trip to Mahon Prison on your way back tomorrow and transport an inmate to High Street for interview." He ignored Liam's gawping. "The governor's expecting you. I'll email the paperwork to him in the morning. Bye."

He cut the call quickly and then, motioning Liam to hold on to whatever wisdom his mouth had just opened to impart for a moment, he left the room to ask a just getting ready to leave Alice to make a call that had nothing to do with his job.

When he returned an eavesdropping Liam was smirking piously. "Cancelling your house viewing? Tut tut, the wife won't be happy."

Craig chuckled as he retook his seat. "The wife as you call her will be ecstatic. She's already fed up with me moaning about complete strangers' bathroom fittings." He sat back in his chair and folded his arms. "So, go on then. Let's have it."

The D.C.I. feigned innocence. "Let's have what?"

"You know you're just busting to have a go about the prisoner I'm bringing up from Mahon."

"Well, if you're asking do I think you're an eejit for doing it, then yes, I do. If the PPS or Ombudsman catch on you'll be toast, and uniformed constable pounding the beat toast at that."

Craig sat forward eagerly, brushing off the warning. "This guy was McElroy's cellmate and they were close. Pete taught him to read and write, so there was trust there-"

The D.C.I. cut him off. "Loyalty too that means. And there's that whole honour amongst thieves crap, don't forget. What makes you think this scrote will betray that? That's if Pete even confided what he was planning in the first place?"

Craig gave an offended grunt. "Oh ye of little faith in my ability to intimidate."

It earned him a sceptical look.

"Ach, wise up, boss. You know if he's in Mahon he's a hard man! He's far more likely just to tell the Ombudsman's office you questioned him and land *you* in the shit."

Craig deflated slightly. "Well...maybe, but it's worth a go for Annette's sake. I don't know that he'll tell us, not for sure-"

Liam shook his head hastily. "Whoa there, now. What's that '*us*' about? I want to keep *my* job!"

Craig continued as if he hadn't spoken. "But it's worth a try, isn't it? I mean we've *got* to help her out of this mess-"

His deputy cut him off in a chastising tone. "By getting us, I mean you, *into* one?"

But Craig wasn't listening now. He had the bit between his teeth.

"The more I think about Pete leaving his prints on the French doors, the more I think there's something odd here. He had no intention of hiding the fact that he'd entered that house. Why?"

Liam looked less disapproving and more interested. "He'd have known his prints were in the system all right."

Craig nodded eagerly. "*Exactly*. Pete wasn't a stupid

man, so that means he must have believed that even if he got ID-ed he wasn't going to get picked up again."

Liam edged forward in his seat, enthused. "He was planning to skip the country! That's what I thought this morning when we were at Annette's. You thought it too."

Craig wasn't convinced that *was* what he'd been thinking, but if it bought him his deputy's help it was as good a working theory as any.

"That on its own warrants a chat with his roomie, doesn't it? So are you on board now?"

The D.C.I. gave a hesitant nod. "OK... but only on the condition that if it gets us sacked you've got to pay me what I'd have earned anyway till I die."

Craig's faith in the theory developing in his mind was such that he gave a decisive nod. The pair descended into satisfied silence for a while then Craig's face suddenly lit up.

"I've just had a brilliant idea!"

Expecting to hear some new revelation about Annette's case the deputy warily asked, "What?" only to be surprised when an entirely different topic was raised.

"What do you think of this? I'm going to suggest that Katy's mum and my mum go house-hunting for us! We can give them our requirements and budget and set them loose. They couldn't possibly bring back a worse shortlist than me."

His deputy immediately thought of a problem.

"Can either of them drive? 'Cos that isn't a chauffeur duty I'd ever have wished on *my* old man."

Craig gave a smug grin. "Katy's mum can. She drives everywhere. My mum *did* learn when she was young in Italy, but she still can't get used to everything being on the wrong side of the road here so she's a lethal weapon on wheels." He shook his head incredulously. "I don't know *why* I didn't think of asking them before. They'll love it. Then Katy and I can go and view the ones on their shortlist after the baby's born."

Problem sorted he turned to his computer and got back to their case.

"OK, let's think about this timeline. Edgar and Nicola Westbury married in oh-five and their son was born late that year, they moved to France in twenty-ten where Bella was born in twenty-twelve and abducted in fifteen. Stuart Kincaid visits Rownton village in sixteen, Nicola Kincaid-Westbury kills herself in seventeen, and then Stuart returns to Rownton in eighteen and gets murdered. With a photo of his niece *hidden* in his jacket, a photo he may well have shown to the village post-mistress in twenty-sixteen-"

He stopped suddenly and lifted his mobile, calling Aidan back and catching him on the A32 to Dromore, where the two detectives were spending the night in a small hotel.

"Do Edgar Westbury's parents still live in Rownton?"

Aidan ignored the lack of preamble and answered as if their earlier conversation had never stopped.

"They died in a car accident in March twenty-fifteen."

Craig was taken aback. Could the accident mean something, or had it just been what it was labelled? It was something more for Davy to check out.

He typed a reminder on his screen for the analyst and then moved past the tragic event to its inevitable follow-up.

"So there would have been a funeral soon after that, and odds on it was a whole village affair, given that the Westburys senior owned the only hotel. I want you to find out the name of all the local newspapers and get them to Davy. We'll need every report on that funeral, including photographs if there are any, to see exactly who exactly was there. Does Edgar have any siblings?"

"One. A five years younger brother called Blaine who's apparently a bit of a waster. He moved abroad. We did wonder about the funeral so we asked Gabriel McCusker whether Bella and her brother were there. He said yes, they were both there with their parents. Blaine was as well, and apparently he got pissed at the wake."

"None of that sounds surprising. If Nicola Westbury mourned her daughter enough to kill herself then she doesn't sound like someone who would have left her kids in anyone else's care, although the drunken brother sounds interesting. One last thing, Aidan; I don't expect Stuart Kincaid went to the Westburys' funeral as they weren't his in-laws, but just check to make sure. OK, good work. Get some rest now and get back to it tomorrow. I'll go and see what more Davy can find."

As he hung up Liam shook his head. "Davy's gone home, boss. He had to do some prep for an early meeting."

"Fine. I'll email him with everything then. And while *I'm* doing that, give me some suggestions on how best to brief the mothers to find us a decent house."

****

Dromore Village - Twenty Miles from Rownton. 8.30 p.m.

The travelling detectives had decided to have some after dinner drinks in the bar of the country hotel where they were staying; not a bad way to spend your evening in Aidan's mind, considering that his usual options were watching TV alone or punishing his body at the gym. Having reached a level of fitness moving beyond which would result in his sinewy muscles being bulked up and every last ounce of visible fat, which he didn't have much of anyway, being shed in a process known to gym junkies as shredding, he was considering very seriously whether something that required endless tedious weightlifting repetitions and swallowing 'healthy' protein drinks that resembled the bottom of a pond was really worth it, or whether he should just eat the odd slice of cake and pizza and be content with the body that he had. The problem was the gym was his only social life and so his only hope of meeting women, but its uber-competitive atmosphere was leaving him with only two ways to go now: shred or quit.

Ryan on the other hand already had a female companion to go home to, Sarah Reilly, a GP that he'd met on a case fourteen months before, and the thought of her curling up soft and warm on their sofa and enjoying a marathon fest of Game of Thrones without him wasn't in *any* way being compensated for by the honey tinted liquid in his glass.

He was just about to say as much when Aidan gave an unexpected groan. "I'm fed up being fit."

Given that they were boozing and lounging and nowhere near a gym at that moment it seemed a curious non sequitur, but the sergeant decided to bite. He set his heavy glass tumbler down and nodded the D.C.I. on.

"OK, shoot. *Why* are you fed up being fit? It must be great to be able to leap over tall buildings in one bound."

Aidan shook his blond head gloomily; averting his gaze from his associate and fixing it instead on the dancing flames of the bar's open fire.

"Not really. First, once you get fit you spend all your bloody time working to maintain it, and second, I'm only doing it because I've nothing better to do on nights and weekends."

Ryan shifted uncomfortably in his seat. Confessions of strong emotions like anger and frustration he was used to from men, but having one of his bosses basically telling him how lonely he was, not as an aside or joke, and in a captive environment where they were stuck together for at least another day, was something that he wasn't *at all* sure about.

It was the sight of the chief inspector's heavy-jawed face falling further that convinced Ryan that it was time to transcend decades of conditioning and their rank difference, and step up and be a mate.

He sat forward with his hands clasped between his knees and girded himself to ask a personal question that he knew would either earn him a friend for life or a metaphorical kick in the balls. This *was* Ireland after all, still a palpably macho country, and they were in one of its most macho occupations, the police. Such discussions rarely occurred, but what the hell.

"How lo..."

His voice tailed away uncertainly, and then after a short pause he cleared his throat and tried again, this time managing to get his intended question out.

"How long has it been since you had a serious relationship?"

As the question hit the air the D.S. recoiled so hard in shock at his own boldness that he was thankful he hadn't chosen a stool to sit on or he'd have fallen off.

As it happened Ryan needn't have worried about any backlash from Aidan because when he pulled his gaze away from the flames there was nothing but sadness written there. As he answered the question it was joined by obvious grief.

"I was engaged once, eight years ago, but..."

He returned to the firelight again.

A surprised but emboldened Ryan decided to push him on it. He'd never heard the D.C.I. speak of *any* woman being important to him, and would have characterised his romantic life as a serious of futile chat-ups and short, mostly physical trysts. Perhaps his ignorance came from only been on the team for a year and the others all knew about this ex-fiancée, but somehow he thought not.

"What...what was her name?"

"Arela."

"That's lovely."

He meant it; he'd always loved Celtic names, especially the girls'. They had a romance about them.

Aidan nodded sadly. "So was she. She was the gentlest woman that I'd ever met."

Ryan was dreading the next question but knew that it needed to be asked. "Why did you split up?"

He braced himself for a tale of selfishness or infidelity, or even a more mundane one such as she hadn't liked the way the brash detective had held his knife. But what came next was far worse, and strangely its seriousness elevated the D.C.I. in his opinion, although he wasn't quite sure why.

"She died."

Aidan went to say more but no words emerged. But what could they possibly have been except, "I loved her", which was obvious, or the name of the bastard or illness that had ended her life? And why would he have *wanted* those painful details to hit the air when they must have done so a thousand times when her death occurred.

The sergeant opened his mouth to say something, *anything*, more; but what words would be useful? What words could *possibly* help? In the end he said, "I'm sorry" anyway, because he was and because the sound that the sentiment made was something to fill the pause.

It wasn't much of a pause because Aidan shook his head briskly, ending the discussion as suddenly as he'd begun it but with a lifetime of loss expressed in between.

Just at that moment a young waiter appeared in front of them, but without a bottle or tray but with a note in his hand it was clear that he hadn't come to serve. He held the piece of paper in the air for a moment, passing it to Aidan on the sergeant's glance. The solemn D.C.I. took it and nodded the youth away, then straightening up his seat like the professional he was he paraphrased the message aloud.

"It's from the station sergeant in Rownton. Some girl has approached the local newspaper about Derek Morrow. They're running a story about the two of them having had an affair in tomorrow's early edition and she's being interviewed on local radio in the morning as well."

Ryan exhaled noisily. "Aw, hell. Morrow's wife won't like that."

Aidan rose to his feet. "I'd say that was an understatement."

The sergeant gazed up at him. "Are you going somewhere?"

"*We're* going back to Rownton. We need to find out more about this young woman before the shit hits the fan."

Ryan glanced meaningfully through the bar's latticed windows to where a gale was blowing a tree outside almost horizontal, and then he looked back longingly at the glowing fire.

"It can't wait till tomorrow?"

A re-energised Aidan was already signing for their drinks. "No, it can't. I want to get in front of this before things blow up in the morning and the Guv reams us out for not being ahead of the game."

His companion rose reluctantly. "Don't you think you're overreacting? Man has affair and affair goes wrong so he tops himself. It sounds common enough to me, so what's it got to do with our case?"

Aidan took out his car-keys, threw them up in the air and caught them before answering the question with one in return.

"How often does a suicide happen within hours of a dead body being found in the same tiny village? Outside an Agatha Christie novel that is. And then it's *always* suspicious."

Ryan conceded the point reluctantly, his gaze back on the bent tree again. "Well...OK, probably not often."

Aidan snorted, back to his usual bombastic self. "*Probably?* Catch a grip, man; you're letting the fire melt your brain..."

As he turned for the car park exit Ryan shuddered,

anticipating the freezing air when it opened.

"...if the suicide Vic and this girl aren't linked to our murder case somehow I'll eat my tie."

The chilly sergeant wondered sourly whether it would have the same effect as a protein shake.

****

Rownton Police Station. 9 p.m.

It didn't take the detectives long to reach Rownton Station and even less time to locate the editor of the local newspaper, The Rownton Recorder, who conveniently owned the cottage next door to the nick. He also kept chickens in a small holding behind it, thereby double-jobbing as the local source of free-range eggs.

The newspaper man awaited them in the station's reception wearing a practiced look of determination on his strangely gnarled face, which later enquiries would reveal was the product of too many youthful punch-ups in scrums during the local rugby sevens' tournaments and a reluctance to seek medical help.

Thankfully the journalist was holding a pen and notepad instead of one of his chickens when they met so his hands were covered in ink instead of the less fragrant alternative, but whichever occupational hat the man was wearing he didn't seem like the sort to co-operate.

"Would you like to give my paper a statement on the body found in the quarry, Chief Inspector? And why you're harassing local citizens?"

Aidan gave the man a scowl that said he would be taking no lip.

"You're here to answer questions, not ask them."

The editor spat back. "You can forget that! I'm only here as a courtesy because Mickey here asked me and we went to school together."

The forty-something Sergeant 'Mickey Here' O'Hare confirmed the words with a nod, from his position of sentinel, standing cross-armed behind the station's high reception desk.

"Well, more insisted than asked. Be fair, Hal."

'Hal' ignored the adjustment.

"I'm only here to get a quote from you lot about the stiff in the quarry, not to give you anything on *my* story."

The statement pissed Aidan off so much that he took a stride forward, closing the gap between him and the short editor in one step.

"What's your name, sir? Hal what?"

It was something that both the barman's note and Mickey Here had failed to reveal, but either Aidan's height or his long stride took the journalist aback so much that he blurted out, "Hector McDonagh but they call me Hal" and then tutted at having squealed on himself.

"Well, Mister McDonagh, *we* won't be giving you any comments, but you *will* be giving us some if you want to sleep in your own bed tonight. Now, we can either do things here in the cold reception, or I'm sure Sergeant O'Hare has a nice warm interview room," he glanced meaningfully at the custody officer, "and some nice warm drinks to boot."

Refusal from either man wasn't an option, as Aidan's rank ensured the room and drinks and both detectives' forward progress ensured that the journalist either moved in the direction they wished or he would get knocked over on to the floor.

Five minutes later the station's front door had been locked and its bell for emergencies highlighted, and all four men were squeezed into a tiny interview room with a ratio of three to one on opposite sides of the table and the solitary figure of Hector McDonagh, journalist and chicken farmer, now looking distinctly perturbed.

Aidan kicked off the proceedings.

"Now, Mister McDonagh, tell us about this young lady who approached both you and the local radio station. What's her name?"

McDonagh tried for defiance. "Buy a paper tomorrow and you'll see."

Ryan wondered whether Aidan would explode but instead the D.C.I. merely rolled his eyes.

"*Really?* You're *honestly* thinking of withholding information from the Murder Squad?"

The editor's eyes grew round. "*Murder?* But the man just drowned!" The eyes narrowed again as McDonagh sensed a scoop. *"Didn't he?"*

Aidan gave him a knowing look. "You'll have to find out *that* answer from The Belfast Chronicle, won't you?"

Ryan suppressed a smirk, seeing where he was going. Dangling a bigger story in front of the journalist if he played ball *might* get him to loosen his lips about the girl.

The journalist lurched forward. "I want the murder story!"

Aidan gave him a look that a head teacher would have been proud of. "You can *want* all you like, sir, but what reason would *we* have to agree?"

"Because the public-"

He was cut off by the D.C.I. raising his palm.

"*Please* don't give me that old 'the public have a right to know' guff. I've heard it quoted by bigger and better hacks than you and it's rarely been their true motivation. Filling column inches is all you're interested in. So, go on..." he held out his hand in a beckoning gesture, "*persuade* me to speak to my boss and arrange for you to be the first to get whatever story emerges once things have played out."

Ryan added, "Give it your best shot" eliciting a smile from Michael O'Hare.

He'd known Hal McDonagh for years but the detectives had only just met him, and yet they'd spotted the man's voracious ambition straight away; although to be fair it *was* a characteristic often found in journalists so it wasn't something they were likely to get much credit for.

All the cops could tell the gamble was about to pay off when McDonagh began chewing his bottom lip.

Whether it was the rhythmic tapping of Ryan's forefinger on the table, or the soaring heat in a windowless room crammed with four people when it had only been designed to hold two, but the chewing intensified so much that the only way for McDonagh to proceed if he wanted to keep his lips from bleeding was to agree to the offer.

He did so eventually with a grudging, "Oh, for God's sake, OK!"

Aidan leaned across the table and stared directly into his eyes.

"You'll give us her name and contacts, *and* you'll remove the article from tomorrow's paper."

McDonagh's eyes became saucers. "*Remove it?* But that'll leave me with half a page-"

Ryan cut in quickly. "That I'm sure you can fill with something else you already have prepared."

His boss nodded and went on. "The deal's only good if neither she nor Derek Morrow are mentioned *anywhere* in your paper. Understand?"

After a few seconds more frowning there was an angry grunt. It was followed immediately by, "But she'll be on the radio at ten."

Aidan rested slowly back in his chair. "Let us worry about that."

He nodded the custody sergeant to find something to write on.

"Now, write down where she is and the name of the radio show and you'll be free to go and change your front page."

As the detectives rose to their feet the journalist glared up at them. "You'd better not renege on this."

Ryan could see Aidan thinking, *"Or what?"*

But the D.C.I. had the diplomatic sense not to say it out loud, simply nod at the pen and paper now in front of the editor.

"Give it to Sergeant O'Hare when you've finished and then take yourself off home."

Ryan glanced at the wall clock and sighed. It was almost ten o'clock. With a trip to wherever Morrow's mistress was located and a visit to the radio jock still to pay, they'd be lucky if they got to bed that night before it was time to get up again.

Chapter Five

Dublin. Thursday, 8 a.m.

"STUPID BASTARD!"

Róisín Casey hissed the words so loudly that her office door flew open and her concerned looking PA rushed in.

"Are you OK, Ms Casey? I thought I heard you call out."

The motherly secretary received no response but a rapidly waving hand shooing her out again, the banker's other one already on a mobile phone. As the door closed behind the woman Róisín dialled a number, her previously shooing hand drumming her desk hard as she waited for the other end to be picked up. As soon as it was she repeated her expletive, adding, in her sharper childhood vernacular,

"I give you one soddin' jab, Arthur, an' you can't even feckin' manage that!"

Arthur Norris had anticipated her anger before he'd taken the call, his online newsfeed from The Rownton Recorder showing him what Róisín Casey had already learnt twenty minutes before, that there was nothing in the newspaper's early edition about Derek Morrow *or* his supposed mistress.

As the elderly businessman opened his mouth to answer, the banker cut him off with,

"How much did you pay her? Whatever it was, it wasn't enough!"

When he heard her inhale for long enough to signal that it was a respite and not preparation for a new assault Norris answered, as quietly and calmly as she had been frantic and loud.

"I paid her well and she agreed to everything, Róisín. I *know* she gave the local news editor an exclusive interview because she told me that he'd promised to make it his front page. I also booked her a slot on the local radio at ten this morning, so even if the journalist did drop the ball, people will *hear* her then and the message will get across and spread."

A quieter, but somehow even more terrifying for that, voice responded. "She'd *better* be on the radio at ten, Arthur, because if she's not *someone's* head is going to roll.

Get your ass down to Rownton and find out exactly what happened to that bloody front page, and get it reinstated, *now!*"

The phone went down before Arthur Norris even got a chance to attempt obsequiousness; at least that was something he had to be thankful for.

****

The C.C.U. Thursday, 8 a.m.

True to his word Craig was in his office at eight o'clock ready to brief, having managed a decent night's sleep the night before because Katy had, which meant that their offspring must have done as well. That had prompted a moment of anxiety about the baby's lack of movement when they'd woken at seven, until its first well aimed kick at Katy's ribs had reassured them that all was well.

But even though the detective was fairly bright-eyed and bushy-tailed he hadn't had time for breakfast, so when his deputy dandered into his office at a minute past the hour with a bacon butty in his hand he almost leapt over his desk to yank it out. Liam spotted the coming assault and shoved the roll in his mouth hastily, fairly certain that Craig was too fastidious to want it after that.

When his boss still came hurtling towards him he became less sure, until Craig yanked his office door open and disappeared off the floor, reappearing five minutes later with a butty of his own and his junior analyst in tow.

"Right, take a seat, Ash. Liam clearly already has. Has Davy told you want we need?"

The dark-eyed analyst nodded, making his gold earring wobble and Liam make a comment that showed not only his lack of tact but his lack of fashion nous.

"What is it with you young ones, always drilling holes and drawing on yourselves? Could you not just scribble on some paper instead?"

Ash shrugged. "I wouldn't know about the drawing part because I don't have any tattoos, but my earring's a national style thing. You know, something I got from my Hindu warrior ancestors, like my winning smile." He glanced at the D.C.I.'s shoes. "Just like your lot probably had giant feet."

Before Liam could retort Craig scored the exchange, "Fifteen love" and waved the analyst on.

He woke up his smart-pad and turned it for them to see.

"OK. Davy said you wanted to know if the vehicles around the hotel were checked when the girl was taken. They were and they were all clear. Same thing with the French equivalent of an Amber Alert. All communications and media were alerted immediately and they checked cars, ports and airports for days afterwards. Bulletins were posted, searches were run and all known paedophiles were brought in, questioned and cleared."

He turned the pad back to face him and tapped again, and a map of the south of France beside a larger one displaying the whole of Europe appeared.

"There were checkpoints set up for miles around and the police checked for anyone travelling with a little girl, but got nothing."

Craig stopped him. "Did they look for anyone travelling with a boy?"

The computer expert shook his head. "No, unfortunately. I actually thought of that last night and checked. It seems obvious that they should have, kids of three mostly looking the same sex except for their hair and clothes, but they didn't." The screen darkened as he went on. "The problem is it would only have taken the abductor an hour to cross from Nice into Italy, so they could have been out of France and into another Schengen country before the blocks went up. From Italy..."

Craig nodded. "It's into Switzerland, Liechtenstein, Austria or by ferry to Malta or Greece."

Liam added glumly. "Then maybe into Turkey or the middle-east."

The words triggered something in the analyst and he tapped and scrolled for a moment until he found what he was looking for, enlarging the page and turning it towards the detectives again. It was an image of a blonde infant with lighter blue eyes than anyone Craig knew.

He asked the obvious question.

"Bella Westbury?"

"Yes. When she was only fourteen months. I found it

yesterday, in an EU-wide mothers' chat-room where Nicola Westbury apparently went to interact after they moved to France. I guess she missed speaking to other mums in English."

Craig sat forward for a closer look, a dozen thoughts vying for space in his head. After a short silence he voiced the first.

"Did other mothers share their baby photos on there as well?"

"Yep. There were dozens on there. But they had to register using their FaceChat accounts and it was password protected too. So pretty secure."

Liam gave a sceptical snort. "Get away with you! You're a flipping hacker, so you *know* how easy those groups are to infiltrate."

Ash didn't argue, but he did qualify his comment. "Infiltration's not the issue. Yes, people can get *into* chat-rooms and even download the photos, but not without leaving some sort of trace-" He stopped abruptly, seeing a smile slowly forming on Craig's face. "You want me to see if the chat-room *was* hacked, don't you?"

"I do. And to trace any hack back and get me a name."

The analyst's normally soft voice became a whine. "But this photo was posted five years ago..."

"Consider it a challenge. You like those."

Before Ash could confirm or deny it, one of Craig's other thoughts came to the fore.

"Not the middle-east, and probably not Turkey, Liam."

The D.C.I. was curious. "Why not?"

"Look at those eyes. She would have stuck out like a sore thumb in an Arab country."

"Don't some Arabs have blue eyes?"

"With olive skin, yes, but rarely with skin that pink. And rarely such a light blue either. The combination marks the girl out as a westerner. Maybe they *could* have fake-tanned her, and cut and dyed her hair, but even so, unless someone has invented tinted contact lenses for babies they couldn't have changed her eye colour. Or if they *did* try to use lenses, she might have rubbed them out. Anyway, tinted lenses always look fake."

Ash laughed. "Don't tell Mary that, she was looking at buying some green ones last week."

Craig rolled his eyes at his constable's seemingly constant need to change her already attractive appearance and went on.

"No. I'm convinced that *someone* would have noticed Bella Westbury in an Arab state."

"So what are you saying?"

Ash interjected. "I know, and I think you're right, chief. I've visited India with my folks, and I'm guessing the middle-east isn't much different; almost everyone has brown eyes of some shade. A child with those eyes *would* have been noticed, and why would a kidnapper have taken *any* risk of attracting attention? It's just asking for trouble. Europol and Interpol circulated photos of the girl across the whole world, including the middle-east, and there was media coverage on her for weeks."

Craig nodded. "Exactly. And those images will be on the Net for years, so if Bella Westbury's not dead then she *must* be somewhere that she doesn't stand out."

The analyst anticipated his next request and pulled up a map of the world, moving the cursor from country to country as he spoke. "Scandinavia, Germany, The Baltics-"

Craig chipped in. "UK, Ireland, Canada, the USA, Australia. Anywhere that blue eyes are common, although they might have aimed for countries outside the EU to be safe."

Liam's face fell. "Damn. You're basically saying we've no hope of finding out where she went."

Craig shook his head. "No, not at all."

He motioned Ash to revert to the map of Europe. "OK, look. There are only two real choices; either she remained in some European country where her eyes wouldn't have stood out, or she was taken *quickly* to somewhere else similar. With the EU media covering the abduction they won't have wanted to cross too many borders, not even the invisible EU Schengen type, so..." he gave a decisive nod as his thoughts suddenly crystallised "...I think she was transported out of Europe within days."

"Not stay in France, chief?"

"With the gendarmes on alert? No."

Liam warmed to the theme. "OK, so how? Plane?"

"Or boat, but plane's more likely. So... flying from the EU countries already mentioned to Canada, America and so on would -."

The D.C.I. interrupted again.

"But there'll have been millions of kids flying every year."

Craig turned back to his analyst. "Children of either sex between two and five, departing around the end of August twenty-fifteen. Can you do it, Ash?"

The younger man frowned. "I can check every country in the world if you give me a realistic deadline for when you want the answer."

It was a dig at Craig's tendency to want everything yesterday.

Liam was shaking his head.

"OK... But what's to say they didn't keep her somewhere till the heat had died down before they flew her out?"

"It could have taken months for the press coverage to wane, and we have to start somewhere, Liam. I think they'll have had her on a flight within hours."

Ash typed some notes on his screen, "OK, that narrows the search parameters a bit."

Meanwhile, Liam had begun tapping the desk thoughtfully.

"Flying with a man or a woman?"

Craig considered for a moment before answering, "Either or both, probably posing as her relatives; maybe even parents. At that age she'd have been accompanied, or if she wasn't then the airlines will have a *very* short list of kids that age travelling alone. They might also have had to put her on her supposed parent's passport to fly, so check the ages for that, Ash. They could vary from country to country."

The analyst typed some further points. "OK, I'll check all that. I'll look for any hair colour in case they dyed it, and coloured lenses would have been spotted by someone in passport checks. Even if the kidnapper spun some story about them being for medical reasons there should be a note of that somewhere."

Liam shook his head. "You *hope* they would have been spotted."

Craig ignored him, mainly because he couldn't afford any doubts that might knock him off path. "And remember, Ash, only eight to ten percent of the world has blue eyes of any shade so that might help."

Liam was surprised. "Eight? Really?"

"Yep. We only think blue eyes are common because they're common around here."

Craig linked his hands behind his neck for a moment, wondering how he could narrow things down even further.

"Distinguishing marks have to be noted on passports, don't they?"

"Yes. But what distinguishing marks would a baby that age have?"

"Birthmarks perhaps? We can ask Edgar Westbury if his daughter had any when we see him later."

Liam sounded a warning. "Without getting his hopes up that she's still alive, boss. You'll put the man through hell."

"Good point. Thanks. I-"

Ash pulled a face that made Craig break off to ask, "What's *that* look for?"

"Well... it's just, aren't we being a bit optimistic here, chief?"

Liam cut straight to the point, although it made him feel sick to say it. "You mean the girl's probably dead."

The analyst swallowed hard and nodded. "Yes. I'm sorry, but... yes. We could just be looking for a straightforward paedophile like Pierre Galvet."

Craig lurched forward. "You've found something more on him?"

"Nothing useful, sorry. He was definitely in the vicinity at the right time, but he had a job picking fruit from six every morning so he would have been at work when the girl was snatched."

"*Prove* to me that he was and I'll strike him off our list."

The Hindu warrior's eyebrows shot up. *"How do I do that?"*

"Dig into the detail. Contact the farmers Galvet worked for back then and get sight of their records. Odds on it'll be a family farm and they'll know all their regular pickers. See when Galvet clocked in and out on the day of the abduction and if anyone *actually* remembers seeing him there. Check the hours he got paid for that month from their tax records –they won't have paid him if he wasn't producing the goods, and with fruit picking the only way to do that is if you're physically there working the hours and have fruit to weigh at the end of the day."

Liam chipped in. "And see if he had the use of a car. It's hard to abduct someone using a bus or train. People tend to notice that sort of thing."

"Good thinking, Liam. Ash, if you need a hand with the French I can make some of the calls for you. Or Andy, he speaks it pretty well I think. "He motioned to his deputy. "Tell the style icon here why Bella Westbury is unlikely to be dead, Liam."

The D.C.I. screwed up his face. "OK. But brace yourself, Millennial, 'cos it's disgusting." He swallowed hard, trying to shut out the images filling his head. "So...whoever took the girl viewed her as a commodity not a person. Paedophiles mostly abuse children and discard them, either alive or dead, within hours of abduction, so either Bella or her body should have been found during the police searches-"

Ash interrupted. "But maybe they buried her somewhere quickly."

"Unless it was very deep there's too much risk of early discovery from wild animals, not to mention that the police use dogs in searches and they're pretty good at finding things. And derelict buildings are out too; they're some of the first places cops check. No, even if whoever took her had their own lockup or house they would've just abandoned her after the attack and legged it, and her body *would* have been found by someone by now."

The analyst wasn't giving up. "But what if they transported her to another country and *then* killed her?"

The deputy shook his head. "You're giving the scum credit for having impulse control, but that's not how they work. They see, they covet, they take, they abuse, and then they kill or abandon. It's an urge that they either can't or don't want to control, and even waiting till they'd driven a kid an hour across a border would be too long for most of them."

The D.C.I. took a deep breath, fighting hard not to vomit at the topic they were discussing. He took some small comfort in the fact that the others were looking just as bad.

"If they *aren't* being driven by impulse then they're being driven by profit, either financial or for the kudos they'll get from their filthy mates."

He stopped dead, his eyes pleading with his boss to pick things up. Craig stared down at his desk as he did.

"Liam's right. The kudos comes from taking and circulating pornographic images of the child to other paedophiles, to establish and maintain their position in that community, and for that to occur the child has to stay alive. Or, God forbid, they're an age preferential paedophile and they pass the child along when they age out of their preferred age group to someone who likes older children. But, *importantly,* in both of those cases the child would still be *alive.*"

The words, "but damaged" hung unspoken in the air, and nobody was even *touching* the pariah topic of snuff movies.

Liam signalled that he was ready to take over again. "The last and best option is that our kidnappers were motivated by money. I mean that the girl was stolen to order for someone who was looking for a kid."

Ash's eyes widened. "You mean to adopt them?"

"We *hope.* Abduction and illegal adoptions aren't as uncommon as you'd expect unfortunately, especially now that a lot of countries are clamping down on adoption tourism."

The analyst looked confused.

"That's foreigners flying into poorer countries and adopting their orphans to take back home. It was tolerated at one stage in some places because of the high incidence of orphans after wars and such like, but popstars taking selfies have-" He broke off suddenly and gawped at Craig. "That's another reason you were harping on about her eyes!"

"Yes."

Ash was staring blankly at them so Craig explained.

"Sadly a great deal of the wealth in the world is still held in western countries, where blue eyes and fair skin are also more common. A lot of people want to adopt a child who looks like them and wealthy westerners can afford to pay. It's a long shot but not out of the question that someone in the western world wanted a blonde, blue-eyed baby and Bella Westbury fitted the bill. Or the abductor might have just stolen her on spec, recognising that her colouring was likely to attract a good price and betting that they would find a buyer eventually."

He shook his head sadly, thinking of Nicola Westbury. "Bella was only left alone in her garden for one minute, so someone *must* have been watching and waiting, and someone who might have planned the kidnapping for money fits just as much as a paedophile, more so in my opinion because of what Liam said about impulse control. That's another reason I don't believe that Bella's dead; she was worth too much money."

Liam had been nodding in agreement but now he screwed up his face in doubt. "OK, I know I'm playing Devil's Advocate here, boss, but would a poacher *really* have taken the risk of stealing such a well loved child for cash? Knowing how hard her parents would hunt for her?"

"We'll find out won't we."

Just then Craig thought of something and turned back to his analyst. "Do you have aging software on your computer?"

"I can easily get some. You want me to age the girl up from this photo?"

"And any later images that you can get your hands on. Let's get a range of what she's most likely to have looked like between her abduction and now."

"What then? Should I circulate them to cops around the world?"

The detectives said "NO!" simultaneously and then Craig added a quieter, "No. Thank you. It could put her at risk. If whoever has her believes the heat's died down they might relax, but if they get wind of us getting close they might kill her just to stay out of jail, no matter whether they're raising her as their own child or not. Just produce the images and let me have them as soon as you can."

He rose to his feet. "Right, that's enough to get on with for now. Tell Davy I'll call him later."

With that Craig opened his office door and they exited. He paused as he passed his PA's desk.

"Alice, we're off to Monaghan now. You have the address. Inform the others that they can call me if they need to, please, and we'll be back in time to brief at six."

He glanced meaningfully at his deputy who was already heading for the lift and added, "Although the *exact* time depends on whether Liam drives like the usual maniac or not, in which case we *may* actually arrive back here before we've left."

It earned him a shout of, "JUST CAUSE YOU DRIVE LIKE A NUN" from the D.C.I., but Craig's intended snappy comeback of, "eighty isn't slow!" was drowned out by a much more cerebral, "time doesn't work like that" from the Doctor Who loving analyst who had just returned to his desk.

The exchange provoked nothing but a raised eyebrow from the secretary, who for her sanity's sake had learnt to tune out most of the team's banter in her months with them, now only ever listening to sentences that began with her name.

Liam's, "I take it that means I'm driving again" as they entered the lift was accompanied by a martyred look that wouldn't have fooled anyone, even if his tone *hadn't* been so gleeful at the thought of the mileage claim he would be putting in.

"I need to think" was Craig's only response, and think he did, not uttering another word until an hour later when they reached the invisible border between Ireland's six and twenty-six counties, and even then only to voice a hope that, "Brexit doesn't bugger this place up."

Liam took it as a sign that political discourse was now in order, and as every person in Ireland regardless from where they hail lives and breathes such debate, with even airport taxi drivers giving up-to-date briefings on the state of the country and indeed the world before their tourist passengers have even reached their hotels, the next twenty minutes was spent as the locals said, 'ripping the ass' out of politics and everyone involved. The result of the debate was that Liam arrived at their destination thoroughly satisfied that he'd solved the whole of humanity's problems, and Craig was left thinking that they should just press the off button, reboot the planet and start again.

But those were minor issues compared to someone dealing with the loss of their child, so the detectives parked the hypothetical for the real and prepared for a *genuinely* challenging discussion, in which for once Liam was happy to let his boss take the lead.

They were surprised, although there was no rational

reason why they should have been, when the front door of the neat detached house that was their destination was opened by a gangly, tow-haired boy. Their next surprise was when Edgar Westbury, obviously the child's father from their doppelganger-like resemblance, came bolting from a back room milliseconds later shouting, "GET AWAY FROM THEM! WHAT HAVE I TOLD YOU ABOUT STRANGERS?" before pushing his son behind him and glaring defensively at Craig.

The detective assessed the situation in seconds: his infant daughter abducted, his wife and parents dead, his solitary sibling a continent away and left with only his precious son to hold. Unless Edgar Westbury remarried and had more children they were looking at the only close family he would ever have, so it was no wonder that he was protective of the thirteen-year-old. Westbury was terrified of losing him as well.

Liam's assessment was less generous and comprised of: weirdo, jerk, and that's going to be one messed-up kid; but neither policeman's thoughts showed on their faces as they produced their IDs.

"Chief Superintendent Craig and Chief Inspector Cullen from Belfast. My PA should have called ahead."

"She didn't describe you."

To be fair that wouldn't have been normal secretarial behaviour, and anyway, what would Alice have said? One sandy-haired giant and one tall dark man, both of them wearing suits? It was the least insulting description that Craig could think of and a straw poll of the squad would no doubt have produced quite a few more that were worse.

Edgar Westbury relaxed his stance slightly but he didn't relax his defence of his son, instead turning to the boy with, "Go and play in your room, please, Simon. I need to speak to these officers."

"Can't I stay, Dad?"

A shake of the head was all that seemed necessary to quash the teenager's resistance, and his caving-in seemed to Liam almost like a Pavlovian response, which begged the question how often had he needed to be told before he'd been trained? With *his* kids he'd be yelling at them till they were twenty before they took the hint like that. The D.C.I. was torn between wishing they were as obedient as

Simon Westbury and thanking God that they weren't.

As the boy trudged reluctantly up the stairs, giving a quick smile at a wink from Craig, his father motioned the policemen into a bright sitting room and offered refreshments, which before Craig could refuse them Liam had accepted with an enthusiastic, "Great," adding the unnecessary detail that, "my stomach thinks my throat's been cut."

In the event it was a useful pause, as Westbury's absence from the room gave the detectives time to confer.

"That man's wound tighter than a clock, boss."

Craig nodded in agreement. "But you can understand it. He hasn't had a lot of luck, has he? The only family he has left is the boy and a brother who could be anywhere in the world."

Liam pulled a face. "Maybe. But he's storing up trouble with that kid. Tight leashes breed angry dogs."

Craig smiled. "One of your Granny's famous sayings no doubt."

Just at that moment their host reappeared, and as he passed around the refreshments Craig got to the reason they were there.

"Mister Westbury, as my secretary said, we're from the Belfast Murder Squad-"

The man's obvious horror cut him short.

"She didn't mention murder!"

Damn. He and Alice *really* needed to have a word. He'd noticed before how she hated saying the word, preferring euphemisms like 'grievous incident' and 'fatal assault'. But it really *did* need to be in the preamble when arranging meetings so that the other party was forewarned.

"I'm sorry, she really should have mentioned. We've come to ask you a few questions about a body that was found on Tuesday."

As Westbury's pale eyes expanded alarmingly Craig realised the significance of what he'd just said and hurriedly added, "A *man's* body."

He felt every bit of the father's pain and relief in his immediate noisy exhalation and wondered whether to apologise for his clumsiness, deciding against it because it would raise the subject of his missing daughter sooner than he'd planned.

Ignoring his deputy's chastising glance Craig forged on. "He was found in a disused quarry south-west of Rownton village, where I believe you were raised?" Without pausing for confirmation he added, staring directly into the widower's eyes, "We now have an ID and he was your brother-in-law, Stuart Kincaid."

The widower's eyes widened again, but only slightly this time, and Craig wondered whether his shock was less because Kincaid was an adult, or could it possibly mean there'd been bad blood between the men. The sadness that immediately followed and darkened Edgar Westbury's thin face said not; he was genuinely dismayed by his brother-in-law's death. But Craig knew he and his deputy could debate that later if necessary, certain that Liam was also registering every expression on their host's face.

The deliberate pause Craig left after his words gave Westbury space to speak, and he asked the same questions that had been raised in their discussions with John and Des the day before.

"But what was Stuart doing in Rownton? And at the old quarry? He lived halfway across the country in Portaferry!"

Liam responded first. "All good questions, Mister Westbury, and things we're looking into. To your knowledge had Mister Kincaid ever been to Rownton before?"

The widower shook his head, but when no elaborating words followed the D.C.I. offered some of his own, watching his face attentively as he did.

"Mister Kincaid was drowned."

The gasp that came from Edgar Westbury was too sharp to have been manufactured, as was his squeaked, "*Drowned?* But Stuart was a strong swimmer!"

Craig cut in. "We did say we were the Murder Squad."

"Yes, yes, but I didn't... believe... no, not believe...listen perhaps. *But drowned?* How does someone drown a grown man?"

He shook his blond head repeatedly as the facts sank in.

"Stuart gone. Oh God... oh God..." They watched as tears sprang to his eyes, "...his poor parents. Both their children dead." His quick glance towards the ceiling confirmed that they'd been right in their assessment of why he was so protective of his son. "I can't think of anything worse, at *any* age."

Craig could see him about to spiral and intervened before they lost him. He knew it was selfish but they'd had a long trip and they *really* needed some facts.

"Mister Kincaid's parents are still alive?"

It was a stupid question given that Kincaid had only been in his early forties. Why wouldn't they be alive? *His* parents still were, thankfully, although even as he thought it he knew that the loss of one of them could come only too soon.

The widower shook his head, but only to clear it. "Yes. They're still only in their sixties. They used to live in Ballycastle but they moved to Cavan last year to be closer to Simon. I take him to see them all the time. We're very close. They're his only grandparents now, and since my own parents died..."

As his words tailed off Craig had a sudden, horrified thought. Had Stuart Kincaid's parents been notified of their son's death? In his haste to find Edgar Westbury he hadn't even thought to ask.

To avoid their grandson innocently bouncing up to them with the news next time he saw them, he nodded Liam to go outside to check, continuing the interview in his absence.

"Luisa Kincaid ID-ed her husband's body yesterday, in case you'd like to contact her."

Westbury nodded absentmindedly. "Yes...of course... Luisa. Poor Luisa. The funeral...I should really go..."

Craig took a deep breath and prepared himself for the likely traumatic effect of his next words.

"Mister Westbury...in your brother-in-law's jacket pocket there was a photograph. We think it had been deliberately hidden because it was folded into the small coin pocket that people rarely use. Also, his wallet had been taken and in my experience that's either done because someone's looking for something specific, like perhaps a photograph-"

Westbury cut across him. "Not for Stuart's money and cards?"

"Possibly, but we think it's more likely the wallet was taken to slow down his identification. His watch was also missing so we can't rule theft out *completely* as a motive, but," he looked solemn, "we *really* don't believe that this was a mugging gone wrong, Mister-"

The widower interrupted again. "You said Stuart drowned."

"*Was* drowned. Someone held him under the water. They left bruises."

"Who found him?"

Craig suddenly realised what was happening. Westbury was trying to keep him on the subject of Stuart Kincaid's murder to avoid hearing something that might hurt him more, even if he wasn't sure yet exactly what that was.

Or... perhaps he feared that the photo Kincaid had been carrying had been of his dead wife, it would have been natural given that they were twins, and Westbury couldn't deal with the reopening of that particular wound.

But as sorry as the detective felt for the man they had to make progress, and he was just about to do that when Liam re-entered the room and put his mind to rest on Stuart Kincaid's parents with a nod. It gave Craig renewed energy, so he took a deep breath and passed on the information that Edgar Westbury had been trying desperately not to hear.

"Mister Westbury, the photograph that Mister Kincaid was carrying was of your daughter, Bella, and we've matched it to one that was taken not long before she disappeared. Do you know why Stuart might have been carrying it?"

Such a complete silence fell on the room that Craig held his breath rather than break it, but broken it was eventually, by a soft whimpering that grew into wracking sobs. The detectives watched powerlessly as Edgar Westbury's pale face grew red and wet and his body crumpled until it was almost doubled in two, and then as the door opened suddenly and the boy who'd been sent to his room like a child re-entered, wrapping his arms around his father with a confidence and compassion that said he'd done so many times before.

Craig rose and signalled his deputy to follow him, nodding to the teenager that they would be outside, and exiting just as he started making soothing noises that made tears gather in both detectives' eyes. They stood mutely outside in the street, until eventually Liam sighed and said what was on both their minds.

"It's brought back everything to him, boss. The girl's abduction, the searching and waiting, what his wife went through..."

Craig shook his head slowly, every shake feeling like a burden he couldn't set down. "How does someone get over so much loss?"

"Some people never do. That's why the mum killed herself."

It was Craig's turn to sigh. "I felt like a shit for making the man suffer again, Liam, but there was nothing else that I could do. I *had* to ask him about the photograph. It's our best lead to Kincaid's killer."

"Ach, now, don't beat yourself up. It'll-"

The D.C.I. stopped mid-sentence, seeing the house's blue front door re-open and a small hand beckon them inside. They returned to the sitting room to find a red-eyed Edgar Westbury clutching a handkerchief in his hand.

"I'm very sorry about that. Sometimes things just hit me."

Craig took a seat beside him on the sofa. "Don't apologise. I'm just sorry that I had to bring it up."

Westbury nodded. "You had to, I understand that. And I *want* to help you find Stuart's killer, if I can."

Liam glanced meaningfully at the boy, who was standing protectively behind his father now. In response Westbury reached out a hand to his son.

"I've told him that his Uncle Stuart has gone, and it's hard on him, but I think it's time that I realised Simon is nearly grown. He can stay with us now. He's a very brave boy."

Craig nodded and withdrew an envelope from his pocket. "This is a copy of the photograph Mister Kincaid was carrying. Are you OK to look at it?"

When Westbury nodded he passed the picture across, watching carefully as the father gazed at the image of his lost daughter for a moment before slowly nodding his head.

"This is the one I gave the French police to use when Bella disappeared. We have the original framed upstairs. It was taken on a trip to Paris around her third birthday a few months before..."

Craig employed his softest tone. "So you don't have any later photographs of her."

The widower shook his head and then said firmly, "Not yet."

The detective didn't say anything to dash his hopes.

"Why would Mister Kincaid have been carrying it, do you know?"

Westbury and his son replied together, in a jumble of, "Copies", "Searchers" and, "He loved Bella."

"So you're saying that Stuart Kincaid was a loving uncle and copies of this photograph were given out during the initial search."

"Yes. Stuart and his wife Luisa didn't have a daughter so they doted on ours, and as soon as Bella-"

He paused and took a deep breath before restarting.

"As soon as Bella disappeared they flew out to France to help us with the search. Perhaps Stuart just put her photo in his coin pocket and forgot about it?"

"Was Mister Kincaid likely to have kept a suit for years?"

Simon shook his head vigorously. "No way. Uncle Stuart was a cool dresser. He was always getting new stuff and giving the old away."

Westbury confirmed his son's words with a nod.

"Stuart must have moved the photo between suits. But I'm not surprised. He was very fond of both our children. We have snaps of his boys as well."

It was the opening that Craig had needed. "So fond that he might *still* have been searching for Bella?"

Westbury looked confused. "Well...Stuart was certainly a *determined* man, but if he *was* searching for Bella why would he have done so in Ireland? And in Rownton of all places? Why not in France where we'd lived at the time?"

It explained why Edgar Westbury hadn't been with his brother-in-law in Rownton.

Liam gave a noisy sigh. "That's one of the things we're trying to find out."

When Craig slipped the snapshot back into his pocket looking as if he was preparing to leave, his deputy coughed meaningfully, reminding him that they had more to ask.

The prompt did the trick.

"Just a few final things, Mister Westbury. We've seen

photographs of Bella at fourteen-months that show her as a very blonde child with striking blue eyes, but this later image of her is slightly more distant and darker, so it's difficult to tell if her colouring had altered at all."

The widower shook his head. "It hadn't. That one was just taken in a bad light. Bella is white-blonde with almost ice-blue eyes like her mother. Nicola kept that colouring all her life so I doubt that Bella is going to darken as she grows."

Craig smiled admiringly at his constant use of the present tense.

"Thank you. Also, did Bella have any distinguishing marks at all? Moles? Birthmarks? Had her ears been pierced? Or-"

His heart sank as Westbury shook his head before he'd even finished.

"Nothing. She's perfect."

But Liam had noticed the boy shaking his head behind his father's back.

"You don't agree, Simon?"

Westbury turned sharply towards his son, the vehemence of his words allowing no room for dispute.

"Bella's perfect, Simon! You know that."

The teenager stuck to his guns. "I love Bella, but no, Dad, she isn't perfect the way *you* mean. She has a mark on her hand. Don't you remember? When we took the trip to Italy and Mum had her hands Hennaed at that market?" He turned back to the detectives. "Mum just did it as a novelty, but Bella cried so much because she wanted a pattern on her hands too that Mum gave in. So the lady Hennaed a little daisy on the back on her hand."

Craig wasn't an expert on fashion fads but he had a sister who was. In her teens Lucia had tried every new trend that had emerged, Henna being one of them, so he thought he knew enough to comment this time.

"But Henna fades, Simon."

The teenager nodded excitedly.

"Yes, Mum's did, but Bella's hand got all red and nasty with the dye and it left the daisy behind."

Edgar Westbury's jaw dropped.

"Oh my God, Simon, you're right! I remember now! We took Bella to a doctor about it and he said there was nothing that he could do; she would have a raised scar there for the rest of her life. It was very red at first but he said it would turn white eventually so we didn't worry too much about it. It faded pretty quickly and left a little flower, and as Bella liked it we didn't fret. But it's there, it's *definitely* there. It's a distinguishing mark."

Craig sat forward eagerly. "Would you by any chance have a photograph of it?"

"Yes, yes, I took several to monitor its healing."

He nodded his son to a drawer. "Bring the last one that I took, Simon."

The boy returned with the image of a chubby left hand with a perfect white outline of a daisy on its back.

Craig took it gratefully. "This is good, thank you. We'll copy it and send the original back. Also, could I have the original of the photograph we found on Mister Kincaid to do the same? The colours have faded in ours."

As Liam went with the boy to retrieve it Craig carried on with his questioning.

"Did the French police include the daisy in their search parameters?"

"Oh. No. We forgot to mention it. Bella had only got it a few months before. We went to Italy in April, just after we got back from my parents' funeral. To cheer us up." Westbury's eyes widened in panic. "Oh my God, we should have said to the gendarmes, shouldn't we?"

Craig shook his head reassuringly. "It's unlikely that it would have made a difference then."

It wasn't a platitude; he was telling the truth. When you're looking for a needle in a haystack, a tiny nick on that needle only becomes important if you find one. He'd read the search outcomes the night before and the gendarmes hadn't found leads on *any* girls that had fitted Bella's description at all.

But the daisy *might* help them now if the girl was still alive.

"I have another question, Mister Westbury. You must have flown to or from France with Bella at times, so how was she was described on your passport?"

"White-blonde hair and ice-blue eyes."

The specificity might help Ash's searches.

"But we didn't fly after she got the scar, so we hadn't got

round to adding the daisy under distinguishing marks."

Which didn't mean that someone hadn't noticed it when she was being taken across a border, or that they wouldn't notice it now if it was made public knowledge.

But for Bella's safety that time couldn't be just yet.

As Craig was asking his next question Simon re-entered the room, followed by Liam holding a framed photograph in his hand.

"Your parents' funeral, Mister Westbury... Stuart Kincaid definitely wasn't there?"

"Goodness me, no. Stuart was only linked to my family through Nicola, so we never thought to ask him."

"That's fine. My final questions concern your brother Blaine. Where is he? Do you know?"

He was rewarded by a frown that said there was absolutely no love lost between the siblings.

"In America somewhere, last I heard. Somewhere on the east coast. I'll be honest with you, Superintendent, Blaine and I never got on. We hadn't been in touch much in the ten years before my parents died and there's been no contact at all between us since the funeral. There was a disagreement over the Will."

"What sort of disagreement?"

Westbury gave a disillusioned shrug. "Blaine isn't the most responsible character and he has a bad gambling habit, so my parents only left him a small lump sum and left the guesthouse to me to run. It was worth a *lot* more than the cash he got, so Blaine was pretty unhappy and he was *very* vocal about it."

"May I ask what you did with the guest house?"

"I put a manager in to run it for a few months, but then Nicola was so upset and... well, my heart wasn't in it anymore so I sold it to a developer. I tried to contact Blaine to give him his share of the proceeds but he'd disappeared off the map. I don't know his address, and I'm sorry but I don't really care. It wasn't just the gambling, he was a bad lot generally."

"Bad lot how?"

This time the boy *was* too young.

"Cover your ears, Simon."

Liam had a better idea. "How'd you like to play with a police siren, son?"

It always worked with *his* kids.

The boy was out of the room before he was and the siren started blaring seconds later.

Craig repeated his question.

"Bad lot how, Mister Westbury?"

The widower sighed. "You name it and Blaine was into it. Drugs, women, gambling, and God knows what else. He hated growing up in a village, he called it Hicksville, so as soon as he could he moved to Belfast. After that Blaine never met a vice that he didn't like and he would do pretty much anything to fund them."

His face darkened angrily.

"Dad was constantly placating the police about him and paying his bloody fines, so to be honest I'm glad he's not around anymore. I'd feel obliged to see him because we're such a small family, and I really don't want Simon exposed to an influence like that."

The detective nodded, trying to shut out the siren which Liam had just cranked up to maximum, and fighting the temptation to go out and shove it up his deputy's ass.

"I understand, Mister Westbury, but we *still* need to speak to him, so if you have a photograph and whatever the last contact details you had for him were, that would be great."

Five minutes and several rounds of white noise later Craig had what he needed.

"Who are your family solicitors? Perhaps your brother has kept *them* up to date if he's moved."

"I doubt it or he'd have jumped on his share of the guest house, and I know for a fact that the money's still sitting in the bank. But I'll happily give you the solicitor's details. We stuck with the one my parents used, a guy called Hector McDonagh in Rownton. He runs the local newspaper as well, so if there's *any* word of Blaine he'll have heard it. You can't miss his offices; they're right next door to the local police station."

It was enough for now. From initially being unsure about him Craig had warmed to Edgar Westbury, so when they entered the street to retrieve his son, now flushed with excitement from his time playing cop, he shook the man's hand.

"Mister Kincaid's parents have been informed of his

death, so it's safe to get in touch with them and his wife about the funeral. But please keep everything that we've discussed today to yourself. If we have any relevant updates we'll contact the Kincaids directly."

'And we'll do the same with you if we find that your daughter is still alive', remained only as a thought in his head.

****

High Street Station, Belfast. 10 a.m.

Andy Angel hated this part of his job almost as much as he hated doing death notifications, and sometimes even more; questioning people when they'd lost a loved one, especially if those questions might taint their memory, was brutal. But he knew that it was necessary and sometimes revealed more than expected, so he had to do it, and if you *have* to do something unpleasant it's better done in the same way you rip a plaster off a hairy arm, quickly, with force, and braced for a scream.

So it was that he had Luisa Kincaid seated opposite him in an interview room, instead of on a soft couch in a relatives' room like the day before. The D.C.I. knew his limitations as well as he knew his abilities, and while he could muster the fast part when he made the effort he'd *never* been able to do the verbal force part of the job, so the cold-walled, neon-stripped ambience of the room would have to act as a proxy for that. As, hopefully, would the brusque constable seated at his side.

While Craig had briefed his D.C.I.s on the Kincaid/Westbury family tree so that he now knew Bella Westbury was Luisa Kincaid's niece by marriage, Andy had decided *not* to update Mary, preferring to see what her ignorant questioning on the subject might expose. Stuart Kincaid being Bella's uncle didn't automatically mean that his carrying of her photograph was innocent; if that were the case no family members would ever be involved in abuse. And there was also the thorny question of how Kincaid had been dead for months and no-one had reported him missing. Not the norm for someone with a family.

Unfortunately the woman in front of him still seemed so dazed from hearing about her husband's death that she looked like she wouldn't have noticed if she'd been a Christian in the Coliseum and he'd been an approaching lion, so after a moment Andy sighed and was just preparing himself to do it the hard way when Mary, who'd had quite enough of what she saw as his underestimation of the widow's strength, masquerading as so-called gallantry, slapped a palm hard on the table and glared at the woman opposite, barking unambiguously, "Why was your husband carrying around a photo of a young kid?"

Andy almost choked at her tone, and only her omission of the word "pervy" stopped him from taking the D.C. outside and reading the riot act. He was just wondering how to rephrase the question less pejoratively when Luisa Kincaid seemed to rouse from her sleep.

"Kid? Whose kid?"

It was Andy's cue to slide their original photo of Bella Westbury across the table, watching her face closely as he did.

It widened into a smile and she whispered, "Bella." A concerned frown followed immediately, "Poor Bella. Why has no-one ever found the dear wee thing?"

Mary spoke again, less aggressively. "You know this little girl?"

Luisa Kincaid's tone took on a 'don't be an idiot' edge.

"Of course I know her! She's my niece by marriage, Bella Westbury. She was the daughter of Edgar and Nicola, Stuart's sister." She shook her head sadly. "She disappeared in France in two-thousand-and-fifteen. Such a terrible thing to happen. It was the death of Nicola."

Andy saw tears threatening so he steered her from emotion back to fact.

"Can you tell us why your husband might have been carrying his niece's photograph?"

He felt embarrassed as he asked the question and if it hadn't been that they'd absolutely *had* to rule out Stuart Kincaid as being a paedophile, he would have been disgusted at their warped minds.

Luisa Kincaid gazed at the image for a moment longer before replying.

"It's simple. Stuart adored Nicola so he adored her kids

as well. He and Nicola were twins you know and they'd been as close as peas in a pod all their lives."

The D.C.I. smiled encouragingly, trying to keep her on point.

"So when Nicola killed herself...well, I know you can't see Nicola well in that photo but she's there in the background, anyway she and Bella were inseparable, so perhaps Stuart just kept it as a memento of them both?"

Mary wasn't buying it and she said so. "There must have been lots of better images of them together."

When she was answered by a shrug Andy jumped in again.

"You're sure it couldn't have been something more than that? Could your husband have been searching for Bella perhaps?"

The new widow's eyes widened incredulously. *"You think he was?"*

"Is it possible?"

After a short pause she nodded hesitantly. "Yes...yes, *definitely* when Bella first disappeared. We *both* joined the search in France. But after that...well, to be honest I half expected Stuart and Edgar to disappear *together* for months to hunt for Bella, but the gendarmes insisted that it was their job and told them not to interfere in case they messed things up."

Andy's eyes widened in shock. "They actually *said* that? It couldn't have been the language barrier?"

It wasn't that he couldn't understand the gendarmes' reasons for the instruction; family becoming too closely involved in an investigation carried pitfalls. They could inadvertently taint evidence or slow the case down, but worse than that, if something they did impacted negatively on the search and the child wasn't found, even if it *wasn't* as a direct consequence, relatives were likely to blame themselves for the rest of their lives.

But 'messing things up' wouldn't have been language that he or anyone he knew would ever have used.

Luisa Kincaid confirmed with a brisk nod that the officers they'd met had.

"That's exactly what one of the detectives said to Stuart. My French is very good. Anyway, so we all stayed together as a family. Nicola needed everyone around her; she couldn't even speak she was so distraught about Bella. But in the end nothing helped her...not company, not doctors or medication. To be honest I think her suicide had just been a matter of time from the day that Bella disappeared."

She opened her handbag and took out a paper handkerchief, stemming the tears that had started to fall. After giving her a moment to compose herself, Andy prompted her to continue by mentioning her husband's name again.

"Yes, Stuart, poor dear man... after Nicola died he became distant from all of us. He was here in body and he went to work every day as usual, but a light had gone out." She stared directly at Andy, "You understand what I mean?"

He understood all too well because unfortunately he'd seen it many times in a parent, lover, child or sibling, even sometimes a friend who couldn't come to terms with how someone close to them had died. Unexpected death in any form could prompt it, but the deliberate brutality of murder and the desperate sadness of suicide seemed to cause the worst effect.

Luisa Kincaid continued, reading the 'Yes' in his eyes.

"Stuart got so depressed that when he disappeared last March I just assumed he'd gone off somewhere to mourn alone. He left a note saying that he needed some space and not to worry, and at first he got in touch every week," her eyes dropped to the table, "but then gradually the frequency of his contacts dropped-"

Mary cut in. "When was the last time you heard from him?"

The widow nodded. "I can remember exactly. His calls dropped to once a fortnight for a while, always on a Monday, but then in July they became irregular, probably because the boys always got so upset that he wouldn't come home. He just kept saying that he needed more time..."

She opened her bag again and withdrew a thick diary, flicking back through the pages until she stopped at the twenty-ninth of October the year before. Ignoring Mary's immediate eager reach she gazed at Andy with pleading in her eyes.

"You must understand. We'd had months of Stuart's

calls being erratic and we'd got to the point where if he didn't call we just got on with our lives. I *had* to for the boys' sake. From July onwards, he'd only called once, to speak to me not the boys, so when I didn't hear from him after this call on the twenty-ninth, well..."

"What about at Christmas? Didn't you get worried when he missed calling then?"

She shook her head, tears streaming down her cheeks now. "I just assumed he didn't want to upset the boys by getting their hopes up again. I don't know why but it never even occurred to me that he'd come to any harm. I was *sure* he would just come home when he was ready. Stuart knew how to take care of himself. He wasn't a big man but he was very fit; he'd been a marathon runner for years and boxed..."

Andy nodded sympathetically, picturing the routine that she'd had to grow into after her husband had left. Forced to cope without him and deal alone with her sons' pain at missing him, a pain increased by sporadic calls that had raised their hopes that Dad would be home soon, only to have them cruelly dashed again. It must have been hell, or limbo at any rate, and when Stuart Kincaid's calls had become less frequent it might actually have been a relief in some ways; a respite from the emotional rollercoaster that she'd watched her children suffer. So when he didn't call for three months, well...

But it raised a practical question, and Andy decided to ask it gently before Mary took a more brutally logical approach.

"Can I ask...who ran the business in your husband's absence? Or did you close it?"

Luisa Kincaid shook her head. "No, we couldn't afford to close it. I've only ever worked part-time because of the boys so it's always been our main income. Stuart had a very good operational director so he's kept things going."

The D.C.I. nodded and rested back in his chair, satisfied that there was nothing sinister in the fact that Stuart Kincaid hadn't been reported missing.

"So you think your husband *could* have been searching for Bella while he was away?"

"Well, it didn't occur to me *then* that he might have gone looking for her; it seemed too long after her disappearance. But now..."

Her expression said that it *might* make sense, but after a moment's thought Luisa Kincaid confounded both detectives by shaking her head.

"No, because Stuart would have gone to France then, wouldn't he? Why would he have been in Rownton? Bella wouldn't have been there, would she? But-"

After a moment of her asking herself questions that were leading nowhere Andy knew that he needed to ask a difficult one of his own, certain that it was only a matter of time before Mary's absent "pervy" *did* hit the air.

He swallowed hard and when he opened his mouth he was surprised to hear his voice emerge as a croak.

"Mrs Kincaid... I... I hate..." He stopped abruptly, hoping that she would take the hint and save him from more agony, but her face was a complete blank so he croaked again. "Mrs Kincaid... is there any...*was* there *ever* any suspicion that..."

When the widow started to gawp at him, his heart leapt. She'd taken the hint! He was saved. All that he would have to cope with now was her anger and indignation, or so he thought, which is why Luisa Kincaid's sudden laugh threw him completely.

"You're asking me if my husband was a paedophile? *Stuart?* Oh my God, just when I thought I would never laugh again."

She rolled her eyes at both cops.

"I suppose you have to ask, but honestly, don't be so ridiculous! Stuart loved kids, but not in the way *you* mean. He loved Bella because he adored Nicola and Bella was her child. He felt Nicola's pain when Bella disappeared like it was his own, so if he was carrying her photograph around then it was part of that. Maybe he *was* still searching for her for Nicola's sake, but a paedophile? *Stuart?* Never."

As Andy's mouth opened again she raised a hand to stop him.

"And before you say, couldn't I be in denial? Couldn't I just be some deluded little wife who never really knew her husband, the answer is definitely no. Stuart had his faults: workaholic, too fond of a drink at times and he *always* drove too fast. But not that. *Never ever that.* You can check his computers, office, whatever you like."

They would.

Suddenly her forehead creased and she looked confused. "But what the heck *was* he doing in Rownton? And in a quarry of all places?" She looked at them both pleadingly. "You *will* find out, won't you?"

It was Andy's cue to take control again and as he rose to his feet he reached out a hand to clasp hers.

"Our team has the highest detection rate in Northern Ireland." He was tempted to add the rest of the UK and Ireland as well, but he needed to check the latest stats. "And D.C.S. Craig won't rest until we've found answers for you."

The pain on her face said that it would provide limited comfort, and as the D.C.I. ushered his junior from the room to give Luisa Kincaid some privacy, he thought once again that the living victims of murder were the hardest part of their job.

****

Ten Miles Outside Rownton

It always took Arthur Norris a long time to get anywhere, partly because he couldn't drive as fast as he'd once been able to, and partly because he often got lost. The first was due to age slowing his thought processes and reactions, and the second to the appalling sense of direction he'd had since youth that meant as soon as he left a motorway and had to make decisions whether to turn left or right, he invariably viewed the map at the wrong angle and ended up returning the way that he'd come.

But even without those impediments, whether the pensioner had covered the eighty miles from Belfast to Rownton Village in one hour or the three that it had actually taken him, it wouldn't have helped him in his mission to ensure that Rio Reynolds made it to her radio interview, because the young woman had been in police custody since the night before. Well, actually an interview that had morphed *into* custody when she'd failed to comply with Aidan's polite requests the evening before not to attend the radio slot and had taken a swing at Ryan and connected with his eye, giving the sergeant a shiner that would make him the centre of attention and jokes for at least a week to come.

So it was that while Hector McDonagh was bemoaning the replacement of his rather inelegant but to the point 'SUICIDAL BUILDER'S MISTRESS ON THEIR NIGHTS OF SIN' headline with a eulogy to the giant turnip that had won the summer before's village fete, said so-called builder's mistress was stewing noisily in a cell in the cop shop next door, and Derek Morrow's wife and family were still mourning him as the faithful man that he had actually been.

When a battered looking Ryan and his boss returned to the station that morning after a late breakfast, they were greeted by a smirk from an obviously amused W.P.C. and a scowl from her far less amused boss. As Mickey O'Hare stepped out from behind his custody desk to greet them, the niceties of, "Good Morning" and, "Good Day" were abandoned in favour of, "When the hell can I let that banshee go?"

Aidan countered with another question. "Have Derek Morrow's wife and family been in yet?"

"Yes. They came to collect the letters he left and now they've gone to the morgue at Omagh to view the body. It took the undertaker a fair bit of time to tidy him up after his PM, what with the hole in his head and all."

Ryan grimaced at the image, empathising with the pain that Morrow must have felt from the shot. The ache in his own head from being punched was bad enough.

Aidan was still on the practicalities of ensuring that the Morrows and Rio Reynolds never met.

"Are you expecting them back here?"

"Nope. Morrow's home was ten miles north in Cooneen so I expect they'll bury him from there."

The D.C.I. rubbed his hands together cheerfully.

"Right then. There's no risk of them bumping into Ms Reynolds and we've nipped her print and radio antics in the bud. We had to get an injunction for the second for the duration of our case, but by the time it's finished she'll be old news and no-one will be interested in her lies." He gestured towards the cells. "If you get her into the interview room we can question her now and let her go."

O'Hare gave a sigh of relief. "Thanks be to God for that!

I've three aspirin in me already this morning because of the noise she's been making." He turned on his heel eagerly, grabbing a set of keys from behind the desk as he passed. "Come on then if you're coming. She doesn't want a brief, and anyway Hector's the only one local and I don't think he'd oblige."

"He's a solicitor too?"

"It's the country. We all turn our hands to a lot of things."

A minute later a screeching Rio Reynolds, who was exposing more flesh than seemed decent at any hour of the day, was seated in the station's small interview room, only pausing her Human Rights' rant long enough to demand a cup of tea.

Ryan gazed pleadingly at O'Hare as he rushed to escape. "And two for us, please."

Muttering expletives, the custody sergeant slammed the door hard behind him, and the detectives turned their eyes to the young woman opposite, considering her as intently as she was now considering them.

Rio, so named because her mother had developed a retro obsession with the eighties' Duran Duran song of the same name while carrying her rather than that she'd spent her pregnancy gazing into the nearest river, spoke first and with a taunt that sounded even nastier than its content, courtesy of her Belfast twang.

"Nice shiner, copper."

Ryan gave a grunt.

"I'm nat sorry I gave it you, pig. You shudn't have stopped me gettin' tee my radio show. Nye I'll have to dee it tomorrow an' I wuz supposed tee work."

Aidan rested back in his seat and crossed his arms. "You won't be giving a radio interview about Mister Morrow. Not tomorrow or any other day."

It sparked a glare of indignation and some crossed arms of her own, which considering the cut of her top created a rather unfortunate look.

"You can't stap me!"

"Oh yes we can. We've got an injunction to prevent it, and if you try to publicise your story in some other way we'll arrest you again, this time on a charge of slander."

Her kohl-lined eyes widened. "*Slander!* What's that?"

Aidan decided to keep it simple. "Saying something that you shouldn't."

The response was predictable. "I can say anythin' I like!"

Ryan volunteered more detail. "Actually you can't, Ms Reynolds, not if it's false and damages Mister Morrow's reputation, which it will."

Her face tightened to match her arms. "It's nat false, it's true!"

Aidan motioned her on. "Prove it then. We've seen the interview you gave the editor of the Recorder, and in it you stated that you and Derek Morrow had been lovers for months. If that's the case then you should have texts, cards or presents from Mister Morrow. And there should be people who can confirm seeing the two of you together; restaurant staff and the like. Give us some of *that* if you want us to believe you."

Her fists bashed the table as she spat back at him.

"We stayed indoors! We didn't want tee go out,' cos we wuz gettin' busy. If you know what I mean, like."

She shot the D.C.I. what was obviously meant to be a seductive look but ended up as a cartoon version of the same.

"My honey didn't want us bein' seen together, in case someone told his old bag af a wife."

Honey indeed.

The words made Ryan snort derisively. "I've seen a photo of Derek Morrow and he was sixty, overweight and balding, so I think if he'd been dating a twenty-five-year-old he would have boasted about it to someone, don't you? Who might that have been, Ms Reynolds?"

This time they were treated to a shrug.

"You're telling us that you don't know the name of *any* of his friends?"

"I didn't say that!" After a moment chewing her lower lip her fake-lashed eyes widened triumphantly. *"Jimmy!* Yeh, Jimmy that he works with. He's Derek's mate."

She'd been briefed well.

They would be interviewing Jimmy Rushton, Morrow's deputy, later, so the story could be easily checked.

"Good. We'll ask Mister Rushton when we're interviewing him."

The girl paled slightly beneath her layers of fake tan.

"Yeh, well, he'll probably lie. Jealous af my honey an' me, he wuz. Like all af them."

Aidan stepped in again. "Any other witnesses you'd like to offer?"

She gave a sharp nod that made her earrings bounce off her cheeks.

"Yeh, yeh, there's Arthur. Arthur No-"

The girl halted abruptly, with a look of alarm that made her eyes saucer and her lips form an 'o'. The shape changed quickly as she tried to cover up with a laugh.

"No, nat Arthur, he's no-one. He's... he's just my dad's best mate."

Another change of heart, likely prompted by the thought of them checking *that* detail as well, brought, "No, he's nat, he's... I mean how wud *he* know anythin' anyway? Arthur knows nathin'. Nathin'."

The two men watched the mythical mistress dig a hole with her red-tinted mouth for a moment and then Aidan decided to end the charade. He leaned forward on the table, making an exaggerated tutting noise.

"If you're going to tell lies you really should keep them straight, Ms Reynolds." Lecture over, his tone hardened. "Now, Jimmy Rushton won't even have *heard* of you when we ask him, will he?"

The eighties band tribute was obviously tiring of the game because all they got from her was a grunt.

"Well, we'll soon find that out. And this Arthur, what's his surname? It obviously starts with 'no', so he shouldn't be difficult for us to locate."

It sparked another brief burst of energy from the young woman, "Arthur's gat..." Almost immediately the lie faded into a shrug. "Ach, I'm fed up with this. I've gat tee get home."

Ryan was both curious and seeking validation for his injury so he asked her what she did. If she worked as a professional cage fighter then being given a black eye by her wouldn't be quite so embarrassing.

The question elicited the first genuine spark of excitement that they'd seen in Rio Reynolds since they'd encountered her the night before.

"I'm a make-up artist. Trainin' in stage an' film. It's

brilliant-"

Aidan cut in again. "It sounds it. Arthur what?"

She glanced up at the wall clock and gave a sigh. "I've missed my class nye."

"You'll miss tomorrow's as well unless you give me his name. Arthur what?"

It brought a practiced tut. "Oh, all right then! Arthur Norris."

"And he is?"

"The old guy who came up tee me at work yesterday."

"Where's work? By your accent you're obviously not from around here."

"McGran's in Belfast." It was one of the last great department stores in the north. "I dee demos on the make-up counter."

The D.C.I. immediately smelled a set-up.

"What did this Norris want from you?"

The girl dropped her eyes to the table, rubbing at an imaginary spot with her finger as she muttered her reply.

"Pay me."

Ryan was incredulous. *"You want us to pay you?"*

He got a rude snort in reply. "Nat you, dummy."

Aidan got things back on track. "Arthur Norris offered to pay you for what?"

"Two interviews." Her kohled gaze shot up to his face again. "He said he'd give me a thousand quid if I did an interview with the local paper an' one on the radio. That'll pay my stage make-up course fees fer a year!"

Aidan sighed noisily. A measly grand for breaking a widow's heart.

"Did you get it up front?"

The girl groaned. "Only half. I'm stupid. Nye I'll never get the rest."

Aidan was tempted to seize the money, but then he considered the girl's age and what the training course might mean for her future and decided on the threat of doing it instead.

"OK, Ms Reynolds, here's my one time offer. Accept it now or not at all. Either you give us *full* details of everything you have on Arthur Norris and exactly what he asked you to do, or we take back the first five hundred as the proceeds of crime."

Her jaw dropped. "You can't do that!"

"I can, or I can tie it up in evidence so long it'll be worth about two quid by the time you get it back. Take it or leave it."

They could see the calculator whirring behind the beautician's eyes, and then the realisation that it was time to cut her losses prompted a grudging nod.

"OK. So tell us what you know about Mister Norris."

She complied with a sneer that would have done a reality show contestant proud.

"He was an old git."

"How old?"

"My granddad's age. Around sixty or seventy."

The D.C.I. gulped: sixty wasn't that far away for some of the squad and he wondered if *they'd* be viewed as old gits too when they were there.

"Describe him, please."

The young woman puffed out her cheeks for so long thinking that Ryan had time to take a drink of tea as he waited, while Aidan watched the process fascinated, half-expecting her to turn blue.

Eventually, "A good head taller than me, grey hair, a beard like Ed Sheeran, an' he had a hat."

"What sort?"

"A cap, like in Peaky Blinders."

What *would* they do without popular culture to aid communication with the young?

"What sort of accent?"

"Belfast, but posh Belfast, nat like me. An' he talked funny. Slow like."

Considering she rattled along at a clip, Aidan reckoned that meant Norris probably just spoke like a normal human being.

"OK, so he approached you when?"

"Abyte five yesterday. I wuz on till six."

He nodded Ryan to make a note of the time. Most department stores had CCTV, so they might be in luck and be able to view the interaction.

"Tell us exactly what he said."

"I can't remember zactly, but it wuz something like, Derek Morrow is a builder an' you're tee say you two had an affair. He showed me a picture af Morrow as well." She gave a look of disgust and added *"As if."*

"And then?"

"Then he gave me money tee train it down here an' stay overnight in some place called Omagh, 'cept thanks tee you I ended up sleeping in a bloody cell instead!"

"Mea culpa."

"What?"

"Just go on."

He really didn't have the energy to explain Latin to her right now.

"The old man said the newspaper an' radio wud be in touch an' then he bunged me five hundred cash." A whine entered her voice. "He said I'd get the rest after the radio today."

"How?"

"Took my bank details an' said he'd put it in." Her face crumpled. "'Cept nye he won't, will he."

The D.C.I. steamrolled over her grief.

"So you never actually *met* Derek Morrow? And if we ask Jimmy Rushton he'll never have heard of you?"

She gave a grudging "No" to both that made Aidan sign off the tape and stand up.

"Stay here."

He nodded Ryan to follow him out, waiting until the door had closed behind them before issuing instructions.

"Call Davy and ask him to pull the store CCTV and run a check on this Norris, and tell him I'll get the girl's bank details so we can see if a payment comes in and trace it back. Then nip next door and ask Hector McDonagh who first contacted him about the interview, and if it was Norris did they just speak or meet up? And get any contacts for Norris that McDonagh has. I'll stay here, tidy this up, and set up the meetings with Rushton and the pub landlord."

Just then his mobile rang and Craig's name came up. Aidan nodded the sergeant to get on with things while he took the call.

"Yes, Guv. What can I do for you?"

"A few things. First, how are you getting on with the interviews?"

"Just two more to do, Morrow's deputy and the pub landlord, then we'll nip down to Mahon on our way back."

He suddenly realised that he'd forgotten the church *and*

Biddy Evans and made a mental note to drop in on both after they'd been to the pub.

"Good. John's just called me about Morrow's PM and his cause of death was exactly as it looked; gunshot to the head. Anything interesting in your interviews so far?"

Aidan leaned back against the corridor wall and reached into his pocket for a cigarette to play with, suddenly remembering, mournfully, that there wouldn't be one because he'd given up.

"The girl claiming to be Morrow's mistress has admitted that it was a pack of lies. She was paid to say everything by some bloke. No idea who he is yet but we're getting Davy to pull some CCTV and do a check."

"Excellent. How much did he offer her?"

"A grand, but she only got half. She's just a kid so I was going to let her off with a warning."

"Fine. And the money?"

"She needs it, Guv, so..."

"Agreed. Let her keep it, but scare her enough to deter her from doing anything like this again. We don't want her getting ideas about becoming a professional fake mistress. Right, I need you to go and see the local solicitor for me when you're done with your interviews."

"Hector McDonagh. He's the local newspaper editor and chicken farmer as well."

"Very enterprising. OK, good, then you already know McDonagh. I want you to ask him about the sale of the Westburys' guest house, especially the financial distribution, and also, see if he has any recent contact details for Blaine Westbury. Ash should be able to send you a photo of him to show around, just in case someone has seen him around the village lately."

Aidan frowned, slightly confused about the relevance of the requests, but he decided not to ask. It would all come out in the wash, aka the next briefing.

"Will do."

"Good. I can't remember if I said this before but we'll be briefing at six, so just park your prisoner from Mahon at High Street when you get back. Call Jack so he knows to expect him."

Jack Harris was the custody sergeant at High Street, the C.C.U.'s nearest police station and the one they favoured for prisoner interviews and overnight stays.

"I'll see you both then."

As soon as Craig had hung up the call he made another one, this time to his junior analyst with the information about Bella Westbury's Henna scar. Just as Ash was scribbling down the details Davy arrived back from his meeting and he called across.

"I'm glad you're back. We've got a shed load of work to do."

Davy slung his backpack over a chair and turned back towards the exit. "Bring your list and let's go for a sandwich. I haven't had breakfast yet."

Just then both of their desk phones rang; Aidan and Ryan with yet more tasks. Noting them down delayed their food break for ten minutes and by the time the analysts finally managed to reach the canteen Ryan Hendron was just re-entering Rownton police station.

"I've spoken to Hector McDonagh-"

Aidan waved him down. "Save it. We're going back to see him again now. The Guv's just called with some new stuff he needs to know and Jimmy Rushton can't see us for half an hour. He's in a meeting."

It raised the thorny decision of when to eat that day. It was eleven o'clock and they had four people left to interview: McDonagh again, Rushton, Finbar Brolly, Biddy Evans, plus they needed to drop into the church, and all that before they had to hit the road by four o'clock at the latest to reach Armagh, collect their prisoner, and then get back to the ranch via High Street for a, more than likely, two hour briefing at six. It left them with the likelihood of no food before eight o'clock that night unless they had something before they left the village. The only question was where.

Thankfully Mickey O'Hare was so pleased to be told that he could release his noisy houseguest that he entrusted them with a secret known only to the locals, and zealously guarded in case Northern Ireland's foodies descended on Rownton in their gluttonous chattering masses and disturbed their precious peace.

"The best Irish stew and Ulster Fry for a hundred miles around are served at our pub. But I'd eat before you tell Finbar that you want to interview him or he's likely to spit in the pan."

Now that was something they *should* tell any of Northern Ireland's glutterati who were thinking of making the trip.

****

Dublin.

Róisín Casey had had enough of waiting, in fact she'd broken her golden rule by doing it at all, making her feel as it always did like a child outside a toyshop with her nose pressed against the glass. She didn't even like waiting when there was something worth doing it for, like a bespoke piece of jewellery from her lover or the arrival of a couture outfit that she'd been measured for weeks before, but she *really* didn't like hanging about when the expected thing was unexciting or never happened at all, which had already been the case twice that day.

The financier banged repeatedly on her computer's 'enter' key as she was thinking, the refreshing website of The Rownton Recorder displaying exactly what it had displayed an hour before, and the Tyrone radio host's voice booming out of the second web window she had open *still* not announcing the anticipated interview with the mistress of the 'Rownton Suicide'.

The double disappointment made the banker irritable, her default mood between diplomatic manoeuvres and *always* exacerbated by not getting her own way, and Róisín definitely hadn't got her own way on Derek Morrow yet, which meant that his suicide might soon draw much more dangerous attention than she'd hoped.

It left her with a decision, something at which she normally excelled, but this one was making her nervous; getting it wrong had the potential to derail an organisation worth a lot of money that had taken her and others years to set up.

Her gaze flicked repeatedly across her neat desk as she considered her options, lingering longest on her landline. Arthur had obviously failed to get the fantasy mistress to cooperate with the interviews, or failed to reach her in time to rearrange them for later which was the same thing, so...did she call him and-

She paused mid-thought, a cold dread creeping over her as she realised the possible reasons for the girl not giving the interviews that day. There were only three: either she'd chickened out, unusual when there was cash involved; she'd *been* that girl in her teens and when you come from nothing and want everything you'll do anything for a buck. Or second, because Arthur hadn't reached her yet to pressure her, the news editor and the radio jock to reorganise the interviews, and if not then why not? It had better be because the old bastard was dead in a ditch somewhere or he would soon wish that he was.

Which brought Róisín to the third reason, the one that was now making her shudder with fear; someone else had got to the girl first and *stopped* her interviews, and the only people with that capability were the cops.

The revelation made her gasp and move into damage limitation mode. Arthur was on his way to Rownton, where, if the police *had* got hold of the girl she could have coughed by now and they might be lying in wait for him. If so, pretty damn soon he would be in an interview room with the bright light of legend shining on his saggy face, and all it would take was a few hundred lux in his eyes and a couple of questions and the old man would give *her* up.

The banker inhaled again, less sharply this time and shaking her head. *No*. Rio or Trio or whatever the hell her name was couldn't *know* that Arthur was on his way to her, so even if she *had* given him up the police would research his details to find him not hang around Rownton waiting to see if he just happened to drive into town.

It left Róisín with an urgent choice: did she rely on Arthur's crap sense of direction making him hours late as usual and call him to warn him off before he reached Rownton... or not? If he was already there and his phone rang the cops might seize it and reverse engineer her number.

But the risk was small: she would use her throwaway mobile so even if the police *did* uncover its withheld number they could never trace it to her. And making risk assessments was her job after all, so the question now was how *big* of one would she be taking by calling Arthur, compared to allowing him to drive on to Rownton and perhaps straight into the cops' arms?

It was a pity that Róisín Casey had broken her golden rule about waiting and wasted time thinking, because life is rarely changed by considered decisions but rather hinges on split-second choices and random events. Timing in life, as in comedy, is everything, and had she been able to view things from a distance she would have seen that Arthur Norris had *already* arrived in Rownton and was entering the offices of Hector McDonagh, newspaper editor, just behind two detectives who wanted to speak to Mister McDonagh wearing his solicitor's hat.

Of course the men didn't know each other; to the detectives Norris just looked like another grey-faced, aging man in a suit, although with the jaunty addition of a flat cap, something which in itself *should* perhaps have made them look at him more closely. But they were busy so they didn't, and neither did Arthur Norris take the two suited men for police officers, so relieved was he at managing to actually *find* the village to notice anything but where he was, and already preoccupied with planning another meeting with Rio Reynolds to get her back on track.

So it was that neither policeman paid attention to either Norris or his ringing mobile as they waited for Hector McDonagh to emerge from his back office, and neither did they eavesdrop on the phone conversation that then occurred, other than to shoot each other a knowing glance that whoever the woman was who was yelling at the old man was giving him one hell of a telling off.

They didn't pay attention to Arthur Norris at all in fact until Hector McDonagh emerged from his office, and then in the briefest of moments all of that changed. The detectives saw McDonagh's eyes flick past them to the cap-wearing pensioner and then widen in alarm, Norris himself not noticing because he had his back to everyone still busy with his call.

Even then, on its own McDonagh's alarm could have meant one of a hundred things; he might have recognised Arthur Norris as a debt collector, an irate customer, or someone that his newspaper had smeared, had not the editor/solicitor's stunned gaze then acquired a layer of fearfulness, shifted immediately to the detectives and been followed by him reversing into his office again.

Arthur Norris had seen none of this, so when he ended his call with a considerably redder ear than he'd begun it with and turned to see if the newspaper editor had appeared, he was greeted instead by two glaring police officers, the taller of which was displaying his ID.

"D.C.I. Hughes. I'd like to ask you a question, sir, if you don't mind."

Norris nodded wordlessly, and either decorum or a fear of authority made him whip off his cap.

"What's your name, please, sir?"

Ryan watched the pensioner's expression alter as all possible excuses for not answering were raised and dismissed by him mentally, and then as he came to the, false as it happened, conclusion that it was safe to respond.

"It's Arthur Norris."

Aidan's own expression gave nothing away. "Would you have anything to confirm that?"

A quick rummage produced a driving licence telling them that Norris' middle name was Geoffrey, his age was sixty-eight, and he lived at an address in Bangor, County Down. As Aidan perused the ID its owner nervously asked the obvious question.

"Can I ask why you need my identification?"

The D.C.I. had already begun making notes so he left his sergeant to reply.

"Because we'd like you to accompany us next door to the police station, Mister Norris."

To emphasise that there were two ways in which the man could do so Ryan produced a set of cuffs.

The land agent chilled, knowing that he was about to be in trouble not only with the police but with Róisín, and definitely fearing the second far more than the first.

He had one last go at salvaging his day.

"But why, Officer? I haven't done anything. I'm just here to see Mister McDonagh."

It was Aidan's cue to open the door to Hector McDonagh's back office and beckon the now cowering local out.

"McDonagh the newspaper editor, the solicitor or the chicken farmer?"

Norris didn't have the wit or reflexes to lie. "Newspaper editor." He scrambled around for a reason. "I'd...I'd like to put in a full page advert."

Ryan responded with a smirk. "About a Ms Rio Reynolds, by any chance?"

Norris didn't even try for an answer this time and as Aidan preferred to play his games sitting down, he mentally kissed goodbye to his Ulster Fry and motioned to the D.S.

"Take Mister Norris next door and book him in for questioning, please. And tell Sergeant O'Hare we'll need his room again. I've a few things to sort here so I'll be with you in ten minutes."

As the front door closed behind the hapless Norris and his escort, Aidan turned back to Hector McDonagh.

"You've obviously met Mister Norris before. When?"

There was a second's delay while the solicitor considered citing client confidentiality then he gave in with a shrug.

"He's a land agent and I dealt with his purchase of the quarry years back."

Interesting.

"And you arranged the print interview with Ms Reynolds at his behest?"

"Yes. And the radio one."

As Aidan then produced a photo of Blaine Westbury and set about gathering the information that Craig had requested, Róisín Casey was miles away basking in the satisfaction of a bollocking well given and congratulating herself on having taken her calculated risk.

It was a choice that would soon give Craig a thread to tug at and destroy everything that she and others had built.

****

The C.C.U.

The analysts' excursion to the staff canteen had proved a voyage of discovery, revealing, amongst other things, sandwiches that for once had been comprised of bread other than thin white sliced and fillings other than egg and cress or ham and cheese. The, seemingly overnight, renamed and renovated 'Blue Line Cafe' had a new manageress who'd seemingly declared it her mission to educate the palates of police personnel, and was establishing a rolling rota of French, Spanish, American, Italian and other world cuisines instead of the usual curled-up Belfast baps and rock hard scones. In celebration of her first week on the job a gourmet version of Croque Monsieur was on sale and after two rounds each of the cheesy delight the analysts were sated and raring to go.

The food acted like rocket fuel on Ash's searches and yielded sufficient results for him to call Craig back far earlier than anticipated and with something very useful to say.

He caught the detective having a meal of his own at a new motorway service station just north of the border that Liam had insisted they try, the D.C.I. viewing such places in the same way a child views an entertainment arcade, with a variety of novelties to experience that he could *never* find at home.

Craig had only just managed to stop his deputy buying a hat that said 'Kiss me, I'm Irish' arguing that with Liam's colouring and freckles no-one could have ever mistaken him for anything else and there were limited occasions on which he could wear it without either getting arrested for harassment or punched, when he'd been tempted himself by a book of international baby names that he thought might help unlock their current stalemate choices of Molly or Marianna for a girl and Tom versus Robert for a boy.

The detective was just averting his eyes from his deputy's plate, which was stacked with such a pick and mix of food from the buffet that it made him feel sick, when the buzz of his phone gave him a legitimate excuse to step outside.

"Craig."

"Hi, chief. It's Ash."

Given that the number on the screen was the CCU's switchboard's and he recognised all his staff's voices the intro was redundant, but it made Craig smile.

"Hello, Ash. What do you have for me?"

"OK, well..." The analyst changed tack suddenly, seemingly without any point. "Actually, where are you?"

"Motorway services just past Dungannon. Why?"

"Good, that means you can still divert to the lab on your

way back."

"Fair enough, but why?"

"Because Des already had the aging software so he's doing the girl's photo for us."

Craig urged him on.

"We've also got some info Aidan wanted."

"Good. Don't tell me about that now, tell Aidan and bring it up at the briefing. Is that everything?"

"*As if.* I'd hardly call you just for that lot, would I?" He didn't wait for the policeman to respond. "OK, so I took the daisy scar and the girl's colouring and something interesting came up."

Craig gripped his phone, hardly daring to believe that they'd had a breakthrough already. They had, but not as much as he'd just started to hope.

"So, there were over forty kids under five who travelled from the areas we agreed within a month of Bella Westbury's abduction."

"Boat or plane?"

"Both. I looked up to age five like you suggested because size varies at that age, so people could have lied about how old she was."

"And?"

"So then I ignored the hair colour because it could have been dyed and her fair skin because they could have tanned it, but using her blue eyes I got it down to fifteen. A mix of boys and girls."

"Excellent. So you're pulling their travel details and passports now?"

"Well...yes..."

Craig felt an axe about to drop.

"But that's where there could be a hitch."

Nothing could ever be simple, could it?

It wasn't the analyst's fault so the detective swallowed his frustration and said, "Mmm..."

"Some of the countries they travelled to mightn't be keen to hand over passport details."

Craig frowned. "Like where?"

"Russia."

Damn. He'd forgotten there were a lot of blue eyes there too.

"Also Venezuela. There were two kids travelling there."

Ditto. Forty percent of the Venezuelan population was of European descent.

A cold chill ran down Craig's spine. Russia and Venezuela. *Of course.* What do you do with someone that you want to make disappear? You transport them to countries where they'll blend in but have no extradition treaty with the UK.

If Bella Westbury *had* been taken to either of the countries mentioned, then how in hell would they *ever* find her and get her back?

The detective became aware that his analyst was still speaking so he curbed his negativity and asked him to repeat his words.

"Sorry, what was that last thing you said, Ash?"

"I said I've contacted the British and Irish Embassies because the Westbury family hold both passports, to see if they can help facilitate the search for details, and I could give the international agencies and D.C.I. Barrett in Intelligence the heads up as well if you think that they'd be able to help?"

Ray Barrett ran the Police Intelligence Unit day-to-day and very well, so although Craig had oversight and responsibility for the division it was normally a very light touch role. But now might be the time to use his senior position there.

"Actually... send that info to me now, Ash, and I'll ask Ray myself. We can call in to see him on the way back from the lab. Yes to the agencies, but don't tell them *why* we're looking specifically."

"Cool. OK, one last thing. None of the passports listed a scar on a kid's hand under distinguishing marks, but I've a hunch about something so I'm going to contact the airlines direct."

Craig smiled at his initiative.

"Good man. Your hunches usually pay off."

He ended the call quickly, his mind already back on the road, leaving the analyst preening himself at the praise and getting ready to make the next in his series of calls.

****

Rownton Police Station.

Arthur Norris hadn't said a word since entering the interview room. In fact his only notable reaction since Ryan had steered him from Hector McDonagh's office had been to look shocked when Rio Reynolds had flounced out of the police station just as they were walking through its door.

Norris had averted his face immediately but the action had proved futile, as the beautician, annoyed by the lecture she'd just received and the fact that the rest of her promised payment was never going to materialise, had already spotted her betrayer and launched herself at him nails out, seeking her revenge.

A moment of screeching, chaos and expletives ensued and had it not been that Arthur Norris knew that he was heading towards a worse fate, he might have been grateful for Mickey O'Hare marching the girl determinedly away down the street. As it was, Rio Reynolds' presence at the police station told the businessman that the game was up, so he positively dragged himself into the interview room where he slid down in his seat beside a uniformed constable and declined to say a word, surreptitiously pushing his mobile deep into his pocket beneath the table and stationing his hand there as its guard.

But Ryan Hendron was neither blind nor stupid so he knew exactly what Norris was at. The question was why? What could there be on the old man's phone that he wanted to conceal? And might it be relevant to their case?

At Arthur Norris' refusal to answer routine questions, the sergeant recited them again on autopilot while allowing his thoughts to go elsewhere. Norris was hiding his phone for a reason and given that there was nothing at all exciting about smart-phones themselves that only left four possibilities. He was concealing someone's number, an image, a website or a file. Which led them back to Derek Morrow. *Why* had Norris paid Rio Reynolds to blacken the dead man's name? What was the point of discrediting anyone *after* their death, unless... it was to deflect from the *real* reason why they'd killed themselves?

The thought prompted Ryan to exit the interview room in search of the custody sergeant.

"Where did Derek Morrow's suicide letters go?"

Mickey O'Hare answered without looking up from the sticking plaster that he was applying to a laceration on his hand, a small but deep wound that he intended to big-up to his wife as having come not from one of Rio Reynolds' acrylic nails as he'd led her away but from a burly drunk who he'd only managed to subdue after a violent fight.

"Like I said earlier. The family collected them on their way to the morgue."

"Did you see what was written in them?"

The sergeant gave him a wry look. "Do I *look* like I'd read someone's suicide note?"

Ryan was tempted to ask what appearance that sort of person might have, but decided on politeness over wit.

"Sorry. Let me rephrase the question. Did you *ask* Mrs Morrow to show or tell you what the notes said?"

O'Hare gave a nod of his greying head. "I did."

"So would you care to share that with me?"

'Care' was a funny choice of word and the local man's strictly honest answer would have been, "No."

He wouldn't 'care' to share *anything* more with the Belfast police. They'd been finding dead bodies and untidying his station for two days now and he'd had enough.

But O'Hare decided to be polite as well, in the hope that it would make them go away soon.

"One letter was just the details of Morrow's bank and Will details and what not, and the other one said he was killing himself because he couldn't cope with the stress of work."

The words made Ryan frown. *Stress of work?* Derek Morrow had been a builder in a tiny village; he'd hardly been constructing a skyscraper in New York!

"Did Mister Morrow *get* much work around here?"

O'Hare leaned back against the custody desk and crossed his arms as casually as if he was standing at a bar as he answered.

"Aye, well, Derek did OK for it. His lads are building some starter homes on the edge of the village, for young families like." He rolled his slightly drooping eyes. "*That'll* bring trouble for us in the future, I'm sure. Teenage delinquents and whatnot."

Considering it had been truanting teenagers who'd found their murder victim the village obviously already had a few of those, but Ryan let the comment pass and carried on.

"That still doesn't seem enough to have caused him stress, so was the firm involved in any other work?"

"Aye, well, Derek does, did, *any* construction needed here about. Out on the farms, the local schools and so on. It was enough to keep his wee team busy, but I'd say he hadn't been *really* busy since he'd worked on the old quarry years back."

The detective felt a sudden tingling down his spine. "The quarry where we found the body?"

"Only one around here."

"So Derek Morrow's men did the excavation work on it?"

"Aye, and they're responsible for maintaining the outbuildings to this day and doing the odd inspection. Not much work there though, I expect; the place has been empty for years. But Jimmy Rushton could tell you more about all that than me."

Ryan nodded and changed tack. "How well did you know Mister Morrow?"

O'Hare moved behind his desk and rested forward on it with his elbows, making Ryan picture him running a pub when he retired. He wouldn't be the first copper to go that route.

"Well, now...I saw him in passing around here every day, but I've *known* him all my life. Derek comes from Cooneen like me. It's a village ten miles from here, so I've seen him about therefor years. He even put in my Ma's new kitchen back in the day."

"So did he strike you as being more stressed than usual lately?"

O'Hare shook his head. "About as stressed as me I'd have said." His smile said that wasn't very much. The sergeant liked a quiet life, preferably one without excitable detectives around.

"Mind you, who knows *what* goes on in a man's mind? Although I have to say that Eileen, that's Derek's wife, seemed surprised by his suicide too. When she came in for the letters she said he'd given no signs at all of being depressed. The whole thing seemed to have hit her out of the blue."

The detective was beginning to feel the 'two men in a bar' ambience himself so he leaned back against the nearest wall and shoved his hands in his pockets before going on.

"Was their marriage strong then?"

"Derek and Eileen? Oh, God, aye. There's *never* been a divorce in that Morrow family, and those two always gave me the impression of being as happy as pigs in muck. The whole idea of Derek having a mistress is a non-runner as far as I'm concerned. And that Rio girl is younger than their kids."

Not that *that* ever stopped people. But O'Hare's assessment of the marriage was ringing true to Ryan and it made him wonder whether there might be something even more 'off' about Derek Morrow's suicide than it had first appeared. Mrs Morrow might need to be interviewed, but not today and hopefully by some other cop.

He nodded in thanks and propelled himself off the wall, turning back towards the interview room and glancing at the clock behind the custody desk as he did. It was after twelve, so where the hell was Aidan? He'd said he would only be ten minutes. Ryan's eyes narrowed. He'd *better* not have nipped off somewhere for lunch.

He shrugged the thought away and beckoned O'Hare to follow him back to the room, ready to take his next step. As Ryan opened the door he was unsurprised to see Arthur Norris still staring into space; the man obviously had a lot on his mind and he was beginning to form a picture of just what that might be.

"Please stand up, Mister Norris."

The older man obeyed him like an automaton, but Ryan saw that one hand was still deep inside his pocket.

"Empty your pockets, please."

When, as expected, Norris didn't move, the detective nodded his local counterpart to perform the task, something that was only achievable by forcibly tugging Norris' hand away from his phone.

The detritus of his and most other men's lives appeared on the table item by item: phone, car-keys, half-eaten packet of mints, and from his inside jacket pockets a wallet and comb. The wallet yielded nothing but the usual cards, ID and cash, which just left Norris' smart-phone as an item of interest.

Ryan gestured to it. "You were holding on to that for grim death. Why?"

When no reply came he nodded everyone to sit and changed tack.

"Why did you try to frame Derek Morrow, Mister Norris?"

He could have added, "For adultery", but he was convinced that the detail of the lie hadn't been its point.

It elicited the first reaction from Arthur Norris in almost an hour, as the man's rheumy eyes widened in shock.

"I didn't frame anyone!"

Ryan leaned forward. "You wanted people to believe that Morrow killed himself because of an affair instead of his real reason."

"I'm not saying anything about that, and anyway, *that* doesn't count as a frame."

"You don't *need* to say anything, Mister Norris. Ms Reynolds already identified you as having been the man who paid her to lie."

As he said the words Ryan was wondering 'why adultery?' *Why* would Norris have wanted people to believe that Derek Morrow had killed himself over love instead of the work stress outlined in his suicide note, especially as by Mickey O'Hare's account *neither* motive was credible?

Just then something occurred to the detective: feeling the need to set up an alternative motive for Morrow killing himself implied that Arthur Norris had already known what was written in the suicide note! At that moment the penny dropped on Ryan, and if it had been professional to have clicked his fingers to mark the victory he would have done. Instead he made do with a grin.

Derek Morrow had worked on the quarry and maintained his involvement with the place for years, and he'd killed himself only hours after they'd found Stuart Kincaid's corpse there. *Somehow* Morrow and possibly the quarry itself were linked to Kincaid's murder, or at least Morrow had thought when they'd found the body there that he might have been *implicated* in some way, so he'd killed himself rather than deal with the fall-out.

But... had Morrow developed a conscience before his death and cited work stress in his suicide note deliberately, to *point* them to something? The fact that Arthur Norris had tried to deflect attention from it as a motive for suicide said that he might have done, *and* that there could be danger for someone still living if the police followed up on something to do with Morrow's work. And although that someone mightn't actually be Arthur Norris, his involvement in the attempted cover-up said that he was somehow implicated too.

That was where Ryan's reasoning hit a wall and he realised that they didn't know enough yet to take things further, so he refocused his assault.

"Your phone, Mister Norris. Why were you trying to conceal it?"

Silence.

"Who called you earlier when we were at the solicitor's office?"

A slight twitch.

The detective pursued the twitch with a hard stare into Norris' face as he asked his next few questions, slowly and in steps, leaving space for the man to react between each one.

"What don't you want us to see on there? ... Is it an image? ...A website? .... A file? .... Or perhaps there's a particular phone number that you're trying to conceal?"

Norris 'only reaction was another small twitch on 'phone number' but it was enough.

There was a number on Arthur Norris' mobile that he didn't want them to see, but they would check the device for all the other possibilities as well. Ryan withdrew a plastic evidence bag from his pocket and reached over to enclose the phone in it. Suddenly galvanised, Norris' hand shot out to snatch the device, to be blocked swiftly by Mickey O'Hare's bandaged own.

"You can't take my phone!"

"I think you'll find that we can, Mister Norris." Ryan rose to his feet. "And I'll be taking you to Belfast along with it as well. I have more questions for you."

A now white-faced Norris went to object but no words

hit the air, so the city sergeant turned to his rural counterpart and requested his help again.

"We've a few more people to see before we hit the road, so would you keep Mister Norris here until then?"

Mickey O'Hare jangled the heavy bunch of keys at his waist meaningfully. "I've got the perfect guest room for him down at the back."

It was time for Ryan to go in search of his disappearing D.C.I.

****

The Labs. Third Floor. The Forensic Department.

Craig and Liam watched intently as Des Marsham enlarged the first image on his computer to fill his screen; the photograph of the fourteen-month-old Bella Westbury that Ash had downloaded from the chat-room. He cleaned it up and sharpened its colour and contrast carefully before activating his aging software to produce an image of the girl at three-years-old, not long before she'd been abducted, while the detectives observed the process fascinated. They watched as the girl's bones lengthened, her curls straightened subtly and her baby-faced chubbiness receded to a slightly more formed toddler shape.

After he'd finished Des sat back and sighed, not in contentment but with an acceptance that the image was the best that the software could achieve. Then he said the words that no-one else wanted to.

"Pretty little thing."

Craig felt regret well up and stick in his throat, until he spat it out mixed with fury.

"Sick bastard! I hope he's six feet under."

His vehemence surprised the others, more used to his calm reticence and Liam being the one to voice such sentiments; but then none of them knew of his once violent experience with a paedophile.

After a moment staring at the image Des responded by opening the second one beside it on the screen.

"OK. This is the *actual* photograph of Bella around that age that was found in the victim's pocket, although I'm using the copy you brought from Edgar Westbury because it's clearer. It was the last photograph ever taken of her and the one used by the search teams."

They compared the images for height and build and all three men nodded at the fit, but when Des enlarged the faces in the two images there were distinct differences.

Liam frowned.

"Why do they look so different? In real life her hair was lighter, and she was finer featured."

"That's because the software can only approximate predicted changes along *average* lines, but a person's genetics and nutrition will always determine the exact results at any given age."

He typed furiously for a moment, his eyes flicking between the two images as he adjusted the growth parameters.

"OK, I've inputted the variance and her parents' measurements, so that should keep things nearer Bella's specific patterns for a few years anyway. Now I'm going to use those specifics to age her forward to six years eight months, the age that she would be now."

Another round of image tidying ensued and they watched as a series of Bella Westburys at her abduction age, and then four, five and finally six years and eight months appeared. A taller than imagined little girl with the age's typical combination of a short trunk and longer, skinny arms and legs.

Liam was the first to speak this time. "Her eyes are still that very light blue like her dad said."

Craig nodded. "And very blonde, just like her mother. She looks just like the photographs we saw of her too. Westbury had some dotted around his house." He shook himself briskly to halt the looming tide of sentimentality. "OK, that's great, Des. I'll need images at each of those ages emailed to Davy and Ash, please."

The forensic lead glanced at him quizzically. "Not just the age she is now?"

Craig shook his head. "It's not enough for what I have planned." He motioned his deputy that they were leaving. "Send a copy of each to me as well, please. And we'll be briefing at six if you and John would like to come."

The scientist shook his head immediately. "Sorry, I

can't tonight. We're holding our annual special metal detecting event from six to six." His excitement was audible. "I don't know where we're going yet, but they're always held somewhere unexpected."

A murmur of, "a Uranium dump," from Liam was answered by a haughty, "*Hardly*. Anyway, I'll give copies of everything I have to John and email these images across now."

Craig saw his deputy's lips part to say something else and shunted him forcefully from the office, knowing from the glint in his eyes that he'd been about to say something rude.

Liam's words eventually hit the air in the lift to the ground floor.

"*An all night metal detecting event?* I mean, what does that even *look* like? A bunch of sad gits in tin hats digging holes by candlelight?"

The lift doors opened and Craig turned towards John Winter's office as he answered. "You're confusing them with alien hunters trying to block signals. Metal detectorists don't wear tin hats as far as I know. It's apt to throw their equipment off."

His reasoning fell on deaf ears.

"Aye well, they should be wearing strait jackets because they're all bonkers! An event he called it, for God's sake! *An event!* I bet they've even sold tickets! Nerds with more money than sense standing around eating burgers and talking about the piece of iron that got away."

Craig was trying not to laugh as he knocked on John's office door but he failed. When the pathologist opened the door he knew instantly what had provoked their mirth.

"Des' metal event?"

"Yes, except *you* make it sound like Iron Maiden's performing."

"I wish." He gave a martyred sigh. "And *I'll* hear every boring detail of it tomorrow, ad nauseam." He waved the detectives to take a seat. "Anyway, what can I do for you two?"

Craig got back to business. "Anything more on Stuart Kincaid's PM?"

"Nope. Just what I told you before. His tox-screen and bloods were normal and he'd had a meal an hour or so before he died. Meat and two veg. Nothing unusual. We didn't need a mineral analysis because we had his ID."

"OK then, anything on Derek Morrow, the builder from Rownton?"

"Not much. I spoke to the pathologist who did his PM and it was a clean angled shot through the roof of his mouth and into his brain. He used a long barrelled revolver. I checked and he had a licence for it. He was a member of a gun club in Enniskillen."

Liam gave a tut of disgust. "I hate those bloody places. Bunch of sad fuck wannabe cops and urban cowboys so desperate to kill something they take it out on the wildlife."

Craig had to agree; most of the people he'd met who shot living things as a hobby had had screws loose, and even worse, in Northern Ireland some of them had links with paramilitaries so there was the danger that legally held guns would illegally meander to them. Someone wanting a gun should be an absolute block on them *ever* getting one in his book. If they wanted target practice why couldn't they just play darts or snooker, or join a flipping archery club?

Liam was already on the next question.

"Did Morrow have anything else wrong with him? Like a terminal illness that might have explained why he'd wanted to kill himself?"

The pathologist shook his head. "Nothing. He was actually pretty fit for a man of sixty. Probably because he'd had a physical job all his life, whereas we're all so sedentary that one day we're just going to melt into giant blobs of cholesterol on the floor."

"God, that's cheery, Doc!"

Craig laughed. "Yes, thanks for that, John. I'll ask for that on my gravestone. Here lies a giant blob of cholesterol who never got off his ass!"

He sprang to his feet just to prove that he could still do it.

"Right. We're briefing at six if you'd like to come. You could cover Des' stuff as well."

The medic folded his arms tightly, indicating that some sort of demand was coming. "I'll come if you *promise* that we can go for a pint at The James afterwards. I haven't had a decent session since..." He thought about it for a moment. "Christmas!" His eyes widened in horror. "That's six weeks ago!"

"You make it sound like the end of the world."

Two gimlet gazes confirmed to Craig that it was.

"Oh OK, let's go for a drink then, but only one. I promised Katy that I'd sort out the mothers tonight."

John unfolded himself and sat forward, his interest piqued. "That sounds dangerous."

Liam stood up, shaking his head. "Nah, he just means he's giving them the job of house hunting, so they need to be briefed in case they go off the rails. God knows, they could end up buying a castle or something."

It wasn't as farfetched as it sounded. Mirella Craig's architectural sense only had two reference points: Tuscan farmhouse or ornate palazzo with nothing in between, and as she'd successfully turned their family home in Holywood into a copy of the former that meant the palazzo was still itching to get out.

So although Craig was hoping that Maureen Stevens' more moderate taste would keep his mother's under control, Liam was already running a book on him ending up living in as close as Ireland could approximate to an Ancient Roman's dream home.

John sniggered, picturing a tormented Craig surrounded by sheaves of estate agents' details and swatches of material, longing for the solitude of his bachelor pad.

"You should have asked me to look for you, Marc. I'd have found you something like our place."

Craig's heart sank; he hadn't even thought of it. And a modern Scandi dream like John's converted chapel would have been the perfect thing. Ah well, at least it gave him something else to add to the search guidelines that his mother would completely ignore.

"Right. We need to go now. We have to call in at the Intelligence Unit before we head back to the office, and there's a lot to pick up before six."

As Liam followed he mimicked choking himself while pointing at Craig's back. It was as accurate a critique as any on the maternal house search chaos that was about to kick off.

****

Rownton Village.

After ten minutes' spent ricocheting in and out of the few communal spaces in the small village: the shop, church and charity co-op, Ryan Hendron's search for his boss finally paid off outside the pub. The smile he saw on Aidan's face as he was exiting The Rocking Chair made the sergeant get ready to whine about him having availed of its Ulster Fry behind his back, until he noticed that the D.C.I. was holding two substantial packs of sandwiches in his hands.

"Are those for us?"

Aidan glanced down at the food as if he'd forgotten that it was there. "These? Oh, yeh, I thought we could eat them on the way to Mahon. We can buy a coffee at the shop before we leave." He glanced back in the direction of the police station. "Where's Norris?"

"Held for questioning. I think we should take him back with us."

Aidan raised an eyebrow but didn't question the decision. He was pleased, as Craig would be when he found out, that Ryan was stepping up.

"Fine. Sorry I was so long, but I was meeting with Jimmy Rushton and Finbar Brolly, the pub landlord."

"Useful?"

"Brolly was. He said Derek Morrow came tearing into the pub on Tuesday in a panic, asking why the police were in the village. Brolly said he was in a real state, and when he said the police would want to interview everyone local Morrow belted out the door."

Ryan gave a whistle. "Guilty as sin about something."

"Exactly. So either Morrow was involved in Kincaid's murder or he knew who was."

"I think it was the latter."

"Hold that thought for a moment. Brolly also told me that Stuart Kincaid came into the pub."

"For a beer?"

"That and to show a photo of his niece around apparently. He asked about the Westbury family too. It *also* turns out Brolly went to the same school as Blaine Westbury. Small town."

Aidan spotted a low stone wall and walked across to sit

on it, beckoning the D.S. to do the same.

"Explain to me why you think Morrow knew who was involved in Kincaid's murder."

Ryan glanced longingly at the sandwiches and then forced himself to respond.

"OK, well, it's obvious Arthur Norris wanted to convince everyone that Morrow topped himself because of love, not work stress as per his suicide note, yes?"

"OK."

"So that means Norris or someone else employing him wanted the focus shifted *away* from Morrow's work. Given that a body was found in the quarry just hours before Morrow's suicide and Mickey O'Hare's just told me Morrow *worked* on the quarry and still had oversight of the place, I think there's a link there."

Aidan nodded, shielding his eyes from the early afternoon sun as he thought. "Rushton confirmed they have oversight of the quarry too, so let's make the link. Kincaid's body's found in the quarry so the police arrive to ask about it. Morrow, whose company worked on the quarry, panics and kills himself. But surely that points to Derek Morrow killing Kincaid and knowing the game was up?"

"Or him *knowing* who did it and being involved somehow."

"And *you're* thinking that Morrow didn't kill Kincaid himself but his reference to work in the note was to help point us to who did. To point us to the quarry *itself* being a clue. Pity that Morrow's oversight of the quarry didn't extend to him being there to prevent Kincaid being drowned isn't it."

"That's if he *wasn't* there when it happened."

It earned him a startled look from the D.C.I. that encouraged Ryan to go on.

"I think this is where Arthur Norris comes in. *Someone* has a vested interest in us not following that work stress lead, and it's either Norris himself or he knows who it is."

Aidan took out his phone, dialling a number and handing it across.

"Take the next step, Sergeant."

Davy's voice came on the line. "Northern Irish Tourist Information. David Walsh here."

"Ha ha. OK, if you're tourist information then I'd like you to find me everything you can find on The West Mountain Quarry for six o'clock, please."

The analyst carried the joke through. "Can do, sir. Strangely we've been researching that very location just on the off-chance."

"Cheers, Davy. We'll see you then."

He cut the call and handed the phone back to Aidan, continuing the thought as he did.

"OK, so we find out who owns or owned the quarry and see if there's anything there. The other thing is that Norris was trying to conceal his mobile so I've taken it as evidence to find out why. There's something on there that he doesn't want us to see, and *I* think it's a phone number. My guess is that it could lead us to whoever wanted Morrow's true suicide motive concealed."

"So you don't think that could be Norris himself?"

Ryan shook his dark head emphatically. "Nope. He's a follower, and a timid one too. I think he's afraid of someone and he's probably right to be. One man's already been murdered." He changed topic. "What did Jimmy Rushton have to say?"

Aidan shook his head glumly. "Nothing useful. He said Derek Morrow was a decent man, good to work for and treated his men fairly. He didn't know him socially but he did say that Morrow had bought a cruise for his wife and himself just last week, leaving at the end of May."

Ryan's eyes widened. "That doesn't sound like a man planning suicide, or an unfaithful one."

"Or a poor one. We need to check Morrow's bank accounts. And if he *did* kill himself because Stuart Kincaid's body was discovered in the quarry we need to find out why, and whether it had anything to do with that photo of Bella Westbury". He jumped off the wall. "Which reminds me. I showed the photos of Stuart Kincaid and Bella and Blaine Westbury to Hector McDonagh, Brolly and Rushton, and guess what I found out."

"Take them one at a time. McDonagh first."

"OK, he told me that Blaine hasn't claimed the money from his parents' estate and hasn't been in touch. He hasn't seen him since the funeral."

"Bit strange for a waster who was always broke."

"Just what I thought. Little Blaine must have come into money. Maybe he married into it."

They were both wondering who the woman might be as Aidan continued.

"McDonagh didn't recognise Bella from the photo, but when I told him her name he said he recognised it as belonging to Edgar Westbury's daughter. He said he'd heard that she was at her grandparents' funeral and agreed to dig out any photos that he might have taken for the newspaper. He didn't seem to recognise Stuart Kincaid's picture at all."

"You believed him?"

"I did actually. Finbar Brolly was the same; didn't recognise Bella's photo but said he recalled her being at the funeral. Stuart Kincaid he *did* recognise as having come into the pub, and he said he'd heard Kincaid had been showing a photo around and asking about the Westburys but he hadn't actually seen him do it, which OK, I suppose he *mightn't* have done. He could have been busy pulling pints."

Ryan nodded.

"Kincaid's bound to have been showing the photo round. I'd have shown it *everywhere* if I was looking for a child."

"Agreed. So anyway, Jimmy Rushton didn't recognise *any* of the photos and he just looked blank when I mentioned Blaine's, Kincaid's and Bella's names."

"That would make sense if he just comes to Rownton to work. Where does he live?"

"In Omagh."

"Thirty miles away. Fair enough. Did you ask Rushton about the huts up at the quarry Liam wanted to know about?"

"Yep. He said there used to be a permanent security guard up there but it was downgraded years ago. Now Morrow's men only go every other week to inspect the place and check for rats."

Ryan glanced at his watch, wondering if they had time to eat. "Right, it's two-thirty now, so we're doing OK for time. I already asked about Blaine in the church when I was looking for you and no joy, so that just leaves Biddy Evans to see before we head for Armagh."

Aidan held out the sandwiches, making the D.S. salivate in anticipation. His hopes were dashed when the D.C.I. added, "She has a cottage at the north end of town. We can walk there in five minutes and dump those in my car on the way past."

Ten minutes later they were seated in the neat living room of a pristine cottage, being plied with tea and iced buns that Ryan would have eaten five of if anything more than two wouldn't have made him look like a pig. Having worked pleasantly through the preliminaries with their hostess Aidan produced his selection of photographs, beginning with the least contentious one of the three.

He set down the driving licence photograph of Blaine Westbury that Ash had mailed through and before he could even ask a question Bridget Evans wrinkled her brow.

"That's Blaine Westbury. I'd know him anywhere."

"Yes, it is. Can you tell me how you know him, Mrs Evans?"

"Why, his parents owned the White Tree Guest House all their days, poor things." She shook her tightly curled greyhead solemnly. "Such a tragic end."

"And you knew the children?"

Her face broke into a smile. "Edgar was in and out of my post-office buying sweets all the time. He was a lovely boy. Always cheerful."

"And Blaine."

She pursed her lips tightly, etching a delicate lace of lines on her upper lip.

"The good Lord says that we should always be charitable but it was very difficult with that boy. He stole from my shop, and got in worse trouble as well. His poor parents were always having to deal with it. Bad to the bone from the day he could walk."

She shuddered. "I'm not sorry he's not around here anymore. I often used to wonder if there was anything that he *wouldn't* do."

Aidan had heard some damning indictments in his time, but that was one of the clearest.

"When was the last time you saw Blaine, Mrs Evans?"

"Well...I saw him at his parents' funeral." Her next words were tinged with disgust. "Everyone did. He was the worse for drink at the wake, and then..."

She fell silent and Ryan knew why.

"I know you feel that the Westburys have suffered, Mrs Evans, and you're possibly worried about saying something to make things worse for them. But we really wouldn't ask if it wasn't important, so if you even *think* you've seen Blaine more recently we really do need to know."

Whether it was the sympathy in the sergeant's words or the quietness of his tone that did the trick they would never know, people not usually being asked to complete satisfaction surveys on how they were questioned by the police unless they are already grinding an axe, but do the trick it did.

Bridget Evans nodded once and continued. "I'm almost certain that I saw Blaine early one morning last November. I was barely awake and I went to the kitchen window to open the curtains."

When she indicated a window towards the rear of the small house Ryan went to look out. The view was spectacular, a vista of rolling fields with a range of high hills in the distance. As he re-entered the living room the post-mistress was expanding on her story.

"He was running across the fields as bold as you like, in the direction of the village. I rubbed my eyes to make sure I wasn't imagining it and when I looked again he was gone."

Aidan felt himself tense eagerly but he looked to Ryan for a confirmatory nod before pushing for details.

"Let me be clear, Mrs Evans. That window looks out towards the old quarry, yes?"

"Yes, that's right. You can't actually see the quarry because it's below the hills, but it's there just behind them."

"And Blaine Westbury was approaching from that direction, crossing the fields towards the village."

"Exactly so. Running, but he wasn't dressed like one of those joggers. He was wearing a shirt and a pair of those jean things." She gave a rueful smile. "That's if I wasn't seeing things, of course." She tapped one temple with a wrinkled finger. "I'm not as sharp as I once was. Mind you, that still makes me a genius compared to most round here."

They were essentially Gabriel McCusker's words but with a sarcastic edge, no doubt born of years of having to put up with Rownton's occupants moaning at her about everything from their late pensions to a lack of stamps.

The retired post-mistress was still talking. "I didn't see Blaine again after that so I dismissed it as my imagination. But I *really* don't think that it was."

Neither did Aidan, and *if* Blaine Westbury had been in Rownton the winter before it warranted a deeper look.

He parked the point and moved onto his second photograph.

"Do you recognise *this* man, Mrs Evans?"

She peered over her glasses and smiled. "Oh, yes, that's that nice Mister Kincaid. He dropped into my post-office."

The D.C.I. felt a spark of hope. "How often did he call in?"

"Twice. The first time was when I still had the post-office, I think it was two years ago. He introduced himself and showed me a photograph of a little girl."

He whipped out the image of Bella they'd found in Kincaid's pocket. "This one?"

"Yes, yes that's it. Sweet little thing. He was asking if I'd ever seen her around the village but I'm afraid I had to disappoint him and say that I never had."

Her face fell, mirroring what both detectives knew must have been Stuart Kincaid's reaction.

"But I *really* don't think she'd ever been here because Rownton isn't big and most people used my shop every day, to buy milk and whatnot. Even visitors at the guest house when it was open. So generally if I haven't seen someone they haven't been here."

She undoubtedly *had* seen Bella, at her grandparents' funeral, but he decided not to point out her memory lapse.

After a moment's regret-filled pause the post-mistress continued.

"The second time that Mister Kincaid was in the village was last winter and I didn't have the shop any longer." Her eyes widened in pleasure and surprise as she recounted the rest of the tale. "But, do you know... he sought me out just to say hello, and then he took me to the Silverbirch Hotel in Omagh for afternoon tea! Such a gentleman."

The kindness made both policemen a little sadder that Stuart Kincaid was dead, but not wanting to lose momentum Ryan urged the retiree on with another question.

"Was Mister Kincaid alone when you met him?"

"Oh, yes, both times."

"And can I ask what you talked about on the second occasion?"

She creased her forehead trying to recall, and then shook her head.

"I'm sorry. My memory isn't what it was. I do know that we discussed current affairs, he was very well read, and I seem to recall him asking something about the old quarry. And the Westburys too, although for the life of me I can't remember what."

"He didn't show you the girl's photograph again?"

"Oh yes, yes he did that too, but I still had to say that I hadn't seen the child because I hadn't." She smiled wistfully. "Perhaps he'll come again someday. If he does then I'll tell him that you called."

They hadn't the heart to tell her that Stuart Kincaid would never return.

They'd covered everything that they'd come to ask and it hadn't been a wasted trip, but the detectives stayed a little while longer in the cosy cottage anyway, almost as much for their own sake as Bridget Evans'.

Chapter Six

The Police Intelligence Section. Malone Road, Belfast.

Craig's and Liam's trip to Police Intelligence turned out to be a wasted one, something that they'd realised seconds after they passed the building's front-line security checks and reached Ray Barrett's office. The Director, not knowing that they were coming and the world of spying, covert observation and intelligence gathering ticking over nicely, had not unreasonably taken the afternoon off to watch his granddaughter play chess for her school.

It had made Craig tut slightly, not from annoyance at Barrett but at the knowledge that he couldn't defer any longer returning to the squad-room to sit behind his desk. It was something that he hated doing because the second his backside hit the chair his PA, be it the demure, ballroom dancing Alice or the bat-eared, no-nonsense Nicky who was only there occasionally at the moment, would swoop in with letters to be signed and reports to be perused, and he loathed paperwork of any sort.

Unfortunately as you ascended the ladder in the police, as in most jobs, there was more and more of the stuff, which probably explained the spread of most senior officers' asses and guts, and he preferred *his* as they were. He wanted to be out on the street where the action was, his dislike of being sedentary so strong that he'd recently turned down the lead in Serious and Organised Crime, an acting Assistant Chief Constable role, and become a member of Sean Flanagan's Chief Superintendent Trinity for his sins.

But Craig's annoyance was nothing compared to that of Róisín Casey, who had been calling her lackey's mobile constantly for the previous two hours and getting Arthur Norris' answerphone every time. She expected the people who worked for or even with her to give twenty-four-seven availability, so the first few messages she'd left for him, asking what had happened with Hector McDonagh and the girl's interview, which she *still* hadn't heard amidst the crappy nineties' pop that the God awful radio hosts in Tyrone had been blasting out most of the day, had ranged from impatient, through irritated, through furious, until finally now a sense of dread had set in.

Arthur wasn't brave enough to *ignore* her calls all afternoon, so that left limited possibilities. Either the idiot had dropped his phone down the toilet or lost the device somewhere and so had a genuine technical reason for not answering her calls; or he was dead, probably because his car had crashed on the way back to Belfast, in which case hopefully his phone had been totalled too erasing her messages; or the last and *definitely* worst option in her book, he'd encountered the local cops *after* they'd spoken and his phone was now in *their* clammy, oversized hands.

She thanked her lucky stars that she'd had the wit to only call him from her pay-as-you-go mobile and untraceable work extension, and then laughed, chiding herself for being ridiculous. The police wouldn't be interested enough in boring old Arthur to hold him for hours, even if the girl Reynolds *had* opened her over-painted mouth. Although... they might be on edge with *all* strangers; the discovery of a dead man just outside such a hick village couldn't be an every day event.

Whatever had happened she couldn't bear not knowing, so she reached swiftly for her burn mobile and then suddenly stopped her handing mid-air, dropping it to her desk phone instead. Her office extension would be safer this time. Calls from the bank's several hundred internal extensions were impossible to trackback because everything was routed through a switchboard in Belfast.

It wasn't Arthur that she was calling this time but the police enquiry number so she adopted her politest tone, altering it to tooth-achingly sweet when the call was transferred to Rownton Station and she heard it being answered by a man.

"Good afternoon, Rownton Police. Sergeant O'Hare."

"Oh, good afternoon, Officer, I wonder if you could help me?"

Mickey O'Hare twitched to attention, but only in small part because of his caller's seductive voice. He was intrigued that not only wasn't the woman's accent local but it was so polite that she sounded like an Irish version of the Queen.

"Yes, Madam. In what way?"

Cue tremulous, anxious tone.

"Well, my elderly uncle was visiting your area earlier and can't seem to get in touch with him. I'm a little worried. He tends to get lost and become easily confused, bless him."

Bless him? Talk about overkill.

Even if O'Hare hadn't been on alert already that would have made him straighten up.

"Name?"

Róisín thought fast, failing to register that the policeman's tone seemed less sympathetic than she'd have expected with a caring niece.

"Arthur Norris."

Even though the sergeant had been expecting to hear the name he still gave a startled twitch. The woman was lying, not about looking for Norris but about her reason for the same. Whatever her motive *really* was, O'Hare's spidey sense said that it wasn't good.

Mickey O'Hare knew that because he was a good copper, one that was only still a sergeant at forty-five because like many of his peers he had stayed at that rank to suit his way of life. Promotion to inspector would have taken him away from Rownton, the village too small to warrant more than a sergeant's presence, and *that* would have taken away his comfortable, know everyone and their kids and grandkids personally, friendly with the locals and home at five on the dot way of life.

But just because O'Hare hadn't *wanted* rank and wasn't au fait with every whizzy new investigation technique didn't mean that he wasn't *very* good at his job, and every police inch of him was tingling now.

He asked a holding question while his brain raced ahead.

"And *your* name, Madam?"

There was no hesitation in Róisín's reply of, "Jessica Thwaite," but O'Hare took that as a sign of the woman's preparedness to lie rather than of anything good.

He was right. Jessica Thwaite was the alias that Róisín *always* employed when she lied, whatever her motive. Right now it was to obtain information about Arthur in any way that she could.

O'Hare was steps ahead, deciding exactly how much she would get from him and how to avoid landing the hapless Norris in the shit when she did. He didn't know Arthur Norris personally and from their brief acquaintance he'd thought the man was an eejit, but compared to this woman Norris was a minnow and as a general rule he preferred to focus his energy on the sharks of this world.

So the sergeant did what all good public servants did when faced with any difficulty, he obfuscated; he'd done it so often in his career that he practically had a degree.

"Norris you say... Norris...Norris..." He set the phone close to his custody ledger and rifled noisily through its pages before speaking again. "No, no, I can't see that name here, Madam, but if he's likely to have got lost then perhaps he's ended up at one of the other local stations instead? I can have a ring around and call you back."

Damn.

Róisín *knew* that Arthur had reached Rownton because they'd spoken after he'd arrived, so either he hadn't come in contact with the police at all or this village plod wasn't as stupid as she'd thought and he was calling her bluff.

She thought fast and decided to play her story through.

"Oh, that would be wonderful. Thank you, Officer. You have my name already, but my number is zero zero three five three one..." A completely fictitious number followed, which like all fictions gives away more than the storyteller thinks it has.

When the call ended Mickey O'Hare tried the number immediately, and then made second call to Aidan, who was staring out the car window at the passing countryside thinking, while Ryan drove his precious BMW to Belfast from Armagh.

"D.C.I. Hughes."

"Hello, sir, it's Sergeant O' Hare here. Can you talk? It concerns Arthur Norris, so you might want to move away from him first."

"Give me a minute." Aidan covered the handset quickly. "Pull over. I need to take this."

His glance at the man in the back seat removed the need for Ryan's looming question, and a moment later they were parked on the hard shoulder with their blue lights flashing, which had an unintentional but beneficial slowing effect on all the passing motorists who were driving too fast.

Aidan clambered out of the car and walked several metres ahead before he spoke again.

"OK, fire ahead."

"Aye, OK, so I've just had a call from a woman asking about Arthur Norris' whereabouts. She said she was his niece and gave the name of Jessica Thwaite."

"You sound like you didn't believe her."

"I didn't. Something about her was wrong. She had an Irish accent that was so posh she sounded like royalty, and she said Norris tended to get lost and confused, which I saw no sign of at all, did you?"

"Quiet but not confused."

"Right, so she was definitely trying to make him sound like some stray sheep that she was worried about, but I sensed something else. Something that made me worried for the man. Anyway, I made a bit of a show of checking for his name and then said that I hadn't encountered him but would ask around the nearby nicks and call her back. But I've just tried the contact number she gave me and it's fake, or at least it won't connect for me anyway, so maybe your lads could check it and her name? It was a southern mobile."

"They'll trace her call to you too if they can. Good work, Sergeant. Right, I obviously can't speak with Norris in the car so if I give you a number to call now, could you ask for Davy Walsh and tell him what you've just told me?"

"Surely. So I should give *him* her name and the number she gave me?"

"And the exact time of her call to your station. All calls are routed through the police switchboard now so they *should* be able to locate where she phoned from. Hopefully we'll find her with all that."

As Aidan ended the call and climbed back into the car, he found himself wondering whether Arthur Norris was someone more to be pitied than blamed.

****

Belfast. 4.50p.m.

As it happened, Craig was saved from returning to 'burial by paperwork' in his office by an instant message on his phone, an innovation introduced just weeks before by the Chief Constable to do away with the unnecessarily long phone calls it often took to inform someone of a simple fact such as lab results being ready or an arrest having been made. His message was more cryptic and informed him that he had a 'delivery at High Street' that he knew could *only* be his prisoner from Armagh.

He signalled Liam to divert to the station, expecting to be shown one prisoner when he entered but instead finding Jack Harris bent over his custody desk muttering about, "Being dumped with two."

Craig greeted the disgruntled sergeant cheerfully. "Hello, Jack. I'm here to see my delivery."

When the sergeant lifted his eyes far too slowly from his registration book both detectives knew that he wasn't amused.

"I was told there'd only be *one* prisoner."

"There is. Ben Frampton from Mahon Prison."

"No, there isn't, there are two! Some bloke called Arthur Norris has just been brought in by your lot as well, and it would have been *polite* if someone had let me know. I've rooms to clean and meals to sort out you know."

He sounded like a boarding house landlady; all that was missing was a lament about his 'housewife's hands'.

But the detectives were genuinely confused about the second guest so Liam took a peek at the sergeant's book.

"Who's the heck's Arthur Norris?"

Jack sniffed as he replied. "I'm damned if I know. Ask your boy Aidan, he brought him in from some place called Rownton."

The penny dropped on the others at once.

"Hughesy's found something for us, boss."

"Norris must be the man who paid the girl to lie. Aidan mentioned something about him when he called earlier."

Craig turned back to the custody sergeant. "What time did the prisoners arrive, Jack?"

"About ten minutes ago. I'm just booking them in."

"Are Aidan and Ryan still here?"

A jerked thumb indicated the staff-room, so they'd showed themselves through to the back where the other two detectives were finally getting to eat their sandwiches in peace. A peace that was shattered by Liam storming in.

"Hello, hello, hello, what's all this slacking then?"

As Ryan went to retort Craig shook his head. "Ignore

him, he's just winding you up. Stick the kettle on, Liam. Mine's a black coffee."

He stared at his D.S. curiously. "Who gave you the shiner, Ryan?"

The answer came in an embarrassed mutter, "Rio Rey-" that was cut off by Liam's guffaw.

"*A girl!* You got a black eye from a *girl*?"

"Yeh, well, she was a real wildcat!"

Aidan's quick snort of derision was a betrayal worthy of Brutus, but Craig decided to prevent what looked like it was about to be a noisy exchange by taking the seat opposite the D.C.I.

"Right, Aidan. This Arthur Norris. He's the man who paid the Reynolds girl to lie?"

Aidan could only nod, his mouth now full of tuna and onion, so Ryan gave the answer.

"Norris turned up at the local solicitor stroke newspaper editor's office while we were there seeing him, chief, and we worked it out from there. I interviewed Norris and he wasn't giving anything away, but he was definitely trying to conceal his mobile so it's at the lab now and we decided to bring him in."

Aidan gulped down his mouthful of food and added, "Some woman called Rownton's nick after we'd left, looking for Norris, but the sergeant there didn't like the sound of her so we're following up on that too. Davy's working on everything now."

Craig took the coffee his deputy was holding out and nodded. "Good work, both of you. We'll see what Davy has on all that at the briefing. What's your general sense of things?"

Aidan motioned Ryan to answer and took another bite of his doorstep sandwich.

"I think Norris is a gofer or fixer of some sort, chief-"

Aidan interrupted with a full mouth, making Craig wince and Liam feel hungry.

"McDonagh said he's a land agent, Guv. He knows Norris from negotiating the quarry purchase."

Craig raised an eyebrow at the links that were developing and waved his sergeant to pick things up.

"Norris is low level, chief. I'm pretty sure someone *ordered* him to get the Reynolds girl to lie and now they want to make sure that he's keeping quiet about it. It'll either be the woman who phoned the station or someone *she's* working for, and the way Norris was hiding his phone I think it might give us something good."

"Excellent. OK, you two keep on that, but let's see what everyone else has before we plan our next steps. Right. Change of topic. Did Ben Frampton give you any trouble?"

Aidan shook his shock of blond hair. "Good as gold, although the Governor looked like his nose was out of joint."

Liam guffawed. "That'll be 'cos he was *ordered* to send Frampton up. Doesn't like being told what to do, like the rest of us."

Craig rose and turned for the door. "Right, we'll leave you to finish your food in peace and see you back at the office. Liam, bring your drink and let's go see what Mister Frampton has to say."

On first encounter Ben Frampton didn't appear to want to say anything except, "Bastard cops!" and "I missed my five-a-side match today because of you!"

Without meaning to the burglar had given Craig an idea.

"Put our guest back in his cell, please, Liam. I need to make a call."

He headed out the station's rear exit to the car park, and ten minutes and another fractious conversation with George Royston later the prison governor had agreed to send through Frampton's activity schedule by the next morning, and Craig had grovelled to Jack and persuaded him to keep at least one of his prisoners overnight.

The length of his other prisoner's stopover would depend on what Arthur Norris had to say, but finding that out would have to wait until after the briefing; so Craig gathered his troops, told the custody sergeant that Aidan and Ryan would return around eight o'clock, and cheekily requested that he should have the kettle on the boil.

****

The Forensic Department. 5.20 p.m.

Lead crime scene investigator Grace Adeyemi was working alone on the third floor of the pathology building but she wasn't doing so in silence; the background musak of beeping chemical analysers and whirring centrifuges was counterpointed by the constant electrical hum and throb of the sprawling lab's neon lights and its sleeping but never shut down PCs.

The cacophony always got on the CSI's nerves, so as soon as the last person waved her good-night and pulled the department's heavy glass door closed behind them, Grace added a soundtrack of her own; a mix-tape of the gospel music that she sang at church every Sunday interspersed with a selection of Billie Holiday and Aretha Franklin tracks that she was trying to learn for her occasional singing gigs, the next of which was the following night at The James Bar in Pilot Street, a place of drink and therefore sin, yes, but as long as she didn't drink alcohol she could manage to reconcile herself with that. After all, she reasoned, who had given her a love of all kinds of music but God?

The reason that Grace was alone in the lab that evening was twofold: there was an urgent job to be carried out on some prisoner's phone, and her boss, Doctor Marsham, who would usually have done it, not being the sort to ask his staff to work late if he wasn't willing to do so himself, had had somewhere else important to be. Where he hadn't said, and she hadn't asked because it had suited her anyway; her singing voice was strong and the cavernous lab offered her the perfect rehearsal space without any fear of incurring her neighbours' wrath.

But that was an aside, and in front of Grace lay the evening's *main* business; a smart-phone that unexciting as it appeared apparently held something of value to the police. Gloved and masked the senior CSI unsealed the evidence bag and slid the phone onto the sterile sheet spread out on her workbench, spending the next ten minutes meticulously printing every inch of its exterior before pressing its on-switch and waiting to see what appeared.

The screen-saver was as unexciting as the phone itself; just the standard manufacturer's logo. But that in itself told her something about the phone's owner so Grace made a note: 'Owner appears to view phone as a utility not a fashion accessory. Older?'

She scrolled through the memory for any photographs

and found only three: a dog, a car, and a mountain. Either the person who owned the phone, she read the evidence label and discovered that he was called Arthur Norris, had no family, or he was so private that he didn't want a casual viewer to know that he had. It gave her something to think about, or rather for the Murder Squad to. *Was* Norris all alone in the world like her? Were the pictures just stock images? And most importantly, if they weren't and Norris was being held for questioning who was going to feed his dog?

Just as the CSI was picturing the lonely animal she was startled by a loud beep; a text from the phone's voice mailbox. She dialled it and listened to the messages, all fifteen of them, all from the same youngish woman becoming increasingly irate at not being called back. Every word was noted down before Grace turned to the phone's contact list, expecting to find at least the numbers of a vet and mechanic there based on the pics, but there was only a single phone number saved, a Republic of Ireland mobile, the same number she'd picked up from the messages, and it was registered as the oddly named 'S.W.M.B.O.'.

It left the forensic lead with only three routine tasks: to perform a data dump, including all websites accessed; to make a list of any recent calls; and to send a request to the network provider for all exchanges that had taken place on the phone in the previous six months.

She was just about to call the C.C.U. with the information already gathered as per her boss' instructions, when the smart-phone buzzed to life again, the ID on its screen saying that 'S.W.M.B.O.' was calling.

Thankfully Grace was a quick thinker, so before she picked up she killed her music and set the mobile to record. Then she hit 'answer' and was just considering saying, "Hello" when 'S.W.M.B.O.' aka Róisín Casey screamed down the line.

"ARTHUR! WHERE THE FUCK HAVE YOU BEEN? I've been calling you all sodding day! There was nothing in the paper and that stupid bimbo didn't go on the radio, so you must have been..."

The words tailed off as the banker suddenly realised that she hadn't heard Norris' usual defensive spluttering coming down the line. Both women held their silence for a moment and then Róisín spoke again.

"Arthur?"

Grace didn't utter a word, hoping that the caller would give more away. Róisín's sharp gasp of realisation, spitting out of, *"Cops!"* and immediate hang-up did. No-one innocent would jump so quickly to the police as an option, not unless they followed the word up with an anxious query about what had happened to their friend. The woman who'd just rung was up to something, and wondering what that was revived a dormant Nancy Drew streak in the CSI that made her want to find out more herself before she passed things on to the police.

After checking that the call had been properly recorded Grace decided to phone the number back, but it dialled out. No answer and no answerphone, so either 'S.W.M.B.O.' had never set one up or she'd just disabled it in case her personal message gave something away.

A call to the network provider made the CSI's heart sink. She'd been right that the number belonged to a Republic of Ireland mobile, but it was unregistered and pay-as-you-go so she couldn't get a name. Although the provider's promise to give up whatever data they could from it as long as they received a warrant meant that perhaps not everything was lost.

It was as far as she was going to get without involving the police, so Grace made a note to recheck everything again in the morning when she was fresher, called the Murder Squad with what she had and then started rehearsing her show for Friday night.

****

The C.C.U. 6 p.m.

"OK, contrary to common belief this briefing *is* actually going to be brief because we're at the point where a lot of things are still up in the air."

Craig ignored the immediate sceptical snorts and adjusted his chair's position, giving Aidan a chance to jump in, gesturing at a coffee drinking Ryan as he did.

"Plus *we* still have a prisoner to interview before we go home tonight."

Craig surprised him with a shake of his head. "I've been thinking about that. Let Norris stew overnight and interview him tomorrow instead. A hard bed and some of Jack's burnt toast for breakfast might just focus his mind."

He acknowledged the grins of gratitude and moved across to the white-board.

"Right, let's tidy things up a bit."

He wrote 'Stuart Kincaid' up on the board.

"We have a dead businessman called Stuart Kincaid, forty-three, who left his Portaferry home in-" A glance towards Andy and "March" came back.

"Left home in March twenty-eighteen, a home where he lived with his wife and two teenage sons."

Another glance and Andy filled in their names and added his opinion that the marriage had been happy.

"OK, good. So, Andy, tell us about the period between Kincaid's disappearance and being found dead, from his family's perspective."

The D.C.I. gave a tight shrug. "He'd been very down since the death of his twin sister, Nicola, and went away, as far as his wife knew, to mourn. At the beginning he called home every week, then less frequently because it was upsetting their sons to speak to him but not be able to see him. The calls became sporadic. The final one was on the twenty-ninth of October but since July there'd only been one other, so they'd been sparse for months."

Craig nodded. "Which is why the alarm wasn't raised about his disappearance."

"Yep. His wife genuinely had no idea that he was dead. She was also adamant that he only had Bella's photo innocently-"

"Because he was searching for her?"

"Not that *she* was aware, although she didn't rule it out. But more because he missed his sister and the girl so much."

Liam had been sitting motionless, resting back in his chair with his feet up on another, but now he came noisily to life, thudding them to the floor. "Now you see, that there's what I don't get."

Craig waved him on.

"If Kincaid was so cut up about his sister then why not carry a photo of *her*? As well as the girl's maybe? Or even one of the two of them together?"

It was a good point and one that Andy thought he might have answers to. "In the clearer photo you got from Edgar Westbury, you can definitely see Nicola in the shadows behind the girl."

Liam was unconvinced.

"Aye, well, it's no substitute for close-up, is it?"

"Ah, yes, but we don't know where Kincaid was *staying*. He might have kept a whole load of photos of his sister in his room."

When Liam couldn't think of a comeback Craig picked up the point by turning to his lead analyst, who he knew would already be several steps ahead. Davy didn't disappoint, just itching to display the slides he'd made on the LED screen by Alice's desk.

A yellow and blue PowerPoint slide so luminous that it hurt Craig's eyes appeared, and his wince saw it being dimmed to a tolerable level as soon as the analyst was alongside.

"OK, s...so. Basic facts on Stuart Kincaid. His business was and is doing well, even with a caretaker manager in charge, and he stayed in a series of four and five star hotels in the months after he left home." He tapped his smart-pad and a map of Ireland appeared. "I've managed to track some of his movements over those months using credit-card payments to petrol stations, restaurants and hotels."

A series of numbers appeared all over the island, showing Stuart Kincaid's transit from his home in Portaferry, number one, to his final stop in Rownton, number twenty-five. The positioning of the rest of the numbers made it clear that his journey had been far from straight.

Ryan pointed at number twenty-four, in Omagh. "There's the afternoon tea at the Silverbirch. He took the post-mistress shortly before he was killed."

Davy nodded. "You can see he meandered *a lot*, around the north, s...south as far as Cork, east and west-"

"Searching for leads."

"Probably, chief. Anyway, the last place Kincaid *stayed*, checking in on the thirty-first of October for five days, was a country house hotel in County Tyrone. I've been in touch with them and the management have confirmed that they held his room for a few days after the booking expired and then packed up his things and put them in storage. They're still there now."

Craig walked across to the screen to join him, "Excellent."

He scanned the group like the fickle finger of fate and landed on Andy and his companion for the day.

"Right, you two get down to the hotel tomorrow and go through Kincaid's stuff. Bring back anything interesting. See what the staff there have to say, and drop in on the diving team Liam organised while you're local, to see how they're getting on."

He turned back to his analyst. "Who paid the hotel bill, Davy?" already telling himself not to get his hopes up of the analyst's answer yielding a clue. Kincaid's killer would've had to have been *very* stupid to go and pay the bill himself.

Davy shook his head apologetically. "S...Sorry, chief. Kincaid had preauthorised his credit card for extras so the hotel just took the outstanding bill off that."

As Craig nodded pragmatically and returned to his seat, the analyst added more hopefully, "But I *did* manage to trace his phone." Another slide appeared. "Kincaid's final call was made at ten-twenty-two p.m. on the second of November to his bank; at that time of night it must have been to check his accounts, but I'll ask. After that noth-"

Liam cut him off. "By nothing you mean no activity?"

"No, s...sorry, I meant no *outgoing* calls. The phone was still receiving calls for another twenty-four hours and there w...were two from his firm. I checked and they'd left messages. The phone provider pulled them for me and it was just Kincaid's manager with updates about work."

"Kincaid was still keeping an eye on his business from a distance, boss."

"Looks like it."

"Anyway, the phone died on the fourth of November and the provider gives its last location as smack in the middle of the reception cell that covers the quarry."

Craig sighed. "Kincaid's killer must have thrown it in the water and its battery took time to die. That means his wallet and watch could be down there too."

Liam wasn't so sure. "Maybe not, boss. Remember we

speculated the killer might have taken the watch. Probably did if it was expensive."

"Was it, Davy? Expensive?"

"Yep. Luisa Kincaid sent me this." Another tap and a photograph of a stainless steel Patek Philippe appeared. "Fifty grand's worth."

Liam nodded smugly. "You see. They wouldn't have chucked *that* away."

"Maybe not. There's one way to find out."

He glanced around, intending to give a refined search order for the divers to Annette, and felt his heart sink when he realised again that she wasn't there.

"OK, Liam, get on to the diving team and tell them to look for the watch and phone specifically. Davy, check with Luisa Kincaid and see what else her husband was likely to have been carrying, then send the dive commander the list."

He turned back to the whiteboard and wrote up the name 'Rio Reynolds' to quite a few surprised looks.

Mary was the first to ask.

"Who or what is Rio Reynolds?"

Liam tutted loudly. "Have some respect, Constable. For all you know you could be speaking about the future mother of my child."

It sparked a series of "Seriously?"s, some with X-rated additions, but Craig took his point.

"Liam's point, Mary, valid if not very elegantly put, is not to judge people by their names."

"Well, she sounds like a stripper to me."

"Make-up artiste actually," retorted Ryan in a pompous voice, then he added, "But she *was* prepared to take money to say she'd had an affair with someone when she hadn't, so she's not the nicest person I've ever met."

Mary wasn't appeased. "As opposed to actually *having* the affair, which would have been *so* much more upstanding of course."

In an attempt to move things on before she had a complete meltdown Craig wrote up 'Derek Morrow' and tapped it with his marker, but he was interrupted yet again, this time by his deputy.

"Rio means river, doesn't it, boss?"

"Yes. Or it's a-"

The D.C.I. cut him off. "So what's this fad for calling your kids after nature?"

The question made Craig smile because he'd had a similar conversation with his mother the night before, accompanied by a lecture about Katy and him not burdening their child with a whimsical moniker, in case they'd even been considering such a thing. Considering that *she'd* named her own pair Marco and Lucia in twentieth century Belfast, she was hardly in a position to throw stones.

Liam hadn't finished.

"And I mean it's always the *nice* bits of nature, isn't it? Like Sky or Rainbow."

Ryan's curiosity made him ask the question that everyone else knew the D.C.I. had been angling to have asked all along.

"As opposed to?"

Craig groaned at the open goal.

"*Weeds*. How does Weeds Reynolds sound? Or how about Manure Reynolds, or Dung Beetle Reynolds, or-"

Craig cut him off. "Yes, thanks for that, Liam. Just what we needed. Twenty-five different ways to say crap."

It brought a sigh and a tut from Alice that made Craig roll his eyes.

"*He* says it twice and there's nothing, but I say it *once* and I get tutted straight away!"

His plea for justice fell on deaf ears because people were laughing so much, so he moved things along.

"Right, that's enough nature for now." He tapped the board again. "Derek Morrow, a construction manager in Rownton, committed suicide hours after we found Stuart Kincaid dead." He held out the marker to Aidan. "Explain the links."

The D.C.I. gave a loud yawn that reflected the busy twenty-four hours he'd had and began.

"OK, well... here's a quick summary. When Stuart Kincaid's body was found, Derek Morrow, who was involved in the excavation of the quarry years back and still held the contract for its maintenance, ran into the local pub in a panic according to its landlord. He was particularly agitated about all the police around the place. Now, that *could* have been because he was afraid of being accused over something to do with his work at the quarry, or it could have been something else."

He leaned back against a desk and folded his arms. "Because only hours later Morrow tops himself, citing work stress in his suicide note, which his wife and family didn't think was a thing and seems unlikely from everything we've heard."

He gestured at John, who throughout the briefing had been doodling quietly on a pad.

"The Doc here said Morrow's post-mortem showed a straightforward shot from a gun that he held legally. He was a member of a gun club."

The words prompted a nod from the pathologist and a disgusted snort from Andy that matched Liam's earlier reaction.

"Back yard warriors we used to call them. Of course the guns are just a substitute for having a small-"

He halted abruptly, remembering that he was in mixed company, but Mary was quite happy to fill in the missing word.

"Dick. Is that what you were going to say?"

Alice palmed her face with both hands.

"It's what I was trying *not* to!"

Craig didn't have the energy to chastise them so he just rolled his eyes and turned back to Aidan. "OK, so Morrow's death was a suicide. Carry on."

"Yes, well, he left two letters for his wife. One was his Will, his bank details and funeral stuff, and the other said he'd killed himself because of work stress, which was nonsense, and we confirmed that when we spoke to his deputy Jimmy-"

Liam interrupted with a smirk. "But the *mention* of work might have been a pointer towards the quarry, given that Morrow had managed the place and Kincaid's body being found there had panicked him."

Ryan jumped in. "That's what we thought, especially with the whole Rio cover up trying to imply that Morrow had killed himself because of an affair. First of all, the custody sergeant in Rownton knew the Morrows and said their marriage was solid so an affair was unlikely, and secondly, why offer the girl money to lie *at all*, unless you're trying to divert attention away from some *other* cause for Morrow's suicide?"

Craig nodded. "Agreed." He glanced from the sergeant to Aidan. "One of you tell me more about Rio Reynolds and Arthur Norris."

Aidan passed the marker to the D.S. and retook his seat, leaving Ryan tapping a finger eagerly on the board.

"OK, Rio Reynolds is a twenty-five-year-old beautician at McGran's department store in town and she was approached yesterday afternoon by an elderly man who offered her a grand to give two interviews, to the Rownton Recorder and the local radio. She was to say that she'd had an affair with Derek Morrow and ended it just the day before his death, the implication being that he'd killed himself for love. She got five hundred up front and will never get the second five now."

He scribbled up 'Arthur Norris'.

"This is the name of the man who paid Rio Reynolds to lie. Norris was encountered by us in the offices of the Rownton newspaper editor and later ID-ed by Ms Reynolds outside the nick. Norris was obviously on his way to the editor to complain about the interview not going into print. He refused to talk to us so he's at High Street now waiting to be re-interviewed."

He wrote up 'Jessica Thwaite'.

"Then, while we were driving back up, a woman calling herself by this name phoned Rownton nick *looking* for Norris. She left a fake southern contact number, but we're following her up-"

Davy held up his smart-pad. "I've got something on that."

Another slide appeared on the screen.

"OK, long st...story short. Grace was examining Arthur Norris' phone about an hour ago and she found some answerphone messages and a number saved under something called S.W.M.B.O."

Craig and Liam smiled simultaneously.

"You know what it means, chief?"

"It's an acronym for 'she who must be obeyed' which tells us a lot about Norris' view of their relationship."

Ryan nodded. "Some woman was yelling at Norris on the phone in the editor's office too. It has to have been her."

Davy nodded. "That makes sense, because while Grace was w...working on the phone it rang and the acronym appeared. This is the number behind it."

A series of digits appeared on the screen.

"It's an Irish mobile number but not the fake one that the woman called Jessica Thwaite gave. Unfortunately it's a pay-as-you-go number, although we'll dig into Norris' phone and see if something else connects. Grace is doing a data dump and some other checks now." He turned to Aidan. "While I'm on phones. Is there any chance Derek Morrow's family will give permission to check his phones and computers?"

The D.C.I. thought for a moment and then gave a nod. "I don't see why not. I'm sure they'd like real answers as to why he killed himself."

Craig sounded a warning note. "They might not like what we find, Aidan, so get them to sign a waiver." He exchanged a wary look with his deputy as the analyst went on.

"Grace said that when the phone rang she answered it but said nothing, and a w...woman on the other end, the same voice that had left the messages, started ranting."

"About?"

"Arthur Norris." He read from his smart-pad. "Her exact words were, 'ARTHUR! WHERE THE FUCK HAVE YOU BEEN? I've been calling you all sodding day! There was nothing in the paper and that stupid bimbo didn't go on the radio, so you must have been...' That's when she stopped talking. Grace still said nothing and after a few s...secs the woman gasped, said, 'Cops!' and cut the call. I have it all on tape if anyone fancies a listen."

Liam gave a slow whistle.

"Bloody Hell. Old Arthur's working for one angry lady, and she'd obviously ordered him to Rownton to find out why the girl hadn't done her job. When S.W.M.B.O. couldn't get hold of him, because *we* had him, she left messages and then tried Rownton nick calling herself Jessica Thwaite. That 'Cops' and hanging up means she was definitely up to no good, boss."

Craig nodded. "Agreed. Anyone who was really concerned about a missing friend would have stayed on to ask how he was. OK," he retrieved his marker, "that leaves us with, who is this woman and what *sort* of no good is she up to? What's Arthur Norris' role in everything, and what if any are the links between this woman, Norris, Derek Morrow and Stuart Kincaid's death?"

As he was scribbling the points on the board something suddenly occurred to him and he turned back urgently to Aidan.

"Tell me again what was in Morrow's envelopes."

"Suicide note, bank account details, copy of his Will and stuff about his funeral."

"No insurance details?"

"Well, the wife probably has the house stuff and-"

Liam's jaw dropped as he realised that Craig was on to something.

"Not house insurance, *life* insurance. Didn't Morrow leave anything about that? It's one of the first bits of info I'd leave for *my* widow."

Aidan looked confused. "No. Well, I mean, it wasn't mentioned."

Craig turned to his lead analyst. "Davy, I need to know *exactly* what was in those letters and the contents of Morrow's bank accounts too. If he *didn't* leave details of his life insurance policy it may be because he didn't have one..."

Liam finished the thought. "Because there's no point having life insurance when suicide never pays out. Morrow must always have known he might need a quick exit, boss."

Craig nodded dolefully. "But actually *planning* for suicide, Liam, that's desperation... What sort of trouble had this man got himself in?"

The question would remain rhetorical until they had more information, so when after a moment Craig noticed his D.S. eager to speak he waved him on.

"Blaine Westbury, chief."

Craig added the name to the board. "Go on."

"Well, we'd only got general stuff on him, like he'd never collected his inheritance and he was a bad lad, until we interviewed Biddy Evans, the ex-post-mistress. *She* confirmed that she'd met Stuart Kincaid *twice* and on both occasions he was alone. Once in twenty-sixteen when he showed her a picture of Bella and asked about her but Mrs Evans said she hadn't seen the girl, and again last winter when Kincaid came to the village and dropped in just to say hello. They talked about the quarry and the Westburys too and Kincaid took her for afternoon tea at hotel in Omagh."

"Sounds like a nice man." Craig finished scribbling note beside Westbury's name and turned around. "So what did Mrs Evans say about Blaine Westbury?"

"Well, she didn't like him, that's for sure. Said Edgar was nice but Blaine had been a bad lot since he was a kid. But when we asked when she'd last seen him, expecting her to say at the parents' funeral in twenty-fifteen, she said she'd seen him in the fields behind her house one morning last winter. In November, so that fits with when Kincaid's phone died and the time the Doc here said he must have died."

Craig's eyes widened. *Had they found the name of Stuart Kincaid's murderer? Blaine Westbury?*

His tone became intense. "Details, Ryan."

"OK, well, Mrs Evans said she saw Blaine running across the fields behind her house towards the village one morning in November, and the direction he was coming from was where the quarry is. It's just behind the hills at the end of those fields. She said Blaine was wearing normal clothes, a shirt and jeans, so he wasn't out jogging or anything and she didn't see him again him after that. No-one else seems to have known that he was there. We showed his photo to everyone we spoke to and there was nothing."

He pulled a face.

"What's the problem?"

"Well, apparently Mrs Evans has slight dementia, chief, so I'm not sure how she'd stand up as a witness. But honestly she was as sharp as a tack when we talked to her, so if she says that she saw Blaine I'd say she definitely did."

A quick nod from Aidan to say that he concurred and Craig wrote the information up on the board, then he sketched an impromptu Westbury/Kincaid family tree alongside that he knew Davy would soon turn into a slide.

"OK. Let's dig deeper on Blaine Westbury tomorrow. I'll need everything about him, bank accounts, travel, down to his height and build. To have drowned Stuart Kincaid he must have been stronger and taller than him."

He glanced at the clock. It was ten-past-seven and the mothers were arriving at the apartment at nine. Just enough time to finish the reports and have his promised pint with John, before heading home to two hours of property hell.

He turned to his analysts to find them conferring over something on Ash's smart-pad. It looked too important to break up, but there was a beer calling his name so he moved on to his best friend.

"John. Anything from you or Des?"

The pathologist had spotted Craig's covert look at the clock and was hearing the siren call of alcohol as well, so he inhaled deeply and summarised in one breath.

"Stuart Kincaid was drowned by force from behind by a tall, strong man gripping his shoulders and pushing him beneath the water, and his stomach contents and blood analysis were normal, and Derek Morrow blew off his own head with a long barrelled revolver."

The sentence ended in a gasp and a round of applause from Liam, who also decided to use the report as an example of how it should be done.

"OK now, the rest of you, listen and learn. That, right there, is the way to deliver information. Straight to the point and short. None of your meandering 'I asked the prisoner and then he said to me' shit, and no interruptions for jokes. OK? Short and sweet in future."

Since *he* was easily the most divertible member of the team Craig was hoping that he'd at least have the decency to laugh, but the D.C.I.'s deadpan expression said that personal insight wasn't his thing so it was left to his boss to point out the facts.

"This from the man who makes War and Peace seem short!"

"I do not!"

Craig just rolled his eyes, said, "Thanks for that, John" and turned to his still conferring analysts.

"Is there anything that either of you would like to share with us? Pithily for Liam's sake, of course."

Ash jumped to his feet and commandeered the screen, exchanging Davy's blue and yellow slides for his waterfall themed own.

"So...I told the chief some of this earlier, but there's

more now on Bella Westbury. I searched using age, colouring and the rest, and narrowed it to fifteen children travelling from any of our designated departure points in the days after her abduction in twenty-fifteen, and I'm working on pulling all of the passports they travelled on-"

Craig cut in. "Any joy yet from the embassies and airlines?"

"Yep. I got hold of seven of the passport photos and eliminated them. Not Bella. Like I said earlier I'm having a bit of an issue with the Russian and Venezuelan travellers but Davy's got onto all the intelligence agencies so we're waiting for them to get back."

Remembering something, Craig turned to his deputy. "Liam, remind me we need to see Ray Barrett in the morning."

"We need to see Ray Barrett in the morning."

It earned him a roll of the eyes. "I meant remind me tomorrow, but you knew that already."

The response was a winsome smile.

"Continue, Ash."

The analyst displayed an image of the back of a child's left hand, the significance of which no-one but Craig and Liam understood.

"OK, I won't bore you with how we got here but Bella Westbury had a daisy shaped scar on the back of her left hand from Henna gone wrong. It was never listed on her or her parents' passports because they hadn't flown since she'd acquired it, and it wasn't used by the gendarmes in their searches-"

Craig's jaw dropped as something occurred to him, and he gasped out, *"Thank God."*

His deputy's eyebrows shot up. "Was that you getting religion, boss, or is it something to do with the case?"

"The second. I've just realised that the *abductor* would have had no knowledge of the girl's scar before they took her unless they'd got *very* close indeed, and if it was never advertised by the police or the media as a recognition feature they're unlikely to have bothered removing it since."

"Which means?"

"I'm not sure yet, I'll come back to you on that. Sorry, go on, Ash."

Just as the analyst opened his mouth to speak again Andy jumped in, making Ash roll his eyes.

"Sorry, but..."

Craig waited expectantly to hear what came next, but it seemed to be being inhibited by a sudden attack of doubt.

"Whatever you were going to say will be fine, Andy, just as long as it's said in the next thirty seconds."

The D.C.I. glanced awkwardly around the group. "Well... it's just that it sounds like we're officially investigating two cases now instead of one." He added hastily. "Which is fine of course, just as long as we know."

"You mean we're searching for Bella Westbury now as well as Stuart Kincaid's killer."

Andy gave a sheepish smile. "Well, yes."

Craig scanned the group. "What does everyone else think? Are we?"

"Yes" and, "Pretty much" came back.

"And is that OK with people?"

This time there was a unified nod. Just as well, because he'd known they'd been investigating the girl's disappearance in parallel for days without admitting it out loud.

"Thanks for clarifying that, Andy. Now, Ash, what were you going to say?"

The analyst had taken advantage of the interruption to perch on a nearby desk, so he continued talking from there.

"OK, so, the daisy also wasn't listed on *any* of the fifteen passports under distinguishing marks, but like the chief just said, if whoever took her hadn't known about it *before* they took her they might have found out too late to have it noted down. So I decided to call my mate Quattro-"

Liam howled with laughter. "His parents named him after a car?"

Ash rolled his eyes, annoyed at the interruption. "It's his nickname, not his real name."

Craig interceded, trying to be helpful. "It means four in Italian, Liam."

But his support just gave the analyst the back-up he needed to push things even more.

"Yeh, 'cos *that's* when he first got called it, Dumbo."

Davy eyes widened at the insult and he jumped in

hastily, trying to prevent a fight. "They're making a new movie version of that, you know. With Colin Farrell."

But Liam was seriously unimpressed by the moniker he'd just been given and glared at the junior analyst. "That's D.C.I. Dumbo to you, you little squit."

Craig wondered whether Liam realised what he'd just said, but Ash wasn't about to hang around till he did so he moved things along.

"So anyway...Quattro works in IT for the central aviation authority and he's really connected, so I asked him what happens if an airport security guard notices a distinguishing mark on someone that hasn't been noted on their passport. Long story short he said that as long as the face matched and the person had got the mark *after* the passport was issued, then they'd just note it down on a separate register and it would be added by the host country when the passport was next being renewed."

Craig tensed at the possible implications and motioned the analyst to pause. "Comments anyone?"

Liam got in first. "That means the bastards had a passport already waiting *before* they took her."

Aidan chipped in. "It mightn't have been one specific to the Westbury girl, just a proforma waiting to be filled in."

"No, because then they'd still have had time to put in the daisy under distinguishing marks."

Craig waved them down. "There's something more here than that. Anyone?"

When nothing came he answered his question himself.

"The kidnappers missed Bella's scar off the passport, so they obviously didn't know about it. But they *must* have been watching her constantly to snatch her in the tight one minute timeframe that she was left alone so why *didn't* they know about it? That tells me her passport must have been prepared so far in advance it was before she'd even *acquired* the scar."

Seeing nothing but blank looks he turned to his deputy. "Liam, when did Edgar Westbury say she got the Henna tattoo?"

"April. Four months before she disappeared."

Craig turned to his pathologist. "John, the father said the scar was red and ugly but faded quickly. How long does it take for a scar to fade to white?"

"For adults over a year, but for a child that young the cell turnover is so rapid that a few months could have done it."

It confirmed what Edgar Westbury had said.

Liam knew which direction Craig's thoughts were going so he headed him off at the pass.

"That scar's pretty small, boss. They wouldn't have noticed it before they took her unless they'd got really close."

Craig shook his head. "They should have when it was red, Liam. The Westburys said it was red and nasty so it would have stood out against her fair skin even from a distance. Anyone watching her would have noticed something on the back of her hand for months even if they hadn't known it was a flower. The kidnappers *must* have made their abduction plan and prepped the girl's passport before she'd got the scar in April, and then only kept her under *distant* surveillance until the snatch."

Liam kept arguing his case. "But they *had* to keep a close enough watch on her to spot the exact time her mum left her alone in the garden and execute the lift."

"Why? They could have been watching remotely and still seen that."

The D.C.I. gasped. "You think their house in France was on CCTV?"

Craig nodded eagerly. "It makes sense. If someone was watching Bella on CCTV the images would have been too grainy to see the scar, but they *would* still have been alerted to any possible opportunities to snatch her like her playing in the garden. It wouldn't have taken long to orchestrate a snatch, especially if she'd already been a surveillance target for months."

Liam was sceptical. "They'd have to have been spot-on in their timings, boss."

"Let's see." Craig turned to his chief analyst. "*Was* the Westburys' house on CCTV, Davy?"

"Sorry, chief, I'm still struggling to find out anything on CCTV beyond the hotel. Everything seems to be 'tomorrow' over there. It must be the heat."

"OK, leave it with me." Their trip to France was reappearing.

But the analyst hadn't finished. "Although if you

pushed me-"

"Consider yourself shoved."

"OK, then, *I'd* say that because the house was in the hotel grounds and therefore part of its property, if the rest of the hotel had CCTV surveillance then it *should* have had as well."

He saw Liam's mouth opening and shook his head.

"That doesn't mean whoever was viewing the hotel CCTV was in on the abduction. Anyone nearby with a bit of tech knowledge could have piggybacked the hotel system and been seeing everything that it saw."

Damn.

"OK, pursue what you can there, Davy."

He turned back to his junior analyst, who was tugging hard on his earring. Body piercings always made him feel nauseous so he averted his eyes as he waved him on.

"OK, so anyway, Quattro said the passport offices at airports hold lists of DMs, that's what they call distinguishing marks, and they copy them to the passport authorities and embassies for the issuing countries. So I asked him to check if any DMs had been noted at *our* listed airports in the time frame we have and he's doing it now. I should have the list by tomorrow."

Craig held his breath at what it might mean, hardly daring to let himself hope that they might still find Bella Westbury alive.

Depressingly, the analyst's next slide was about Pierre Galvet.

"These are the records from where Galvet was working during the period Bella disappeared, and you were right, chief. The farm's owners knew him well and said they docked his pay on the day of the girl's disappearance, because although Galvet clocked in as normal at six he left the farm at eleven and was missing for the rest of the day."

Andy couldn't believe his ears. "*How the hell did the local cops miss that?* All the statements I read said Galvet had a solid alibi. He was picking fruit all day long."

The analyst shook his head glumly. "They didn't really check, that's why. I suppose they were under pressure looking for the girl, so after they'd searched Galvet's digs and found nothing they must just have just taken his word."

Human error.

To be honest Craig wasn't that shocked. There'd been cock-ups in their own backyard and there would be plenty more in the future, although never any of *that* magnitude thankfully and he'd be lodging a complaint with the French about this one when their case was done.

"Did Galvet have a car, Ash?"

"Not one registered to him, but I'm sure nicking one wouldn't have been tough."

Craig frowned, thinking about what they'd heard for a moment before speaking again.

"OK, bear in mind that this is all just speculation at the moment, but if it isn't...logistically *could* someone have been watching Bella from a distance for months, piggybacking onto say the hotel or other local CCTV? Then when they spotted a gap when her mother left to go into-"

Liam cut him off. "Rewind a bit, boss. Say the bastards *were* watching on CCTV and spotted the girl and her mother go into the garden. The boy's older, so at school, and it's a nice sunny day, so they're likely to stay out there for hours. Yes? That makes the watcher zoom in to take a closer look, maybe even move Galvet to somewhere close-by on the off-chance, hence why the scrote was away from his fruit picking for most of the day. Then the watcher sees Nicola Westbury go into the house leaving the girl alone in the garden and spots his chance..."

He paused, waiting for Craig to comment.

"I'm not sure that part could work, Liam. It could have taken too long for the watcher to alert Galvet and we know the mother was only gone a minute." Craig was working out the steps as he spoke. "But... if you're right and Galvet got orders to go down there and wait... he leaves the farm, steals a car, sits in it near the Westburys' house, somewhere that he can keep their garden *in view*, then he's close enough that *as soon* as Nicola enters the house he spots it and he can rush to snatch Bella, take her to car, drive somewhere else and pass her on."

Aidan wasn't convinced. "But Galvet's a paedophile, Guv, so would he *really* have had the self control to do all that without taking advantage of the girl?"

Liam answered first. "Galvet's a Hebephile. They like kids eleven to fourteen. The Westbury girl was too young."

Craig nodded vigorously. "And remember if he was being watched the whole time on CCTV he *couldn't* have harmed the girl without getting caught, not if he'd wanted to get paid. He was on the clock too, and if someone was going to all that trouble to steal that particular girl they wouldn't have wanted her harmed." He shook his head. "No, all Galvet was there to do was grab Bella and transport her to whoever was watching. It was easy money for a lowlife like that."

Aidan made a face. "Even so... using a paedo of any sort was risky."

Liam was on Craig's side. "What other sort of criminal could they have persuaded to get involved in snatching a child? Most other crooks would have dobbed them into the police out of disgust, or hoping for a reward."

There was silence for a moment while people took everything in, and then Craig shrugged.

"Like I said before this is all just speculation until we get some facts to support it. OK, we need to find Galvet. Andy, take the lead on that, please. Right, anything else, Ash, before we wrap it up?"

"Yep."

He tapped up his next slide and Des Marsham's aged-up photographs of Bella Westbury appeared.

"These are from Doctor Marsham's aging software and show Bella at different ages from three to the almost seven year-old she is today. I've sent them to social services in every country I can think of in case she's become known to them over the years, also to Vice downstairs and Child Exploitation and Online Protection, so they can use their contacts to check the..."

He didn't need to finish the sentence; everyone was well aware that they would be checking the photos against an international database of children's images, gleaned from porn websites, videos, DVDs and magazines, and they all hoped Bella's image wasn't found amongst them at *any* age.

Craig broke the uncomfortable silence with a question. "Did you manage to do that other thing I asked, Ash?"

The analyst brightened up. "Sure. I also sent the images to the heads of all the photography databases across the world: Getty Images, Reuters, the intelligence agencies and others, to check if she's in their databases, even innocent images that might have appeared in newspapers. They'll have copies of everything from photos of school sports teams and choirs to randomers just taken for interviews."

It made Liam laugh despite the seriousness of the topic. "So if anyone's been stupid enough to allow her photo to appear in their local school magazine we might get them?"

Craig nodded. "Yes, but it's a long shot. If these people stole the girl to order they'll have raised her to be camera shy."

"Still. Good call."

Craig set down the marker that he was still holding; noting idly that it had stained his fingers bright green.

"OK. This is good progress, and we'll make more tomorrow. Everyone, go home now and be in tomorrow bright and early." He turned to the pathologist. "Pub?"

"Pub."

"What about you, Liam? Fancy a pint?"

The D.C.I. unfolded himself from his chair, nodding. "Just give me a second, will you, boss?"

Before Craig could say "Yes" he'd loped across to the LED screen, ready to give the team's junior analyst a clip round the ear.

"You needn't think I'd forgotten that Dumbo crack, son."

Thankfully for Ash he was smaller and nimbler than the lumbering policeman so he ducked just in time and wove away between the desks, calling out, "D.C.I. Dumbo, D.C.I. Dumbo" and generally dicing with death until Craig finally managed to drag his deputy out the door.

Chapter Seven

Dublin. 8 p.m.

Róisín Casey was torn between two options. Not because she was indecisive you understand; she would rather die in a ditch than admit to something so weak. No, it was just that having *made* the decision that she had two options and carried out a risk analysis on each, the pros and cons were so finely balanced that she was genuinely unable to choose.

The banker sensed that the net was closing in on her, the silent respondent on Arthur's phone had told her as much; even if the people wielding that net weren't yet aware of what they might want her for or even who she was. But the way they'd known to hold their silence and let her use the pause to hang herself meant that they *had* to be working for the cops.

So the police had the old man's phone and it would soon yield... well, what *would* it yield? The numbers of her burn mobile and the bank's switchboard certainly, because she'd called Arthur from both; perhaps even her first name because he might have saved her numbers under it, or perhaps *she'd* said it when she'd left him messages, she honestly couldn't remember whether she had or not. Even in the best possible version of events those things would bring the cops close to her within a day or two, not to mention that if they had Arthur's phone then they also had the old man himself.

Hence her two options. Did she stay put, carry on with life as normal, and bluff the police when they arrived? After all, what could they actually prove? Even if Arthur talked all he could say to get her in trouble was that they'd worked together on the quarry and cut some corners environmentally, and he'd paid the girl to deflect from Derek Morrow's possible role in that. The old man knew nothing of the much bigger venture in which she and Derek had been involved.

Or... did she disappear? Temporarily, until the noise died down, somewhere warm and impossible to extradite from, or even permanently, by faking her death? She had the resources stashed away to do either, but... Róisín pictured a future where her capital shrank and offered diminishing returns, and her five star lifestyle of champagne and penthouses was degraded to a weekly spritzer and a bungalow, and shuddered violently. True, that would only happen in the *distant* future, but it would happen all the same, and as someone who had clawed her way out of poverty she had no intention of *ever* going back.

The issue was how did she choose? A normal person when flummoxed would ask the opinions of their nearest and dearest, but she had no friends and was estranged from her family, which left her with only one person that she could tell. But if she worried him without knowing whether the police were even close then she might risk his anger, and she was well aware of what happened to people who did *that*.

The argument was circular and repetitive and lasted until the sun came up heralding a new day, a day in which the controlled and calculating banker would make a mistake that Craig would cause her to regret.

****

Laganside. Katy's Apartment. Friday, 5 a.m.

Right now the detective was busy with other things, which considering that it was five o'clock in the morning he would really rather not have been; but, as with on-call medics and other professionals that deal with the unpredictable side of human nature, his responsibility for criminal behaviour and all its consequences was no respecter of time. That was why he was standing in the apartment's hallway, hair on end, eyes half-shut, with his mobile clamped to his ear and trying hard not to yawn down the line.

He'd grabbed the phone on its second ring, years of conditioning making him react instantly to its trill, and left the still-dark bedroom, closing the door quietly behind him so as not to disturb his new wife before whispering, "Hello."

In truth he expected the caller to be Liam, his deputy's uncanny ability to learn about crimes in Belfast almost before the criminals had been booked a product of thirty years policing there, *and* knowing almost every cop and bad lad within its forty square miles. Not to mention the favours that he'd done endless local coppers through the years that ensured he was always the first to get the tip-off about tasty things.

But this time the caller wasn't Liam, and Craig was surprised to hear a sheepish voice on the line that sounded like it belonged to Des.

"Hello, Marc."

"Des? Is there something new about the case?"

Although what sort of forensic finding could constitute a five a.m. emergency, the detective's sleep addled brain was struggling to name.

After an embarrassed swallow the forensic expert answered him.

"Mmm... no, sorry, not about the case... it's just...well...it's just..."

Craig was awake enough now to detect another sound behind the scientist's stumbling words.

"Is that a station tannoy?"

Des' immediate, *"Ah"* conveyed confirmation, relief and shame in one syllable but moved them no further on, so Craig thought he should probably issue a prompt.

"You're in a police station, so which one?"

As he asked the question he was wondering *why* Des had sounded ashamed, given that his work took him to police stations all the time.

This time the forensic lead answered with more confidence, as if with fact she was on solid ground.

"High Street."

"So you've been called to collect evidence from a prisoner."

Even as Craig said it he knew that had to be wrong; no station sergeant would summon the head of forensics for the whole country to do the job of a junior CSI.

It was then that the penny dropped, and his next words cut across Des' mumbled, "Not exactly."

"You're the prisoner!"

He heard relief in the scientist's next words, as if even though the truth was unpalatable he was glad that it was out.

"Yes...yes, sorry, I am, Marc. I'm afraid I've been

arrested and I wasn't sure who else to call but you."

Dismissing a serious offence instantly, not because everyone, including Des, wasn't *capable* of committing one, but because the scientist's placid personality would have made it just too much of a chore, Craig ran through the list of possible misdemeanours that the man could have committed in the time since he's last seen him, landing on something involving alcohol. Des *had* been known to punish a pint or six in his time.

Without bothering to ask more Craig said, "Pass me over to the custody officer."

Jack Harris' night-time counterpart Angus Thompson came on the line, the recently immigrated Scot's world weary tone undoubtedly accompanied by his favoured habit of rolling his eyes and his head at the same time.

"Yes, sir. Angus Thompson here."

"Doctor Marsham told you who he was phoning, Sergeant?"

"Several times, sir, in entitled, obstreperous and then pleading tones."

Craig chuckled at the man's wit, vividly picturing Des's indignation at finding himself on 'the other side of the wire'.

"Well, Angus, care to tell me *why* he's been arrested?"

"Oh, it isn't just the Doc, sir. I've got ten of them here. *And* all their equipment."

The drollness of his delivery was so perfect that a comedy career obviously lay ahead.

"Equipment?"

Images of Des carrying a jemmy, a blowtorch and a bag labelled 'swag' filled Craig's mind.

"Metal detecting stuff and shovels, sir. The bunch of them were found in the grounds of Cranross Castle an hour ago by Lord Cranross himself, digging for so-called treasure. There were warnings issued to another lot in Fermanagh for digging at Tully and Monea Castles recently."

This time Craig *did* laugh. A bunch of middle-aged men sneaking around in the middle of the night like they were members of the Hatton Garden Gang. It was bizarre, although oddly *not* the strangest thing that he'd ever heard in his job.

"OK. So what do you propose to charge them with?"

He heard Thompson move somewhere quieter as he lowered his voice.

"I'm not. I'm going to keep them here for a few hours and then let them off with a warning. If they'd actually found anything and taken it we would be looking at theft and court, but thankfully they're hopeless at what they do. But the castle *is* private property and they left some pretty big holes in the grass so I can't vouch for Lord Cranross not taking a civil case."

Craig was wondering what metallic objects had prompted the detectorists to dig in the first place as the sergeant carried on.

"Anyway, I've put the fear of God into them, so that should work. I'll pass you back on to the Doc now, shall I, so you can calm him down?"

"Before you do that, how long were you planning to hold them?"

"Long enough to underline things, so I thought it'd be the cells till eight, then give them some breakfast and chuck them out."

Craig made a decision that he knew Des wasn't going to like, the scientist's reason for calling him so early undoubtedly to get set free.

"What time does Jack come on?"

"Around then. Eight-thirty's his scheduled start, but he's always here before then."

"OK, then can I ask you a favour? By all means lock Doctor Marsham up with the others but let him out just before eight. He works with Jack a lot and it might undermine him in his eyes."

Unlikely but possible.

The Scot sounded surprised. "I can do that, surely, but I actually thought you'd want me to let him go now."

Craig was tempted, but nepotism was a slippery slope and he was already halfway down it with Annette. Her case was *really* serious, and when it came out that he'd been investigating it without approval, and he had no doubt that it would soon, if he'd got caught *also* using his influence for Des it might make people question any justification that he managed to find for her release.

He tried to extinguish the guilt he felt at leaving Des in

jail and adopted a serious tone.

"No. They all need to learn a lesson or the next time they *will* end up in court. Just tell Des that I'll call him soon after eight."

Craig hung up before he relented, and with there being no hope of further sleep he made himself an extra strong coffee and took a seat at the kitchen table to think about their case.

He was never sure whether he loved or hated this stage in an investigation, when there was nothing but unanswered and new questions, and strands that wouldn't seem to knit. It was exciting because he never knew whether the tiniest clue could be the answer to everything, but nerve-wracking because all it took was *missing* that tiny clue for a trail to run fatally cold.

On balance he decided that he probably loved it, and what that said about his personality only a psychiatrist could assess, but as he'd had as much sleep as he was going to get and it was too early for breakfast, he decided not to waste the extra hours daydreaming and take himself into work.

When Craig entered the dark, quiet squad-room thirty minutes later and turned on the overhead lights, he was taken aback by the sight of his junior analyst slumped at his desk, slack jawed and snoring, while his computer display was changing image repeatedly at high speed.

A quick scan showed that Ash was wearing different clothes to the day before which meant he'd also come in absurdly early, but *why* he'd felt the need to be there at six a.m. was something that Craig wanted to find out. The detective tip-toed across the floor and whispered, "Ash" in his analyst's ear several times, finally giving an impatient shout of, *"ASH!"* when he didn't wake.

It prompted a cartoon like sequence of head jerking, eye widening alarm, followed by the analyst straightening up in his seat and grabbing for a pen in an attempt to look hard at work.

"What are you doing here so early?"

The analyst glanced around him frantically for the words' source, until his blurred vision eventually cleared and he realised that the speaker was Craig.

"What? Me? I'm in early all the time, chief."

A sceptical look from the detective provoked a second, more honest answer, with Ash motioning at his computer as he spoke.

"The time difference with the passport countries was slowing things up and I wanted to get on with it."

"So anything useful yet?"

In reply the younger man sat forward and began to type. "Give me five minutes."

"Fine. I'll make us some coffee."

True to his word, five minutes later they were sitting together in front of the analyst's screen while he pointed out what he'd found.

"OK, some basic stuff first. Davy checked the rock types and rainfall levels and they fit with the quarry holding a lot of water last winter when Kincaid was drowned. We've also got the department store CCTVs and all the tapes and newspaper coverage of the protests now, so someone will need to view those."

Craig thought for a moment. All his detectives had work allocated for that day and neither he nor Liam was going to spend their time doing the tedious and essentially junior job. So who did he give it to?

As the answer became obvious he sighed, not because it was an onerous task or he'd decided on the wrong person, but because he knew that the right person, Mary, was going to moan. But handling staff grumbles was part of his management role, so he set himself a reminder to call Andy at seven-thirty to notify him he'd be going to Tyrone alone, and another to phone the constable after that to say that *her* road trip was off.

Decision made the detective turned back to his analyst. "OK, Mary will view the photos and CCTV. But can you or Davy nail down the reason the quarry shut, please. And don't forget we still need the names of whoever owned it as well."

"I'm pretty sure Davy's already got something on that. I'll check."

As the analyst scribbled himself a note, Craig had had another thought.

"Who was looking into the photography paper for the photo found in Kincaid's pocket?"

"Davy. It was French, same as in the original pic you

brought from the Westburys' house. Nicola Kincaid must have had both prints made while they lived in Nice."

"OK, good. And I'm presuming Davy did Kincaid's and Morrow's criminal checks as well?"

"Yep. All clear. Do you still want us to look into Kincaid's company?"

Craig nodded. "When you find time. I don't imagine you'll find anything, but just for completeness sake."

Suddenly he noticed a file on the analyst's desk that definitely wasn't one of theirs.

"Is that the French file on the abduction?"

"Yep." He glanced pityingly at Craig the Luddite. "It came through by email late yesterday, but I know how much you like paper, so I printed the whole thing out."

"You make it sound like it's papyrus! I just like to hold something in my hand as I read."

Ash's pointed glance at his smart-pad made Craig feel old and abandon the debate. He lifted the file and began to flick through it, then he stopped himself; it could wait for half an hour.

"Carry on with what you were saying."

"OK, still on the old stuff. Davy checked on the Westburys' car accident and they were sideswiped by a jack-knifing lorry. He checked the police and insurance files and there's nothing weird there."

"Fine."

Another loose strand snipped off.

"And I'm trying to get into that mums' chat-room again. I managed it for a while but it locked me out again. Its firewalls are pretty good. I haven't detected any other attempted hacks so far but I'll keep looking."

Craig smirked. "I have every faith in you."

The analyst's hacking ability was legendary in the force and they'd availed of it several times, not always strictly legally. It gave the detective an idea, *also* not strictly legal.

"Ash, nothing to do with this investigation, but how would you fancy checking something that might help Annette out?"

The analyst nodded so hard his earring got caught in his long hair.

"Any time. I can't believe they're giving her such shit."

He realised just how loud swearing sounded in an

empty office and gave a sheepish smile, but Craig hadn't even heard the expletive, his mind on far bigger crimes.

"You'll need to keep this completely to yourself. No confiding in the rest of the squad or your mates."

"Not even Davy?"

"Davy's fine, but the fewer people who are involved the better. I'd like you to see if Pete McElroy had any social media accounts, net diaries and so on. Anywhere at all where he might have recorded his private thoughts."

"Sure. But two problems. One, he's dead so they might be locked now, and two, how could he have accessed them in Mahon?"

As the analyst ended his question they both laughed; Mahon's lax cyber-security had been a factor in their earlier case there.

"Point taken, chief."

Craig stifled a yawn that made him remember it was still the middle of the night.

"Even if Pete didn't access them *inside* Mahon, he'd been out for a few hours before he went to Annette's place so he might have done then."

"What sort of thing are you expecting to find?"

Craig had a fair idea, but shook his head to signal that it was best he didn't influence any findings.

"Fair enough. I'll take a look." The analyst gestured at his still changing screen. "Do you want the up to date stuff now?"

"Fire ahead."

"OK, so, Quattro's sent me through the list of DMs from the airports. And who knew? There were *three* flowers listed on kids' hands."

Craig stopped him. "Three out of fifteen?"

"Yep. It seemed a bit much to me too, people going around tattooing their kids, but maybe it's down to different cultures and all that stuff."

The detective wasn't so sure. "Hang on a minute. *Tattoos?* You're *sure* they were tattoos? They couldn't have just been those transfer things that children stick on themselves? I remember plastering myself with mini pirates when I was a kid, and my sister walked around so covered in flowers she was like Botanic Gardens."

The look Ash gave him said he hadn't a clue what he

meant, so Craig lifted his nearby smart-pad and found an example of a transfer in the shape of a Minion. The analyst still looked perplexed.

"They soak them in water and they stick on?"

"Yes, that's it. You didn't have these when you were a kid?"

"Nope. We just drew on ourselves and the walls with markers like normal kids. Anyway, what you're saying is that not all three of the flowers might be real tatts or scars, but it doesn't matter anyway because at least it's narrowing things down while I'm waiting for the passports to run. The bad news is that one of the three kids went to Russia. The others went to Canada and the U.S."

Craig nodded; he could live with a two in three chance of retrieving the Westbury girl. It was better than none.

Just then Ash's desk-phone rang, making him arch a dark eyebrow in surprise.

"Who's calling me at," he checked his computer clock, "a quarter to seven!"

He'd stated the time as if no-one normal could possibly be awake at such an hour.

"There's one way to find out."

When the analyst lifted the phone a voice that they both recognised came down the line.

"Hi Grace. How come you're calling this early?"

He set the call on speaker as she replied.

"Because I'm stupid, that's why. I came in early to re-check something I rushed through last night and discovered that I hadn't looked deeply enough. That man Arthur Norris, the one at High Street, well, the woman who called his phone left a lot of messages, and as well as the ones from her pay-as-you-go phone I've just found a second number. A Belfast one. I called it and it's the switchboard of a Merchant Bank. The switchboard's based here in town, but when I checked the bank has branches all over Ireland and the U.S., so I'm not sure how much use the switchboard will be to you without an extension number, but do you want its number anyway?"

Craig passed him a pen.

"Fire ahead."

As Ash scribbled down the information Craig mouthed a question.

"OK, the chief's asking if you know how many extensions the bank has."

"What's *he* doing there at this hour?"

When Craig answered her his smile was audible. "Good morning, Grace. I'm here because I couldn't sleep."

He omitted to say that it was *her* boss who had woken him up.

"Oh, sorry, sir, I wasn't being cheeky."

"Didn't think you were for a second. So... the number of extensions?"

The answer came in a satisfied tone that said she was sure of her ground.

"Seven hundred and forty two. Three hundred and ten of them are in Dublin, so, bearing in mind that the woman's mobile had an Irish number too...."

Craig gave a thumbs-up.

"That's great, Grace. Thanks."

"OK. I should have that data dump over to you before ten too."

Suddenly remembering that Des *was* her boss, Craig lifted the receiver. "Just to say that I spoke to your boss earlier and he may be in a little late this morning so just carry on."

Des was bound to go home at eight to change after his night in the slammer, so he would phone him to grovel then.

The CSI frowned quizzically and then shrugged. Des must get even less sleep than she did, but then maybe that was how he'd got to be the boss.

When he hung up Craig stretched and yawned noisily.

"OK, I'll leave you in peace to get on with things, Ash. I'm heading down to the canteen to get some breakfast; can I bring you anything back?"

Ten minutes later he was ascending the stairs with a bag of food and his mind on how best to re-interview Ben Frampton. The man would view him as the enemy because cops and prisoners were never cosy, but that animosity was bound to be increased because he was a cop from the same squad as Pete's wife. Even if George Royston hadn't been explicit as to *why* Frampton was being transported to Belfast he *would* have been told by whom, so there was no question that the burglar would continue to be on his guard.

Frampton owed Pete McElroy loyalty for teaching him how to read, and in his experience loyalty often grew stronger after death, tinged as it often became with a rose-tinted hindsight where the deceased had never done *anything* wrong during their life. His father had once caustically referred to the phenomena as being 'retrospectively elevated to the sainthood' which was just one example of how his staunch childhood but now very lapsed Presbyterianism and his mother's still devout Italian Catholicism had sometimes butted heads over the years. Only the former's relaxed approach to life had stopped religion becoming a deal breaker between them and leading to two seriously confused kids.

The upshot was if he went in hard against Pete then Ben Frampton could either be vigorous in his defence or clam up, and once *that* happened there would be little he could do to make the man cooperate; the usual threats of arrest, charge, court and prison tended to mean very little to someone who was already there.

So... if the big stick approach was out that just left the carrot. The thought spurred Craig to dump the bags of croissants and doughnuts that he was carrying on his analyst's desk and speed into his office, lifting his phone receiver and dialling before he'd even sat down. The call he made was to Mahon Prison and it was the first of four, the others made to inform Andy that his trip to Tyrone would be solitary and tell Mary that she was to come into the office, which thankfully reached her answerphone so he was spared having to repeatedly explain why in answer to her accusations of sexism, juniorism and whatever other 'ism' happened to be the politically correct flavour of the week.

His last call was timed for just after eight o'clock and was to Des Marsham; the call he'd been looking forward to least of all. Craig's lack of enthusiasm was justified when the scientist answered his mobile in a dull voice that said despite Angus Thompson undoubtedly having treated him with kid gloves his experience in lock-up hadn't exactly been a thrill.

"Hello."

"Hi, Des."

Silence. It could mean one of two things; either, optimistically, because he was calling from an office extension the scientist might not be sure yet who was speaking, or, more likely, because he was furious.

When he added, "It's Marc" to test the water, a lengthy pause was followed by the musical tones of Annie Marsham coming on the line.

"Hi, Marc. He says he's not talking to you."

She sounded amused enough that Craig decided to push his luck and broach the subject head-on.

"Sorry about last night, Annie, but I couldn't have got him out without being accused of nepotism."

She relayed the words verbatim to her husband, albeit dispersed between instructions to their two sons to put on their shoes and coats because they would soon be leaving for school.

The scientist's reply was relayed disjointedly as well.

"Des says... Stop that, Martin! Don't hit your brother... *What?*...I told you, your gym gear's in the dryer so just go and take it out... Des says he thought you two were mates but you couldn't even do him a favour so you're obviously not."

Craig could hear her husband's huffiness in the words even when relayed in her cheerful tones and went to explain further, but after a couple of words he stopped speaking and gave an exaggerated tut.

"Annie could you just set his mobile on speaker, please, and I'll explain everything so that he can hear."

"Gladly. Martin has Raff in a headlock now so I need to go anyway."

Craig heard the mobile being set down and the echo of a speakerphone cutting in, and pictured its owner standing with his arms crossed listening while he tied himself in knots trying to explain.

"Des, I need you to keep this to yourself, but I'm involved, without permission, in trying to follow up a new theory on Pete McElroy's death-"

He smiled as he heard the speaker cut out immediately and knew the father had done so to keep whatever came next from inquisitive little ears. When the line didn't go dead Craig took it as a sign to keep on speaking.

"I'm calling in favours, including having Pete's cellmate

at Mahon brought up for interview at High Street, and I'm aware it could all land me in the shit. But I don't care as much about that as that someone could try to negate whatever I *do* find to help Annette by saying it's been manufactured from nepotism, which would be more likely-"

He was cut off by a grudging, "Which would have been more likely if you'd also shown nepotism by getting *me* out of jail last night."

"Yes." Craig softened his tone. "I'm sorry, Des. Any other time I would have done my best to get you *and* your friends released, but I just couldn't this time. Can you understand why?"

He could almost feel the scientist's sulk draining away and the response when it came was hurt but logical.

"I understand, Marc, but I'm still pissed off with you. I didn't get a bit of sleep on that plank Angus Thompson calls a bed!"

Craig reached into his, admittedly fairly limited, psychology kit and pulled out, "I can hear you're angry and I don't blame you. Look, I tell you what. I'll ask Liam to see what he can find out about the odds of a civil case being pressed by Lord Cranross for you digging holes in his grounds. He's probably just pissed, so he might be amenable to you just paying-"

He was cut off by a whine. "*We thought it was public ground!* I mean, who the hell owns a castle nowadays apart from the Queen?"

"Quite a few people apparently. There've been digs at two others in Fermanagh that have caused disputes-"

"Well, nobody told *us* we couldn't dig there or we wouldn't have gone!"

"Nobody told you not to dig up Royal Avenue either, but you wouldn't have *dreamt* of doing that!"

There was renewed silence until the detective spoke again, more sympathetically.

"OK, look, leave it with me and I'll get Liam on it. In fact, I'm sorry, I should have thought of him when you first called me but I didn't. I just know that *I* can't be anywhere near this with Annette's case at such a delicate stage. OK?"

"Well...I suppose..."

"Good man. Liam will be in touch later. Oh, by the way,

Grace called us with some info earlier and I told her you might be in late-"

"You didn't tell her I-"

"God, no! She probably thinks you're at the dentist or something. All I meant is that you can take your time going in because she seems to have things in hand. OK, I have to go and interview Pete's cellmate now. I'll buy you a pint next time we meet."

As he was putting down the receiver, "Ten pints. I'm still annoyed you know" came down the line.

****

The C.C.U. 9 a.m.

While Andy was on his way to Tyrone a huffy Mary was taking out her annoyance at missing her road trip by thumping items around on her desk and banging its drawers deliberately hard, and was being studiously ignored by everyone in the office except Alice, who could hear the racket even with her earphones on and was punctuating each sound that the constable made with a loud, "TSK". It was odd how put-out Mary seemed considering how much she'd moaned about the cold when going to see Luisa Kincaid, but it seemed that the appeal of visiting a hotel and a diving expedition had overcome that.

Whatever its cause Davy had had enough of the sound combo *very* quickly and was tempted to take the D.C. to task, but with Mary not being his direct subordinate and no cops being present to do it for him escape seemed his only option, so he jerked his head towards the squad's new staff-room as a signal for himself and his junior to decant there and discuss their outstanding work in peace.

The space wasn't ideal, workplace kitchen-diners never exactly being cosy, with their regulation vinyl floors and Formica surfaces for ease of cleaning, but the room's warm apricot walls and personal touches of colourful mugs, a high-end coffee percolator and arty posters that were arranged far more prominently than the obligatory fire notices and safety hints, all unmistakable signs of Annette's hand in its design before Christmas, made it somewhere that both analysts could at least tolerate.

The major plus of the room was that it was quiet and far away from Mary's sulky clattering, so Davy closed the door behind them, hopeful of peace; in the gap between early morning coffees and elevenses they *should* be undisturbed.

He sat down at the table, smart-pad at the ready, and began to run through his list.

"OK, passports. Where are you with those, Ash?"

"Eight checked now, and I'm chasing three kids with flowers listed as DMs."

Davy crinkled his forehead quizzically. "Three? Three people tattooed their children?"

His junior smiled. "That's exactly what I said, but the chief said they might have just been those transfer things, so I've contacted the airports and asked them to dig for photos or archive footage so that I can take a closer look."

He paused for a second and took a sip of the energy drink that he'd brought with him, its pale blue colour always making Davy think of the cleaning stuff that his Mum put down the loo.

"Also, I've a call out to the photo agencies that the chief listed. I sent all the images of the girl through and said I'd give them twelve hours. They insisted it shouldn't even take that long with their face recognition tech so I'll give them a bell when I get back from checking on any progress with Vice."

Davy glanced at the wall clock. "What time are you heading down there?"

"Ten. Then with Vice and the photo-journos checks out of the way that just leaves me with social services in the different countries to chase up, plus the chief's asked me to do some checks on Pete McElroy's media as well."

He sighed at how long the work was likely to take and to his surprise his boss smiled.

"You *seriously* sent the pics to each countries socials separately? What time w...were you here till last night?"

Ash gave a wry smile. "Eleven and back in at five. Me and the chief had a chat here this morning around six. He didn't sleep much either."

Davy raised an eyebrow at the information and turned back to his smart-pad, tapping it several times and then turning it so his junior could view the screen.

"What am I looking at?"

"Interpol, Europol and the FBI."

"Yeh, I know that much. But *why* am I looking at them?"

"Because they and the other in-country agencies can run your pics through their social services databases in a tenth of the time."

Ash's brown eyes widened. "I'm thick! GCHQ might be able to help as well. On the intelligence side."

"And you've still got contacts there from the Miskimmon case."

He was referring to a murder by hacking case they'd worked on in twenty-fifteen; where two siblings had almost destroyed a satellite network not to mention tried to kill Katy, Craig's now wife.

"Or, you *could* ask D.C.I. Barrett to do some of this for you. I'm pretty s...sure it's part of his job. If you send the requests before you go down to Vice we could have answers by the end of today."

Ash was about to say thanks, but a second thought of, 'why don't *you* send them and help me out?' stopped him.

Hi boss read his mind and smiled.

"*I'll* be busy chasing the CCTV in France, following those numbers that Grace sent through from Norris' phone, and I've just had an email to say Derek Morrow's wife's given permission to examine all his computers, phones and money accounts."

Satisfied that they were both going to be glued to their computers all day and not just him, Ash felt more magnanimous, and demonstrated it by asking something that he knew he should have asked before.

"How'd that meeting go at Queen's?"

Davy shrugged in the universal shorthand for 'not bad'.

"They made me do the presentation to a panel and then asked me questions on it. I think they wanted to be sure I w...wouldn't disgrace them at the conference, seeing as I'll be flying the university flag."

"Sounds brutal."

The senior analyst locked his hands together behind his neck and rolled his eyes. "A bunch of dusties asking tough questions, so pretty much as expected. Then my tutor followed me out afterwards to pick things up, told me it had counted as my midway assessment for my PhD and I'd passed. They might have bloody w...warned me beforehand."

Ash's small tinge of regret and jealousy that he hadn't pursued the doctorate path himself when he'd been offered it, preferring a life of holidays, women and wine, was pushed aside quickly in favour of, "Congrats, mate. I'll be calling you Doctor Walsh soon."

"There's a good few years till then, but yeh, thanks, it's good. You should do one too. The chief will help fund you and you'll get time off to study. You could do it on s...something like police and intelligence agency IT liaison maybe?"

It was a mouthful but definitely worth a thought.

Davy sprang to his feet in a fluid motion as he continued speaking.

"The best thing is Maggie's coming to Geneva with me for the conference, so it'll be like a mini-break. Right, w...we need to get on with things. It sounds a bit quieter out there now so hopefully Mary's stopped chucking stuff about."

The sight of the constable with her iPod buds in her ears, a bag of sherbet lemons in her hand, and her feet up on her desk watching footage of the quarry protests, said that peace would probably reign for as long as her movies did.

****

High Street Station. Friday, 9.20 a.m.

Jack Harris was normally a sociable man. He liked having his mates round on a Saturday to watch footie on the box, with a few beers and whatever grub his wife, a gentle creature and a brilliant cook that he thanked God at least once a week he'd married, had taken it into her head to prepare. He didn't mind his kids bringing friends home either, or even taking part in the occasional dinner party his dearly beloved inflicted on him, just as long as he had some say in choosing the guests, her amateur dramatics group too airy fairy and painful to talk to in his book; there was only so often he could listen to debates on Shakespeare's Women or what Nietzsche had said about evil before he wanted to tape up their pretentious mouths.

But, although socialising had its place, in Jack-World that place *definitely* wasn't his police station, and having it invaded, nay *colonised* by the Murder Squad was giving the custody sergeant the definite hump.

Bad enough that he'd arrived for work an hour before to have Angus Thompson tell him there was a bunch of metal detecting beardies in his cells waiting for discharge, which of course as daytime officer *he'd* had to process and arrange, but no sooner had he pointed the last of the satisfyingly exhausted hobbyists towards the street than, first Aidan Hughes and his dark-eyed D.S., and then Craig and his big galloot of a deputy had appeared, presenting themselves at his reception desk with dumb looks and demands to see their prisoners tout suite, or "Nye" as Hughes had said in his thick Belfast way.

Jack had been irked by the hobbyists and annoyed by the first pair of detectives, but when Craig and Liam appeared as well he decided it was time to work to rule.

"Sit over there. Sirs."

The order was accompanied by a jabbed finger directing the pair to the reception bench.

Craig followed the instruction absent-mindedly, his head full of a million different things, but Liam spotted that there was fun to be had with the irritable desk sergeant and decided to give him a prod.

"Who rattled *your* cage then?"

Harris rose straight to the bait.

"Who rattled *my* cage? *Who rattled my cage?* I'll tell you who! Your sodding teammates, flouncing in here and demanding to see people 'Nye', that's who!"

Liam turned to his boss knowingly. "Hughesy."

"Had to be. No-one else on the squad can mangle a vowel like that." Craig looked past his deputy to the sergeant. "Sorry, Jack. I'll have a word with him."

Not planning to be mollified quite so quickly but having the wind taken out of his sails by such a ready apology, the uniformed sergeant came back with a half-hearted, "Aye well, just be sure that you do. Sir."

The post-script addition of respect made Craig laugh. "I bet if you were telling me to fuck off you'd add sir at the end as well."

"I could try it if you'd like."

Liam reared in mock offence. "Here now, I'm not having that."

Craig waved him down, knowing, which Liam didn't, that Jack had arrived that morning to find his station full of metal detectorists and their muddy equipment, and giving him a pass.

It paid off. The sergeant having walked to the cliff edge felt much better for it, and as thanks to Craig for not tipping him over he motioned the pair through to the cell corridor.

"Your friends are in interview room one with Sandi observing, so I'll have to put you in number two. Go on down and I'll bring Mister Frampton through."

As Jack left reception in search of his prisoner Craig shook his head at his deputy who was already hot on his heels.

"I need you to do something before you join us, Liam."

Explaining quickly what Des had been up to and how he'd left him to languish in jail overnight, to increasingly astonished and chastising looks from his deputy, Craig finished up with, "There are no criminal charges to be answered but I'd like you to call Lord Cranross."

The D.C.I.'s eyes almost popped out. *"Me?* You're trusting *me* to talk to a Lord?"

"He's only a man, Liam, and you can be charming when you want to, you know that. Just see what he plans on doing about things, and if he says he's bringing a civil case for damages then ask for the lowest figure that he'll settle for without involving solicitors."

Liam's astonishment changed to a knowing smile. "You're going to pay it, aren't you?"

"It depends how much it is, but probably. I feel bad for leaving Des locked up all night. Even though I couldn't have intervened personally I *should* have called you to handle it, I just didn't think of it at the time."

The D.C.I. shook his head. "There were other people digging too, and I know you feel guilty about Des but you can't pay for them all."

"We don't know what it'll cost yet."

"No, I mean you *can't*, at least not without speaking to Katy first. You're married now and you can't go around spending money anymore like you're not."

The words made Craig frown. He *really* didn't like the idea of his freedom being curtailed, and anyway he wasn't sure that he agreed with his deputy, after all *he* never asked Katy what *she* spent money on. But it was a debate for another time because Jack was beckoning him through.

"Look, just make the call and get a settlement figure, Liam, and then join me in the interview. We can argue whether marriage means the complete loss of an individual's autonomy some other time."

As a perturbed looking Craig advanced down the cell corridor he did so having completely missed his deputy's smirk. Liam rubbed his hands gleefully in self-congratulation; having failed to wind Jack up properly that morning he'd just managed it with the boss.

****

High Street Station. Interview Room One.

Aidan Hughes was getting bored, which granted happened pretty quickly, especially without nicotine to take off his edge, but the fact that Ryan, someone whose lifelong deafness in one ear had meant that he'd often had to ask patience of others in repeating their words and also possessed more than a smidgeon of the virtue himself, was bored too, said that the stalemate they were in with Arthur Norris *needed* to break.

The D.C.I. leaned forward heavily on the table between them and the pensioner, whose habitual grey-facedness was now tinged with red blotches from a combination of poor sleep and an allergy to the woollen blanket he'd been given to cover himself with the night before, giving a heavy sigh as he did so.

"Mister Norris. We can sit here all day if you like while you say 'no comment'-"

He was surprised by the first sign of life from the man in an hour.

"I *didn't* say 'no comment'. I didn't say anything."

The insistence and speed with which the land agent uttered the words made Ryan sure of something. Norris was frightened of something or someone, and by the shouting of the woman he'd been arguing with in Hector McDonagh's office and her S.W.M.B.O. nickname on his phone it was almost certainly her.

He signalled Aidan that he wanted to try something and got the nod; Norris' silence finally having been broken they now needed to open things up.

"Mister Norris. Would you like a solicitor to be present? I know you refused earlier, but we could get you one now."

"No."

"Because you feel that you've done nothing wrong?"

When the question produced a definite wince the sergeant followed up quickly.

"Or you feel you *have* done something, if not exactly wrong then something that you're not proud of, but you feel you can't *tell* us in case someone else finds out?"

To his surprise the man stared straight at him for a moment and then gave a small nod.

"The set-up with Rio Reynolds? Is *that* what you're not proud of?"

This time he was answered by a shake of the head and Norris added a stumbling, "Well, yes, I am... I mean I'm not happy that we did that...."

We.

"... but that isn't what I'm most not proud of. If that makes sense."

Ryan gave a small smile of understanding and sat back in his chair to ease the tension, hoping that Aidan would follow suit. He did, and folded his arms in a signal for the D.S. to keep going.

"This other thing that you're not proud of, Mister Norris, are you afraid that you'll land someone else in trouble if you tell us about it?"

This time the response was an unambiguous, "Yes."

"And you care about that person, so you don't want to do that, do you?"

When the elderly man shook his head quickly, Ryan knew that they were on the right track.

"Would I be right if I said this person might be a woman, a woman that you're fond of?"

Norris' instant astonishment made him feel like a mind reader, when really it was simply far easier to read people than was often thought. Plus he *had* already heard that female voice yelling down the phone.

Arthur Norris leaned forward on the table as if he thought he'd just found a friend, and as he did so the neon light overhead highlighted every crevice and mark of aging on his face, making Ryan feel more kindly towards the man.

"She's young, you see. Well, not young young, not a girl, but *much* younger than me. And I don't want to get her in trouble."

Young, and yet... also someone to be feared?

Ryan nodded comfortingly. "I understand. You feel *protective* of her. But perhaps you're worrying for no reason? Perhaps *no-one* will be in trouble. But we'll only find that out when you tell us everything. You could be worrying unnecessarily, you know."

The first sign of doubt appeared on the older man's face, and it was followed by a genuinely questioning look.

"You think so?"

Before the sergeant could reply Norris' eyes fell to the table and he started muttering to himself. Aidan doubted that the tape would pick up his words so after a moment Ryan prompted gently with, "I didn't quite catch that, Mister Norris."

The pensioner shook his head. "I'm sorry. I was just thinking out loud. Wondering whether you were right and I am worrying unnecessarily. Perhaps the insurance might cover things after all."

Insurance? Against what?

Some judicious questioning followed, and five minutes later the detectives knew that the reason Arthur Norris had been so reticent was because he'd been worried that, as well as the dead body that had been found at the quarry, something that had had *nothing* to do with him, the police had been in Rownton investigating possible environmental pollution there; pollution that he as land agent for the purchase worried that he and the owners might be found liable for.

As Derek Morrow had also worked on the quarry and was still managing it, Norris had been worried that his suicide could have increased police attention to the place, and that the suggestion of an affair as a motive for Morrow killing himself might have diverted that.

As the words came tumbling out in a torrent that said the elderly businessman was relieved to *finally* be able to explain his actions, the two detectives were fighting hard not to look shocked. They'd had no idea that there might be environmental concerns at the quarry, but what was ever more interesting to them was how frequently Norris' explanation was peppered with, "we", "they", and "she".

Before they got into that Aidan offered the land agent a tea break and summoned Sandi in to sit with him, then he ushered Ryan out to the car park where they could speak without being overheard.

"Well done for getting that out of him, Ryan, but what the hell does it all mean?"

The D.S. drew a hand through his jet-black hair, still without a single grey in his forties and not through dye.

"Well, we now know that Norris, and whoever this mystery S.W.M.B.O. is, bought and maybe even owned the quarry together, probably along with others, and when *we* turned up in the village Norris was worried we'd discover pollution there. We need to get the Environment Agency to check that there isn't any."

"Agreed, although I doubt that Derek Morrow killed himself over a chemical spill. But OK, so given that Norris is obviously subordinate to this S.W.M.B.O. woman it's likely she's running things and he just does as he's told."

"But what things? The old man obviously thinks everything's about pollution, but we don't know that *she* does. She might know something about Kincaid's killing and just not have told Norris. I'd say he'd be pretty easy to control if someone set their mind to it." He kicked a stone at his foot, watching it skitter across the tarmacked car park as he thought. "We need to talk to S.W.M.B.O."

Aidan stared at him sceptically. "That means Norris giving up her name, and I don't think he's there yet. He might see it as a betrayal and clam up again if we even ask. We need to hold him here until Davy gets something off his phone."

"Do we have grounds?"

The D.C.I. nodded. "We can hold him another few hours for questioning anyway, but he paid the Reynolds girl to lie about a suicide victim so I'll give the duty solicitor a call and see what kind of charge might apply there if we need longer. Meanwhile, you ask the environment people to go in after the divers have finished. And see where Davy's got to with the quarry's ownership as well. Let's see if we can give this mystery S.W.M.B.O. a name."

As they were making their calls Liam was in the station's reception struggling not to laugh down *his* phone at the butler that he was speaking to, who was informing him in a Jeeves' accent that, "Lord Cranross has instructed me that all business must be conducted through his family solicitors, Russell, Cuthbert and Mogg. They have offices in Chichester Street in Belfast. Good day."

It made the D.C.I. wonder something; if the butler spoke like that then what did the Lord himself sound like? He pictured the ventriloquist's dummy Lord Snooty and was glad it would be Craig and not him finding out.

Liam's stifled laugh became a full-on guffaw just as Ryan entered reception to call Davy on the landline, having belatedly realised that his mobile was still on the bedside table where he'd left it to charge the night before. It made him wonder, and not for the first time, *why*, if scientists were clever enough to send a man to the moon, they couldn't invent a bloody phone that could detect its owner leaving without it and summon them back.

His, "Hi, Liam" became, "bye, Liam" as the deputy headed down the corridor to join Craig in Interview Room Two, giving a cheesy grin through the two-way mirror at Jack Harris as he took his seat opposite Ben Frampton but saying nothing to interrupt his boss' flow, which wasn't yet in full flood mode because Craig had only just managed to drag the recalcitrant burglar through the preliminaries of date, name, age and address.

"Right, Mister Frampton, it's my understanding that you're in Mahon Prison serving a ten year sentence for burglary, and that you have five years of that term left."

It didn't require an answer and Craig didn't get one, so he filled the silence by tapping the page in front of him on the table. It was Frampton's prison schedule, and the detective was hoping that if he needed something to incentivise the mane might find a possibility there.

"I can see from your prison schedule that you're currently taking a lot of drama classes. I take it you're involved in a prison play?"

There was a pause while Frampton assessed whether he would be giving away any secrets by confirming the assertion. When the decision was no, he offered up, "West Side Story."

Appropriate given the number of gang members in Mahon perhaps, although was it strictly advisable? Perhaps a show that didn't involve gang fights and death would have been a better choice, not to mention the challenge to find someone who could hit Maria's high notes.

As Frampton volunteered that he was a Shark in the production Craig willed his deputy not to crack the obvious, "A toothless one" joke because of the gaps in the man's lower teeth.

As a diversion he hurried on with, "So you have songs to learn, and that requires you to read. We know Pete McElroy taught you to read so you must have been very grateful to him."

It prompted a crossing of arms and a tight-lipped, "I was. Still am."

It was a warning that his loyalty didn't expire after death, just in case they were hoping that it had.

"So you two were friends."

The words provoked a suspicious squint.

"But Mister McElroy's gone now."

That brought a sneer, "Killed by his pig wife!"

Craig corrected him calmly. "Ex-wife for many years, and you must know that the reason for the divorce was that Pete didn't treat her well. I've checked your record, Ben. You've got no history of violence towards either men or women and you've got a wife and two daughters who love you at home."

The arms tightened. "So?"

"Don't you have an opinion on men who hit women?"

Now the lips were pursing. "Pete was good to me. We were mates."

Craig's comebacks started to speed up, making Frampton speak faster too.

"Which means?"

"*We* never had any argy bargy, so she must have provoked him."

"Just like the man he shivved in his first prison provoked him."

The convict leaned forward slightly and Craig could feel his deputy twitching to shove him back. A sideways glance told him not to.

"Yeh, that guy must a pissed Pete off too."

Craig wasn't pausing for breath now and it made his deputy smile inwardly; he was trying to make the burglar trip up.

"So Pete was just an angel who taught you how to read."

"Yeh."

"You must have been close."

"We were mates, like I said."

"So you must have been shocked by his death."

"No." Frampton's eyes widened as he realised what he'd said and he began to backpedal at speed, "Yeh, I mean yeh. Yeh, I was shocked."

It was his first stumble and the last thing they needed was for him to pick himself up so Craig drove on.

"You said no because you *were* expecting his death, or half-expecting it. You knew."

"No, no, that's not it."

Frampton looked to Liam for support but all he saw was a cop whose glare said he would like to eat him for lunch.

"Don't look at him, look at me, Ben. You knew or you suspected that Pete was going to die that night, didn't you?"

The convict wasn't even trying to form words now, his eyes darting wildly around the room.

"Because Pete had told you, hadn't he? He'd planned the whole thing. And he trusted *you* to help cover it up."

Craig could feel his deputy's shock but he kept his eyes fixed straight ahead, watching as Ben Frampton's eyelids flickered and then stretched wide open as he realised that something he'd just said had given Craig an in. Until now the detective had just been shaking his prisoner hard to see what fell out, and finally something had; he'd had his suspicions for days about to Pete's *exact* motivation for entering Annette's house that night but now it was time to confirm.

He was speaking so quickly now Liam hadn't realised

he was capable of it.

"Pete trusted you to help him cover up the planned burglary at his wife's house, didn't he? Maybe you even helped him plan how to break in? Breaking into a cop's house, do you know how many years that could add to your sentence, Ben? You'll miss your daughters' childhoods. Maybe get free just in time to walk one of them up the aisle."

Frampton's lean forward became a lurch, and Liam's hand shot out to hold the burglar back just as his panicked words spat out.

"You can't do that! I'm doing my time quiet. You can't blame me for what Pete did!"

Craig didn't relent; the only sympathy he felt was for Annette.

"We can if you knew about it in advance! We can if you knew he *planned* to break and enter his wife's house and possibly kill her. We can if you knew he planned to harm her partner and child. You could be looking at serious charges here, Frampton, and all because Pete was a mate!"

All resistance to Liam's hold evaporated as the convict shrivelled in his seat like a punctured balloon. Craig paused long enough to let the man's own thoughts do his work for him, and when he saw Frampton's once defiant expression change to tearful anxiety he uttered his next words in a slower, more solemn tone.

"You *knew* that Peter McElroy planned to break into his ex-wife's house, Mister Frampton, and you didn't tell the governor or the cops. Keeping that knowledge quiet made you an accessory. *Peter McElroy* made you an accessory in *his* crime."

The burglar's mouth opened and closed silently as he went on.

"*You* might have thought that he was your friend, but friends don't do that. Pete would have known that you'd be looking at an extended sentence if you were caught, but he didn't care, did he?"

"But he taught me how to read..."

It was said in a shaky voice, as if Frampton was questioning whether Pete had only ever done so in order to use him.

"Is gratitude for that enough reason for you to serve

more time away from your family? Is it?"

The burglar shook his head and as the detectives watched his expression became one of pleading, even though he didn't dare say the words. Craig paused again, but only to regroup; the man was already on the ropes so there was no need to hit him again.

"All right. Here's what I want from you, Ben, and as long as I get it and you're prepared to make a signed statement and testify in court if necessary, I'll send you back to Mahon in time for tea."

Hope made the prisoner's eyes brighten.

"No more years?"

"No more years. But only if I get everything from you. If you hold *anything* back then you'll be charged."

One eager nod from the now completely toothless Shark and Craig motioned to his deputy. "If Jack can supply some tea and biscuits we'll get this all on tape."

A clatter from behind the mirror said that the sergeant was already on the move and five minutes later they were ready to record.

"OK. Tell us what happened in your own words, Mister Frampton."

The burglar gripped his mug of tea, rolling it between his hands occasionally as he spoke.

"Pete McElroy was put in my cell in January last year. My last cell mate had been gone months, so I knew someone was coming, but I wasn't best pleased when I found out it was McElroy because I'd heard that he'd shivved a bloke. But pretty soon we started getting on and he offered to teach me to read. I'd bunked off school a lot when I was a kid so I'd never learned, but I'd wanted to for years so I worked hard."

Craig raised a finger to halt him. "Liam, check if Pete requested to share with a burglar especially."

As the D.C.I. scribbled a note to himself his boss nodded their prisoner to continue.

"Pete got depressed a lot. He said he'd fucked-up his life over some girl."

The affair that had eventually led to Annette requesting a divorce.

"He said he'd lost his wife and kids over it and he got pretty down about that."

"Did he ever go to see the prison doctor?"

Frampton shook his head hard. "No way. Pete said that was for mugs. He said no quack could tell him more than he already knew. All they would do was shove pills into him and he wasn't having it. But..."

"Yes?"

"The closer he got to his discharge date the more miserable he got. It was like he felt there was nothing for him on the outside anymore."

Given that he would've been unlikely to ever get a teaching job again, Annette had moved on with Mike and he was estranged from his kids, Craig could understand why.

"They told him in October that they'd be giving him a trial period outside before his real discharge, like they do with lots of us now. He was going to be staying in a hostel over Christmas." The convict shook his head. "I think the timing really got to him, after all the family Christmases he'd had. Anyway, that's when he said it to me."

"Go on."

Frampton swallowed hard and when his next words emerged they were almost a whisper. "Pete said he was going to top himself."

Craig wanted to shout with relief; it was what he'd suspected but hadn't dare voice. Pete McElroy had wanted to die, and he was pretty sure that he knew what his preferred method had been.

But he was still a long way from proving that, so he refocused his attention on the man across the table and watched as Frampton's small eyes widened, pleading for understanding.

"You've gotta understand. *Lots* of blokes say that inside, especially if they're missing people. I've said it myself sometimes, but you'd never think of really doing it."

"So you didn't believe Pete?"

"No. Not at first. But then he kept on about it, talking about how he'd do it. Hang himself, drown himself, throw himself in front of a train-"

Liam cut in.

"Never a less violent method like pills?"

It prompted a shake of the burglar's head and then a note of pride entered his voice. "Nah. Pete wasn't that sort of bloke. He was big. Macho. He used to go to the gym every day."

As befitted an ex-PE teacher.

"If *he* was gonna go down he was going down hard. That's just what he was like." Frampton dropped his eyes to the table. "That's when he said the other thing. It was about a fortnight before his leave period and I didn't listen at first because I was busy rehearsing for our Christmas concert, but then he kept saying it again and again."

"What?"

"That he was going to kill himself when he got out on leave, and he was going to take the bitch who'd put him in prison down when he did."

Craig murmured the words, "Suicide by cop" and then closed his eyes in relief, hardly even registering his deputy's astonished, *"What?"*

It was what he'd been thinking for days and now he had confirmation from the man that Pete had been closest to in his final year. Pete McElroy had committed suicide by cop. The bastard could no longer control Annette in life but he was going to have a damn good go at it in death.

A warning note sounded in Craig's mind, making him open his eyes again. They needed proof to get Annette off, and on its own a convict's word wouldn't be enough.

He sat forward and gazed at Frampton intently, ready for any hint of a lie.

"Tell us *exactly* what Pete said about how he was going to do it."

"That was-"

"*Don't* tell me that was everything. If you're not going to get charged then you need to tell us the *whole* truth."

The burglar gave a defeated nod. "OK. Pete said his wife was a crack shot and he knew where she kept her gun. He planned to break in, kill her new man, and then go at her, knowing that she'd shoot him to protect herself or her new kid."

"But what if her gun was locked away?"

"Pete said he knew her password. He'd watched her put it in a safe-box for years and she'd never changed it once. He was planning to take the gun out while she was asleep and leave it beside her, then kill her man and launch himself at her so she'd shoot him dead."

The detectives exchanged a look. Annette's gun not being locked away that night had just saved Pete a step; he'd been planning to leave it where she could reach it anyway.

"McElroy didn't want *her* dead as well?"

The convict shook his head firmly. "No, he was crystal clear on that. He said he wanted her to suffer in prison. He said he wanted the bitch to lose everything just like he had. Her job, her kids' respect, her freedom. But he *definitely* wanted her new man dead. Pete used to go on about how she'd bagged herself some posh doctor and was living in luxury while he was rotting away in jail."

Craig wouldn't exactly have described Annette's home décor as luxurious, especially not with a toddler throwing food at the walls, but he understood the point.

"What was Pete going to use to kill her partner?"

"His bare hands. He was planning to strangle him or suffocate him with a pillow. Like I said; Pete was strong."

McElroy had gone to the house unarmed knowing he wouldn't have needed a weapon to kill Mike, and that the *lack* of one would have made things look ten times worse for Annette. And because he'd never planned to leave the house again he hadn't been concerned about leaving his prints.

But this was still all hearsay. They needed evidence.

"We need something more concrete than this. Did Pete leave a suicide note with you?"

"No." The burglar shrugged. "And they took all his stuff from the cell, so if it wasn't in there…"

The way he allowed the words to tail off bothered Liam. Frampton had told them just enough to save his own neck but the D.C.I. *knew* there was something more.

He signalled to take over the questioning.

"You realise that unless we see proof this is all just bullshit, don't you? You'll still be under suspicion and charged. Pete McElroy had no experience of breaking and entering yet he managed to get into that house without breaking the lock or making a sound? There's *no bloody way* he did that without someone giving him a masterclass in B&E, and who better to do that than old Benny the Burglar himself? Eh?"

As Frampton went to object his eyes turned to Craig,

sensing that he was the more sympathetic of the pair. The cynical gaze that greeted him left him disappointed, and Liam's addition of, "Tick-tock, Benny Boy, it's almost charging time" made the thief finally concede defeat.

"Oh, for fuck's sake, all right then! Pete had a new solicitor!"

Liam sat back with a satisfied look and left it to his boss to tidy up.

"Name?"

"Floods in Belfast. Some mate of Pete's came to visit about a week before Christmas and helped arrange it."

"Arrange what?"

"Pete wanted some papers held for safekeeping, and he didn't trust his defence lawyer not to look at them and shoot his fat mouth off."

As he would have *had* to if he'd realised that break-in was planned.

"But *any* solicitor would have told the police if they'd suspected a crime was about to be committed."

"Pete said that because he was using a middle-man this Flood lot wouldn't know anything about his charges, so they wouldn't suss he was a con. They'd just think he was some straight punter leaving papers for when he died."

"The name of Pete's mate?"

It prompted another shrug. "Search me. Just some bloke."

"And the papers?"

"Letters. Some to his kids I think, and he didn't say what the rest were."

Craig could guess. One would be a suicide note dated to be opened on some date in the distant future. Probably just in time for Annette to finish a long stretch in prison for manslaughter.

He rose to his feet and leaned his fists on the table. "Right. This will all be typed up minus the expletives and you're going to sign it, Mister Frampton."

"As long as I'm not being done for anything."

Craig took his time in answering to make him suffer. Ben Frampton had withheld this information for almost two months, and if they hadn't had the wit to question him then Annette would more than likely have gone down. He *really* wanted to charge the bastard but they needed his testimony, so when he thought he'd left the burglar hanging for long enough Craig nodded his head.

"No charges for what we've discussed here, *if* you sign it and agree to testify if called." He turned to his deputy. "Liam, sort that out, please. I need to find this Flood's address and say we're coming."

An hour later Ben Frampton was awaiting transport back to his cell for one and they were heading for Flood and Son's Solicitors in Belfast's Oxford Street, with a still stunned Liam grilling his boss about exactly how and when he'd figured Pete's suicide by cop plan out.

****

County Tyrone. 10.30 a.m.

Andy was quite enjoying his solo outing. He didn't get that many of them, usually paired up with Aidan or Mary, and although he liked company he also liked being his own boss. In theory he *should* have been the boss in both of those pairings too, being the most senior D.C.I. after Liam; but as Aidan was naturally bombastic and he was naturally quiet he usually let the lanky exercise addict take the lead, knowing that if it was ever *really* necessary he could crack the whip. Well, that was the theory anyway.

Mary was a different case. She was a woman, and fortunately or unfortunately he'd had chivalry bred into him along with good manners; and that, as well as having no sisters and going to an all boys school, had left him with an awe of the fairer sex that had resulted in him being walked over in two marriages, and all without managing to wise up one little bit.

Mary also had the added 'otherness' of being unpredictable, inclined to eccentricity in her attire and physical accoutrements such as tattoos and piercings, as well as in her approach to life. It made Andy regard her with both amusement and a 'light the blue touch paper' wariness, that meant that while entertaining she wasn't the easiest person to spend hours with in a car.

But today he could revel in his solitude and also play whatever he liked on disc, which was a CD of ocean wave music, something that soothed the, in his case, very small savage beast. After mellowing out for seventy miles the car's sat-nav announced that the detective had arrived at his destination, The Valley Hotel.

Small and architecturally beautiful, the early Victorian building perched on a hill overlooking a shallow, heavily wild-flowered valley that Andy later learned had been planted by a famous gardener of the time. The artistic D.C.I. was just picturing elegant ladies in bustles picking their way delicately through it on summer evenings, when a very tall, very anxious looking man approached his car and he climbed out to shake his palpably twitching hand.

"Chief Inspector Angel?"

"Yes. You must be Mister Abernathy, the manager."

"Yes, yes, yes." The visibly perspiring hotel manager turned quickly on his heel. "Follow me, follow me, please and I'll take you to Mister Kincaid's things. Yes, things, *lots* of things."

The human version of Lewis Carroll's White Rabbit gave a rapid and frequently repetitive commentary as he led the way.

"I have to say we were most shocked, most, most shocked when we heard what had happened to Mister Kincaid." He shuddered. "Such a nice man. Charming, charming, and so pleasant to the staff. I only wish all of our guests were like that."

He stopped in his tracks and rolled his eyes extravagantly. "You wouldn't *believe* some of things that happen here. Shocking, shocking, the things people get up to in hotels. Shocking. If the newspapers only knew."

Andy was picturing rural orgies and about to ask for details when Abernathy returned to the subject of their murder victim.

"As soon as we realised that Mister Kincaid wasn't returning, it took a while of course to be sure, yes sure. Well, we cleared his room and secured his possessions in the storeroom, for his family you know. Nothing has been touched since last November, no, no, no, nothing at all."

But not before you took payment of the bill from his credit card, the detective thought cynically.

"What made you decide Mister Kincaid wasn't coming back?"

"Well, he'd only booked the room for five days, and we

left it for seven more at the end of that before we removed his things."

A week to give up on a man; business was a savage game.

As they'd been speaking Abernathy had led the way through the hotel's reception to a storage area, and he threw open its door indicating a large suitcase and a cylindrical leather bag.

"I don't know that you'll find anything useful in the luggage, Chief Inspector. Not that I looked, of course not, no, no, no, but the chambermaid who packed the items said that they were mostly clothing. Yes, clothing. So that would be suits and shirts and so on, I imagine."

Unless Kincaid had been into kaftans or cloaks, it was a fair bet. There was further fashion commentary to come.

"Mister Kincaid dressed very smartly. That's what the maid told the other gentleman who came to look at his things."

Andy turned sharply to face him. *"What other man? When?"*

The manager was startled. "Oh, well, I wasn't on duty that day, so I'm not-"

The detective cut him off. "I need to speak to whoever was then. And *why* did they let him see Mister Kincaid's things?"

The hotelier's eyes widened so far in indignation that Andy spied the edges of his contact lenses. It diverted him slightly; he was getting short sighted and had been thinking of trying lenses out himself. His reverie was ended by Abernathy's barked response.

"We did *not* let him see Mister Kincaid's possessions! As if we would do such a thing indeed! This is a respectable establishment, respectable. We've had politicians staying here, I'll have you know!"

A pretty dubious endorsement in Andy's view, but the manager hadn't finished yet.

"And that film star. You know, the one who played an old farmer when he was twenty-one."

He was left no more enlightened.

"So I'm shocked at your suggestion, Chief Inspector. Yes, shocked. In all my born days, I don't think I've ever been so offended. No, no, no, I don't think I have!"

It took the D.C.I. a good five minutes to calm the man down, and then he asked a question that he knew would make Abernathy substitute defensiveness for offence.

"How long do you keep your CCTV tapes for?"

The manager's barricades went up immediately.

"CCTV? *CCTV?* We're just a small hotel and it's a matter of economy."

Current financial climate, expenditure, blah, blah, blah.

"If we were part of a large chain we would *never* have to wipe them because we'd have a digital system... but then we would lose our individual charm. Our charm is very important."

Right now it was wearing thin.

"How long, please, Mister Abernathy?"

After some hesitation he confessed that they wiped them every month.

The D.C.I. allowed himself a mental *'Damn'* and then berated himself for having unrealistic expectations. It was unfair to expect such a small hotel to keep its tapes for longer, after all they probably hadn't *had* many guests murdered, although judging by the ages of the ones he'd passed in reception they'd probably had a fair few natural deaths.

Andy forced himself to smile at the hotelier. Abernathy had done his best to be pleasant and helpful, even if his twitchiness *was* putting him on edge.

"I'll need to see the chambermaid who packed up Mister Kincaid's room, and whoever spoke to the man who came asking to view his possessions, please. And I'll be taking the bags with me for examination."

It sparked a round of foot shuffling and several, "Oh dear, oh dear"s that made the detective wondered how on earth the man coped with running a business when even a few questions made him lose his cool.

"What's the problem now, Mister Abernathy?" The question was accompanied by a weary sigh.

"Well, it's just... well... I mean... Freya is on her day off today, and I'd have to check the Rota to see which junior manager was on the day that the gentleman called."

Talk about making a mountain out of two small hills.

Andy glanced at his watch and made a decision.

"Right. You have them both here for twelve and I'll return then."

It was on the tip of Rufus Abernathy's tongue to ask him where he was going when he decided that he couldn't cope with the answer and reiterated the time instead.

"Twelve o' clock then. Twelve noon that is. That's just over an hour from now..."

Andy left the speaking clock to it, already heading for his car and the quarry to see what, if anything, the divers had found.

****

Flood and Son's Solicitors. Oxford Street, Belfast.

It took the detectives ten minutes to get to Oxford Street and ask Colum Flood nicely for Pete McElroy's effects, and another hour in the street outside trying to think of ways around him when the solicitor refused. There was the option of contacting Amy and Jordan and asking *their* permission to see their father's effects, but that would have meant alerting the two students to their suspicions and upsetting them before they had proof, not to mention that they might have told their mother and raised Annette's hopes that they'd found something to help her case before they were sure.

Craig had then decided that trying for a warrant was best, citing the need to view Pete's papers as part of an investigation. True, it wasn't *their* investigation, but he'd felt there was no advantage in splitting that particular hair. It had fallen to his deputy to be the voice of sanity for the second time that week, something that Liam didn't intend to make a habit of, and point out that telling lies to a judge to obtain a warrant would be career limiting for them both.

In the end they decided to try again with Colum Flood using judicious questioning, so, having managed to get the lawyer to agree to answer anything he felt wouldn't be breaching Pete McElroy's confidentiality, they sat down in his modern office again to begin a session of yes/no.

Liam kicked off, flashing the young solicitor his most winning smile.

"Mister Flood, will you confirm that Mister Peter

McElroy, now deceased, was a client of yours?"

The pleasantly plump young man, who wore long sideburns and a three piece suit that made him look like a character from Dickens, smiled and shook his head. "No, I won't confirm that. That knowledge is privileged."

It made Craig roll his eyes and try a different way.

"We already have that information on record from Mister McElroy's cellmate at Mahon Prison, who also told us that Mister McElroy planned to commit two criminal acts before he died. One was breaking and entering his ex-wife's home, and the other was to deliberately and falsely incriminate her in his death. We believe that an admission of both is contained in a letter he deposited with you. Deposited with you *deliberately* rather than with his criminal lawyer knowing that *you* wouldn't be suspicious, and thereby making you complicit in his crimes. Now, does that change your attitude?"

The young solicitor had been visibly shaken by the word complicit and was adjusting his collar nervously, but he still shook his head, although his next words *did* give Craig some hope.

"I can't confirm that Mister McElroy was a client *or* release any of his papers unless compelled to by a court order."

It wasn't a yes, but it *was* a hint that McElroy's papers were in his possession. Rephrased and taken to Sean Flanagan with Frampton's statement it *might* just be enough to earn them a helping hand.

Craig nodded to the lawyer and made quickly for the door, leaving Liam struggling to keep up and losing him at the lift. They connected again outside the Laganside Courts opposite where Craig was perching on a stone bollard and talking on his phone. He ended the call just as his deputy approached.

"Who were you calling? The Chief Con?"

Craig shook his head. "Annette." At Liam's immediately wary look he shook his head. "Don't worry, I was careful, but I managed to get her to confirm that the kids received calls from Floods last month to come and collect letters Pete had left for the pair of them. Just general 'I love you' stuff but unfortunately nothing to take their mum off the hook or Annette would definitely have been told. At least it's confirmation Pete left letters with Floods to hold."

The D.C.I. hemmed and hawed for a moment and then gave a nod of approval. "OK, so you've confirmed that Flood *was* Pete's solicitor and that the scrote left letters for his kids just like Frampton said. Surely that's enough leverage to ask the C.C. to get a warrant and find out if Pete left a third one for Annette?"

Craig squinted up at him, shielding his eyes from the sun. "Tell me how. *Exactly.*" He gestured back at the office they'd just left. "*Flood* won't confirm there's another letter, and *we* only know it exists because we've been gathering information illegally-"

"*Irregularly,* not illegally. We haven't broken any laws."

"I've bent a few regs at least. Bringing Frampton in for a fishing interview wasn't exactly kosher. But we've *got* to see that third letter or this whole thing will have been pointless and Annette will go on trial. It's Catch sodding 22."

Liam grinned suddenly. "We could break into Floods tonight and nick it."

"Oh, yes, brilliant. That definitely *would* be illegal, so then there'd be three cops going to jail. Still, you and I could keep each other company in Maghaberry at least."

The D.C.I. shook his head hastily. "No way in hell am I sharing a cell with *you*. You'd be nagging me all day long about how much I eat. So, OK, if we can't nick the letter because we don't want to go to the bin, what *do* we do then?"

Craig hopped off his impromptu seat.

"For now you call Jack and tell him to hold on to Frampton a bit longer. We may need to speak to him again. I'm going to phone Davy."

He found the analyst having to shout to make himself heard.

"What's that racket?"

"Mary and Ash are getting into it about s...something as usual. I've given up trying to work out what."

There'd never been any love lost between the junior analyst and the constable and at any other time Craig would have made an effort to discover what they were fighting about or knocked their heads together, but his analysts had too much work to do right now to allow delays so instead he told Davy to put him on speaker and yelled, "SHUT UP!"

The background noise lowered instantly and then tailed off, and Craig pictured the squabbling pair looking around for him, panicked, and then slowly realising that he hadn't just walked in but was on the phone.

When there was complete silence he went on.

"Mary. Whatever work you're doing, move it into my office and *remain* in there until I get back. Ash, stop squabbling and get on with your job. Liam and I will be back in a while and I want results. Take me off speaker now, Davy."

The senior analyst obliged and watched with a smirk as the D.C. grudgingly gathered up her things.

"Are they doing it?"

"Yep. Mary's on her way into your office and Ash is getting back to work. To be fair, she *was* w...winding him up deliberately. She's been driving me mad as well."

"Then I'll give *both* of you lessons in restraint after I've spoken to Constable Li."

The computer expert gave a cheeky laugh. "What did you call for anyway, chief? Is there something you need?"

"Yes. How's it going with Pete McElroy's media accounts? Have you got anywhere at all?"

In lieu of a reply Craig heard the receiver being covered and the familiar click of the call being transferred. The next voice he heard was his junior analyst's, its tone overly polite to deflect the detective's anticipated criticism of his earlier shouting match.

"Peter McElroy had several social media accounts and an email account, sir. I've tried to crack them but the social media firms have got picky about security recently and tightened up."

His frustration was clear and made Craig stifle a laugh. Anyone else would have been pleased about the extra security but for a hacker it was just an obstacle.

"All the better to protect them against people like you, eh?"

"You think? Anyway, I *can* hack them but it'll take me a bit more time, so couldn't we just ask his family for his passwords and access them the old-fashioned way?"

"NO!"

Craig softened his tone slightly. "Sorry, Ash, but no. Just keep hacking and get what you can, please. Pass me back to Davy."

The quieter voice of his senior analyst came back on the line. "Yes, chief?"

"How's everything going otherwise?"

"Honestly? There's still a lot to wade through. I've been given access to Derek Morrow's stuff by his family so I'm on that now, and Mary's been watching the CCTV."

"OK, I'll speak to her in a minute, but I just wanted to say gather together whatever you have for lunchtime. I'll be doing a mini-briefing then. Now, transfer me to my office."

His extension was answered quickly, but Craig could feel his constable's hostility from her silence, although his past experience of her *might* have contributed to the impression as well.

"Mary?"

He didn't know why he was phrasing it as a question; there should be no-one else in his office unless it'd been burgled since he'd left.

"Yes."

Craig gave an exasperated sigh at her sulkiness and counted mentally to ten, only reaching five before he spoke again, deliberately quickly, any pauses likely to give her room to object.

"Pierre Galvet. If you haven't already begun researching his whereabouts I want you to do that as soon as you've completed what you're doing. You know what to look for. You can return to your desk in an hour and I'll need everything for the lunchtime briefing. Thanks."

He hung up before she could draw breath, knowing that neither his approach nor her hour long detention was mature management but not really giving a damn. He had too much to get through to waste his energy arguing with a huffy millennial, although the knowing look that Liam was giving him said that he could only delay dealing with Mary's behaviour for so long.

****

The West Mountain Quarry.

Quarries are always a sorry sight, their stark appearances rarely enhanced by the bleakness of winter. High, brutally hewn walls, human beings and their machinery having none of nature's eons of finesse, and at their bases dark, cold, stagnant water, its surface so filmed with algae that it might have lain undisturbed for decades.

Andy knew that *this* quarry's pool had been disturbed much more recently than that by Stuart Kincaid's body, and now he watched as it was disturbed again, this time by rubber-suited human tadpoles rasping and gasping their way to its depths, placing all of their trust in artificial lights and tanks.

The D.C.I. picked his way down and through the stone rubble at the water's edge towards a small woman who looked like she was in charge, his hints taken from her dark trouser suit and the sunglasses shading her eyes from the pool's reflected glare.

"D.C.I. Angel, Murder Squad."

She smiled with her gaze still fixed on the water. "Inspector Ella Davis. Heading up the search. I take it you're here to see what we've found."

"That would be great."

It prompted her to turn towards him, revealing a raw looking burn on her right cheek that she quickly explained away with, "Oxyacetylene torch slipped last week" as if it was something that happened every day, which it might well have done on her adventurous squad, and added, "You're in luck on the finds. This way."

She motioned Andy back up the way he'd come and followed, until they reached a high-sided van alongside which men were stripping off their wetsuits to reveal full body thermals, and drying their barely-there shorn hair with worn police-issue towels.

One quick rap and the back doors of the van opened revealing another officer, and a few murmured words later a sheet of plastic was laid out on its running board and on it were placed some items in clear evidence bags.

Davis spoke again.

"This is what we've found so far. Anything look useful?"

Andy scanned the treasure trove and lit upon a, once

black but now faded almost to grey, credit card. There was no doubt about it; the card had belonged to Stuart Kincaid. His name was embossed along its lower edge and its expiry date still hadn't been reached.

"This was our man's. We're still missing his phone, wallet and watch."

One of the undressing divers, now clothed in jeans and a jumper, piped up.

"We've just retrieved a phone, Guv. Your old man has it."

Before Andy could say anything the inspector had called out to a large man hunkering at the pool's perimeter.

"DOUGIE. BRING THE PHONE, WILL YOU."

The man gave an acknowledging wave and unfolded himself to his full height, which Andy saw was a good head taller than Liam. He was tempted to invite Dougie back to Belfast with him just to see the deputy's face.

The diver appeared beside them a minute later, smiling down affectionately at his petite wife and boss and passing the evidence bag across as he did.

"What part of the lake did you find it, love?"

Lake. It was a definite promotion for the murky pool.

"A fair way in. Right hand side about forty feet from the shore."

Either floated there out of Stuart Kincaid's pocket or thrown by his killer, and thrown seemed more feasible.

Andy tried to live up to people's expectations of a detective and squinted at the item as if he could identify its owner at a glance. In truth he had no idea what Stuart Kincaid's mobile looked like, but he knew a man who would. A call to Davy confirmed it; the soggy device was just as Luisa Kincaid had described her husband's mobile, and the odds of finding two the same in the remote pool had to be slim.

"I'd like to take this and the credit card with me, Inspector, if that's all right? Our analysts might be able to get something off them."

In reply Davis swept a hand over the rest of the bags.

"You can take it all if you sign."

The collection of coins, keys and a miniature Batmobile made Andy wonder why people seemed to think chucking their crap in water was preferable to putting it in a bin.

"Thanks, but these will do for now." He scribbled his name on a sheet thrust his way. "If you find a wallet and watch let me know, please?"

He handed over his mobile number and headed back to the hotel, to find a chambermaid called Freya Dalkey and a not long out of university management trainee called Tristan Rodgers lined up in its reception like soldiers on parade, with Rufus Abernathy on full alert alongside them.

"Relax, all of you. I just need to ask some questions. Is there somewhere quiet that we could go, Mister Abernathy?"

The manager led the way, more calmly than earlier, into a large back room whose trestle tablets set along each wall suggested that it was the hotel's venue of choice for buffets. He took up position intimidatingly behind his two, now seated, employees, folding his arms with a solidity that suggested any request by Andy to speak to them alone would result in immediate refusal and the hotel's lawyers being trotted out.

Resigned to his audience the murder detective turned first to the chambermaid, and after getting the usual boring details to help Davy confirm that she was who she said she was and wasn't wanted for some crime, police forces having been embarrassed many times for missing such people for lack of simple checks, Andy set aside his notebook and rested back in his chair, attempting to relax the thirty-something woman with a smile.

It didn't work, the chambermaid still so tense that she was wringing a corner of her overall as if she was trying to remove a particularly resistant stain, so the D.C.I. stared pointedly at her boss and then not so subtly jerked his head towards a chair, the threat clear if Abernathy didn't comply and sit down.

It eased the tension in the room slightly and the wringing softened to a fidget.

"Now, Ms Dalkey. Can you identify this man for me?"

A photograph of Stuart Kincaid looking business-like, and more importantly alive, was produced.

"That's Mister Kincaid."

"And can you tell me how you know him?"

A nervous glance at her employer gained nodded permission to go on.

"He stayed here twice. Once a few years back, and the second time last winter for a few days. I took care of his room both times. I always take care of the rooms in Marchmont Wing."

"Good. But can I ask you why you know his name? You must have a great number of guests and you surely don't remember them all."

She gave an unexpected smile, as if she was recalling something pleasant.

"Mister Abernathy told me it earlier, but I remembered anyway because Mister Kincaid was nice to me. He asked my name and we chatted about our families."

If such simple civility impressed her then it didn't say much for the rest of the hotel's guests.

"Did he tell you why he was in the area?"

She thought for a moment and then nodded.

"He said his sister used to have relatives nearby, which seemed a bit strange. I mean, wouldn't they have been his relatives too?"

Not if they were in-laws, as the Westburys had been.

The maid continued, volunteering. "He seemed a bit sad."

"About his sister?"

"No, generally. But he was always nice."

"Is that all he said about his reasons for being here?"

"No. He said he was looking for something too. He went out early every morning and didn't come back till late."

Andy edged forward on his chair.

"Do you have any idea what that something could have been?"

"No, although he did keep looking at a photograph he carried. It was of a young girl. He told me she was his niece."

"And he definitely said he was looking for *something* and not *someone*?"

The woman's lips formed an 'O' that suggested the distinction might carry some weight, but when after a moment's further thought clarity was still elusive she ended her search with a sigh.

"I'm sorry, I can't remember. All I know is that Mister Kincaid was in the area looking for something, or someone maybe."

It was enough to suggest that they were on the right track.

Andy smiled at her to relax and turned to her companion, noticing that the young manager seemed *far* more at ease, his posture a slouch and his hands looking very at home in his trouser pockets.

"Mister Tristan Rodgers."

As the freckled youth's mouth opened Andy half-expected to hear, "That's my name, don't wear it out" emerge, and he felt sure that it would have done had Abernathy not been only feet away.

Instead a clipped, "Yes, sir" hit the air, accompanied by a grin that said the young man was thrilled at being questioned by the cops and would be regaling his mates with the tale as soon as he got home.

"You were the junior manager on duty when a man came inquiring about Mister Kincaid's things. Tell me about that, please."

The hands came out of the pockets and Rodgers sat forward enthusiastically as if he was about to tell a tale.

"Yeh, well, he turned up one day last November just after I'd come on duty." He glanced at his boss. "When Mister Abernathy told me you'd be asking I went back and checked the exact date. It was the fourth."

The day that Stuart Kincaid's phone signal had died.

"How can you remember so accurately?"

"Because he turned up when I was watching the footie. It was Man City v Southampton, premier league. Brilliant match. Anyway, it was a quiet Sunday, so I was in the back office watching."

The detective glanced at Abernathy, expecting to see horror that his employees took time away from their duties for such things, but instead the hotelier mouthed, "Great game", making him warm slightly to the man.

Rodgers spotted the exchange and grinned. "Don't worry, when we're not busy Mister A *lets* us to watch telly, just as long as the guests don't see." The youth snorted rudely. "*They* like to think we all stand in a cupboard somewhere just waiting for their call."

A squint from Abernathy said *that* had been a step too far, but the young manager was on a roll now so he carried on.

"Anyway, so I was in the back room watching the footie when the desk bell goes. I come out to reception to see what's what and there's this man standing there-"

Andy stopped him. "Tell me what you remember about him, please. Physically first. And take your time."

The youth screwed up his face and as he did so Andy noticed that his freckles coalesced curiously to form the shape of the Isle of Man. The map remained intact for several seconds until Rodgers spoke again.

"Taller than me."

Andy stood up. "Show me exactly."

He was five-ten and Rodgers was around the same, so he expected him just to point above or below his head. Instead he gestured to his boss and Rufus Abernathy obligingly came across, at which point Freya Dalkey nodded.

"Yes, he *was* about Mister A's size."

"Of course. You saw him too, didn't you?"

"Only for a minute."

"But you both agree that he was Mister Abernathy's height."

"Yes."

Around six-three. Andy retook his seat and the others followed.

"OK, carry on."

"So he was that height with dirty fair hair."

"Not brown?"

"No, dark blond. I can't be sure about his eyes-"

Freya interjected. "They were greeny-grey, and he had really heavy eyebrows. Darker than his hair, so they made him look like he was scowling, even though he wasn't I don't think."

Andy smiled and turned back to Rodgers. "Anything else on his physical appearance?"

"He was kind of swarthy. And fit looking. Slim, but you knew there were serious muscles under his clothes."

"Age?"

"Not as old as the boss but a bit younger than you."

"Older than Ms Dalkey?"

"Oh yeh, older than Freya but younger than you."

Around forty would be his guess. Andy turned back to the chambermaid.

"Does that description fit?"

"Yes."

He scribbled everything down before going on.

"OK. Now, what was he wearing?"

"Shirt and jeans."

"With shoes not trainers." The maid leaned forward eagerly, adding, "And he had a ring on. Not a wedding ring, but one of those gold ones people wear sometimes with initials on them."

A signet ring.

"Did you see any engraving on it?"

"No, sorry, he was standing too far away."

"Mister Rodgers, did you notice anything else?"

The young man shrugged. "I didn't even see a ring."

Andy turned back to the maid for more detail.

"Which finger was it on, Ms Dalkey?"

"His little finger, I can't remember which hand. I noticed because it's not that usual to see men wearing jewellery even nowadays. He wore a big watch as well. It looked heavy."

An alarm bell rang in Andy's head but he parked the detail and went on.

"OK, very good. Now, both of you, was there anything unusual about his voice or accent?"

It was Rodgers who replied. "Yeh, he had one of those weird accents."

"Not from here?"

"No, but like he had been once, maybe a long time ago. I mean it sounded like he'd come from here somewhere but had lived away. It was weird."

Unfortunately weird wasn't a linguistic category and the chambermaid wasn't able to shed any further light.

"OK, we're almost done. Now, tell me exactly what this man said to you, Mister Rodgers."

The answer began with a snort and continued with, "Aye, well, now *there's* a sorry tale..."

The expression sounded so incongruous coming from the youth that Andy knew he must have heard his parents or grandparents use the phrase.

"...he pitched up at the front desk, but I think he only did *that* because you can't get up to the rooms without us opening the security door, or opening it with your passkey yourself and-"

The detective stopped him. "Do guests get a passkey?"

"Oh, aye."

"But *he* didn't have one?"

"That's the strange thing, he did, but it wasn't working on the security door so he had to call me-"

Andy stopped him again. "Could I see one?"

Abernathy immediately produced a cream plastic rectangle from his pocket and passed it across. "That's a master key for everywhere in the building, but the guests' passkeys are only encrypted for their room and the security doors."

"And that's done when they check in?"

The hotelier shook his head. "The security door codes are embedded on *all* our keys and then a new room code's randomly generated by the computer for each guest. People walk away with their keys all the time and we don't want them coming back and being able to access the rooms."

The detective nodded and turned back to Tristan Rodgers. "Go on, please."

"OK, so, he buzzes me and says he can't get up to his room, so I ask which number it is and he says nineteen." He dropped his voice conspiratorially. "Except *I* knew Mister Kincaid was staying in nineteen so my antenna starts to twitch. I ask him his name, all casual like, and he says *it's* Kincaid too, cheeky as you like."

"Did you challenge him about it?"

"Yeh, and then he says he's not Stuart Kincaid, he's *Paul* Kincaid, Mister Kincaid's brother, and he'd asked him to come and get something from his room-"

Freya jumped in. "That's when *I* walked into reception and saw him. I thought it was a bit fishy because he didn't look like Mister Kincaid and he hadn't mentioned a brother, but I didn't need to say anything because Trist here already had it under control."

The youth preened himself. "Anyhow, then I said I was sorry, but brother or no brother we couldn't give access to anyone's possessions without a court order. He looked really pissed, and then all of a sudden he just took off."

"Did he take the key with him?"

"No. Threw it on the desk when he walked."

"But if the passkey *had* worked he could have reached room nineteen without anyone seeing."

"Yeh, it was a bit of luck it failed, wasn't it, but it happens a lot. They're rubbish those plastic keys. We're always having to reprogramme them. I went up and checked it in Mister Kincaid's door afterwards and it didn't work there either so the key must have been a dud, although it was definitely one of ours."

The information made Andy frown. A dud or damaged by the quarry pool's water? Had the man taken Stuart Kincaid's key from his body after he'd killed him, or had he just got hold of a proforma from somewhere else? The whole episode didn't say *definitely* that the man was Stuart Kincaid's murderer but it certainly put him in the frame, so they needed to ID him. And officially, in case it was needed in court.

Suddenly the D.C.I. had what he knew was a ridiculously optimistic thought.

"I don't suppose you kept the key?"

The young manager's face fell. "No. Sorry."

His boss interjected pointedly. "And neither did he report the episode to the police, although you would *now*, wouldn't you, Tristan?"

It prompted a glum nod from the youth as Abernathy went on.

"Normal procedure in such an episode would be to call the police, give them any evidence, CCTV, the key and so on, but Mister Rodgers was still being trained so..."

Damn. They'd lost evidence because of inexperience.

Still, they had two people who could identify Kincaid's possible killer now, and they had his luggage with whatever the man had been searching for presumably still inside. Andy decided he was going to have two companions on his trip back to Belfast.

****

Annette Eakin's House. East Belfast.

Had Craig known what had been happening across town that morning he would have had to decide whether or not to try and stop it, and that would have put him between two rocks and a hard place and handed him a conundrum he couldn't possibly have solved without putting *someone's* nose out of joint.

Hearing about it ten minutes before his briefing from a laughing so hard that she could barely speak Katy, he chided himself for *not* having anticipated the situation, knowing *all* of the women involved and their personalities, in particular his mother, who all her life had been like a runaway train. Even when under the calming influence of Maureen Stevens his mother Mirella was impossible to control, something that his father had accepted soon after they'd married fifty years before. But he'd reckoned without Maureen Steven's kind nature actually *adding* to the force of that eccentricity, which on this occasion it most definitely had.

Through her laughter Katy had explained that she'd casually mentioned to the pair that Annette was feeling depressed alone at home all day and also that she had a toddler daughter, Carrie, and they'd taken it as an invitation to kill several birds with one stone: cheer the inspector up, practice their grandmothering skills, and get a third opinion on what sort of place their own grown-up children, and more importantly their future grandchild, might one day call home.

So it was that Annette had trustingly answered her front door that morning, surprised to see Mirella and Maureen but merely thinking that Craig had told them of her situation and they'd come to offer tea and sympathy, only to find herself and her young daughter being propelled into respectable outfits and hustled into Maureen Stevens' little red car, in what minus the affectionate laughter might have counted as a kidnapping.

The outing turned out to be less a pity party for Annette than a cheerful, ricocheting, road trip, where she and Carrie were chauffeured all over Belfast via numerous stops at coffee and toy shops, to view houses that ranged from chic magazine centrefolds, through overly sensible boxes that she couldn't picture Craig living in *ever*, to the other extreme of homes that were so covered in mirrors, zebra print and ornaments that Liberace would have thought that they were too much, although her toddler's cries of "Sparkly, sparkly" did result in several indulgent,

"Ahh"s.

As an abstract concept the outing had car-crash written all over it, but as an experience it worked brilliantly, with the group ganging up in different combinations against the others to curtail their wildest instincts of gaudiness, boring common sense and romance, and end up with a shortlist of places for the newlyweds to view that had even been obligingly road-tested by a tearaway child.

But Craig wouldn't learn of that success until much later, so to add to his worries about work he spent the rest of his day picturing the good, the bad, and the sensible creating chaos all over town.

****

The C.C.U. 2.30 p.m.

The postponement of the team briefing until Andy arrived back from Rownton had allowed Ben Frampton and Arthur Norris to be squeezed for information again until their pips squeaked, although not with anything particularly juicy coming out, and for the squad's more deskbound pursuits to be progressed as well. By the time the whole team was assembled, coffees in hand and a clean whiteboard standing alongside the previously annotated one it was almost two-thirty, and one hundred miles away there was a *far* less orderly scene playing out.

Róisín Casey's ruminations the evening before had sparked an angry telephone conversation that had had at first two, then four and then seven people on the line in a conference call. It was a format that she used comfortably every day in a business context but this time she'd felt ganged up on.

She was in the doghouse and no amount of underlining was convincing the others that *she* hadn't been the one to draw the cops' attention to them; it had been the murder, and worse the careless disposal of Stuart Kincaid that had caused that. Nor had pointing out to them that she, as the more visible of the two of them currently in Ireland, was the one in the hot seat gained her any sympathy, so when the call ended the banker was left with the words, "Bloody well sort it out!" ringing in her ears. How she was supposed to do that was left entirely up to her, but do it she better had and Róisín knew it; her partners in this particular enterprise were people who sanctioned murder whenever necessary and they wouldn't draw the line at killing one of their own.

But while the financier was working out how to ensure the police investigation hit a dead end, it was ramping up in Belfast. The squad had reached an impasse on Stuart Kincaid's death unless they got some new information and Craig was praying that this briefing would give them that.

He cracked the clean whiteboard hard with his knuckles to say that they were starting, making several other people wince as he did it but seemingly hardened to the pain himself.

"OK. This briefing is important so give me everything you've got, but as tidily as possible, please. Let's start with..." He gazed around and lit on Aidan, who was chewing energetically on a piece of nicotine gum. "Aidan and Ryan. You were together in Rownton and you interviewed Norris, so off you go."

Seeing that the D.C.I. was going to choke if he tried to swallow his gum too fast Ryan rose to his feet, taking the marker that Craig was holding out.

"OK, to summarise yesterday and today. We interviewed half the village and they led us to the woman that you've all heard about, Rio Reynolds, who had been paid by a man, Arthur Norris, to lie to the newspapers and radio about the reason that a local man called Derek Morrow committed suicide."

He scribbled up 'Norris' and 'Morrow' and went on.

"Derek Morrow was a local builder who also managed The West Mountain Quarry that was excavated between twenty-twelve and fifteen. His firm was involved in the excavation but also continues to manage the outbuildings to this day. Other than that they were building a new housing development at the edge of the village and did local odds and bobs."

Craig held up a hand to stop him. "So definitely not as stressed with work as his suicide note would have had us believe."

"Exactly. But even so, Arthur Norris or whoever *he* works for wanted *no* suggestion of work as the reason for

Morrow's suicide, hence manufacturing a romantic affair and getting Reynolds to lie about it." He wrote 'work - deflection?' beside Morrow's name.

"OK, so if Morrow's work *is* something that someone's trying to deflect us from, then what aspect of it and why?" He tapped on Norris' name. "That brings us back to Arthur Norris, who paid the girl to lie, and who it turns out *also* had an involvement with the quarry, as the land agent for its purchase. Norris said *he* feared we were in Rownton because of some environmental pollution issue at the quarry and that Morrow's reference to work would make us look deeper at that, so he was trying to divert from any discovery of the pollution with the girl's story of an affair."

Craig stopped him and turned to the others. "Theories, anyone?"

Liam's came first and pithily. "Bollocks. No-one kills themselves over a bit of environmental whatsit. Anyway, surely any pollution wouldn't have been Morrow's fault? He was just a builder."

Aidan had freed his mouth of gum and decided to play Devil's Advocate. "But he *was* supposed to be caring for the quarry, so he *might* have thought he'd missed some pollutants and felt guilty, what with the local kids paddling about there."

Craig raised an eyebrow. "*You really think that?* After interviewing Norris?"

"Nope. But I'm advancing a theory like you asked."

Craig rolled his eyes. "Let's limit it to sensible ones. OK, anyone else?"

Andy pictured the quarry. A deep grey canyon with a stagnant pool at its base; not somewhere he would fancy a swim but he hadn't seen any signs of pollution there.

"Most of us have been to the quarry, me just today..." Mary's jaw jutted out in a sulk at the mention of her cancelled road trip. "...and all right, I know pollution *can* be hidden, but did anyone notice *any* signs of it there? I know I didn't."

When the answer was a clear "No" Davy decided to contribute some facts to the debate.

"After Norris mentioned pollution I asked the divers to test some s...samples of water, and the first results say there's nothing strange."

Andy nodded, vindicated. "So... Morrow mentioned work in his note and I think that was deliberate, trying to point our attention to something-"

Liam cut in. "Why not just spell it out?"

"Because that might have been construed as him *admitting* to something and he had his family's feelings to worry about."

Craig retrieved his marker and wrote 'Pointer' on the board.

"OK. If Morrow *wasn't* pointing us towards pollution but something else, perhaps something to do with his work at the quarry or perhaps linked to some other work he was involved in, then *why* was he telling us?"

He turned back to Aidan, regretting his earlier 'sensible' jibe and hoping that the D.C.I would ignore it.

He did.

"Guilt, that's why. Morrow felt guilty about something he'd been up to and he was pointing us to it. I'm tempted to say that because he killed himself just after Stuart Kincaid's body was found that he'd actually had something to do with Kincaid's murder-"

"Murdered him you mean? He couldn't have. Morrow was the same height as Kincaid; I saw his file."

The D.C.I. shook his head. "No, Morrow didn't actually kill Kincaid, but maybe he knew about it? Or felt that we were going to catch him for something else while we were in Rownton. He was definitely panicked by us being there. The pub landlord told me."

Craig nodded. "Agreed. It might have been both. Morrow could have known something about Kincaid's murder and *also* been up to something else, and us finding the body somehow risked blowing everything open."

He was surprised by his deputy shaking his head.

"Yes and no. I agree Morrow didn't murder Kincaid, boss, because if he'd been feeling guilty about something to do with that it would have been the easiest thing in the world to write 'work stress because of the quarry' and point us specifically to his involvement with the place. Instead he wrote 'work stress' in general *knowing* that no-one who knew him would believe it, not even his wife, and we would start to dig far deeper."

"So you're saying that Kincaid's murder was the least of

Morrow's worries."

The D.C.I. thought for a moment and then nodded. "Yeh, that's exactly right. Morrow was feeling guilty about something that in *his* mind was worse than murder, and he thought that us turning up in town was going to blow it apart. I *also* think he pointed us to it after his death *hoping* that we would find out what it was and stop it, but killed himself because he couldn't live with what would happen to him if we did."

Craig furrowed his brow in thought and after a few seconds he nodded. "OK, I agree. Morrow could have been involved in something serious that we don't know about yet."

He wrote 'Guilt – cause?' on the board and glanced around the group expectantly for the next gem. He didn't have to wait for long.

Davy clambered to his feet and reached for the marker.

"Right, so we got permission to examine Derek Morrow's phone and computers and I've been w...working on those for a few hours. It w...wasn't long enough to get through everything so I focused on his finances, and Morrow had..." he wrote a number on the board,"...four bank accounts."

Liam snorted rudely. "So what? I do as well. Savings, current, post-office and an ISA, and Morrow would've needed a business account as well."

The analyst gave him a cool look. "Can I finish?"

"Go on then. Dazzle us."

The look became wry as Davy went on.

"We found four bank accounts and something else interesting. Three of Morrow's bank accounts were a business account for his building firm, and a current account out of which he transferred money every month to a savings account. All of those were with the same bank and the shortcut to it was pinned on his computer, and accessible with a click and using the right passwords. Morrow listed them in the letter he left for his wife, s...so no mystery there at all."

He perched on the edge of a desk and went on. "He wasn't wealthy but he *was* earning a decent amount, so his firm was solvent and he and his family w...were living within their means. It's Morrow's fourth account that I'm still trying to crack." He smiled triumphantly at Liam. "In the Cayman Islands. He didn't leave a password for it. Or for this."

He pressed a key on his smart-pad, displaying an icon on the LED screen.

"This icon was encrypted and placed in a *hidden* folder on Morrow's laptop. I haven't got past the encryption yet, it's heavy duty, but I've identified it as belonging to a cryptocurrency site."

He got just the uncomprehending looks that he'd expected from everyone but Ash and rolled his eyes in mock despair.

"Cryptocurrency? Yes? No? Doesn't *anyone* but Ash know what I'm talking about?" He turned back to Liam. "Surely *you* do? You knowing so much about accounts, after all."

Craig gave him a moment to make the D.C.I. feel deservedly uncomfortable before saying, "Move it along, please, Davy."

The analyst did so with a smug grin. "OK, cryptocurrency is essentially cyber currency, so it exists in bytes of data rather than as coins or notes and all exchanges take place in the Ethernet. The best known version is Bitcoin, but this icon links to another firm."

Andy perked up. "I've heard of Bitcoin. There's something called a blockchain as well, isn't there?"

"Yep. A blockchain is like an accountant's ledger. Basically it's a running record of the cryptocurrency transactions."

Craig nodded. "OK, so Morrow's icon led to one of these cryptocurrency sites? Couldn't he just have been investing in it?"

The analyst pulled a face. "Yes, but... OK, so it's not out of the question for Morrow to have got on the cryptocurrency trail, especially years back when it was cheaper, but there are two weird things here. First, he had the icon hidden and heavily encrypted. Why? Second its log, I managed to get into that because its encryption was weaker, says that the site's been accessed repeatedly over the past few weeks. S...Several times a day."

"Which tells us?"

"Morrow must have been trading *very* heavily. Why

else access it so often? And he must have been making the payments from his Cayman account because there's no activity on his other accounts that fits."

Craig noticed that Ash was looking puzzled.

"Ash? You have something for us?"

The computer expert's mouth opened as if he was reaching for something, but as they watched it slipped from his grasp.

"Damn! There was something I read about crime linked with crypto recently, but I can't remember it." His slim face brightened with determination. "But don't worry, I will."

"OK. Then you and Davy work together on that and on unlocking Morrow's Cayman account. They could be important."

"We'll need to take it slowly, chief, or we could w...wipe things."

As Craig nodded he suddenly felt that the line of enquiry was going to prove very important although he honestly couldn't have said why.

"OK, keep going with those, Davy, they could be the key to why Morrow *really* killed himself. Right, let's tidy up Arthur Norris. Aidan and Ryan, bring us up to date."

This time it was the D.C.I. who stood up. "OK, so we know the environmental pollution angles a crock now-"

"Norris might have believed it."

"I'm pretty sure he did and does, Guv, but what I was going on to say was, I don't think we're going to get anything else useful from Norris except for maybe who employs him."

Ash raised a finger. "I've got something on that. Norris is a retired business consultant."

Liam gave a grunt of disgust. "What the hell *is* a business consultant anyway? They don't actually *run* a business but they feel free to tell other people how they've made a hash of running theirs?"

The analyst came back at him like a flash. "What, you mean like *you* don't actually commit crimes but you tell others how they made a mess of committing theirs?"

He grinned, displaying his perfect white teeth and making the D.C.I. conscious of his own slightly tea-tinted ones.

Craig chortled at the quick retort. "Be honest, he got you there, Liam. Carry on with what you were saying, Ash."

The analyst ignored the D.C.I.'s disgruntled glare as he did.

"OK, well, Norris used to work for one of the big firms specialising in mortgages and finance, then he took retirement at fifty and set up on his own. He does some work in Belfast as a mortgage advisor and he also acts as an agent for some properties."

"Of which the quarry was one."

"Yes. That basically entailed him processing all the planning and council applications before it was opened, contracting Derek Morrow then and now, and liaising with the owners."

"Like the mystery S.W.M.B.O. who called looking for him perhaps? I'm still waiting to hear a real name here."

Davy looked glum. "Sorry, chief. The quarry's owned by a consortium and we're struggling to get behind the front."

"Keep trying." He turned back to Aidan. "What more do you have on Norris?"

"He's so protective of this mystery woman it's like she's his kid."

Even the chivalrous Andy laughed at that. "More likely his mistress, that's if he's married."

Ash nodded again. "He has been for forty years. One son. He's a vicar."

Liam chuckled. "I bet *he* wouldn't be pleased if Dad was playing away, now-"

Craig interjected wryly. "I don't suppose Mrs Norris would be enchanted either. Did Norris give you the woman's name, Aidan?"

"Nope, and short of using thumbscrews on him I don't think he will."

A glance at Ryan said that he concurred.

"OK, but she must be the woman who phoned Rownton nick looking for him-"

Ash cut in. "And the woman who left the messages on his phone. No name unfortunately, but Grace got an earful from her that says she isn't half as delicate as Norris thinks."

The words made Aidan frown. "That fits. We got the impression that he was a bit scared of her as well as feeling protective of her. Weird relationship. Almost S and M."

Before Liam could say something rude, Craig jumped up and rapped the board again.

"OK. Where are we with tracing those calls from the southern mobile and merchant bank?"

Ash replied. "We reckoned if the same woman was using both lines we were looking at someone working in a merchant bank down south. Probably Dublin. The fake number she gave the Rownton sergeant had a Dublin prefix too."

Even when telling lies we give something about ourselves away.

"I'm waiting for a list of the bank's extensions there and I've put a trace on her pay-as-you-go mobile, so we'll pick that up if she uses it again. At the moment its signal's completely dead, which means she's smart enough to know to take the battery out."

"OK, good. Keep going on that."

Craig tapped his nose for a moment in thought before he spoke again.

"Has anyone else noticed how finance seems an important factor here? Morrow's cryptocurrency, Norris' mortgage business, our mystery woman's links with a merchant bank?"

If they hadn't noticed before they did now. Craig was just pondering if there were any implications beyond greed when he noticed someone familiar enter the squad-room.

"Right, let's take a ten minute break. We'll restart with Andy, then Ash and Mary."

He was across the floor before anyone could respond, a broad smile on his face as he greeted the woman standing by Alice's desk.

"Nicky! How are you?"

She smiled back, looking healthier and happier than she had in months, "I'm good, sir." She nodded towards his office.

"Could I have a quick word?"

Craig's heart sank instantly. Was she about to tell him that she wasn't coming back? He could see that Alice had had the same thought, although whether it had perturbed her was impossible to tell.

A minute later they were in his office and Nicky was

reassuring him.

"I'd like to start back at the beginning of March, sir, but only part-time."

Craig swallowed his disappointment. He knew part-time was better than no time but the truth was that, although he liked Alice now and they'd got into a rhythm of working together, she was a bit too quiet for him and he missed his old PA's sparkiness.

Hopeful of changing her mind he asked a question.

"How's Jonny?"

Nicky nodded hesitantly, quickly touching the wooden arm of her chair as she did.

"Improving, touch wood. He's attending his counselling regularly, and he's been clean now for two months, but he's starting back at school on Monday and that'll bring pressure and maybe the temptation to use again, so I want to be home more of the time just in case. He's not out of the woods by a long way and we can't afford a relapse."

"I understand."

"That's why, sir, if possible, I'd just like to work between ten and two. So I can see him off in the morning and be there after school when he comes home."

She gazed at her boss hopefully but instead of the eagerness that she'd hoped for, and honestly anticipated after all of their years working together, she saw consternation on Craig's face.

"You don't want me back?"

The question made the detective sit up straight and end his calculation on working hours and their costs right away.

"God, no! I mean yes, yes, of course I do!"

Even part-time, Nicky was the best PA on the force by a mile.

"It's just you looked really worried."

"Did I? Sorry. I was just wondering how to go about things logistically. If you're only going to be part-time then I can't let Alice go back into the pool or we'll be in trouble. But with both of you here, who sits where and when? But I think I have a solution for that, or soon will have. That's if you're OK with Alice sticking around that is?"

He watched as she chewed her lip for a moment and knew there was a question she wanted to ask.

"Yes... but, it's just... I mean... who'll be in charge?"

It made him smile; same old bossy Nicky.

"You will. Alice won't mind, you're more senior on the scale than her anyway. I'll chat to her about working hours and how we do this, and then let's all meet up next week. How would that suit?"

It brought another, this time satisfied, smile.

"That'll suit very well."

The PA rose to leave.

"I'd better go now. I'm taking Jonny shopping for some new shoes."

Craig rose as well. "And I have a briefing to finish. People will keep bumping each other off in this place."

When he'd walked her to the lift he reached over and gave her an unaccustomed hug. "It's lovely to see you, Nicky. And welcome back soon."

As Craig retook his seat amongst the group, sipping the coffee that a curious Alice had handed him on his the way past, he got straight back to business, or was about to anyway when Liam stated the obvious.

"That was Nicky."

"Well spotted."

"When's she coming back?"

Craig shook his head firmly, ending the discussion before it started with, "I'll update you later" before turning to Andy with a smile.

"Right, D.C.I. Angel. You're up."

The always relaxed detective was so low in his seat it looked as if he was about to fall asleep.

"I could report from here, chief."

A brisk wave said it was the whiteboard or nothing so he grudgingly obliged.

"OK, well, I went to the hotel where Stuart Kincaid stayed. I went twice, the first time to speak to the manager and pick up Kincaid's stored luggage, and then I returned on my way back from meeting with the divers to interview two members of his staff. Before I get to *them*, the divers found a credit card with Kincaid's name on it and a mobile phone that matches the description Luisa Kincaid gave us, so I dropped those and his luggage in with Des on my way back here."

"Excellent. No sign of his wallet and watch?"

"Not yet, although I might have something on the watch later. They were still diving when I left and I don't envy them their job. That quarry looked freezing." He shuddered and then turned unexpectedly to Liam. "One of them was almost a foot taller than you."

Head, foot, what's in a little exaggeration?

"Freak."

"Jealous."

The exchange was ended by Craig rolling his eyes, so Andy hurried on.

"The stuff was found about forty feet in from the right hand side of the pool. It might have slipped out of Kincaid's pocket or been thrown in; I'll check with Doc Winter how that fits with his PM findings when I go back to see what forensics have found."

He rubbed his hands together as if he was about to get to the good bit.

"OK, so then I met with the chambermaid who'd tended Kincaid's room and a young manager. I'll take the maid first. Her name's Freya Dalkey and she remembered Kincaid well because he was very nice to her. Pleasant generally, although she mentioned that he seemed sad too. He'd stayed at the hotel twice, the second time last winter-"

Craig cut in. "Was the first time in twenty-sixteen?"

"She just said a few years back, but I'd say yes." Seeing Craig's eyebrows rising he added hastily, "I'll check to be sure. Anyway, Kincaid talked about his sister, saying that she used to have some relatives nearby-"

Liam cut in. "The Westburys."

Andy nodded. "Had to be, otherwise he'd have said that they were his relatives too. OK, so then Kincaid showed her Bella's photograph and said she was his niece, and that he was in the area looking for something, or someone, Freya couldn't remember exactly which."

Craig allowed himself a small smile. It confirmed what they thought they knew.

"Then I met with a young management trainee called Tristan Rodgers, not long out of Uni." The D.C.I. reached into his jacket and withdrew his notebook, reading aloud. "A man turned up one day inquiring about Kincaid's things and Tristan was on duty."

"When?"

"The fourth of November. A Sunday afternoon. He remembered because there was a football match on and he'd been watching it in the back office when the man rang the bell in reception."

Aidan nodded. "I remember that match. Man City won six-one. I lost twenty quid on it."

Andy shrugged indifferently. Sport wasn't his thing.

"Rodgers described the man as..." he turned over the page, "...around six-three with dark blond hair, greeny-grey eyes, and dark, heavy eyebrows that made him look like he was scowling-"

Craig stopped him. "That's quite a detailed description."

His sceptical tone said that most young men rarely remembered details beyond how many limbs someone had, especially when they were raring to get back to the footie, so he wasn't surprised when Andy responded with,

"It was a joint effort with Freya."

"OK, carry on."

"The man also had a swarthy look, and was described as fit looking, not fat. Slim and muscled."

Mary commented for the first time in an hour. "Sounds just my type."

"Only if he wore earplugs."

Craig made a show of looking around for who'd made the jibe, shooting his junior analyst a warning but not entirely unsympathetic glance as he passed.

"Go on, Andy. What was he wearing?"

"Shirt and jeans, with shoes not trainers."

"Age?"

"Around forty waste guess. The maid added that he was wearing a signet ring on his little finger but she couldn't read the inscription."

Pity. A nice set of initials could really have narrowed any suspect list they eventually managed to produce.

Andy paused for effect before delivering his next line. "And she *also* said that he was wearing a big watch."

Craig sat forward urgently. "Do you think she could ID it?"

"I'm planning to check later." He looked at the analysts. "If one of you could get me a photo of the model Stuart

Kincaid wore?"

"Can do."

Craig was hopeful as his D.C.I. looked. "OK, good. Go on, Andy."

"Both of them said the man had a strange accent. As if he'd come from somewhere in Ireland but had lived away."

Liam nodded knowingly. "Mangled. Like that mid-Atlantic twang you get with people from here that move to the States. They keep changing accent mid-sentence like they're confused. Torn between two worlds."

Craig rolled his eyes. "Thank you, Sigmund Freud. OK, so this man rang the bell in reception and Rodgers came out. What happened next, Andy?"

"That part was interesting. Rodgers said he probably only rang the bell at all because you can't get through the security doors to the bedrooms without using a passkey. The man had one but it wasn't working."

He produced a sample key from his pocket, nodding Liam to pass it around.

"That's one they gave me. *Every* key has the codes for the security doors embedded in it, and then the hotel programmes them with a randomly generated code for their bedroom when a guest checks in. The random codes are changed after each stay because people walk off with their keys all the time. Anyway, the stranger told Rodgers that he couldn't get up to his room so Rodgers asked for the room number and was told nineteen. He knew that Stuart Kincaid was staying in nineteen so he asked the man his name and he said *it* was Kincaid too. *Paul* Kincaid, Stuart's brother. He said that Stuart had asked him to go to his room to collect something, but the chambermaid said Kincaid had never mentioned a brother to her."

Davy interjected. "He definitely didn't have one."

"Exactly. Anyway Rodgers was well on guard, and said brother or no brother they couldn't allow access to anyone's room or possessions without a court order. Apparently the man looked really angry, threw the key down and left."

Craig sighed. "But if the key *had* worked he could have been in and out without anyone seeing a thing."

"Yep. Lucky break for us it failed. Apparently it happens all the time and they have to reprogramme them."

Liam rolled his eyes. "Don't I bloody know it. Usually when you've already carted suitcases up ten flights of stairs and then you have to traipse all the way back down to the main desk."

Spoken like a man who'd spent years acting as a packhorse for his kids.

Andy carried on.

"Anyway, it was a stroke of luck that it failed. The question is, had the man taken Kincaid's key from his dead body, or had he just got hold of a proforma from elsewhere? Unfortunately Rodgers was only being trained then so he didn't think to keep the key, and he didn't report it to the police..."

Damn.

But not everything was lost.

"...so then I thought, we could at least get a *sketch* of this Mister X, so they're both downstairs with the artist now. The hotel manager wasn't best pleased I was stealing his staff for the day, but tough-"

Craig grinned. "Excellent work, Andy. I'll send Alice down to sit with them, and as soon as we get the sketch Ash and Davy can run it."

He went to speak to the PA, and had just returned to the group and was writing 'Stuart Kincaid's killer?' on the board when suddenly he had another thought.

"Davy and Ash... Blaine Westbury. What does he look like again?"

It was the senior analyst who replied. "Thirty-eight, fairish hair. I have his driving licence photo but not his height, but I can call his brother and find out."

"Do that now, please, and then one of you take a photo of him downstairs after we're done. But wait till the hotel pair have finished their sketches first. I don't want to taint their IDs."

Liam frowned at what he was implying. "You think Blaine might have been the man at the hotel? But why would *he* have killed Stuart Kincaid?"

Craig shook his head. "I don't know yet, Liam, and I'm well aware that I could be reaching, but I want to rule him out. Remember the post-mistress said she saw Blaine running from the direction of the quarry around the time Kincaid was killed, and she described *him* as wearing a shirt and jeans as well."

He turned back to his analysts. "Let me know what you get on that immediately. Right, Ash, give us whatever you've got, then I'll take Mary on the CCTV and Galvet, and Davy can add anything that we've missed."

He held out the marker but the younger man shook his head, motioning the group to widen the misshapen circle they'd gathered in so that everyone could see the screen by Alice's desk.

"OK, I'll go through the negative findings first to rule things out." A bullet point appeared on the screen. "The Vice Squad has run the various aged images of Bella Westbury through all their databases and there's nothing that fits. No images of abuse, no images of her at all."

A quiet sigh of relief ran through the group, apart from Liam who gave a noisy, "Bloody brilliant news."

"Yes, but we haven't got the results back from the intelligence agencies yet, so I wouldn't cheer just yet. But it's definitely hopeful. Vice's image database is huge."

That brought not so quiet grunts of disgust.

He tapped up a second bullet point. "OK, next, looking at social services registers for child abuse the story seems to be the same. No sign of Bella. The same caveat that not everything's in yet applies, but it's good news so far."

Craig was just opening his mouth to ask something when the analyst shook his head.

"No answers from the photo-agencies yet, chief, if that's what you were going to ask, but I did manage to get back into the mums' chat-room."

Bullet point number three appeared.

"I tracked back to the date Bella was born and there was nothing on her other than that photo I already found, so Nicola Westbury obviously wasn't that into social media." He shook his head in despair. "Honestly, you should see the kids' photos that people post there."

Craig's eyes narrowed. "Nasty?"

"No, not that. Just innocent ones of their kids asleep, in the bath, swimming, but if a perve managed to hack that chat-room they'd be in bloody paradise."

Craig made a mental note that no images of his child were *ever* going to be posted online.

The analyst paused to take questions but when none

came he moved on. "OK, Davy, join in on this bit when I get to it." A fourth bullet point appeared - 'Abduction'.

"So Davy and I went right back to the beginning and we think we've worked out the steps to the girl getting taken out of the country."

Davy tapped his smart-pad and a timeline of Bella Westbury's disappearance appeared. Both analysts began typing on their copies of the slide simultaneously and projecting the additions onto the LED screen.

When he got some free time Craig planned on asking them how just they'd done it, but for now everyone just sat in silence and watched as, 'Playing in garden', 'Mother enters house', 'Bella snatched', right up to, 'flies out of Italian, Swiss or Greek airports' appeared.

Ash walked across to the screen. "This was where things got tricky." He tapped on the word 'snatched'.

"Davy?"

The senior analyst remained where he was and added a text box containing some technical language that made Craig shake his head.

"Explain."

Davy did so with a smile. "OK, the French hotel's CCTV, which you were right *did* cover the W...Westburys' house, was being viewed by the hotel's under-manager that afternoon but the gendarmes checked and he was clean. S...So then we got lucky. The hotel never deletes anything; they just back it up digitally to an off-site archive. I asked to view it, and I guess the gendarmes must have missed it but there was *definitely* the footprint of an unknown computer on the CCTV system."

Andy's eyes widened. "Their CCTV was hacked!"

"Yes. From the outside. It had been since the end of March that year."

March twenty-fifteen? Craig frowned. Something at the back of his mind had just shouted for attention but he couldn't work out what it was.

Andy saw his perplexed look and offered up. "Stuart Kincaid left home in March *last* year."

Craig considered the information and shook his head. "Thanks anyway, but it's something else I'm looking for. What date in March twenty-fifteen, Davy?"

"It was a randomer. Wednesday the twenty-first. No

idea why someone started watching the Westburys then."

After a minute's more fruitless wracking of his brains Craig shook his head and moved on. "OK, so someone watched Bella Westbury for five months until they spotted their chance to take her."

The analyst nodded. "The old traces showed that the hacker was s...somewhere to the east of the hotel and within five miles of it. Sorry, but I can't be any more accurate than that without a live signal. They would've been able to view everything at the Westburys' house, which means the scenario you and Liam suggested w...was possible."

Someone had watched the house for likely opportunities to arise when Bella might be left alone, and then sent a man there ready just in case.

Craig sat forward urgently. "Can we *prove* it was Pierre Galvet who took her or is this all still just theory?"

Davy allowed himself a satisfied smile. "We can prove it now. After the girl's abduction the gendarmes seized all street, business and private CCTV and mobile phone footage in the surrounding ten miles, as well as everything they could already access from the hotel, motorways, border posts, airports and ports. I've had access to everything s...since this morning and here's the relevant clip. Just a warning to everyone; it shows the girl's abduction."

Craig scanned the group to check that they were ready and nodded to start. They watched as Bella Westbury played innocently with her mother in the back garden of their house in France and then as a silver Renault, later confirmed stolen from an area called La Gaude, parked in the street opposite. Ninety minutes later, and just seconds after Nicola Westbury had left to enter the house and get her daughter a drink, a man exited the car, sprinted the short distance to the garden, and left it again almost immediately with the girl wriggling in his arms and his hand clamped hard over her mouth.

The next image showed the boot of the Renault opening and closing and then it accelerating east in the direction of the French Italian border. After another few seconds' viewing, Davy paused the tape and darkened the screen.

"The next clip shows the car on the A8 east and then it

pulls off and loses the cameras on the back roads."

There was silence for so long that Liam was tempted to swear just to break it, but Craig got in just as his deputy was opening his mouth, not daring to look at the faces of his team when he spoke because he knew their expressions would magnify the horror that he was feeling himself.

"Questions, Davy. You've ID-ed the kidnapper as Galvet?"

"Yes. Face match from his arrest records."

"And the car?"

"Stolen that morning from La Gaude, a village close to the fruit farm. Galvet must have left the farm, nicked it and driven it close to the house to park."

Liam nodded. "But not nicked *too* far in advance of the snatch, in case the police had been alerted to look for it."

Craig sighed. "Galvet must have got a call from the hacker watching the girl, saying that today was the day."

Liam shook his head. "Not likely, boss, they couldn't have *known* they'd strike lucky that particular day. Galvet had probably been called to wait loads of times before and just not got the chance to take her. Or maybe they had other paedos on alert other days and it was just his turn. The thing that this *does* tell us is that the Westbury girl was targeted."

Craig met his deputy's eyes and nodded. Bella Westbury had been chosen for some special purpose, and the attention paid to her said that purpose was *very* unlikely to have been transient, like abuse or porn.

"Agreed. The options for why are: abuse, but that would probably have resulted in her death and there's been no body found; porn, but Ash has almost ruled that out; trafficking, but she's too young to have been of use to anyone for physical labour-"

Their ex-Vice D.C.I. shook his head solemnly. "It doesn't rule out trafficking *for* abuse, Guv. Just because her images aren't out there doesn't mean she still wasn't taken by a paedophile ring to be passed around. I've seen it happen before."

It made Craig shudder and shake his head violently.

"No! No, I can't believe that."

"No-one wants to, but we can't rule it out."

Craig hit back vehemently. "*And I say we can!*"

He took a deep breath to calm himself before going on.

"This was *too* careful, Aidan, and that tells me this *specific* child was important to someone, *even* if we look at the fourth possible option, that she was stolen to order for someone to adopt. If someone had just specified that they wanted a blonde, blue-eyed girl then one could have been snatched *much* more easily. There must have been lots of families on holiday in Nice that year."

He shook his head slowly. "This targeting was too patient, and the attention to detail... hacking a CCTV feed, watching and waiting for *months*? No. There's something else going on here that we've missed."

Liam nodded. "They wanted Bella Westbury and no-one else."

"Yes, yes, and we need to find out why. Why *her*? What was so special about that little girl?" He turned urgently to his analysts. "Davy, was there *anything* that stood out on her background or medical history?"

A quick check of his screen brought a shake of the head. "Nothing, chief. Normal health, she had all her vaccinations, no hospital attendances except the ED..." As he gazed at Craig his eyes widened in horror. "You're not thinking organ donor, are you? That someone stole her to order for *that*?"

It brought gasps from even the most cynical members of the team and they waited breathlessly for Craig to deny it, growing more horrified when he took his time to speak and then responded with a question of his own.

"Did she ever have blood taken, Davy?"

A speedy tap brought the words that Craig had wanted to hear.

"No. Never."

The detective eased out a sigh of relief. "Then I don't think we're looking at organ donation. To be truthful I was thinking more of pre-adoption screening. Organ donation hadn't occurred to me until you mentioned it."

Liam was first out of the gates with, "You're a ghoul, son."

The analyst muttered defensively, "I saw it in a movie last week."

Craig nodded. "And it was an important suggestion that thankfully you've now been able to rule out. To make her a viable donor they would've had to have tested her blood group at a minimum and more likely had her tissue typed, but as she hadn't been tested she would have been pot luck as a donor, therefore why not just snatch *any* girl?"

He shook his head again. "No, I'm more and more convinced that Bella was stolen because of *who* she was and not what she was, although her physical appearance might have influenced what her kidnappers did with her after she was taken."

Andy had been frowning since the end of the video so Craig thought it was time to ask him why. He was one of the brightest people on his squad so he had a feeling that the reason would be good.

"You're looking troubled, Andy."

Liam snorted. "After what we've just been talking about? I wonder why?"

The arty D.C.I. shook his head. "Yes, that bothered me of course, but it's more what you first said about her being abducted to order, chief, and now that it was because of *who* she was. What if all of this was about the parents rather than the girl herself? What if someone wanted to destroy the whole Westbury family? Maybe because of a grudge?"

Liam's jaw dropped in surprise. "What sort of-"

Just at that moment Alice returned to the squad-room carrying a page and Craig raised a hand to halt the discussion. The PA hurried across the floor and handed him their witnesses' agreed sketch of Mister X.

"Davy, display Blaine Westbury's photo, please."

Westbury's driving licence photograph appeared on the screen and Craig walked across to it with the page in his hand, glancing repeatedly from one to the other. After a moment he passed the sketch around for everyone to look. Opinion was united; the man in the sketch *was* Blaine Westbury.

"We still need to be certain. Davy, call Edgar Westbury now and check his brother's height. Ryan, arrange a photo array of males the right age and insert a photo of Blaine Westbury, then take it downstairs and do a witnessed ID with both of hotel staff separately. I want this identification airtight. Do that right now, please, while we carry on."

He motioned the rest of the group to focus and continued as if the interruption hadn't occurred.

"We'll come back to what Andy just suggested, but let's take Mary while the ID's being sorted out. You were looking at the protest CCTV, the funeral coverage and Pierre Galvet, Constable Li."

For once the D.C. did her job without any backchat, taking everyone by surprise. It seemed that even Mary had finer sensibilities when it came to an abducted child.

"The funeral coverage didn't show anything unexpected, just the Westbury family en masse with no sign of Stuart Kincaid being there. The CCTV of the quarry protests didn't reveal much either. I checked for Arthur Norris, Stuart Kincaid, Derek Morrow and Blaine Westbury, and none of them were in the crowd. The protestors were mainly environmentalists, people linked with national and international Green groups. In the end the gold yield was so small the place closed down after three years anyway."

She displayed a few slides of people carrying placards, and one of some diehards camping outside the quarry's gates.

Liam gestured at the image.

"Here, when did those gates come down? I didn't notice them when we were there."

"I don't know."

"It must have been before Kincaid got killed, boss, otherwise how did he get in? And his killer. But they should put them up again now if the local kids are using the place as a paddling pool."

Craig nodded. "Good points. Check when they came down, someone, and sort out getting them re-erected with the local sergeant before somebody falls to their death."

As Liam scribbled himself a note the constable changed topic to Pierre Galvet, and an image of the man from his criminal records appeared on the screen.

Liam glanced up for long enough to give his verdict

"Ugly looking bastard. My granny would have said that his black soul had chewed its way through to his outside."

Craig burst out laughing and almost spat out his mouthful of coffee. When he'd stopped spluttering he shook his head.

"That's brilliant! And thinking at some of the criminals we know it seems pretty accurate. I wish I'd met your grandmother, Liam."

It brought a nostalgic smile to the deputy's face. "Aye. She was a fierce woman, I can tell you. She used to put the fear of God into every kid for miles around."

Craig turned back to his constable, still chuckling. "OK, Mary, tell us about Galvet."

"I know where he is now. He's in a nick in Manchester doing two years for indecent exposure."

Aidan wanted the details. "Spill."

"He exposed himself on an express train between stations."

"Thereby giving himself a captive audience for a while. It was well thought out at least."

She rolled her eyes. "Yes, well, part of that audience was male so he got pinned to the floor pretty fast. Dirty devil."

Craig was still on Manchester. "Why is he serving his time in England? Didn't the French want him back?"

"I queried that. It seems they were quite happy to be rid of him for a while so he stayed put."

Liam gave a guffaw. "He'll be in nick a lot longer than two years when they see Davy's CCTV footage. Child abduction will end him up in the Bastille."

Craig smiled. "The Bastille hasn't been a prison for two centuries, but I take your point. We're obliged to share Davy's findings on Nice with the French now that we have them, but we'll need to speak to Galvet *before* they get hold of him or we could be wading through red tape for years before we find out what happened to the girl."

He tapped his chin thoughtfully for a moment and then shook his head, defeated.

"OK, let me think about that for a while. The solution will come to me. "

Just then Ryan reappeared with a broad grin on his face.

"We've got him!"

He held out two signed statements to a startled Craig.

"*Both* of them ID-ed Blaine Westbury from the photo array?"

"Not a single doubt. They picked him out separately and instantly."

Craig waved him to take a seat and turned to his senior analyst. "Davy, what's the word on his height?"

"His brother's just told me Blaine was between six-three and six-four. That's what the hotel people said too. Easily big enough to have pushed Stuart Kincaid under the w...water and held him there."

Craig stared at the floor, his mind racing.

Biddy Evans had seen Blaine coming from the direction of the quarry around the time that Stuart Kincaid was murdered, and now they'd confirmed that Blaine had attempted access to Kincaid's possessions. There was no doubt in his mind that Blaine Westbury had killed Stuart Kincaid, but what had he been looking for in his bags? And why had Kincaid been at the quarry at all?

He looked up to see everyone gazing at him expectantly, something he'd had to get used to since becoming a boss but something that still always surprised him. He knew that people believing that he had all the answers *should* make him feel good, but the day it did was the day that he would quit.

"OK. It looks pretty certain that Blaine Westbury killed Stuart Kincaid, but before we start cheering we need to know why." He turned to Andy. "Andy, get down to forensics after this and find out what was in Kincaid's luggage and phone. Everything."

Davy interrupted. "Remember I've already got a list of his calls, chief. And his card purchases. Nothing exciting there, just petrol, hotels and meals."

Liam frowned. "If Kincaid was buying petrol he had a car, so where did *that* go when he disappeared?"

"I looked into that too. He drove an Audi and it seems to have vanished, so it's probably in a scrap yard s...somewhere now. I've a call out to every single one in the country."

Craig shook his head. "Don't waste too much energy on it, Davy. It's probably crushed or burnt out by now. Right, let's finish up the reports and then we can list what needs to be done." He turned back to his junior analyst. "Ash, have you got anything more for us?"

The response was the hacker crossing to the LED screen again, this time to display images of three small hands bearing flower motifs.

"OK, so thanks to my mate we now have photos of the distinguishing marks. Remember, these *weren't* listed on the kids' passports but *were* noted at the airports they travelled from."

He tapped on an image that was obviously a transfer tattoo, its black ink flaking around the edges.

"You can see that what was described as a flower tattoo definitely wasn't in this case. The border guard was just too stupid to spot it was fake and ask the parents to rub it off."

The image was discarded, leaving only two.

"I wanted to be sure of my ground so I contacted Edgar Westbury and got him to resend the photo of the girl's daisy scar that he gave the chief."

The uploaded photograph joined the other two on the screen, separated from them by a gap.

Ash pointed to its exact match in the pair. "It's identical to this one."

The unmatched image was binned, leaving just the two identical images side by side.

"I didn't trust my eyes, so I asked Grace to examine both of them in the lab. Measuring them, looking at any surrounding pores, pigment and so on, and she's confirmed that it's the same hand with the same tattoo. Or in this case, Henna scar."

Craig tentatively asked a question, praying that he got the answer he was hoping for.

"Which airport and what destination, Ash?"

The analyst gave a slow smile. "This mark was noted on the hand of a four-year-old boy flying out of Fiumicino Airport in Rome on the thirtieth of August twenty-fifteen, heading for Boston, USA. One day after Bella Westbury's abduction."

Craig kept praying. "On the American passport?"

They were in luck.

"Yep. The embassy got me a copy of it and I've checked the images. The kid was definitely Bella Westbury, disguised as a boy a bit older than her and flown directly to the States."

Craig wanted to punch the air. But they weren't out of the woods yet; America was a huge country.

"You're trying to pick up her trail?"

"Yep. I know she flew into Boston on a boy's name and

when, and I have the passport details of the woman she flew with, although they'll be false for sure. It gets tricky after they leave the airport because they'll probably have changed Bella back to a girl again, but I've contacted the FBI and explained the situation so they're on the trail."

Craig's dark eyes widened in alarm. "I don't want them approaching if they locate her! Make it clear that I need to be notified first. Whoever has her could panic and harm her."

The analyst's eyes widened just as much. "I didn't think of that! I'll contact them as soon as we've finished here."

He tapped his smart-pad hastily and a woman's picture appeared. She wasn't anyone that they recognised.

"This was Bella's companion, and the FBI have her picture as well now. I'm also trying to navigate the adoption system over there, but it's tortuous."

"Don't waste your time on the state system, Ash; it can take years to arrange adoptions that way so the kidnappers won't have touched it. If the girl *was* adopted then it was done privately and the FBI should know who's involved in that sort of thing. Stay on it."

Craig paused and dragged a hand down his face in exhaustion. Yes, they'd had a breakthrough in that they now knew that Bella Westbury hadn't been killed, but finding her would take more hard slog so it wasn't time to relax yet.

But his team had worked miracles so it *was* time to be positive. His next words were heartfelt.

"This is astounding work, all of you. Thank you. But we can't stop here, so..." he motioned Ash back to his seat, "...next steps." He stood up, flipped over the whiteboard and wrote 'Arthur Norris' again, followed by 'Pierre Galvet'.

They'd been investigating two cases in parallel for days: Stuart Kincaid's murder and the abduction of his niece; but were they related as he'd always suspected? Craig shook his head sharply. He hadn't proved that definitively yet, and until he could *point* to a link he had to assume none. Then it occurred to him that he and Liam were investigating Annette's case as well. Three cases at once; it was a first even for them.

He focused back on their murder investigation; after

all, that *was* supposed to be the squad's job.

"OK, Aidan, do you think Norris is going to give us anything more?"

"No. We've squeezed him dry and we're running out of excuses for keeping him."

Craig nodded and turned to one of his other D.C.I.s. "Andy, I want you to get a warrant to tap Norris' mobile before he's released."

He glanced at his senior analyst who was grinning.

"*Yes, Davy,* so that you can listen in. As soon as our mystery woman turns on her phone or Norris connects with her I want her address."

As the analyst gave him a thumbs-up, Craig turned back to the squad's fitness freak.

"Aidan, you and Andy get a photo of Stuart Kincaid's watch and run it past the witnesses to see if it's the one they saw on Westbury, then go to the lab and dig into Kincaid's effects. I want everything in his luggage pulled apart. I want to know *why* Kincaid went to that quarry and what Blaine Westbury was looking for at the hotel."

He looked at his D.S. "Ryan, I need you and Mary on the next flight to Manchester to interview Galvet. Alice can sort the paperwork for you. Find out who paid him to snatch Bella Westbury and who he passed her on to. Tell him we've got him on camera doing it but if he cooperates we'll put a word in for him with the French police-"

Liam snorted in objection. "The only word *I'd* be putting in would be guillotine. We can never allow that bastard back on the streets, boss."

"I wouldn't worry, Liam. I very much doubt the French will let Galvet walk *anywhere* until he's on a Zimmer, but we'll need him to believe that they might, to get him to cooperate."

As Mary and Ryan took to their feet, both grinning at the idea of a trip, Liam was grumbling, "No south of France for me then."

"Sorry, Liam, maybe on the next case. Or who knows, we might be asked to give evidence about the girl's abduction in the French courts."

The D.C.I.'s face lit up as he completely missed his boss' joking tone.

"Ash, you'll already have enough to do, but Davy, I'd

really like you to keep digging into Derek Morrow's computers."

"I meant to say, chief, Stuart Kincaid's computers were clear of child porn."

Andy nodded. "Just like his wife said. Kincaid wasn't a paedophile."

The analyst gave the small smile that usually indicated he'd found something interesting to pursue. "I've already got something else on Morrow. There's a WatsUp group on his computers and phone that's as heavily encrypted as his crypto icon."

Craig raised an eyebrow. "*Is there indeed?* I'd be very interested to see who was in his little group of buddies, *and* what they said."

Liam pulled a face. "It'll be nasty for sure. Why else would you encrypt a chat group unless something in it makes you look bad?"

It was a fair bet; there'd been recent court cases where people's private social media exchanges had revealed some very unsavoury things.

Just as Craig nodded in agreement his deputy nudged his elbow. "What about us then? What'll we be doing?"

"We'll be going back over everything we know about Blaine Westbury. I want that bastard."

Liam looked at him sceptically. "He won't still be in Ireland! He'd have to be thick."

"He was stupid enough to kill someone in the village he was born in and then go to his victim's hotel, so who can tell *what* he'll do next. He must have heard Kincaid's body been found by now."

"How? We kept it out of the papers."

"Only his name. The press mentioned a man's body was discovered in Rownton, so if Westbury *did* kill Kincaid it won't have taken him long to work out that that body was him. Then what would *you* do in his position?"

The D.C.I. ruminated for a moment. "That all depends on how big a bastard I am. And how brainless. If I was smart I'd just skedaddle off to a warm country with no extradition. But if I was thick and vicious I'd..." His face broke into a smile. "*You* think Westbury's going to want to tidy up loose ends."

Craig nodded. "I'm *hoping* that he's that stupid. If he is

we need to work out what those ends might be and get there first."

"Ach, sure that's easy. He'll kill anyone he thinks might know something about Kincaid's death and be able to implicate him. So that's... well, maybe just Arthur Norris and whoever S.W.M.B.O. is, now that Derek Morrow's dead. That's if they all *knew* about Kincaid's death."

"Agreed, but we'd better keep a watch on Biddy Evans too, just in case Westbury saw her that morning she saw him. Call the Rownton sergeant now, will you, Liam, and get him to post someone at her house until everything's sorted."

Ryan had a practical question for Craig before he left for the airport.

"What's Blaine Westbury using for money, chief? He's a waster and he didn't collect his inheritance, so how could he have afforded to flee?"

"I'd say the fact that he didn't collect his inheritance means that he didn't need to, Ryan. He's obviously found cash from somewhere, but we may not find out where until we pick him up."

He turned to the rest of his team and called out over the growing hubbub.

"Everyone, let me know what you've got as and when." He glanced back at his deputy. "I'm going to arrange a plain clothes officer to tail Norris when he's released, Liam. When you've called Rownton join me in my office. Ash, I'll need you for five minutes as well."

Craig left the now buzzing group behind him and entered his room, just finishing up his call to plain clothes when the others joined him there. He waved them to take seats and handed out coffees without asking for preferences, his mind full of other things.

"Right, Ash, I'll let you go and get on with things in a minute, but first, have you or Davy found anything interesting on Pete McElroy's media accounts?"

The analyst nodded so hard that his gold earring began to oscillate, fascinating the D.C.I. by his side who'd come from the short back and sides era of masculinity and couldn't make up his mind whether he thought male adornment was ridiculous looking or whether he secretly envied the young their freedom to try things out. If *he'd* worn an earring when he was young some hungry bullock would have chewed his ear off, that's if his father hadn't first.

Liam's thoughts were disturbed by the analyst setting his smart-pad on the desk and eagerly opening a page.

"OK, so, at first look there was nothing exciting on any of Pete's accounts. Photos of his kids, some football clips, just the usual. So I went into his email account."

Liam cut him off. "How'd you know he had one?"

It brought a pitying roll of the eyes. "DOH! *Everyone* has an email account."

"I don't."

Even Craig was surprised. "You *must* have. How do you keep in touch with friends?"

It was the deputy's turn to look pitying. "Well, you see, there's this old-fashioned thing called meeting face-to-face that we country folk favour."

"Very droll. But you have to organise that somehow."

"I've also got another old-fashioned thing called Danni who organises my every waking move on her flipping phone."

"Bet she'd love being called a thing."

"Ach, you know what I mean. Don't be going all politically correct on me."

Craig waved the analyst on with a smirk.

"OK, so everyone in the world *except Liam* has an email, and as most people cut their teeth on one of three or four well-known free email sites, Pete's account was easy enough to locate."

"You got his password from the provider I take it?"

"DOH again. No-oo. That would have left a paper trail. I hacked it like any decent analyst."

Craig raised his eyes to heaven, wondering how many more like him there were around.

Liam was completely disinterested in the technicalities and impatient, so he gestured at the smart-pad.

"So? What did you find? An email saying 'I'm going to kill myself and implicate my ex-wife' would be good."

The earring began to swing again. "Nothing. I went back through months of it, and boy was it boring. Football and rugby."

But Craig knew that the analyst's earlier enthusiasm

meant he had *something,* and *he* didn't have the time for a long lead-in.

"Just cut to the chase, Ash. What *have* you got?"

With a pointed sigh the smart-pad was turned around so that they could read its screen and the hacker pointed to an incoming email.

"That. It's from another email provider."

"But Pete didn't send it-"

"It was sent *to* Pete to verify his ID while he was setting up a second, *new,* email account. He set it up in October last year but never actually emailed anything from it so there's nothing in the sent or trash folders, but he *did* do the old spy trick of writing an email and saving it as a draft. Undetectable unless you know where to look."

He opened the email and read out the words that they'd been hoping to hear. Peter McElroy's suicide note clearly stating his intention to break and enter his ex-wife's home and murder her partner, hoping that in the process she would end his life.

The email wouldn't be admissible because they'd obtained it illegally, but now they knew what *had* to be in the papers stored at Floods. With this knowledge behind him, the solicitor's hint and Ben Frampton's confirmation of what Pete had been planning, Craig was fairly sure he could make a decent case for Sean Flanagan to request a warrant for *all* Pete's communications, being careful not to reveal that they already knew what they would contain of course.

Annette would be in the clear apart from a reprimand for not locking her weapon away, and a potential 'drunk while in possession of a firearm' charge that the PPS would find impossible to prove.

The detective hadn't realised that he'd gasped until he noticed the others smiling at him and then Liam suddenly slapped Ash so hard on the back that the slight analyst almost found himself propelled across the desk.

"Well done, son! You're not so bad really, are you?"

Between coughs the younger man managed to say that he hadn't realised the fact was ever in doubt.

"No, well it's a turn of phrase, isn't it. Like, you're not as big a ballax as I thought you were."

Craig translated. "Take it as a compliment, Ash, this is

astounding work." He would be recommending the analyst rose up the pay scale from next week. "Now, do whatever's necessary to cover your trail. You were *never* in any of Pete's accounts, OK?"

Liam was perplexed. "You're not using this, boss?"

"I'll have the knowledge that it exists to bolster my write-up on Frampton's interview, but no-one can *ever* know we accessed it, Liam, understand? I'm going to try to persuade the C.C. to order a warrant for *all* Pete's communications on the basis of what we know legitimately. And if we manage it, Annette will owe *you* her freedom, Ash."

All *might* still be well that ended well, but Craig knew that he'd gone against all sorts of rules even interviewing Ben Frampton so he was probably going to get his ass handed to him in a sling somewhere down the road.

The, now blushing, analyst was on his feet ready to leave. "OK, great. I'd better get back to work then."

As he dashed from the room, obviously embarrassed by the approval of his elders, Craig changed topic with a speed that caught his deputy off guard.

"Is Biddy Evans being watched, Liam?"

"What? Oh, yeh, they've sent some W.P.C. to stay with her."

"And Arthur Norris will be followed and listened to, so hopefully the next couple of hours will reveal who our mystery woman is."

The D.C.I. frowned thoughtfully. "I know it's a stretch, boss, but...you're not thinking *she* might have been the one who travelled with the Westbury girl, are you?"

The question was answered with a shrug. It *was* a leap to think that Arthur Norris' mystery S.W.M.B.O. was the same woman who'd flown to Boston with the abducted Bella Westbury three years before. After all, there were billions of women in the world, so why *should* she have been? Which didn't mean that Liam was wide of the mark.

"We'll see. Let's just say I'm not ruling it out. OK, back to Blaine Westbury. Any suggestions on how we find him?"

Just then there was a gentle knock on the door that could only have belonged to one member of his team.

"Come in, Davy."

The senior analyst entered holding two sheets of paper

and wearing an expression that confused them; he looked distressed and triumphant all at once.

"I think you should see this."

Without waiting for a response he handed a page to each detective and watched them intently as they read.

Liam spoke first. "It's a list of names. About twenty. So what?"

The computer expert pulled up a chair, about to start explaining, when Craig did so first.

"These are all missing children, aren't they?"

"Yes."

Liam was puzzled. "How'd you know that? And *you*, where'd you get them from?"

Davy dug into the detail. "I set up a Europe-wide search as soon as I heard about Bella, looking for abducted children over the past ten years where a body had never been found."

As Craig's lips tightened in understanding his deputy wasn't feeling enlightened at all.

"Explain quickly someone, before I pull my gun."

Craig waved him down. "He's saying that Bella was only one of many children who were taken, before and after her, and these are the names of the others."

Davy nodded. "S...Some of them. The ones in the EU during that time. If I widen the search to include other nearby countries, eastern European and Nordic, about a dozen more names pop up."

He held up his smart-pad seeking permission to show them something and Craig motioned him on. A map of the EU zone appeared with red dots scattered across it, including in Ireland and the UK.

Craig sighed.

"These names, Davy, they're all modern. That means these children are all very young."

"I only looked for the ones under five."

Liam was frowning. "I still don't get it."

"Very young children will forget who they w...were eventually, but any older than five and it would be hard to give them a new name and family."

The D.C.I. thought of his own children and shuddered violently, knowing that the analyst was right. His youngest, Rory, was six, and he could imagine that after a few weeks of being called by a new name in a new country he would *completely* forget who he'd been before, especially if they fed him enough gummy bears.

"Fuckers!"

Craig was outraged too but they needed to maintain focus. "Explain the logistics to us, Davy."

"I'm just pulling the details of each case now, chief. I searched for disappearances where no dead body was ever found and there were no viable s...suspects, so these cases are all still marked open, they've just hit dead ends."

"You think we could be looking at a ring, don't you? An abduction ring with the children stolen to order."

The analyst nodded. "And they only take the very young because if even one kid remembered their past life it could blow everything."

"Taken for adoption, boss?"

"Hopefully, Liam. Although like I said earlier, with Bella Westbury there was another reason as well. I'm sure of it."

Davy nodded. "Adoption is the most logical reason but... we can't *completely* rule out an age preferential paedophile ring."

Craig palmed his face in despair and said nothing for a moment, so his deputy filled the gap.

"The level of organisation this would have taken is crazy."

The analyst responded by bringing up a fresh screen showing the airports closest to each of the twenty-odd abduction sites, and then superimposed all of their departure routes to the United States.

Craig's mouth fell open in astonishment.

"*Every* abduction happened near an airport that flew into Boston?"

Davy nodded slowly. "Every s...single one. I cross-matched *all* the flight routes worldwide available at the time of each abduction, including those from an airport so small it only flew to *anywhere* twice a week, and the *only* destination available from every s...single airport was Boston, Massachusetts."

Craig was stunned by the arrogance it had taken to transport abducted children to a country with tight laws and an extradition treaty with the UK.

"*Shit*. That's where Bella flew into as well, boss."

Craig felt sick. "You know what this tells us, Davy."

The analyst nodded his head.

"Boston is twenty-two percent Irish American, the highest percentage of any city in the USA; next biggest is Pittsburgh with sixteen. S...So if the abductors have Irish connections, north or south, they would blend in immediately. And as English speakers they wouldn't stand out in most of Europe either-"

Liam cut across him. "They were reckoning they could hide in plain sight. Time to bring in the trafficking team, boss?"

Craig shook his head sharply. "No, no, not yet, not until we have actual proof. At the moment, while this is brilliant work, it's *all* still circumstantial. *Maybe* abducted children, *maybe* linked to each other with maybe a link to Boston...maybe Blaine Westbury killed Stuart Kincaid who was maybe on to something, it's all maybes..."

He shook his head again more slowly. "No. We need a *definite* way in. Some key that opens this up for us so we can say for certain what we've got." He stared hard at his head analyst. "My money's on you and Ash here, Davy." A gleam of enthusiasm lit the younger man's eyes. "There's something here that *we're* still missing, so get back to it and find out what it is."

As the door closed quickly behind the analyst Craig returned to his earlier point.

"What do we know about Blaine Westbury, Liam? From the beginning."

"Thirty-eight-year-old loser. Ruined his parents' lives with his petty crime and debt, always broke yet never claimed his inheritance, and probably killed Stuart Kincaid."

The summary made Craig smile. "Succinct. Right, let's look at that piece by piece. Broke but didn't claim his inheritance, and if he killed Kincaid he didn't do that for money either. He didn't even steal his credit card."

"He might have worried any transactions could have been traced to him. But if he took Kincaid's watch that's worth something."

"Only if he sold it which I don't think he did."

"OK, then he might have gone looking for something

else to sell in Kincaid's luggage."

Craig made a face. "I'm not saying a definite no, but it doesn't feel right. Blaine *could* have used Kincaid's card several times quite safely before anyone had known he was dead yet we know he didn't, and he was probably wearing Kincaid's watch when he went to the hotel. So...if a gambler and waster *doesn't* need money, that can only mean one thing."

"Two. He's either taken a vow of poverty, or he's already got enough from somewhere. That means..." The D.C.I. raised his eyes to the ceiling and reeled off the standard list, "...rich friends, drugs, theft, tax rebate, job, legal or illegal-"

Craig cut him off. "The first and last. Drugs are risky, a tax rebate's too slow, he's too lazy for a legal job, and theft would involve the cops fast. Either Blaine's hooked up with a rich group or a rich partner or he's doing something nasty to generate cash. It could even be both. But if he *has* set himself up in some crooked business he'll have needed capital to start."

"OK, so we need to see his tax and bank accounts from here and abroad."

"Yep, but Davy and Ash are already overloaded so let's pay Ray that visit and give the other section I supposedly manage some work to do. We need tax details, bank accounts, and immigration and travel info for Master Blaine."

****

The Atlantic Way Merchant Bank. Dublin. 4 p.m.

Róisín Casey was considering not only her future but her existence more carefully than ever before. She would be in mortal danger from her business partners unless she complied with their instructions, and if they *didn't* decide to kill her they could still take everything that she possessed with a single click of a mouse.

The knowledge had urged her to discuss things with the one person who really mattered to her in the group, but he was in agreement with the others so the conversation had left her with a serious decision to make alone.

Did she cut and run elsewhere without him before everything unravelled? True, she would be lonely and risking future poverty but she would still be *free*.

Or did she do as she'd been *told*, not asked? Kill anyone left who could cause problems for their venture, namely Arthur, and stay put trusting that the cops would be too stupid to follow through any leads.

The first option guaranteed that half the world would be off limits to her forever if she valued her liberty and she would probably die alone in some rat-ridden hole, the second that she might *just* keep her life, the man she loved and her income and luxuries, but only if the police really *were* as thick as shit. For a woman only skilled in risk analysis when all other factors were equal it was an impossible choice; like balancing the chances of contracting malaria against the future price of beans. Interestingly the immorality of killing didn't even enter into the banker's equation, but then if she'd possessed *morals* it's doubtful that Róisín would *ever* have got where she was.

But the financier's struggle was wasted because the decision was about to be made for her, unwittingly, and by a man she'd manipulated for years using a combination of sex and fear, creating a hold so strong that he was completely dependent on her now.

As Arthur Norris claimed his belongings and left High Street Station he missed the car tailing his taxi, so engrossed was he on his mobile phone. Heaving a sigh of relief that he'd managed to keep his mouth shut for so long that the police had been forced to release him, and then one of pleasure that he would get to boast of his stoicism to the woman that he'd done it for, his first call *wasn't* to his wife of forty years but to Róisín Casey's pay-as-you-go mobile, although as he'd suspected it might be the line was dead.

It had happened before when Róisín was in one of her Greta Garbo moods, but the land agent's need for praise was greater than any respect for her solitude so his next call was to the switchboard of The Atlantic Way Merchant Bank.

Davy Walsh hunched over his desk listening as the call was answered briskly and Norris asked to be transferred to a particular extension number, and then as a woman on the other end first said her name, "Róisín Casey" and then, when the first syllable of "Hello" emerged from Norris' mouth, as she immediately cut the call.

They had her! They had the woman who'd called to shout at Arthur Norris as if she ruled him and had lied to the Rownton sergeant to find him, the women who'd almost certainly ordered the cover-up on Derek Morrow's death, the woman who'd done God only knew what else.

As soon as the phone went down Davy reverse-checked its number, tying it to the bank's branch in Dublin Docklands, and while he listened to Norris call again he pulled up an internet search on a Ms Róisín Casey, the bank's Vice President of Mergers and Acquisitions.

He clicked open her company biography, complete with smirking photo, and sent it across to his junior with the instruction to, "Check her pic against that woman's passport", then he stopped listening to Norris for a moment and called Craig.

He caught the two detectives just as they were leaving the Police Intelligence Section, Ray Barrett having been suitably briefed.

"Yes, Davy."

"Norris did it, chief, he called her! Her name's Róisín Casey and she's high up in The Atlantic Way Merchant Bank in Dublin. VP at their Docklands branch. I've got Ash running her photo against the woman's passport now."

Craig punched the air. "Brilliant! Get that info to D.C.I. Barrett, and say we want the same on her as he's getting for us on Blaine Westbury. Movements and money. I want to know what she's been up to."

As they reached the car he set his mobile on the roof and put it on speaker. "Right, tell us *exactly* what was said on Norris' call, Davy."

"Hang on a second, chief. Ash is waving at me." He covered the receiver for a moment. "Are you about to say the passport woman's Róisín Casey?"

"Yep. No doubt."

He uncovered the phone. "Casey's the woman who flew out of Rome, boss."

Craig gave a gasp of relief. They were heading the right way.

He realised that Davy was still speaking and grinned at the eagerness in his voice.

"OK, so Norris had just got into his taxi when he tried her burn mobile, but it was dead, like you'd expect if the battery's been taken out. Oh, by the way Mary got a clear pic of him from McGrans' store CCTV. Anyway, then st...straightaway Norris rang the bank switchboard and asked for extension three-ten. It's their offices in Dublin's Docks. Anyway, Casey answered with her name but Norris hardly got out 'Hello' before she hung up. He's been calling the extension back since but it's dialling out."

Liam smirked. "She's worried someone'll trace her, boss. Why else cut the call?"

"Agreed. She already guessed we'd got hold of Norris, that's why she called Rownton station, and now she's terrified that he'll lead us to her. Davy, tell them to lift Norris again, and redirect Aidan to High Street to face him with Casey's name and see what he says. Liam and I will head for the labs."

As the detectives began their next steps, Róisín Casey was taking her rage out on her shoes again, but only for a minute this time; the situation had grown too serious for even a spectacular tantrum to solve. If the police had been listening then Arthur had just led them straight to her, and even if they hadn't there was no telling what the stupid bastard might tell them once he realised she wouldn't be taking any more of his calls. No one liked being dropped and in her experience men reacted particularly unpredictably.

Either way she could never reach Arthur in time to kill him now, so her options had just narrowed to one; skip the country. But she wasn't prepared to lose the man that she loved so she had to find some way of making *him* understand that they both had to go. They'd had a great time in Europe while it had lasted but now it was time to cut and run somewhere better for their health. Luckily they had contacts all over the world.

But Craig had other plans, and after a moment's discussion Liam got on the buzzer to Garda Headquarters to request their assistance in a case that if they were right might involve police forces in half the world.

The D.C.I. strolled away into the distance as he was

talking and when he returned to the car he was wearing a smug smile.

"That was a bit of luck. I've just spoken to an old mate of mine."

"Anyone I'd know?"

"Probably not."

Liam had encountered half the cops in Ireland during his career whereas Craig had worked in London for fifteen years.

"His name's Pat Goodall. Used to be my D.I. in Newry way back. He was always talking about moving down south and it looks like he finally made it. He's a Superintendent in the Garda in Dublin now. Sound man, but a lousy Gaelic player."

The ultimate insult. Liam was skilled in almost every sport that involved a ball; except for cricket, because the bat handles were too small for his giant hands.

"I'm surprised the Garda took him then."

The comment had been so dry Liam had to check Craig's face to see how it had been meant.

"Oh, I see. Very droll. Anyway, Pat's just checked and he says Madam Casey's got two outstanding speeding tickets handily enough, so he's going to bring her in for a long chat."

"Two hours long by any chance?"

The time it would take for them to drive from Belfast to Dublin.

"Three to four I'd say. I told him we had to go and check some forensics first."

"Excellent. We'd better get to the lab then."

Ten minutes later a shame-faced Craig was standing in Des Marsham's office, with the head of forensics giving him a chastising look that he knew had nothing to do with their investigation but everything to do with his overnighter in the cells.

His first play was a curt remark. "Does it really take three of you to look at the contents of some suitcases?"

Liam answered for all of them. "We're a close team."

"But not necessarily a loyal one."

The dig made Craig wince and his deputy wasn't having it.

"Here now, there's no need for *that*. I've been on to

Lord Whatshisname's butler about any damages and the boss here's offered to pick up the tab."

It was Des' turn to look embarrassed. "You don't need to do that, Marc."

Liam nodded. "That's what I said, and I bet his missus will say so too."

When Andy, who'd been listening to the discussion increasingly puzzled, opened his mouth to ask what on earth they were talking about, all three men said hastily, "Let's move it along" and as a distraction Des pointed quickly to Stuart Kincaid's bags, both empty now and with their contents arranged neatly alongside.

"Andy said you were looking for something to indicate Kincaid was following leads on his niece's disappearance, but the only items I found of possible relevance were these."

He lifted a small leather folder from amongst the possessions and opened it to display some papers, motioning Craig to take a look. As the detective unfolded the first piece of paper he gave a gasp; it was an almost identical list to the one Davy had shown them shortly before!

He passed it to his deputy and unfolded a second page that held a list of car registration numbers. Andy, who'd been peering over his shoulder, pointed in astonishment to one halfway down.

"That's the car Pierre Galvet stole!"

Liam peered at the number. "Bloody hell, boss, he's right. And these are the names of Davy's abducted kids. Kincaid was streets ahead of us!"

Craig reached behind him for a stool and almost fell on to it. "He was really on to something, *or* someone. *That's* why he was killed."

Des and Andy were looking confused, so Liam brought them up to speed on Davy's theory of an abduction ring while Craig removed the two remaining items from the folder and set the first of them on the desk. It was a series of head and shoulder images of young children, each one set against a grid.

Andy's eyebrows shot up.

"That's a facial recognition grid! Look, it says something at the top. 'Les Gendarmes Nice, France.' And there's a date. December twenty-seventeen."

"What-" Craig stopped abruptly and thought for a few seconds before starting again. "OK. So... Stuart Kincaid got this from the gendarmes seventeen months after his niece's abduction."

Liam looked perplexed. "But why? Her photo's not there."

Andy had noticed something else. "Look, there. That bit translates as these are missing kids that the police *found*."

That was the advantage of studying languages.

He frowned. "But why would the gendarmes have given Kincaid anything at all? He was a civvie."

Craig gave a small shrug. "He must have paid someone to access info the gendarmes gathered after the girl's abduction."

Liam gave a whistle that said he was impressed. "A private eye. It must have cost him a bundle. And he must have paid them in cash because Davy didn't find anything on his card."

When he saw that his other D.C.I. was still looking confused Craig turned to him inquisitively. If Andy didn't support something immediately it was usually because there was another layer to be found.

"OK, so I understand about the lists of missing kids and cars. Kincaid obviously believed that Bella had been kidnapped not killed. But *what* took him to Rownton? Bella had never lived there, and she went missing in France not Ireland."

Craig dropped his eyes to the floor in thought for a moment. When he looked up again there was a glint in them that everyone saw.

"Stuart Kincaid was a *very* clever man. When no body was found he felt sure Bella wasn't dead and followed the same thought processes as us. He thought of a stolen car being used in her abduction, hence the list of registrations, and through researching, maybe paying a private detective, he discovered that there were far more missing children in Europe than just his niece. Agreed?"

No-one argued.

"He also worked out that Bella *might* have been taken for another reason, just as we did-" He stopped abruptly mid-thought and took out his phone. "Hold everything for a minute. I need to speak to Davy again."

As he disappeared into the corridor Liam rolled his eyes. "Bosses. Huh!"

Andy seized on the pause to ask about something else that had been puzzling him. "Two things. One, Doc Winter's just confirmed the location of Kincaid's possessions in the water fits with his findings, and two, what was all the moody stuff about earlier on, Des?"

The scientist looked offended. "I wasn't moody!"

Liam started at him sceptically. "Not much, you weren't." He decided to enlighten his team-mate. "He took the hump with the boss because him and his mad metal mates decided to dig a hole in a castle garden last night and got themselves nicked. Einstein here called the boss in the middle of the night asking him to bail him out, but the boss made him wait till this morning so he's been sulking all day. Boo bloody hoo."

Just as Des was about to retort Craig reappeared, knowing from the sudden silence that greeted him that his ears should have been burning but too absorbed in what he had to report to care.

"Davy's just confirmed something for me." He pointed to the list of names. "He hasn't got info on all of them yet, but at least eight of these children were snatched off the street."

Liam tutted. "Filthy scum."

"Yes, but they watched and waited to take Bella so someone *specifically* wanted that little girl, so much so that they were prepared to invest time and money in surveillance. Right. Everyone give me your thoughts on why."

"Pretty."

"There are lots of pretty children."

"Blonde and blue-eyed so she'd fetch a good price."

"Ditto."

Liam ventured. "Maybe she was born to someone other than Edgar and Nicola Westbury and her birth parents wanted her back?"

Andy rolled his eyes. "You've watched *way* too many soaps, mate. I saw her birth weight and location in her file on Ash's computer. She was definitely the Westburys' kid." He repeated what he'd said at the briefing. "A grudge.

Revenge. Someone wanted to hurt the Westbury family."

Craig nodded emphatically. "Yes. A grudge. I think you're right." He expanded his reasoning. "Stuart Kincaid was exceptionally close to his twin sister, so it makes sense that she would have told him things over the years. Things about how bad Edgar's relationship was with his younger brother, about Blaine causing their parents pain by being a waster, him getting drunk at their funeral *and* about how they'd left almost everything to Edgar in their Will. Yes?"

Liam nodded. "My sisters tell me all *sorts* of stuff about their in-laws."

"Right. So when Kincaid began investigating his niece's disappearance, especially after his sister's death when he became almost obsessed through grief, *something*, either something that Nicola had said or something that he'd learned independently, made him suspect Blaine Westbury of being up to no good. Maybe he hadn't connected Blaine with Bella's abduction exactly, or maybe he had, we can't know, but *something* made Stuart Kincaid suspicious and I think he went to Rownton hoping to find out more about Blaine."

"A fishing trip you mean?"

"Yes, but led by an informed hunch. Once there perhaps Kincaid unwittingly asked questions of people who liked Blaine and they tipped him off."

"Who?"

Craig shook his head. "We'll probably never know. Some misguided childhood friend perhaps. But if Stuart Kincaid *was* getting close to unravelling something they'd have wanted rid of him, and if Blaine *did* drown him then it makes sense for him to then try to access Kincaid's possessions to see what evidence he had and get shot of it."

Andy gestured at the folder. "The sad thing is if Kincaid had brought all this to the cops last year instead of acting like a lone wolf we would have been months further on."

Liam tutted. "And he would still be alive. He thought he could do it all on his own and it got him killed. Stupid Joe Expert."

Craig shook his head. "Or the police *might* just have treated him like an obsessed, bereaved man and ignored everything. We'll never know." He sighed heavily. "You have to admire the man for what he achieved."

Liam pulled a face. "Mmm...OK. But getting back to the kidnappings; if Blaine Westbury could abduct his own niece and not care about the damage, then those other kids probably didn't cost the fucker a thought."

Craig nodded wearily and was about to open the final piece of paper when Andy spoke again.

"This is all grand but it *still* doesn't tell us why Kincaid went to that quarry."

"Maybe Blaine had something to do with the place? If he had then Kincaid could've been looking around for clues, boss."

Craig responded by spreading out the paper and displaying another list of names. He recognised two of them but not the rest. Róisín Casey and Blaine Westbury.

"What are the odds *this* is the consortium that owns the quarry? If it is then it explains why Kincaid went there looking for Blaine. He's one of the owners."

And he could guess where he'd got the money to buy into the enterprise.

He turned briskly to his second D.C.I. "But that can wait for a while. Let's follow what we have for now. Andy, Arthur Norris is being taken back in High Street, call Aidan and say you'll be joining him for his re-interview. He'll bring you up to speed on everything. Liam and I are heading down to Dublin to interview the Róisín Casey who's on this list. We believe she's S.W.M.B.O., the woman Norris is working for."

"Looks like I missed a lot in a short time."

"You can thank our analysts for that." Craig turned towards the door but Andy stopped him with some more information.

"By the way, the hotel maid ID-ed the man's watch as being Kincaid's."

Another loose end tied off.

"Good. OK, I'm grateful to all of you. OK, Des, Andy can bring you and John up to speed on anything else relevant before he leaves. There'll be a briefing at some point when hopefully we'll be a lot further forward. I'll let you know when."

As he was walking back to the car Craig realised that another thing he probably shouldn't do now that he was married was simply disappear overnight, so he called Katy, who was giggling as she answered. Liam sensed an unwarranted lovey-dovey moment approaching so he took the opportunity to get offside and make a call of his own.

"Hello, pet. I've got to go to Dublin now and we may need to stay overnight. I just wanted to let you know and check you were feeling OK."

He could hear other people laughing in the background and recognised his mother's musical trill.

"Don't worry about me; I'm having a whale of a time here. You know how the mothers high-jacked Annette and took her and Carrie house hunting with them? Well they're all here now telling me about it. Honestly, Marc, it's better than a comedy show. Your dad's here too, in the bedroom trying to find some peace to read. The best thing is they may even have found us a few decent houses to view already tested by a toddler."

As he pictured the scenario Craig smiled. "Houses with chandeliers and marble columns knowing my mum."

The only answer was a giggle that he took as a yes, so he got off the line quickly before she elaborated. Meanwhile, Liam's call to Mickey O'Hare had informed him that the Rownton locals had torn down the quarry's gates as soon as they'd been erected in protest so neither Stuart Kincaid nor his killer would have needed a key to get in.

Another box ticked, the D.C.I. pointed the car south and hopefully to the solution to their case.

Chapter Eight

The C.C.U.

"Davy, come and look at this for a minute."

The senior analyst shook his head. "I'm busy, Ash, what is it?"

"You'll want to see it, honest. I think I'm on to something with the crypto icon."

Even as technologically advanced as he was the concept of cryptocurrency still intrigued Davy, so he dropped what he was doing and rode his wheelie chair across to his junior's desk, following Ash's pointing finger to his PC screen, which was displaying a sample blockchain.

"OK, so we know blockchains are central to the way cryptocurrencies work. One key feature of them is that information added to a chain can't be changed without a *major* effort, and there's always a digital evidence trail. Signed and time-stamped so that the person who put the info there can be traced."

"Presupposing they haven't created a false identity."

The junior analyst puffed out his cheeks for a moment and then nodded. "I suppose there's always *that,* but it'd be hard to do. They'd have to have created false bank accounts to transfer their funds from as well, and *they'd* leave trails too."

A sceptically raised eyebrow by his boss said that it wouldn't be a first.

"OK. Well, anyway, the theory is that this information lock on a blockchain stops people removing information, making fake transactions or manipulating their account balance. Yes?"

"OK..."

"But a few months back, the amount of data that could be added to some blockchains was increased. *Big time.*" He gestured at the sample chain on his screen, "And one of them was the blockchain Derek Morrow was accessing."

Davy was loath to admit it but he was starting to get confused. "S...So that means what?"

"People *had* only been able to add small pieces of text or web links to blockchains, but then suddenly it became possible to add *huge* files, really enormous ones. Then I remembered what I'd heard about criminals using crypto sites. The files *they'd* been adding to the chains had included *images*, in an encoded format."

Davy felt the hairs rise on his naked neck.

"A few weeks back the English police discovered images of child abuse embedded in a blockchain. A bunch of perves were using it as a secret distribution network, so that anyone anywhere with the right info could look at the photos without getting caught. The police got the guy who uploaded them and it can't happen again on *that* blockchain, but there aren't *universal* safeguards in place yet to prevent uploading, or spot and remove any images." He tapped Derek Morrow's icon. "And there are *none* on the blockchain this shortcut leads to."

Davy slumped back in his chair, knowing where he was heading. "You're saying Morrow may have been accessing the crypto-chain via this icon to view images rather than to trade." He frowned. "It could make s...sense. I've just cracked his Cayman account and it has a *lot* of dosh in it. There was some paid to his crypto site, but only small amounts."

Ash nodded eagerly. "Then he must've just spent enough to *access* the blockchain but not trade on it. I'm not saying I've *found* a definite link to images, but when I followed the icon it threw up some *seriously* weird code. I've been in crypto sites before and I've seen nothing like this, but I didn't want to dig deeper in case..."

"You found child pornography. You were right."

"Yeh, I *really* don't want to see that stuff. But also just in case Morrow put a kill sequence on the site and I wipe everything."

Davy gave a sharp nod and stood up. "W...Work on something else till I speak to the chief and see what he wants to do. This is a brilliant catch."

He reached Craig twenty-five miles south just outside Banbridge and explained the situation. It took the detective a minute to get his head around the tech side but then he knew exactly what to do. He'd been feeling guilty about neglecting Cate Pine and it was the perfect way to set that right.

"I'll call you back in a minute, Davy."

Luckily the IT Crime Superintendent was eager to

working with them, especially when Craig explained that she'd not only be working with *his* staff but with the head of Vice, Emrys Lomax. If there was even the *tiniest* chance of illegal images popping up on his analyst's screen he wanted an expert sitting there when they did, to cover everyone's ass.

By the time he got round to calling his chief analyst back they were almost at Dublin Airport and Craig grimaced at the signs for it, wondering whether children had been smuggle through it as well. He had a feeling that a *lot* of unsavoury information was going to be revealed over the coming weeks.

"Right, Davy, here's the plan. I've spoken to D.C.S. Pine from Information Technology Crime and D.C.I. Lomax down in Vice and they're coming to look at what Ash has. Move everything into my office when they arrive, please, I don't want anyone else accidentally seeing something unpleasant. And let me know what you get ASAP. My phone will be on unless we're in an interview."

The words made him wonder whether Pat Goodall had lifted Róisín Casey yet and decide to make that his next call.

****

The Atlantic Way Bank.

Róisín Casey was mid phone argument with her lover when her office door flew open and several uniformed Gardaí burst in, with her flustered PA close behind them counterpointing their noisy announcement of their intentions with, "I'm sorry, Miss Casey, I'm so... they just stormed past me... they didn't even give me time to knock!"

It only took the man at the other end of the line ten seconds to ditch both the call and his girlfriend; although Róisín wouldn't learn that she'd been dumped until much later. For now her loyalty to her lover remained such that she refrained from calling out his name for assistance as the police approached. But *his* loyalty was non-existent so his next move was to rip apart his mobile, microwave it and his laptop to remove all traceable tech and then grab his go-bag from the bottom of the banker's fitted wardrobe and take her apartment block's turbo-lift down to his hire car.

When Craig heard that Casey's call had been to her apartment's landline he gave a heavy sigh, and an even heavier one when twenty minutes later the Gardaí reported that they'd found no-one at her home.

It had always been a possibility that any accomplice she'd had might have been waiting there for her, and if they'd been in Belfast he would have had officers at Casey's apartment before arresting her just in case, but he was in another force's jurisdiction and relying on their goodwill to bring the woman in, so swearing mentally and saying "Thank you" was all that he could do.

But they weren't *totally* powerless, not while they had a hacker like Ash on the team, so when Craig received a call back from Pat Goodall to say that one of his officers had overheard something when they'd entered the banker's office, a smile twisted the detective's lips.

"You're sure you heard Casey say Caracas?"

"One of my lads did. That's the capital of Venezuela isn't it?"

"Yep. I'll check the flight times and get back to you in a minute."

Craig caught Davy just as he was taking Cate Pine into his office.

"Davy, I need you and Ash, so I'm afraid your crypto thing's going to have to wait a minute. Unless you want to let D.C.S. Pine have a go at it first?"

"She's waiting for one of her computer guys so we won't be starting for a while anyway, chief. What was it you needed?"

"Two things. I need you to check direct flights from Ireland to Caracas today and the ones from the UK too, just I case they plan to connect there. Then I'll need Ash to hack into the airports' CCTV and departure check-ins. How long will that take?"

"The first one will take five minutes, and he w...won't need to hack. We have reciprocal agreements."

The analyst smiled to himself. *Hack;* he was pretty sure Craig just liked the frisson attached to the word.

He was right, and a thwarted Craig let it show in his

disappointed tone.

"No hacking? Really? Oh, OK then... No, I mean that's great, *really* great. Right, call me back."

Five minutes later the analyst called back to say that whoever was flying to Caracas had to be leaving from either Dublin or Heathrow Airports. In the absence of Róisín Casey coughing up her caller's name in the next few hours they would have to keep their eyes peeled for the only person Craig thought it could possibly be. Blaine Westbury.

"OK, Davy, get Blaine Westbury's photograph to all check-in, search and security staff at those airports and tell them we need him detained. He's a person of interest in a murder case if they ask. Sorry, I know it's a lot of work but get Alice to help you. I'll alert the police."

Twenty minutes later the metaphorical gates were locked as tightly as possible and everyone was on alert. But in reality, although they *thought* they'd tied Casey's call to her Dublin apartment, Davy knew it could just as easily have been routed to appear that way and been to anywhere in the world. It prompted another round of calls to the European and US security services to be on the lookout at direct and connecting airports as well, that finally left the analyst feeling that he'd done everything he could.

Craig didn't notice until his last call had ended that he was in Dublin City Centre, and in fact parked outside a police station. He turned to his deputy in surprise.

"We're here? Headquarters?"

"Yep, so haul ass."

Craig glanced around him at the narrow one-way street. "Can't you find somewhere better to park? Like in the station grounds?"

Liam gave a disgusted tut. "I've been asking you about that for the past five minutes without getting an answer!" He restarted the engine grumpily. "Honest to God, there's no pleasing some folk!"

After a minute of Craig trying hard not to laugh they were admitted to a secure car park, and the grudging admission that the move might have saved him a ticket was accompanied by an improvement in Liam's mood, but only a marginal one. As they walked towards the station's reception his sulk was still so obvious that it made his boss tut.

"Who rattled *your* cage?"

"You did! You barely said a word to me all the way down because you were on the phone. And I couldn't even listen to Mantovani because *you* were trying to hear. Two bloody hours of a one-sided conversation! The least you could do is bring me up to speed now, before I walk in there and look like a prat!"

Craig conceded the point, more from expediency than any sense of guilt. The last thing he needed was an overnighter with Liam in a state of wounded pride. It would be like spending twenty-four hours with a grizzly that hadn't been fed.

A summary of all things crypto-icon, arrest, Venezuelan and airport followed and it earned him a grudging nod of approval and an astute comment.

"You realise that if we solve this one, it'll all be down to the geeks. You should buy them a robot or something each to say thanks."

It wasn't a bad idea, but it wasn't one they would discuss further just then because a man with a large head and an equally large grin was approaching them, and his loud northern, "'Bout ye, big man" said that he couldn't have been anybody but Liam's old friend.

"'Bout ye, yerself, Pat! Ye big Newry hallion. I see you finally swapped the green for the blue."

It was one of the island's many anomalies that the Republic of Ireland's police wore a blue uniform, whereas Northern Ireland's, in the UK, wore the traditionally Irish green.

"I have indeed. This must be your new boss, then. D.C.S. Craig, isn't it?"

He extended a hand for Craig to shake.

"Good to meet you, and thanks for doing this for us, Superintendent Goodall. We'd better bring you up to date with what else we're planning on doing on your turf."

Just then Davy called again; the airport situation was developing fast.

"W...We're heading into your office to view the crypto stuff now, but I thought I'd let you know that I decided to widen the airport w...watch. We're looking at all departures today to *any* non-extradition country just in case they decide to get slippery, and I've put all the airports on general alert."

"Connecting airports in Europe and the US too, Davy?"

"Yep, and I'll update you soon as."

"Good. And can you update Ryan on your theory about the abduction ring before he sees Pierre Galvet, please."

"Email already sent."

Craig ended the call thanking heavens for his excellent team and turned back to the Garda. "You got all that?"

Pat Goodall whistled. "And all from one word that lassie Casey said. I hope my boy wasn't hearing things."

"Don't worry, there's more than that behind it."

As they brought him up to date on why they wanted to speak to Róisín Casey, Goodall puffed out his cheeks and shook his head.

"Well now, I'd reckoned on the killing part, what with you being Murder Squad and all, but the kids' stuff is worse."

Craig nodded solemnly. "What are your limits on what we can ask her, given that you only brought her in on speeding offences?"

The burly Garda folded his arms, displaying muscled forearms that said he worked out and reminding Craig how long it had been since he'd done the same.

"As far as I'm concerned just go for it, although she's called a lawyer so how far you'll get is anyone's guess..."

"Understood. Was there a message for me from your commissioner by any chance?"

One of his many calls on their journey down had been to the Chief Con, and when he'd explained why they were heading south and requested his assistance, Flanagan had promised to call the new Garda commissioner, who just happened to be a woman that they all knew well from TV: Ruth 'Rusty' Bradley, so called because of her flaming red hair. There was constant speculation whether Bradley chose to front press conferences so often because she saw her hair's fieriness as emblematic of the fight against crime, or she just liked looking at herself.

Goodall's eyes widened in alarm, "I completely forgot about that!" He rummaged in his shirt pocket for a moment then withdrew a note and passed it across.

Craig read it and passed it to his deputy with a smile.

"Rusty says we can ask her anything we want, so if Casey's got herself a good lawyer we could be here all night."

****

Manchester. England.

It was handy that Burnage Prison wasn't far from the city's airport, and even handier that Pierre Galvet had agreed to talk to them as soon as he'd been asked, and the only possible reason Ryan could think of for *that* was because the Frenchman was bored. It was one of the biggest problems with any incarceration, but an even bigger one probably when you're stuck on a protective custody wing because out amongst the general population your sex offences would earn you a severe kicking for being a nonce. Whatever the reason it was their gain.

The next plus was that the entrance to the wing wasn't through the main prison but via a side door that opened conveniently close to the interview room. Even though the D.S. *had* asked his constable to dress circumspectly, a request that for once Mary hadn't argued with, she couldn't conceal her face, and the reception given to any woman in a male prison wasn't a pretty sight never mind one as young as her.

Predictably Galvet leered as soon as he saw her, and when Ryan reported it afterwards Craig would kick himself for sending a woman to interview the sex offender at all. Yes, Mary was a police officer so perhaps such regret *was* just patriarchal anti-feminist self-indulgence on his part, or something 'woke' and complicated like that, and if so he was sure that someone, most probably the constable herself, would point it out to him, but he was *still* uncomfortable exposing women to certain situations and with the best will in the world he knew it would take him years more to get past his upbringing on that. And another decade for his mother to forgive him for doing so.

Perhaps it was a touch of that same conditioning that made Ryan surprised to see that Galvet had a young female solicitor beside him, or perhaps it was just that he'd expected everyone to share his repugnance at the paedophile's crimes. Nevertheless, the sergeant pushed his feelings to one side, checked that there were no language barriers and ran through the formalities quickly, hopeful that either Galvet would answer all their questions immediately or refuse to answer them at all, so that they could get away from the creep quickly and catch the late flight home.

The desire made the sergeant cut straight to the heart of the matter.

"Mister Galvet. Did you work at Le Petit Raisin Fruit Farm in Colomars in the summer of two-thousand-and-fifteen?"

The skinny Frenchman wheezed quietly and picked idly at the raw end of a cigarette that he was obviously dying to smoke. Society's laws made him control *that* habit indoors, but obviously not his untidy one of flaking tobacco all over the place.

His wheeze intensified as he answered, "Oui."

"In English please, for the tape."

"Yes. I work there for many summers."

His lawyer leaned forward, interceding. "What was the relevance of that question?"

Both detectives were surprised when her client raised a bony hand and waved her back.

"Let them ask what they want, ma chère. I need entertainment today."

They would play any role they had to if the Frenchman told them what they wanted to know.

"And which months were you employed there that year?"

As Galvet closed his eyes trying to recall, Mary noticed curiously that the white lumps of fat she'd noticed below his eyes were repeated on their lids. She was still staring when the Frenchman's faded brown eyes reopened and he gave a sly smile at catching her gaze.

She didn't look away, staring the paedophile down so hard that Ryan thought 'Good on you' and Galvet eventually transferred his gaze to the solicitor by his side.

"I think August until October that year, but I cannot be sure."

It confirmed what they already knew.

Ryan asked his next question without much hope of a

truthful answer. Bored Galvet might be, and so willing to confirm neutral details to prolong the meeting, but he doubted that the man fancied incriminating himself.

"Do you recall leaving the farm one day in August that year and going into La Gaude?"

The village the Renault had been stolen from.

The lawyer moved forward ready to object again, but her charge merely smiled, revealing yellowing teeth and badly receded gums.

"Oui, I went to La Gaude that summer, but I do not recall the date."

"Did you go there often?"

It earned the detective a shrug.

"When we were free perhaps. They worked us hard on that farm."

Ryan decided to come at it another different way.

"On the day in question you stole a silver Renault car. Do you remember that?"

This time the lawyer didn't wait for permission. "Don't answer that!"

The detectives watched as the sex offender turned towards her almost teasingly. "But why not? What can they do to me that God has not already done?"

Quite a lot if they were proved right, but Ryan decided not to point that out just then.

"Yes, I took the car. I left it many miles away that night."

The D.S. could hardly believe his ears, but he maintained his cool façade and leant forward at the table, keeping his hands firmly beneath it in case he was tempted to grab the sex offender by the throat.

"That wasn't all you took that day, was it, Mister Galvet?"

The leering smile returned, making Mary want to slap him.

"La jeune fille...ah, oui, elle était très jolie."

Ryan thought he understood the words but he needed them in English for the tape.

"In English, please."

Galvet's constant background wheeze grew louder.

"I say... the young girl. Yes, she was very pretty."

The sergeant's jaw clenched so hard he couldn't speak

for a moment so his constable did instead.

"Can you describe the girl?"

When Galvet's eyes closed this time she hoped they would *never* reopen, but they did, with a smile, and the words that they'd travelled there to hear yet had half-hoped they wouldn't emerged.

"She was three years or so. Very blonde, almost white, very blue eyes. Light. She wore blue dungarees, a yellow cardigan and white shoes. They had little rabbits on the toes."

It was the exact outfit that Bella Westbury had been wearing when she'd disappeared and the pleasure the man took in its description made Mary feel sick. But Galvet's follow-up sickened her even more.

"Her name was Bella Westbury. Belle. Oui, elle était belle."

Ryan didn't want to know what that meant in English, even the sound of the man saying it made his skin crawl, but he *did* want to know how the scumbag knew the girl's name. Had Bella told him herself? It seemed unlikely when she'd been so young.

"How do you know her name?"

Galvet was twisting his lips in pleasure now, playing with the sound. "Bella, Bella..."

Ryan's hands appeared suddenly and slammed down on the table. *"How do you know her name?"*

It made the sex offender cough at length and when his choking ended he gave a rueful smile. "I did not touch her you know. Not in that way."

"HOW. DO. YOU. KNOW. HER. NAME?"

It prompted a sigh. "Again with the same question. Ah, well, I will answer so that we can move on. I knew her name because I was given when I told to take her. Not for me myself. No, I did not touch her in that way, she was too young." He shook his head. "Not for anyone that way. She was too valuable. Taken only for money. You will have heard of such things, no?"

Not this side of hell they hadn't. Ryan noticed there was no defensive bluster from the solicitor now; instead she was arching away from her client, a look of disgust on her face.

Galvet's answers confirmed everything in Davy's email,

but Ryan couldn't understand why the paedophile was offering everything so freely when he *must* have known that it would keep him in prison for life.

He knew it was tempting fate, but he had to ask the reason. The question was greeted by a shrug.

"Because why not? You think I care about more years in here? No. It is boring yes, but not so bad. Besides, I will die before long time."

He smirked at Mary and then pointed to the lumps beneath his eyes. "Fat. You noticed. Too much cheese perhaps. And they say that inside I am full of it, even though I am skinny. I have already two heart attacks so I know I will soon have more."

He waved a hand around the small interview room. "I am not strong enough to work now and if I cannot work I will starve, so better to die here with food and in the warm."

He picked at his cigarette again for a moment in silence, this time deliberately brushing the flakes off the table onto the floor, and then he stared directly at Ryan.

"So... perhaps I will give you what you want and you will give me something?"

"Like what?"

The dead man walking held up his now half-cigarette. "Many of these. I *love* these, they make me happy. Also perhaps they make me die quicker. Yes?"

Everyone goes to hell their own way.

The sergeant's reply was ambivalent, loath to confirm that they would give such a pervert anything.

"We'll see what we can do. Now, back to the girl. You said money was involved. Were *you* paid to take her?"

The Frenchman gave a rude snort. "A pittance! *Merde.* I take all the risk and get three hundred Euros. Pigs."

Ryan's voice became eager. *"Who? Do you have the pigs' names?"*

"I have the names they gave to me, but I know that they were fake. Brad and Taylor, like the pop girl. Who ever heard of Irish called Brad and Taylor?"

The detectives' eyes grew round.

"They were Irish? How can you be sure?"

"I watch movies. I hear the voices. Different voices but both Ireland."

"Would you recognise them if you saw them again?"

"The man, yes. I gave him the Bella girl. The woman," he shrugged, "it was only her voice I heard, when she called me to arrange the first time. After that I spoke only to the man. The same man on the phone and took Bella."

He shook his head wistfully. "I wonder where she is sometimes. I wonder where they all are."

Mary jumped in.

"All? All children?"

"Ah, oui. All very young. The oldest I took was still only four years. Boys and girls, all *very pretty.*"

"All in France?"

"But no. From many places in Europe. Me and others."

"Can you remember exactly where and when?"

The Frenchman smirked. "Yes, but that will cost you *very* many cigarettes."

Ryan nodded; as far as he was concerned Galvet could smoke out of every orifice at once as long he gave them what they needed.

He took back the questioning.

"First, Bella. Give us everything about her to show you're telling the truth. Would you recognise this Brad again?"

Galvet gave a sceptical snort. "But of course. It is my heart not my brain that is failing."

"Describe to us exactly how you took her."

The Frenchman shrugged again.

"It was simple. This Brad watched her from far and when he was ready he called me to wait nearby. I waited, I see a chance so I lift the girl over the wall, drug her with a pad Brad had sent me and drive her to meet him in the woods. He paid me; I left the car there and return to the farm another way."

He made it sound as mundane and unemotional as doing his weekly shop.

"What if the opportunity hadn't arisen that day?"

"We would try again. I had stolen many cars and waited many times for this Bella before."

Shit! It looked as if once this Brad had a child in his sights he didn't give up.

Mary wasn't so sure, so she sat forward signalling to ask something.

"Did you wait so many times for *every* child?"

It prompted a laugh.

"No, never. Usually I just see in the street, I snatch, I hand over, but with this Bella Brad was obsessed. Just with Bella."

It was something to report to Craig. When she sat back Ryan nodded a 'well done' and continued.

"What happened to the children after they were taken?"

It prompted another shrug that this time said 'don't know, don't care'.

"I know they were valuable, but how I do not know."

Ryan decided it was time for a break and he nodded the others to join him outside.

He turned to the solicitor.

"We need to get an ID on this Brad. Are you OK with your client doing a photo array?"

The solicitor nodded, far more subdued than when they'd started. "Please believe me; I had no idea about any of this. I was only appointed to represent him today when you called to say you were coming."

Ryan gave a weak smile.

"We all have our jobs and not every part of them is pleasant. OK, Detective Li here will contact Manchester Police Headquarters to arrange an array here with our suspect's photo amongst them, and meanwhile you and I will get some more details. We're heading outside for five minutes to make some calls and then we'll restart."

With Mary in tow he called Craig, and caught him and Liam in an interview room awaiting Róisín Casey.

"Yes, Ryan. How're things going?"

"You won't believe it, chief. Galvet's coughing to everything!"

Craig set his mobile on speaker. "Be exact."

"He's admitted stealing the Renault and taking Bella for money, three hundred Euros."

"My God!"

Craig could hardly believe his ears.

"But he says he didn't assault her, just drugged her and drove her to be handed over to a man who called himself Brad. Galvet spoke to both him and a woman called Taylor to arrange things, but he says they were obviously false names because both of them were Irish. He never saw the woman but he *did* see the man when he passed on the Westbury girl, so we're going to set up an array with Blaine Westbury's photo included. Is that OK?"

Liam's mouth was hanging open in disbelief at the break they'd just been handed, but Craig managed a weak, "Yes."

"That's not all, chief. Galvet's saying he and others took lots of kids across Europe, both sexes, all four years and under, and he's going to give us everything he can remember on them. We're just starting that now-"

Mary jumped in. "He commented how pretty they all were."

"They're all pretty at that age."

Ryan interceded.

"I don't know, it *did* sound like he was making a point, chief, like *how* attractive they were was important. He was also adamant that the children weren't to be harmed or touched; they were taken only for money, that's what he said. Whatever that means."

Mary jumped in again. "But the Westbury girl was the only one Galvet said he saw so much effort taken with. The rest were snatched but with her they watched and waited. He said this Brad was obsessed with her."

It underlined their grudge theory.

Suddenly Craig's suspicious side kicked in. "Why's Galvet giving us all this when he must know that we'll lock him away forever?"

Ryan sighed. "He knows that, but he says prison's not such a bad place to die as long as we give him enough cigs to smoke. He's not a well man. Wheezing, coughing and skinny as hell, with lumps of fat around his eyes and he says fat inside too. He's had two heart attacks already so I just think he's hoping that the third does the trick."

Liam had been listening silently but now he said, "Xanthelasma."

"Bless you."

"Very witty, but it wasn't a sneeze. That's what they call fat round the eyes. One of my brothers has it. It's a sign of high cholesterol."

They were back to melting into blobs of fat again.

Ryan understood. "That would explain Galvet's crack about cheese. Anyway, will we go ahead with the array, chief?"

"Yes. Get an ID on this Brad and as soon as you have it notify me, then keep going on the children's names Davy sent through and this Taylor. This is amazing work, both of you."

The sergeant sounded a warning note. "It'll cost you a lot of cigs, and I doubt that'll be Galvet's only demand by the end."

"Whatever it costs it'll be a small price to find those children."

Craig cut the call and fell back in his chair, astonished at what they'd just heard. He waited for his deputy to say something and Liam didn't disappoint.

After several "Bloody hell"s the D.C.I. made a rational contribution.

"I think we should defer Casey's interview till they call us back with that ID, boss. That way we can face her with *proof* of Blaine Westbury's involvement."

Craig nodded. "You're right. We need to be better armed before we question her. Go and tell your mate we're pushing her interview back an hour, will you. I need to think."

After a moment of that he dialled Andy's number. The D.C.I. left his interview with Arthur Norris to take the call.

"Yes, chief?"

"What's happening with Norris?"

"Not much. I really think he believes this is all something to do with pollution, I don't think he's got a clue about anything else. When we faced him with Róisín Casey's name he admitted that her bank financed the mortgage business he runs in Belfast and that he's acted as an agent for her at times. Mainly to do with the quarry, although the whole Rio Reynolds' thing shows he does gofer work too. But beyond that..."

"What has he said specifically about her role in the quarry?"

"That she's one of the owners, so she must have been hiding her name behind that front company Davy found. The quarry itself was just a plain old goldmine that ran out of gold, and the protests were just legitimate local anger against the planned excavation."

"And Stuart Kincaid's death?"

"Norris still seems to believe it was just a shocking local murder. He doesn't appear to have a clue beyond that."

Craig tossed up on updating the D.C.I. about the other things they'd discovered and decided against it just then.

"OK, Andy. Try to get the names of the partners in the quarry if Norris has them and call me back."

"Where are you?"

"Dublin. We'll be interviewing Casey in an hour, so call back before then if you can. But *don't* tell Norris we've got her in custody. Oh, and casually ask him if he knows anyone called Brad or Taylor, will you."

When a puzzled, "Grand..." came back Craig ended the call.

He made another one to his secretary. "Alice. I need you to do a little job for me."

The PA wasn't quite sure if she liked the sound of that and he heard it in her hesitant, "Right..."

Nicky would have said, "Hell, yeh."

"It's all above board, trust me, Alice."

"Then go ahead, sir. Where are you now by the way?"

"Garda Headquarters in Dublin. Right, I need you to contact the PA of Róisín Casey, Vice President at The Atlantic Way Merchant Bank in Dublin Docklands. Davy will have the extension number. Confirm Casey's movements from the twenty-ninth of August twenty-fifteen for about a week, and tell her that we can get a Garda warrant if we need to. We're pretty sure Casey was in Rome then but I want independent confirmation."

He might be pushing it on the warrant, but relationships between the two forces were good.

"I need to know *exactly* where Casey was then. Call me back ASAP."

Just then another number appeared on his phone and he was surprised to see that it was his sister Lucia's. She rarely contacted him at work so he knew that he'd better take the call.

"OK, thanks, Alice, I have to go."

He swopped to his second line. "Luce, what's up? I really can't talk, I'm busy."

Lucia Craig smiled to herself, knowing that she was about to deliver a bombshell. She'd had to vie with several other people to be the one to drop it but she'd *really* wanted to hear the shock and panic in her normally cool brother's voice.

"I'll be quick then. Katy's gone into labour and we're leaving for the hospital. Bye."

Craig gripped his phone hard.

"What? No, don't go! You can't!"

"But you said you were busy, big bro. So, ciao."

She sat in silence for a few seconds enjoying his terror, then felt guilty and spoke again.

"OK, look, we just thought you should know, well, all except Mum who thinks this is women's business that you should have no part in, and Katy who didn't want you bothered at work. I don't know what you did to deserve that woman, Marc, honestly. She's a saint. I'd be *screaming* for attention. Anyway, everything's fine and Katy says it could be eight to eighteen hours before the baby appears, first labour and all that, so there's no rush to get back."

Craig felt cold sweat start to drip down his back. The baby was too early.

"She can't be in labour! The baby's not due for another ten days."

"Okey dokey then. I'll just tell it to stay in there, will I? Because you said so."

Just then Liam reappeared and was taken aback by the pallor on his boss' face. Craig held out the phone weakly to him and Lucia explained things again, finally ending the call with, "Katy's fine, the baby's fine, it's all fine and we don't need him here, so just calm him the hell down, will you, Liam."

The D.C.I. had other ideas. "We'll come back up the road now."

"Don't you dare! And that just came straight from Katy shouting across the room at me. She's got enough people here fussing over her without Marc pacing the floor and winding her up. Now goodbye."

As she cut the call Liam slumped into a seat. "You're not wanted, but are we heading home anyway?"

Craig gave a heartfelt sigh. "I really want to but I know I won't get any thanks for it. Katy told me months ago that she *really* didn't want me at the birth; although she said she'd cope with it if I insisted. Even *that* was said very grudgingly."

"*Are* you insisting?"

Craig gazed at him despairingly. "I'd like to be there for her but I really think she meant it when she said that I would just make her more stressed. Maybe it's a doctor thing. She said she doesn't actually want *anyone* there. She'd prefer to deliver by herself in a small room and just appear with a smiling bundle."

Liam's weary snort came from the shattered illusions of a father of two. "*You'll* be lucky. They don't smile for weeks. Danni wouldn't have me there either, she said I'd just panic. *As if.*"

Craig furrowed his forehead. "I wonder if it's a healthcare thing? Because she's a nurse and Katy's a doctor? The way we wouldn't want *them* there at a crime scene."

Liam roared with laughter. "Comparing the birth of your child to a crime scene! Talk about putting your foot in it! For God's sake don't let the missus hear you saying that."

"That's not what I meant! You know-"

Craig was rescued by his phone ringing again and he was relieved to see that this time the call was about work.

"Yes, Ryan. You have the ID?"

The sergeant sounded stunned. "Galvet picked out Blaine Westbury first pop! Called him Brad too. Then he said that he'd handed loads of kids over to him and that he was the boss of everything, although there are others at the top too. But you're not going to believe how many kids Galvet's claiming to have taken, boss. I can hardly..." he swallowed hard. "He said he took *fifteen* between twenty-ten and fifteen alone and about the same number after that. All young. And there's worse. Galvet says he's not the only one this Brad paid to take kids..."

They hadn't even scraped the surface with the children on Davy's list.

"... but he says he'll only give us the names of the other middle men if he gets a few more luxuries in his final years."

What was an advantage for if not to be pressed?

Craig allowed himself a few seconds of imagining Galvet being guillotined and the thought calmed him enough to focus on the task ahead.

"Like what?"

"He doesn't want to be sent back to France. As *he* said, 'they will not be so nice to me I think.' He also wants weekly conversation classes with someone French so he can speak his native language, some books to read and some sunshine in the summer. He's accepted that he's never getting out. Actually, he doesn't want to."

Craig felt sick to his stomach at the idea of giving the man anything; he was walking filth. But...how many children were they talking about and where had they all gone? How many families like the Westburys had been broken over the years?

He tried to think how *he'd* feel if he was a parent with no idea where their child was and knew they *had* to give those families peace if they could, even if it meant bargaining with a pervert like Galvet.

"Yes. Tell him yes to everything, Ryan."

The French government *might* fight to transfer the paedophile but they could deal with that if it happened; by the time any extradition process was complete they should have all the information they needed and Galvet might already be dead.

"Get those names, Ryan, and get the list to Davy as soon as you can."

He met his deputy's eyes in disgust and cut the call feeling tainted, but they had to get the bastards who'd organised everything, and hopefully with Galvet's information and one final thing from Alice they would have both Róisín Casey and Blaine Westbury boxed in.

****

Róisín Casey's Riverside Apartment. Dublin 2.

Blaine Westbury hated doing things in a rush; planning was his forte and he was a virtuoso at it, despite his parents' certainty that he'd had no talent at anything much. Perfect plans and their meticulously timed delivery, with every risk predicted and fail-safes and contingencies in place were something he and Róisín had always had in common, that and their love of money of course. Her for her lifestyle, him for his card games and high stakes trips to Vegas; they certainly had lived the high life together over the years.

He opened the boot of his, deliberately anonymous but high performance in case he had to run, beige Mercedes and dropped in the bag that contained everything he needed for his future. Then, with a final look at the River Liffey and the apartment building that he'd called home on and off for over a decade, he pulled out on to City Quay and headed over the Talbot Memorial Bridge towards the port. From there it was through the port tunnel and he would hit the airport in an hour, and if that had *really* been the end of it he would have been home and dry and the police could have spent the rest of their naturals chasing his smoke.

But there was the inconvenient matter of the Garda having lifted his girlfriend and, had he but known it, the even stickier issue of the north's best detective squad being on his tail, brought there by his own carelessness over Stuart Kincaid's death.

Unaware of that, Westbury drove with the window down and his mind racing as fast as the air outside was rushing past him, thinking of the past and the future and then the past again, and believing in his heart that his only mistake had been arranging for his own niece's abduction, but he just hadn't been able to resist the delicious spectacle of his big brother in distress.

Edgar the big brother, the perfect son and heir, held up to him all his bloody life as the person he fell short of. Good, clean, kind and following his parents into the hotel business, whereas he'd been worthless, dishonest, lazy and would never amount to anything.

He found himself shouting aloud as he sped through the tunnel. "Whose fault was *that* then, Mum and Dad?"

Tell a child that he's a failure and he'll become one, tell him he's dishonest and maybe that's what he'll learn to be. OK, maybe he *had* stumbled a lot, but the helping hand he'd had a right to expect from his only brother had *never* been there to pull him to his feet. Still...he wished he'd never seen Bella at his folks' funeral and decided to snatch her; he *should* have left her alone, not on moral but on common sense grounds. Her abduction was too close to home for comfort and *had* to be why the cops were on his tail. He'd just never expected Nicola's sodding twin brother to make the link and begin to snoop.

He emerged from the port tunnel into the daylight again and put his foot down hard, raking up through the car's gears hard and shifting his thoughts from the past to the future again. He would start again in South America and Róisín would follow if she could. Their buyer networks and infrastructure were still intact there so there was no reason why the future couldn't be even more profitable than the past for them. And if Róisín *didn't* follow, well, there'd be plenty of new girlfriends where he was going. He just had to hold his nerve and board a plane to get there, and in a few hours time he would.

As he pulled off at the exit for Dublin Airport, intending to park and wait in his car until the last possible minute before his flight, Blaine Westbury had no idea *just* how many people were trying to find him, assisted by one of his own grubby gang.

****

The C.C.U.

Craig's small office was a hive of activity. Cate Pine was peering over the shoulder of her analyst as she worked at Craig's computer, and Ash was working in parallel on his laptop with Emrys Lomax looking over his. Davy entered the room at intervals to update his junior on what more was needed and left again with various scribbled notes in his hand.

By seven p.m. Craig knew that the woman who'd accompanied Bella Westbury from Rome to Boston in twenty-fifteen had *definitely* been Róisín Casey, Casey's PA confirming she'd flown into that same airport just two days before and hadn't returned to her work at the bank for a week. Between that information and the match on her passport photo they now had Casey linked *directly* to the abduction of Bella, and Blaine Westbury linked to far more than that.

Davy checked his PC again for updates on the airport surveillance, and when he saw nothing he entered Craig's office yet again, just in time to see the joint effort of two exceptional analysts come to fruition and the cryptocurrency icon on Derek Morrow's desktop finally spring to life.

A series of flashing screens and rabbit-hole 3D effects that would have looked at home in The Matrix ended in both Ash's and his opposite number's computers going dark, making the hackers gasp and exchange a panicked look. If the currency site had crashed that *could* mean it was protected by file wiping software, and despite all of their hard work everything would be lost.

The room was deathly quiet for what felt like minutes, with all eyes trained unblinkingly on the computer screens and no-one daring to breathe, then, after first a small boot-up circle appearing and then the analysts' screens gradually brightening, the soft, round face of a small child appeared.

It was followed by another and another and another, until the screen was filled with children's photographs arranged in rows. Side by side head and shoulder images, all staring blankly at an invisible camera without a single smile. Every possible ethnicity of girls and boys; all young, all bewildered looking, their faces scrubbed, their hair neatly combed and their clothes pristine.

The two detectives in the room gawped at each other but the analysts didn't *dare* lift their eyes from the images, fearful that at any moment they might disappear.

The person brave enough to break the silence was Emrys Lomax.

"We need to click on one of them."

Davy was more cautious. "Ash? What do you think? W...Will it wipe?"

"I don't think so. Do you two?"

Cate Pine's analyst shook her head immediately, and slowly Davy concurred, adding a caveat.

"Take a screenshot first, just in case they disappear."

They took several: on phones, Craig's PC, a laptop and two smart-pads, as well as printing out a sheaf of them, until finally ten minutes later they were ready to proceed.

This time Cate Pine took charge.

"Choose one to click on."

Just then Ash pointed to a square near the bottom of

the screen, looking stunned. "That's Bella Westbury! Derek Morrow was in on her kidnap!"

Davy nodded heavily. "Or he knew about it anyway. Fuck him. I'm *glad* he killed himself now!"

It was a rare outburst from the gentle computer expert, but one which everyone approved.

As Ash calmed himself and steadied his cursor above the girl's photograph they all held their breath again. A single tap led them not to darkness as feared but to a PDF file, and when the hacker repeated the action to open it what was written there made Davy want to vomit.

The file's opening page was headed 'Bella Westbury Adoption' and listed the girl's colouring, age, ethnicity and details of her parentage and upbringing, as well as a transaction code, the eye-watering price that had been paid for her, and the name of who had her now. Bella Westbury was now Olivia Stanger the daughter of Donald and Brook Stanger, residents of Manhattan, New York.

Emrys Lomax thudded on to the nearest chair and dropped his face into his hands for a moment. When the Vice D.C.I. looked up again he didn't try to conceal the tears in his eyes.

"I've seen people do things that you wouldn't believe but I've *never* seen anything like this. This is the depths of depravity." He swallowed hard. "How many kids are on that screen?"

It was Ash who answered, his own disbelief at what they'd found showing in his hoarse voice.

"Around two hundred, but..." He shook his head as if to clear it and then continued, "I think there are other screens behind this one. We can't be sure until we strip it back, but this blockchain's huge so it can hold a lot of data."

Cate Pine joined the other detective sitting down. "They can communicate with each other through the blockchain from anywhere in the world?"

"Yes, but this layer of the blockchain is encrypted, otherwise any user could have seen these images and reported them to the police. Morrow must have been uber cautious because he'd encrypted his shortcut icon as well. We managed to bypass the need for a password by hacking, but anyone else would have needed one."

Davy had a tech question for his junior.

"Can you get names for everyone who's accessed it?"

"Eventually, but we've a lot of work to do before then. The FBI's analysts can help us generate the locations of the kids in the States, and Europol's ditto in Europe, but this is gonna take a while."

Cate Pine turned to Davy. "You'd better update D.C.S. Craig. He needs to be happy before we go any further. If things get out to the agencies too early there could be a leak, and there's no telling what some of the adoptive parents might do to those children to keep themselves out of jail."

It was clear from *all* the analysts' horrified expressions that the possibility had only occurred to the cops in the room.

Davy said nothing for a moment, thinking through the ramifications, and then he nodded, indicating that he'd made up his mind.

"You two keep w...working on the photos and back-up three copies of each kid's PDF. That's the first priority in case things crash. W...We need to know who they were, and who and where they are now. But don't pass those files on *anywhere* till-"

Just then the door flew open and a flustered Alice rushed in. "Davy, your computer's making a noise like it's going to explode or something!"

His alarm. He'd set it to go off as soon as Blaine Westbury was face-matched.

He tore out to his desk, tapped his keyboard repeatedly, and then grabbed the phone and connected with Craig.

"Chief, Westbury's just entered the short-term car park at Dublin Airport. Block A. It's the closest to the terminals. There're no direct flights to a non-extradition country today, but there's a connecting one to Caracas via Newark in the States. The Newark flight leaves at nine-thirty from Terminal One so he has to be on that. He obviously fancies his chances of getting through US security, probably because he's bluffed them so many times before. Anyway, it's half-seven now so you'll need to move!"

Craig had just begun his interview with Róisín Casey and he hoped that the banker had overheard Davy's words. They'd just shown her Blaine Westbury's picture and outlined a hypothetical scenario linking the pair of them to something grave, although without giving the full details, and he wanted her to realise *just* how close they were getting to her partner and start to sweat.

He took the call into the corridor, leaving Liam in the interview room to keep the banker on edge.

"Has he appeared in the departure area yet, Davy?"

The analyst tapped several more times before replying. "No sign of him in either terminal. He'll probably w...wait in the car till check-in's almost closed, so I'd be prepared for him to make a dash for the check-in about an hour before the flight."

If Westbury had a gun he could take a hostage or even shoot people that got in his way, and in a busy airport that meant a lot of people could get killed.

"Right, hike up the airport alert. Liam and I are heading out there now."

He rapped the interview room window hard and beckoned to his deputy, nodding Pat Goodall to return his prisoner to her cell.

Liam was quick on the uptake.

"Westbury?"

"Dublin Airport, so let's get on the road. I'll call Pat from the car. We'll need Garda backup out there."

A bewildered and then panicked Róisín Casey was deposited quickly back in her cell. The banker was quick on the uptake and she'd guessed from the giant cop's expression as he'd left that he thought they'd just cracked their case.

She also had no illusions about human nature and knew her lover *very* well. Where Blaine was concerned he would protect himself first and last and to hell with the rest, so unless she got ahead of things now and cut a deal he *definitely* would, and *she* would be the sacrifice.

As the financier calculated how long she had to play with, and what was the minimum she could tell the police without ending up in prison for life, the murder detectives were racing through Dublin towards its port tunnel with two response cars following close behind.

Craig called his senior analyst again on the way. "Talk to me, Davy."

"Westbury's still not inside the terminal building, so he must in the car park. From Block A he could sprint to departures in minutes. He was snapped on entry in a beige metallic S-Class Mercedes."

Liam gave a whistle. "If he bolts in that thing even *I'll* never keep up."

"Then we stop him, even if we have to crash the car to do it."

Davy continued as if they hadn't spoken; keen to get his information across.

"I could ask the gate guards to s...search for it, chief, but the car park's huge."

Craig shook his head hurriedly, his urgency reflected in his voice. "*No, don't!* We don't know if Westbury's armed but they *definitely* won't be. OK, update me on what else you've got."

"I'll try to hack into the car park CCTV while we're talking. OK, other stuff on Westbury or the crypto?"

"Take your pick."

"W...Westbury first then. He could be flying under one of two names. I've got the passenger manifest and they're the only names that fit by sex and age, but I can't see the passport photos till they check in."

"Names?"

"Jacob Reiss or Bradley Rockenham."

"It's the second."

"How do you know?"

"He called himself Brad when he dealt with Pierre Galvet."

The analyst rolled his eyes. Bradley Rockenham sounded like an extra on 90210.

"OK, the airport will send me their photos the minute either man checks in, and now we're sure which country W...Westbury's heading to I'm going to look for a money trail. He must have transferred assets in advance to live."

Craig glanced at the speedometer in passing and winced; Liam was doing well over one-hundred-and-twenty miles an hour. He focused back on his call.

"Don't worry about Westbury's assets for now; we can do all that after we have him. Tell me what's happening with Derek Morrow's crypto link."

As the analyst outlined their process in the least technical language that he could manage without sounding patronising, Craig felt himself going cold. Rows and rows of young children, each with a price on their head, paid for by people who'd ordered them to suit their needs like they were a fitted kitchen or a new car. It explained Galvet's emphasis on how attractive all the children were. He'd been pointing them to its perceived value in the world of designer adoptions.

It was callous, disgusting and would take forever to undo the damage done to the kids, who'd spent years believing they were with their birth parents only to soon find out that they'd been traded like a commodity.

Commodity trading! The thought made Craig catch his breath. He'd jumped to the conclusion that Blaine Westbury had been the mastermind behind everything and Róisín Casey his supportive partner, but trading was *her* world and *she* would have been the one with international contacts. Had Westbury been the follower and *Casey* the one in charge?

The detective shook his head hard to clear it. He was getting ahead of himself. Who'd led and who'd followed was irrelevant right now, they could sort that out once they had *both* the scum in jail.

Davy's clear voice cut across his thoughts. "Did you hear me, chief? D.C.S. Pine says it's your case so we can't do anything more than gather the names and addresses of the kids without you s...saying how to proceed."

Craig shut his eyes as he responded, hesitantly at first, his words forming at the same time as his thoughts.

"There's a risk here... if the adoptive parents... get spooked...they could...probably will...kill the children to avoid jail. And for all we know they could all be in touch with each other...it's unlikely but not impossible." He became more confident in what he was saying and opened his eyes, "So when we go in for the kids they'll *all* have to be approached at the same time."

He straightened up in his seat assertively. "This will require massive co-ordination with agencies across several countries, Davy, and that will take a lot of preparation, so although I know the urge to do something now is overwhelming we can't. We need to get everything ready for one big swoop and disable all possible communications between them beforehand."

The analyst pushed aside his urge to blow the doors off

in favour of Craig's logical approach.

"OK. I s...see that."

Just then Craig glanced out the window and saw a sign stating that Dublin Airport was only ten miles away.

"Right, quickly, get me D.C.S. Pine and D.C.I. Lomax on a three-way. I need you to put the armed airport police on alert and then come back and join in."

A moment later he had the others cops on the line, and reiterated his approach.

"Thanks both of you for your assistance today, but it's imperative that this is a meticulously planned and coordinated swoop across time zones and countries before even *one* child is approached. We'll need to work through the details before either the birth or adoptive families are alerted."

There was no argument from Lomax but Cate Pine's agreement was grudging.

"If it was my kid-"

Craig cut her off sharply. "But it's not, Cate. And if one child is killed because of our carelessness then we'll *all* deserve a place in hell! This is my Op and I'm running it my way. I'd like assistance from both of you, but only if you can agree to follow my lead. I've informed the C.C. of everything already."

He hadn't, but he knew that even if he couldn't trust Cate Pine's self-control he *could* trust her desire not to mess up her career.

Her follow-on, "I understand" was less grudging and more subdued, but Craig knew that he'd *better* call Sean Flanagan in the next hour or she'd check and he would be screwed.

Just then Davy rejoined the call.

"Davy, I'd like you to collate the children's details and make sure no electronic or hard copies are taken off the floor."

That earned him the expected tut from Pine.

"Emrys, Cate, thank you and I'll contact both your offices on Monday and arrange a meet. Now, I need to speak to Davy alone."

When the others had quit the call Craig repeated his instructions to his analyst even more firmly, adding that he needed all of the children's PDFs encrypted and all paper copies locked in his office safe, then he phoned Sean Flanagan and ran quickly through the day's findings, to his driver's increasing astonishment, obtaining the Chief Constable's agreement that he could have whatever time he needed to plan before any other agencies made a move.

Craig had timed things well, because on the next occasion he glanced out the window they were on the slip-road for the car park. He signalled Liam to pull in before they reached its entrance and wait for the response cars to catch-up, then he motioned everyone to get out.

"Right. We believe Westbury's booked on a flight to Newark leaving at nine-thirty, under the name of either Bradley Rockenham or Joshua Reiss. Actually, Liam, ask Davy if he's checked-in before we enter the car park, will you."

A few seconds later the answer was no, neither man had checked-in, and there was still no sign of Westbury inside the terminal.

"That means we have to assume he's waiting in a beige metallic Mercedes inside this car park, somewhere pedestrians will be constantly leaving and collecting cars. We don't know if Westbury's got a gun but it's likely. Either way he'll be desperate and *extremely* dangerous."

He turned to the Gardaí. "Are any of you armed?"

The answer was a round of shaking heads that made him want to say "Damn", but he didn't. Instead he regretted the fact that police officers in the north felt that they *had* to carry weapons all the time, such was the continuing dissident threat to their lives.

"OK, well, we both are, so we'll go in alone. Meanwhile you cover the entrances and exits and prevent anyone new entering, and follow *but do not stop* Westbury if he tries to leave. He could kill you."

Just then Davy called again and Craig put it on speaker.

"Chief, I've just had a Superintendent Goodall on. He's spoken to the airport and asked for a lockdown on all the terminals and car parks, so nobody can enter or leave."

"Good." He should have thought of that himself. "That should cut the numbers of possible hostages for Westbury to grab in the car park at least."

"Yep. Also the airport's patched me into their CCTV and I scrolled back to when W...Westbury entered. He's in section closest to the terminal building. I've sent the layout to your phone. I can't pinpoint his space exactly because one of the cameras there's on the blink, but look for a beige metallic Mercedes. I'll text the reg number to you now."

"OK, good. And to the Garda officers too, please. He definitely hasn't entered the terminal yet?"

"No. That's the other thing I called about. Joshua Reiss has just checked in and he's not W...Westbury, so you were right, he must be travelling as Bradley Rockenham. It won't be long before he'll start running, because check-in closes in fifteen minutes. I'll text you again in five minutes if I have more info."

"Noted."

He cut the call and turned to the others. "You all heard that, so you men get to your posts. No lights or sirens, just sit quietly, and if that car comes out, follow it but keep your heads down and we'll catch you up. Time to go, Liam."

They passed the gate guard with a flash of ID, Craig directing his deputy incrementally through the car park according to the layout on his phone. Liam drove quickly at first and then as they approached the relevant section more slowly, then he pulled up to wait for Davy's text. It came exactly when promised but it didn't hold good news. Blaine Westbury was a clever bastard. He'd chosen a parking space in the section's far back corner, at the end of a long row of cars and right up against a wall.

It made the Mercedes inaccessible from either the sides or rear, leaving only a frontal assault possible and giving Westbury sight of anyone approaching from several car widths away. It would give the murderer plenty of time to drive out and ram them, or shoot if he had a gun, making an advance dangerous if you were driving but absolutely fatal for anyone on foot.

Craig motioned his deputy to park three rows up out of sight and switch off his engine.

"Are your binoculars in the boot, Liam?"

"Yep."

With that the D.C.I. slipped out the driver's door and hunkered his way to the rear of his Ford, returning a moment later with the equipment to see his boss frowning in thought.

"There are still pedestrians around. If we call Westbury out we'll get a standoff and someone will end up dead."

The D.C.I. shrugged. "What's the option, boss? We can't sneak up on him; he's positioned himself too well for that."

Craig's response was to take the binoculars and, ducking down, weave quickly through the rows of parked vehicles until he was hunkered in one just ahead of Westbury's car. He trained the binoculars on the Mercedes' windscreen, adjusting them until he could make out a man's shape, then he focused the lens so precisely that he could almost count the hairs on Blaine Westbury's upper lip. They were drenched in sweat, a full slick of it, a film repeated on the fugitive's forehead.

Craig watched for a moment as Westbury's pale eyes flicked repeatedly from the windscreen to his hands and then to the car's passenger seat and he realised exactly what they were facing. A quick trip back and he was inside the Ford beside his deputy, who was looking less than amused.

"You might have warned me you were bloody going that close! Well, what'd you see, Rambo?"

Craig gave a tight smile. "A very nervous looking man. He's sweating hard. He kept looking out, then down at his hands, and then at the passenger seat."

Liam nodded. "Attackers, gun, money. He's armed and he has his money and possessions on the seat beside him, ready to make a run for the plane. Well, seeing as he's expecting someone to come at him, it'd be a pity to disappoint him wouldn't it?"

Craig's smile widened; both of them wanted nothing more than to put a bullet between Blaine Westbury's eyes for all the misery that he'd caused. But they wouldn't unless *absolutely* forced to, not because the scumbag didn't deserve it, but because for the moment's satisfaction it would give them it would deprive all the families that Westbury had destroyed of justice, not to mention that they might both end up out of a job with bills to pay.

Craig shook his head with obvious regret. "I'd love us to take the bastard on, Liam, but we don't need to. He's boxed in whichever way he looks at it, so I *have* to point that out and give him a chance to surrender. However... *if* he decides to go full Clyde on us and shoot his way out then all bets are off."

As he went to make another call Liam retrieved the binoculars and opened his door.

"I'm going to take a closer look, boss."

"OK, but keep your head down, you're a big target. Davy? It's me again. We have Westbury in sight. He's in his car and I think he's armed, although I can't see the gun. Liam's gone to look again. How's the timing for his check-in?"

"It's just closed, and he must know that."

"So he guessed that the airport was on alert. He's boxed himself in so we can't approach any other way but from the front, so that leaves us either trying to negotiate his surrender or ordering a full-on assault. Does he have a mobile?"

"The hire-car has a phone so I'll text you the number now."

"Do tha-"

Just then Liam jumped back into the car. "He has a bloody Heckler and Koch MP5K!"

A machine pistol holding fifteen to thirty rounds per magazine.

Craig cut his call. "*Shit!* He means business. Did he see you?"

"Can't have or I'd have a bullet in my ass, but he looks wild stressed so I wouldn't be surprised if he ran soon."

Craig thought fast. They'd both got close to the Mercedes without being seen or they would have been shot at, so now it was time to try the other way.

"OK. Five minutes then I'll call him out." Just then Davy's text with the car-phone number came through. "But I want to make sure this area's clear of civilians first. Stay down, I'll take the right side and you take the left."

"And if we find any?"

"Get them back in their cars, on the floor and quiet." He opened the passenger door and slipped down. "Back here in five."

Pat Goodall's lock-down had worked. The only person they found was a woman struggling with so much luggage that she must have entered the car park before them but not started towards the terminal yet. A quick flash of Craig's badge and a hand over her mouth just as she was about to speak and she was lying down in her car's rear foot-well and quietly saying her prayers.

By the time they reconvened at Liam's car, its owner had revised his opinion on their target.

"I think Westbury *might* have been about to run, boss. Something about his face."

Just then the Mercedes flew past the end of their row proving him right. They jumped into the Ford and Liam threw the car into reverse while his boss hit the siren and lights and called the waiting Gardaí as they gave chase.

"Westbury's heading for you if we can't stop him. Follow only. He has an MP5."

He cut the call and turned to his deputy. "If he reaches the motorway in that car we'll be eating dust. Get as close as you can and I'll try to shoot his tyres out before he hits full speed."

Liam's boot hit the floor, but the Mercedes' speed picked up in response until they were racing through the network of short streets, longer thoroughfares and ramps that made up the multi-storey car park, praying to God that no pedestrians from the interlocking car parks appeared taking a short-cut. The last thing they needed was a dead civvie or a hostage situation.

Craig was hanging so far out of the passenger window now that only his feet hooked around the edge of his seat stopped him falling out and under the Ford's tyres, and with every turn and ramp up to a higher floor he got shunted, rising and falling as his deputy skidded or lost connection momentarily with the tarmac's surface and then thudded down hard on it again.

He ignored the pain and the risk of falling, shutting out everything but the wheels burning rubber just feet front of him and searching for his chance, determined not to waste his limited bullets until he knew that he had the shot.

It came just as Westbury was rounding a left hand corner. The sharp turn made the Merc decelerate until it was only a car length in front of them, and a slow, smooth squeeze of Craig's trigger released a missile that found its way home, blowing out the saloon's offside rear tyre and making its backend flick out and round until it had spun the vehicle three-sixty and impaled its front end on a concrete pillar that all the revving in the world was never going to get it off.

The driver's door flew open almost immediately and a dark blond head appeared momentarily as Blaine Westbury rolled out on to the ground and then scuttled away. Craig was out of the car and after him in a second with his deputy in hot pursuit, both of them yelling, *"ARMED POLICE. STOP!"*

They followed the bobbing head through the floors and mazes of cars for several minutes, Craig in front and his deputy just inches behind, as Westbury fruitlessly tried every driver's door that he passed, hoping to steal something else to drive. After a while the head stopped bobbing and their target took up position behind a blue Toyota. Craig waited for several seconds and then shouted out again from where they were now concealed.

"ARMED POLICE! THERE'S NOWHERE TO RUN TO, WESTBURY. THERE ARE ARMED COPS AT THE EXITS AND IN THE TERMINALS. YOU KNOW WE CAN'T LET YOU GO SO IT'S TIME TO GIVE YOURSELF UP. THERE'S NO POINT SOMEONE DYING."

"FUCK OFF!"

Liam snorted. "Charming. Can we shoot him now?"

Craig shot him a sceptical look and tried again, with the same expletive-laden response.

"The bastard's hoping someone will walk past so he can take a hostage, Liam. There's still a tiny risk of it but we can't let it happen."

They shuffled closer until they were only a single row away, then Craig lowered his head to look beneath the cars.

"I've a clear shot at his legs."

"Just like he has of yours, if he thinks of it first. We need to distract him."

The D.C.I. moved quickly to the end of the row.

"You're the better shot so I'm going to do it, boss. As soon as you hear me shout, shoot the legs out from under the git."

Before Craig could say yes or no his deputy began racing across the road-wide gap between parking rows, taunting the killer as he did.

"WHAT SORT OF A BASTARD COULD DO WHAT YOU DID TO THOSE KIDS, WESTBURY?"

"YOU KNOW NOTHING ABOUT IT! PLENTY OF

THEM ARE HAPPY. HAPPIER THAN WITH THEIR OWN PEOPLE I BET."

It was Westbury's anger at his parents playing out but Craig didn't have the time to listen to his self-indulgent crap. Liam was doing his bit so he had to do his.

Just then he heard a run of shots and a loud, "OW! FUCK!" from his deputy, but he couldn't let himself be distracted from what he had to do. He tightened his focus on the hunkered down legs twenty feet in front of him and chose the biggest target; the thigh. A double tap later and there was a loud cry and a groan, and then a clatter as Westbury's submachine gun hit the ground when he doubled up in pain.

Craig moved in swiftly before he could retrieve the weapon, speeding between cars and kicking the MP5 away just as Westbury's blood-stained hand was reaching out. A second later Liam appeared holding his arm.

"Is it bad?"

"Flesh wound," he added huffily, "although I could have been dead for all *you* knew. You didn't even shout to ask me."

"I didn't get time. Besides, I reckoned you'd be swearing too loudly to hear."

The D.C.I. saw the sense of it and turned his attention to their prisoner, kicking cheerfully at the hole in Westbury's thigh.

"Here, now, that looks wild painful. You'd better get a doctor to look at that."

Craig didn't know how he could bear to touch the man, not even with his shoe, when he could barely look at Westbury without wanting to shoot him again. Not trusting himself not to the first time had felt so good, he stepped away and made the call to emergency services, gratefully accepting the appearing Gardaí's offer to accompany Westbury to the nearest hospital once the ambulance arrived and promising that they would return to interview him after he'd been patched up.

Twenty minutes later Craig left the ambulance staff and cops to it and loaded his, now neatly bandaged, deputy into his car, then he turned it back towards Dublin and Pat Goodall's banker houseguest.

Chapter Nine

Garda Headquarters.

By midnight yet more pieces had slotted into place, courtesy of Róisín Casey's desperate efforts to save her designer ass. In the deluded hope of negotiating some sort of leniency, and despite Craig's *clear* warning that no such indulgence would be forthcoming and that she and her lover would probably spend the rest of their lives fending off attempts by various countries to plug them into the mains, the banker obligingly filled in some gaps.

The names she gave them went on and on like some depraved roll-call in Hell. Middle-men abductors like Galvet, staff in private adoption agencies across the globe, passport forgers, airport staff who'd colluded in smuggling the children in and out of countries, IT specialists who'd set up their finance and communications networks plus the crypto-library of children that Ash had uncovered; the list was seemingly endless. The Bonny and Clyde team had had more people in their employ than most multinationals.

And of course, Róisín had explained that *everything* had been Blaine Westbury's idea. She was just a helpless woman who'd fallen in love and been trapped by her man's threats of violence if she'd refused to assist him; or that was the complete tripe she was proposing to trot out in court anyway.

In Blaine Westbury's case, *he* was reclining in his hospital bed not even *trying* to lie about what he'd done, revealing the details of Stuart Kincaid's murder almost gloatingly and citing as justification that Kincaid had been, "Snooping around my village and quarry asking questions about me", the drowning itself easily managed because Kincaid had been a much smaller man.

When Craig had asked curiously why he had turned Kincaid away as he'd killed him, the answer, "He reminded me of Nicola and I liked her even though she married Edgar", confirmed the semi-personal element to the killing that he had speculated about. The murderer didn't hold back on his hatred for his big brother, and the answer as to why he'd begun watching Bella in March twenty-fifteen was given with a shrug.

"I saw her at my folks' funeral and decided to take her a week later when I found out that Edgar had been left practically everything in the Will. I wanted to hit him where it hurt."

Pathetic bastard. Westbury had torn a child away from her family simply because he'd thought that his own hadn't been fair.

As much as uncovering such tragedy could ever be, it was a satisfactory end to the case. They'd solved Stuart Kincaid's murder, arrested some unspeakable bastards, and were without a doubt going to arrest more. They'd also sparked something far bigger that would hopefully unite hundreds of stolen children with their real families.

In another few days they would uncover even more on the specifics of their case. That Arthur Norris had just been a clueless land agent and gofer who they would eventually release without charge, although with a warning of what would happen if he *ever* paid someone to slander a person again. But they were resigned to the fact that the elderly businessman would probably *never* believe evil of Róisín, the woman he was infatuated with, no matter how long he lived.

They would also learn that Derek Morrow, while legitimately inspecting the quarry the winter before, had witnessed Blaine Westbury murdering Stuart Kincaid, and instead of calling the police had thought he'd found himself a Golden Goose. It had been a short road from witnessing the killing to blackmailing Westbury and getting pay-offs into an account in the Caymans, giving Morrow the nest-egg that he'd never had at last, although how he'd planned for that money to reach his family after death without leaving them the password to access it would take Davy a while to work out. Morrow had played no part in the child abductions but his access to the blockchain was a sure sign that he'd been well aware of them, so he was as guilty as sin. His only redeeming act had been pointing them obliquely towards the venture in his suicide note, but his cryptocurrency link had been the key that had really opened the door.

In a few more days the squad's analysts would find another key when they cracked Morrow's WatsUp group and linked him definitively with Blaine Westbury, Róisín

Casey, and several other high-level players in the abduction ring that they so far knew nothing about; players who had so carelessly chatted about their revolting business venture in the group believing that they were safe. Some of their names were also on Stuart Kincaid's quarry investors list but there were others that were new, and they would all be hunted down no matter where in the world they lived.

But acting on all of that information would have to wait for its discovery and tonight Craig just wanted to get the hell back to Belfast and find out what was happening in his personal life.

Chapter Ten

The C.C.U. Monday, 8 a.m.

The squad-room was deserted and silent and Craig stood in its centre relishing the peace after the weekend he'd just had. Not the excitement of childbirth, that had turned out to be a false alarm so Katy was back home in waiting mode, but the noise of two mothers, his dad, and Lucia and her fiancée all talking at once in their small apartment had made him want to run for the hills.

He'd finally kicked everyone out the evening before, the mothers clutching the final shortlist in the great house hunt and instructed to take a further look, with his father along as a fresh pair of eyes, and then he and Katy had fallen asleep together on the sofa like a couple of old married folk.

He'd left her still asleep in bed an hour before because he'd wanted to be first in to inspect his newly, and covertly, renovated kingdom, and as Craig stood gazing around him and smiling he wondered what his team would make of the work, one member in particular.

He didn't have to wait long to find out, because a run of thudding footsteps that shook the floor and a hard slap on the back that made him cough informed Craig that his deputy had arrived.

"Congratulations! What was it, boy or girl?"

Craig turned towards the D.C.I., shaking his head. "False alarm. Katy was home in hours. I told you it was too early."

Liam seemed unsurprised. "Aye, well, that happened three times with our first. Just the wee bugger winding you up. Fairly shakes you up though, doesn't it."

The sweary title for his offspring sounded strangely affectionate in Liam's country accent and made Craig laugh; meanwhile the D.C.I. had already moved on, striding towards the back of the open-plan office, his gaze narrowing quizzically as he did.

He jabbed his forefinger at a door just ahead of them.

"That door wasn't there last week."

Craig walked ahead of him to stand in front of it. "I had some work done at the weekend."

He threw the new door open dramatically and waved his deputy into a twelve by twelve foot office, complete with external window, desk and chair.

"What do you think?"

Liam snuffled his way around the space suspiciously, like a bloodhound. When he stopped he was wearing a bemused look.

"It's an office."

Craig tried for shock. *"No, really?"*

"Ha ha. Funny man. So I take it you're shifting office into this one. But why? You can't see the river from here and you know you're obsessed with the bloody water." He craned his neck to look out of the window. "Mind you, there's a great view of The James from this one. You'll be able to see as soon as it opens."

"Tempting as that sounds, this isn't *my* office, Liam."

It earned him an unexpectedly angry squint.

"I knew it! You're bringing in someone above me! All those times you suggested I should go for promotion, and now you've got fed up waiting and brought in a new Super!"

Craig smiled kindly and shook his head. "If you became a superintendent it would be great, but a *new one* on the squad? No, thank you. God, Ash was right when he called you D.C.I. Dumbo, wasn't he-"

"Here now, there's no need for that."

Craig reached into the desk drawer and pulled out a nameplate for the door, sliding it into its holder and watching his deputy's face as he read out the name incredulously.

"D.C.I. Liam Cullen. Deputy. *That's me!*"

"Not so Dumbo then."

Liam's small eyes widened. "This is *my* office?"

"Yep. I got fed up tripping over those files piled beside your desk."

"You did this for *me*?"

"Yes. Well, that and I was trying not to break a leg."

The Banbridge man's jaw dropped and Craig was sure that he could see tears in his eyes.

"Oh, God, you're not going to cry on me are you?"

It was payback for every 'big girl' crack Liam had made at *him* when he'd gone 'all Italian' over the years.

The response was a swift punch to the shoulder that Craig *really* felt.

He rubbed it hard. "Next time just say thanks, will you. I value my limbs. Now, I know you won't want to use the room all the time because you're a nosey bugger who *likes* being out on the floor, but you can lend it to others for meetings, viewing CCTV tapes, writing reports in peace, whatever you choose as long as it's for work."

Liam plonked himself down behind his new desk. "Over my dead body they'll use it."

"Fine. Whatever. I'll be moving Alice to a desk outside it at the start of March because Nicky's coming back part-time, so you might need to moderate your language or negotiate a truce with her."

He motioned the D.C.I. to get up again. "Don't get comfortable, you and I are going to see the C.C. to grovel for a warrant for Pete's communications. I emailed him my report explaining yesterday and I've a paper copy for him in the car. Then it'll be the Ombudsman and PPS before we can *hopefully* tell Annette she's off the hook."

"You grovel while I spit in their eyes."

Sounded fair enough.

"Agreed. Then we'll have a week's work to do unravelling this abduction ring before we do a coordinated swoop."

Liam gawped at him. "*A week!* That'll never be enough!"

"It'll have to be. Flanagan phoned me on Saturday to say it's all he can give us. The Trafficking Unit's got wind that there's something big happening and he doesn't want him running away with things before we've got a serious grip. I'd warn Danni she won't be seeing you till Friday if I were you."

He'd been joking, but as his deputy began sizing up his new kingdom for a sofabed it occurred to Craig that putting one in both of their offices mightn't be such a bad idea.

They were just heading off the floor when Davy entered so Craig repeated the one week deadline to the immediately panicked analyst and got on the road.

Twenty minutes later they were standing in Sean Flanagan's office where Craig was indeed grovelling, to a man who was trying to look stern as befitted a Chief Constable and not bemused like he actually felt.

"Well done on the abduction ring, both of you, but why are you asking *me* to request a warrant, Craig? Why *would* I when you're perfectly capable of doing the job yourself?"

"The warrant's not linked to the abduction case, sir."

It earned him a raised eyebrow.

"You're working on another as well?"

"Well...yes, in a way."

The puzzled C.C. turned to Liam for enlightenment, which he was only too pleased to give.

"We need a warrant for Pete McElroy's communications."

Craig jumped back in. "I did email you a report on this yesterday, sir. Here's a paper copy." He set down the document that he'd brought from the car.

Flanagan's quizzical look became a frown, and when he spoke again there was more than a hint of steel in his tone.

"And *why* is Peter McElroy any of your business, Chief Superintendent?"

Seeing that Flanagan hadn't read his email and the meeting looked likely to last longer than the five minutes they'd originally requested, Craig glanced questioning at some chairs. The detectives were briskly motioned to sit, however, the welcoming sign of refreshments was nowhere in sight.

"I can explain, sir," Craig paused and then added, quite cheekily his deputy was pleased to see, "if I could just have five minutes without any questions."

With no signal from Flanagan that such an amnesty would be forthcoming Craig decided to continue anyway, determined not to pause for breath in case he cut in.

"We all know the details of McElroy's breaking and entering and subsequent shooting by D.I. Eakin before Christmas, but this week we were informed that, following the Ombudsman's report, the PPS was considering a charge of manslaughter. Annette is very distressed."

He stopped reluctantly to inhale, fully expecting someone to say something. Happily no-one did so he hurried on.

"But there was something that made me suspicious of the events, namely that McElroy had left his fingerprints, which he *knew* were in the system, on the French doors through which he entered-"

Flanagan raised a hand to halt him, frowning as if he hadn't been aware of the detail. "Meaning?"

Liam volunteered the answer. "Either he didn't care if he got caught and sent back to the nick or he wasn't planning on being around when his prints were ID-ed."

The Chief Constable's eyebrows had risen on 'nick', but when he said nothing about the slang Craig carried on.

"Given that McElroy was due for release only a short time later, the more likely thing is that he believed he wasn't going to be around when he got made. Also, the French doors were intact, meaning that he'd broken in very expertly without a sound-"

Liam jumped in helpfully. "And the Governor at Mahon *finally* admitted on the phone to me yesterday that McElroy had *specifically* asked to share a cell with a burglar last January. Royston thought it was because Pete was trying to be good, i.e. he didn't want to share with someone violent who he'd get in fights with, but he must have been thinking of a possible break-in for a year."

Although Craig was wondering just how much pressure Liam had applied to elicit the admission from George Royston, his glance said, 'Good man'.

Flanagan raised a hand to stop their flow. "You're implying that Peter McElroy had sought lessons in breaking and entering, but that's irrelevant as the prints he left behind would have shown up on the system immediately." He nodded slowly in realisation. "Ah... I see. You mean he didn't want to be *heard* entering and was planning to go on the run afterwards."

Craig shook his head emphatically. "No, he wasn't going to run, sir. With what resources? Ones that he could have accessed, I mean. And where could he have gone without being pursued? Annette would have alerted everyone he was the burglar the moment he'd left the house."

The C.C.'s next words were irritable. "*Well, what then?* Get to the point, man!"

Craig bit back his urge to respond, "if you'd read my bloody report you'd already know all of this" and laid things out in a calm tone.

"It occurred to us that Pete McElroy had *never*

intended to leave that house."

Liam knew that he was getting credit for something that hadn't even occurred to him, but decided that now wasn't the time to demur.

An astonished expression appeared on Flanagan's face but Craig ignored it and pushed on.

"McElroy wasn't a burglar yet he broke in smoothly leaving the door's lock and glass was intact, so we wondered where he'd learned to do that. I enquired and found out that while in Mahon he'd shared a cell with a Ben Frampton, so I decided that we should have a chat."

The Chief Constable found his voice. *"A chat?"*

"Yes, sir. A chat."

Liam gave him five points for sarcasm and five more for managing it while still sounding polite.

"It turned out that Frampton was a notorious burglar, which was particularly interesting because of the break-in, so I had him brought to High Street last week and questioned him under caution. He revealed that in exchange for McElroy teaching him how to read *he'd* taught McElroy how to break and enter."

The C.C.'s eyebrows rose again.

"He also said that McElroy had been severely depressed about his future prospects and had talked of suicide several times. He'd also stated that he wanted his ex-wife to suffer what he had after he died."

Liam had been champing at the bit to say something and spotted his chance.

"That means he wanted *Annette* to lose her freedom, her kids and her job. He wanted *her* to do jail time just like he had."

Craig gave a small smile and carried on.

"McElroy was clear with Ben Frampton about his intent to break in and *kill* Mike Augustus, Annette's new partner, placing her in a position whereby she would feel threatened and draw her gun. If the gun hadn't already been handy Pete had intended to place it beside her. He had the code to her lockbox, having watched her secure her weapon every day for years when they were married. Frampton also confirmed that Pete knew Annette was a crack shot. In other words, if she fired at him she wouldn't miss."

Flanagan's eyebrows had jumped so high he looked like a mime.

"In the weeks prior to the episode McElroy employed a new firm of solicitors, Floods in Oxford Street, and deposited some letters with them. We asked Colum Flood could we see the letters but he wouldn't even confirm their existence, however we've since found out that Pete's two children received letters from Floods in the past few weeks. It's my belief that one of the other letters Colum Flood is holding will be Pete McElroy's suicide note. I *also* believe that he'll have dated it to be opened years from now, approximately when he would have expected Annette to be freed from prison if she was convicted on his death." He fought to keep sarcasm out of his next few words. "It's all in my report, sir."

Liam added helpfully. "That's so she'd have to serve *all* her sentence before people learned the truth."

Flanagan finally roused himself to comment. "Yes, I got that, Chief Inspector."

Craig was beginning to feel more confident so he stared directly at the Chief Constable and re-issued his earlier request as a demand.

"We need a warrant for those papers *and* all of McElroy's electronic communications, because it's my belief that we'll find a step-by-step outline of how he set up Inspector Eakin in a deliberate suicide by cop."

There was absolute silence in the room. How long it might have lasted they would never know, because the next moment the door was rapped and thrown open and Donna Scott, Flanagan's eternally cheerful PA, bounced in.

"Call for D.C.S. Craig, sir."

Flanagan snapped at her. "It'll have to wait, Donna!"

She stood her ground, grinning. "Can't, sir. It's his son saying his first hello."

The blood drained from Craig's face, and although his mouth opened not a whisper emerged. It was left to his deputy to race out and lift the telephone, to hear an ecstatic Katy say, "Tell Marc everything's fine. The baby arrived very quickly and the ambulance is here now. We'll be at St Mary's when he gets down."

Liam heard another woman's voice say, "End your call, dear. We'd better get on our way" just before the line went dead.

He swaggered back into the office and thumped Craig on the arm for the second time that day.

"Cigars all round! The wife says they'll be at St Mary's."

Craig was still gawping. He'd left Katy fast asleep only two hours before! That meant she'd been alone when the baby was born; in fact she must have delivered it herself! She'd got her wish after all.

Sean Flanagan brought the detectives back to earth.

"Congratulations, Craig. Your first?"

Liam guffawed. "And last, judging by the shock on his face."

"Well, let's finish up here quickly and you can be on your way to the hospital." He turned to Liam, seeing that he was going to get no more sense from his boss. "You have this statement signed by Frampton, D.C.I. Cullen?"

Liam mustered his best professional tone. "Yes, sir."

"And he mentions the same solicitor Inspector Eakin's children received their letters from?"

"Yes."

"Yet the solicitor didn't confirm that?"

"He said he couldn't confirm anything without a court order, but surely the kids' letters are confirmation enough?"

The reply was a frown. "The Ombudsman won't like this, and I don't want a precedent established for his investigations being challenged by anyone who simply doesn't like the outcome."

Liam thought he detected a hint of Flanagan preparing to give them what they wanted through his grumpiness, and decided a sober, "I understand" would work better as encouragement than, "hurry the hell up!"

The Chief Constable's flinty next words poured cold water on his hopes. "Also, the police *aren't* above the law, and we can't be seen to be trying to thwart an investigation into one of our own."

Craig suddenly heard things slipping away from them and woke up.

"But surely neither can we proceed against an officer incorrectly *just* to appease the public, sir? If it comes out later that McElroy had openly expressed his intention of committing suicide by cop, then people will say taking

Inspector Eakin to trial was a complete waste of public funds."

He'd mentioned money very deliberately, knowing how close Flanagan's budget was to his heart. It did the trick.

The Chief Constable nodded briskly and stood up.

"Right. D.C.I. Cullen, wait outside until I can organise a warrant, then you can execute it at Flood's yourself. If we find what you believe we'll find then D.I. Eakin *could* be off the hook, although you'll both still have some explaining to do to the Ombudsman and PPS." He added ominously, "*And* me, for interfering in an investigation this way."

As he turned to Craig again he allowed a smile to play on his lips. "I advise *you* to go and see your son. And congratulations again." Then he motioned abruptly at the door. "Now, get out of my office, both of you."

As they left the room Craig turned to his deputy. "Please explain to Annette why I couldn't be there to tell her in person."

"I'm pretty sure she'll understand, boss."

"And remember, the idea that Pete hated her enough to set her up will be a shock after them being married for twenty years, so be prepared for her to get upset."

"Aye, aye, I'll be Officer Sensitive." Liam pointed firmly towards the exit. "Now take yourself off to see Luigi or Spaghetti or whatever you're calling him, and I'll see you whenever."

As Craig took off at a run his deputy was already making a bet that he'd be back in the office the next day. After all, he had someone new to work hard for now.

His speculation was cut short by a shout from Sean Flanagan summoning him back in and handing him a search warrant.

"Take this to the court and get it signed. There's a judge waiting. And I want a call as soon as you've opened whatever papers you find at Floods."

An hour later Liam would oblige him, but not before he'd already read the suicide note that Pete had left over the phone to Craig, who listened while staring at his baby son as if he'd just landed from space.

"Exactly the same stuff as in his email, boss, but the bastard dated it not to be opened till twenty-thirty-five."

"As we expected, he wanted Annette to serve her whole

sentence. OK, follow the C.C.'s lead on when to tell her, Liam, but emphasise that Annette's extremely depressed so if it could be done *yesterday* that would be good."

"Leave it to me. I'll *emphasise* it so hard that Flanagan won't be able to sit down afterwards. Anyway, how's Cannelloni? Cute like his mum?"

Craig smiled at a sleeping Katy as he answered. "No-one's *that* cute, but he's astounding. Now, go away, Liam. I want to talk to my son."

THE END.

Core Characters in the Craig Crime Novels

Detective Chief Superintendent Marc (Marco) Craig: Craig is a sophisticated, single, forty-seven-year-old of Northern Irish/Italian extraction. From a mixed religious background but agnostic.
An ex-grammar schoolboy and Queen's University Law graduate, he went to London to join The Met (The Metropolitan Police) at twenty-two, rising in rank through its High Potential Development Training Scheme. He returned to Belfast in two-thousand and eight after fifteen years away.
He is a driven, compassionate, workaholic, with an unfortunate temper that he struggles to control and a tendency to respond to situations with his fists, something that almost resulted in him going to prison when he was in his teens. He loves the sea, sails when he has the time and is generally sporty. He plays the piano, loves music and sport.

His girlfriend of four years, Katy Stevens, is a consultant physician at the local St Mary's Healthcare Trust, but Craig still lives alone in a modern apartment block in Stranmillis, near the university area of Belfast. His parents, his extrovert mother Mirella (an Italian concert pianist) and his quiet father Tom (an ex-university lecturer in Physics) live in Holywood town, six miles outside the city. His rebellious sister, Lucia, his junior by ten years, works as the manager of a local charity and also lives in Belfast.
Craig is now a Chief Superintendent heading up Belfast's Murder Squad and Police Intelligence Unit. The Murder Squad is based in the thirteen storey Co-ordinated Crime Unit (C.C.U.) in Pilot Street, in the Sailortown area of Belfast's Docklands.

D.C.I. Liam Cullen: Craig's deputy. Liam is a fifty-two-year-old former RUC officer from Crossgar in Northern Ireland, who transferred into the PSNI from the RUC in two thousand and one, following the Patton Reforms. He has lived and worked in Northern Ireland all his life and has spent over thirty years in the police force, more than twenty of them policing Belfast, including during The Troubles.

Liam is married to the forty-one-year-old, long suffering Danielle (Danni), a part-time nursery nurse, and they have a seven-year-old daughter Erin and a five-year-old son called Rory. Liam is unsophisticated, indiscreet and hopelessly non-PC, but he's a hard worker with a great knowledge of the streets and has a sense of humour that makes everyone, even the Chief Constable, laugh.

D.I. Annette Eakin: Annette is Craig's lead Detective Inspector who has lived and worked in Northern Ireland all her life. She is a forty-eight-year-old ex-nurse who, after her nursing degree, worked as a nurse for thirteen years and then, after a career break, retrained and has now been in the police for an equal length of time. She divorced her husband Pete McElroy, a P.E teacher at a state secondary school, because of his infidelity and violence. They have two children, a boy and a girl (Jordan and Amy), both at university, and Annette also has a baby daughter, Carina, with her new partner, Mike Augustus, a pathologist who works with Doctor John Winter.

Annette is kind and conscientious with an especially good eye for detail. She also has very good people skills but can be a bit of a goody-two-shoes.

Nicky Morris: Nicky Morris is Craig's forty-year-old personal assistant. She used to be PA to Detective Chief Superintendent (D.C.S.) Terry *'Teflon'* Harrison. Nicky is a glamorous Belfast mum married to Gary, who owns a small garage, and she is the mother of a teenage son, Jonny. She comes from a solidly working-class area of east Belfast, just ten minutes' drive from Docklands.

She is bossy, motherly and street-wise and manages to organise a reluctantly-organised Craig very effectively. She has a very eclectic and unusual sense of style, and there is an ongoing innocent office flirtation between her and Liam.

Davy Walsh: The Murder Squad's thirty-year-old senior computer analyst. A brilliant but shy EMO turned Hipster,

Davy's confidence has grown during his time on the team, making his lifelong stutter on 's' and 'w' now almost unnoticeable unless he's under stress.

His father is deceased and Davy lives at home in Belfast with his mother and grandmother. He has an older sister, Emmie, who studied English at university.

His girlfriend of five years, Maggie Clarke, is a journalist and now News Editor at The Belfast Chronicle newspaper. They became engaged in early 2017.

Doctor John Winter: John is the forty-seven-year-old Director of Pathology for Northern Ireland, one of the youngest ever appointed. He's brilliant, eccentric, gentlemanly and really likes the ladies, but he met his match in Natalie Ingrams, a surgeon at St Mary's Healthcare Trust, and they've been married now for over two years and have a one-year-old daughter called Kit.

John was Craig's best friend at school and university and remained in Northern Ireland to build his medical career when Craig left. He is now internationally respected in his field.

The pathologist persuaded Craig that the newly peaceful Northern Ireland was a good place to return to, and he assists Craig's team with cases whenever he can. He is obsessed with crime in general and US police shows in particular.

D.C.I. Andrew (Andy) Angel: A relatively new addition to Craig's team and its second D.C.I., Andy Angel is a slight, forty-three-year-old, twice divorced, perpetually broke father of an eleven-year-old son, Bowie, who lives with his mother. A chocoholic with a tendency towards lethargy, he surprises the team at times with his abilities, particularly his visual skills, which include being a super-recogniser, a title given to a small number of individuals who possess exceptional visual recognition abilities. It is something that has proved useful in several investigations.

Andy's spare time is spent sketching, painting and collecting original Irish art. He is also constantly on the search for a new relationship, but without much success as romantic subtlety isn't his strong point.

D.C.I. Aidan Hughes: Originally seconded to the Murder Squad in twenty-sixteen from Vice, Hughes has now become a permanent addition to Craig's team.
Single, mid-forties, tall, thin, and with a broad Belfast accent and a tendency to tan so much at his parents' home in Spain that he resembles a stick of mahogany, Hughes has known Craig and John Winter since they were all at school together. A newly reformed heavy smoker, exercise addict and joker, he is a popular member of the squad.

Doctor Des Marsham: Des is the Head of Forensic Science for Northern Ireland and works with John Winter at their laboratories in a science park off the Saintfield Road in Belfast. They often work together on Craig's murder cases.
Instantly recognisable by his barely controlled beard, Des is married to the placid and hippyish Annie, and they have two young sons, Martin and Rafferty. The scientist is obsessed with Gaelic Football, both playing and watching it, and spends several weekends each year metal-detecting with his university friends on Northern Ireland's Atlantic coast.

D.C.S. Terry (Teflon) Harrison: Craig's old boss. The sixty-year-old Detective Chief Superintendent was based at the Headquarters building in Limavady in the northwest Irish countryside but has now returned to the Docklands C.C.U. where he has an office on the thirteenth floor. He shared a converted farm house at Toomebridge with his homemaker wife Mandy and their thirty-year-old daughter Sian, a marketing consultant, but Mandy has now divorced him, partly because of his trail of mistresses, often younger than his daughter, so Harrison has moved to an apartment in south Belfast.
The D.C.S. is tolerable as a boss as long as everything's going well, but he is acutely politically aware, a snob, and very quick to pass on the blame for any mistakes to his subordinates (hence the Teflon nickname). He sees Craig as a rival and is out to destroy him. In particular, he resents Craig's friendship with John Winter, who wields a great deal of power in the Northern Irish justice system.

Key Background Locations

The majority of locations referenced in the book are real, with some exceptions.

Northern Ireland (real): Set in the north-east of the island of Ireland, Northern Ireland was created in nineteen-twenty-one by an act of British parliament. It forms part of the United Kingdom of Great Britain and Northern Ireland and shares a border to the south and west with the Republic of Ireland. The Northern Ireland Assembly, based at the Stormont Estate, holds responsibility for a range of devolved policy matters. It was established by the Northern Ireland Act 1998 as part of the Good Friday Agreement.

Belfast (real): Belfast is the capital and largest city of Northern Ireland, set on the flood plain of the River Lagan. The seventeenth largest city in the United Kingdom and the second largest in Ireland, it is the seat of the Northern Ireland Assembly.

The Dockland's Co-ordinated Crime Unit (The C.C.U. - fictitious): The modern high-rise headquarters building is situated in Pilot Street in Sailortown, a section of Belfast between the M1 and M2 undergoing massive investment and re-development. The C.C.U. hosts the police murder, gang crimes, vice and drug squad offices, amongst others.

Sailortown (real): An historic area of Belfast on the River Lagan that was a thriving area between the sixteenth and twentieth centuries. Many large businesses developed in the area, ships docked for loading and unloading and their crews from far flung places such as China and Russia mixed with a local Belfast population of ship's captains, chandlers, seamen and their families.
Sailortown was a lively area where churches and bars fought for the souls and attendance of the residents and where many languages were spoken each day. The basement of the Rotterdam Bar, at the bottom of

Clarendon Dock, acted as the overnight lock-up to prisoners being deported to the Antipodes on boats the next morning, and the stocks which held the prisoners could still be seen until the nineteen-nineties.

During the years of World War Two the area was the most bombed area of the UK outside Central London, as the Germans tried to destroy Belfast's ship building capacity. Sadly, the area fell into disrepair in the nineteen-seventies and eighties when the motorway extension led to compulsory purchases of many homes and businesses and decimated the Sailortown community. The rebuilding of the community has now begun, with new families moving into starter homes and professionals into expensive dockside flats.

The Pathology Labs (fictitious): The labs, set on Belfast's Saintfield Road as part of a large science park, are where Doctor John Winter, Northern Ireland's Head of Pathology, and his co-worker, Doctor Des Marsham, Head of Forensic Science, carry out the post-mortem and forensic examinations that help Craig's team solve their cases.

St Mary's Healthcare Trust (fictitious): St Mary's is one of the largest hospital trusts in the UK. It is spread over several hospital sites across Belfast, including the main Royal St Mary's Hospital site off the motorway and the Maternity, Paediatric and Endocrine (M.P.E.) unit, a stand-alone site on Belfast's Lisburn Road, in the University Quarter of the city.

Thank-you for reading this book. If you enjoyed it, why not leave a review on Amazon and recommend it to your friends?

Discover the other titles in the series at:
www.catrionakingbooks.com